THE
THOROUGHBRED
BUSINESS

By the same author

HORSERACING AND RACING SOCIETY

THE THOROUGHBRED BUSINESS

JOCELYN DE MOUBRAY

Hamish Hamilton   London

For Lucy

HAMISH HAMILTON LTD

Penguin Books Ltd, 27 Wrights Lane, London W8 5TZ (Publishing & Editorial)
and Harmondsworth, Middlesex, England (Distribution & Warehouse)
Viking Penguin Inc., 40 West 23rd Street, New York, New York 10010, U.S.A.
Penguin Books Australia Ltd, Ringwood, Victoria, Australia
Penguin Books Canada Limited, 2801 John Street, Markham, Ontario, Canada L3R 1B4
Penguin Books (N.Z.) Ltd, 182–190 Wairau Road, Auckland 10, New Zealand

First published in Great Britain 1987 by
Hamish Hamilton Ltd

British Library Cataloguing in Publication Data
De Moubray, Jocelyn
The thoroughbred business.
1. Thoroughbred horse —— Breeding ——
Finance
I. Title
338.1'36132   SF293.T5

ISBN 0–241–12379–8

Produced in Great Britain by
Butler & Tanner Ltd, Frome and London

═══ Contents ═══

List of Illustrations

Between pages 78 and 79

Inside the Keeneland Association's Sale Pavillion. (*John C. Wyatt*)
Johnny Jones II of Walmac International.
Robert N. Clay of Three Chimneys. (*Doug Saunders*)
Gainesway, Kentucky. (*Tony Leonard Inc., 1980*)
Walmac International, Kentucky. (*Tony Leonard Inc., 1985*)
Chief's Crown at Three Chimneys. (*Doug Saunders*)
Inside Tattersalls' Newmarket salering. (*Gerry Cranham*)
Michael Goodbody, Omar Assi and David Cecil. (*Laurie Morton Photography*)
David Pim. (*Laurie Morton Photography*)
Alan Lillingston of the Mount Coote Stud and Arturo Brambilla of BBA Italia.
(*Laurie Morton Photography*)
Major W. R. Hern, the Queen's trainer, and Robert McCreery. (*Laurie Morton Photography*)
Rhydian Morgan-Jones. (*Laurie Morton Photography*)
Sir Philip Payne-Gallwey Bt. (*Laurie Morton Photography*)
Anthony Stroud, Sheikh Mohammed's racing manager.
(*George P. Herringshaw, ASP.*)
David Minton. (*Laurie Morton Photography*)

Acknowledgements

The author would like to thank the following for their help: Perry S. Alexander, Holly Bandaroff, Nancy Beavis, T. E. Beckett, Charles H. Boden, Patrick Burns, Mrs John A. Chandler, Tony Chapman, Tote Cherry-Downes, Mauritio Conti, Robert N. Clay, Coutts & Co, Richard Craddock, Luca Cumani, Mrs A. J. Cuthbert, Ghislain Drion, William S. Farish, Tom Goncharoff, Chris Harper, David Harris, Michael Harris, David Hedges, Harry Herbert, Elizabeth Hearn, Penny Hoare, R. D. Hubbard, Ian Irvine, Johnny T. L. Jones Jr, Dieter Klein, Edward Kesley, Captain N. E. S. Lees, Alan Lillingston, Greg Magruder, Mr & Mrs Robert McCreery, Robert S. Miller, David Minton, Rhydian Morgan-Jones, Ron Muddle, Anthony Oppenheimer, Anthony Penfold, Major C. R. Philipson, Richard Pilkington, Tim Preston, Grant Pritchard-Gordon, Kirsten Rausing, Martin Rennie, Nicholas Robinson, E. Barry Ryan, John Sanderson, Ed Sczesny, Sam Sheppard, Anthony Speelman, Anthony Stroud, the Marchioness of Tavistock, Duncan Taylor, James Underwood, John Warren, Barry Weisbord, Norman Weisbord, James Wigan, Laura Williams, Hugh Young

══ Introduction ══

This book is about gambling. Horseracing is, and always has been, intimately concerned with gambling. There have been attempts in countries in which gambling is proscribed by religion to stage horse-racing purely as a spectacle, but they have not been altogether successful. In some cases the collective scruples have been overcome by including an entry in a lottery as part of the fee for admission. However, the fact remains that horseracing without betting is of interest only to those who are active participants in it.

The central role gambling plays in horseracing is immediately obvious. For most people who go racing the day's enjoyment lies in making decisions, placing bets, and then being proved right or wrong. The excitement of the sport lies in its immediate and competitive nature. This was charmingly illustrated by a film the French racing authorities made for a television advertisement to encourage people to go racing in Paris. It opens with a barely clothed girl lying on a bed whilst a scruffy young man in jeans is absorbed in a football game on television. "Encore le télé," the girl moans. Then someone suggests they go racing. The scene changes and we see the same couple, now immaculately and glamorously turned out, jumping with excitement as a group of thoroughbreds roar past the Château's stables at Chantilly. The horses approach the finish, and amid cries of "Allez! Allez!" the young lady's choice wins and she flings herself ecstatically into her man's arms. Besides any other implications the film reveals racing to be both quick and exciting, thanks largely to the decision and the gamble.

However, horseracing as a whole is far too large a topic to be examined succinctly, and if this book is to be at all coherent its scope will have to be narrower. Questions related to the administration of horseracing and of racecourses, and the motivations of trainers and jockeys, will be left on one side. Instead, the book will be concerned with the bloodstock business and its participants. The desires and attitudes of the racegoer and the racing fan will only be relevant to the degree to which they influence the decisions and activities of the relatively small coterie of insiders who make up the bloodstock world. The bloodstock business is exclusively concerned with producing and selecting potentially successful racehorses. The sites of its action are the stud farm and the sale ring, and its members are either breeders or owners, or representatives of the mass of auxiliaries who support them: the bloodstock agents, auctioneers, transporters, advertising agencies, insurance brokers, lawyers, accountants, veterinarians and grooms. The members of this world, and particularly those in senior positions, are unlikely to have much interest in gambling upon the result of a single horserace.

Many of those who habitually gamble upon the result of individual races believe it would be possible, with the right information and contacts, to derive a regular income from their labours. If only they knew what the stable thought of the horse's chances and whether its trainer expected it to win, they would be able to place their bets with confidence. In fact, those within the bloodstock world will often receive such confidences and be aware of a myriad of other pertinent rumours, and yet, such sources do not constitute a reliable guide to selecting winners. Insiders may occasionally bet, like the young French lady, for the sake of an inexpensive thrill, but they are unlikely to rely upon betting to pay for their next horse or stallion season. Not every owner and breeder is so pragmatic, but they will all be aware that the possible rewards for success within their own field dwarf any potential gain from betting. The person who buys a stallion of the future as an inexpensive yearling, or who is in a position to sell a half-brother to last year's Derby winner, has secured a jackpot which is more lucrative than any offered by a bookmaker or totalizator. There was a time when the betting mentality, the desire to hoodwink the bookmakers, permeated every level of the horseracing industry. Now the business offers rewards large enough for betting on the result of separate races to be of only marginal interest to all but its least successful participants.

But if betting is playing an increasingly minor role within the blood-stock business, the motivations and desires of its protagonists are still closely allied to those of the gambler. Horseracing has in many ways the ephemerality of the casino. Every season its adherents familiarize themselves with and learn a whole catalogue of names, results and statistics, most of which will be completely irrelevant, even in their own eyes, within a year. This avid collection of information which is of only transitory interest is not as pointless as it may appear, for it creates a shared language and memory. Membership of the bloodstock world does not necessarily preclude any outside interest, but when communicating with each other its members tend to presume that it does, and restrict themselves to discussing the business that is the centre of their lives, relying upon this shared language and memory to facilitate relations.

Introduction

The racing man, like the gambler, habitually takes chances. The central transactions of the bloodstock business are the buying and selling of seasons* and shares in stallions and the buying and selling of yearlings and broodmares. In every such transaction each party realises it may either be wasting its money completely or selling a gem for the price of a bead. This habitual risk-taking leads on to another parallel with the gambler, for the racing man is always optimistic and never learns from defeat, nor is he satisfied with winning once. Like the gambler, he wants to win continuously. The person who buys a Derby winner as a yearling is unlikely to withdraw from the sale ring as a result, but will be back the following year bidding with renewed vigour and enthusiasm. Similarly the man who buys a hugely expensive yearling which never even appears on the racecourse is unlikely to despair; he too will be back the following year, more determined than ever to select the right one. These two characteristics are not only typical of those who buy at yearling auctions; they can readily be observed in the members of almost any branch of the bloodstock business.

A final correspondence between the bloodstock business and the world of gambling lies in the source of what is the chief joy and excitement for a participant in either activity—the pleasurable-painful tension undergone between the moment of decision and the revelation of the final outcome of the game. In the casino the result may be clear after a few seconds, but for the breeder or the owner the tension is drawn out over two years or more. From the moment the hammer drops and you have bought a yearling, or from the time your brood-mare conceives, there is a period of expectation, rumination and worry before it is revealed whether you have bought or bred a champion, or for those with less exalted aspirations a winner. On almost any level the joy of the bloodstock business lies in the uncertainty which obscures the outcome of any move in the game. The possibility of success, however remote, allows the gambler to forget for a time the likelihood of failure. The same could be said of anyone who buys or breeds a thoroughbred. Most members of the bloodstock world were attracted to it by sentiment and a love of horses, but at the same time many are drawn by the gamble and the thrill of this tension. Indeed there is a sense in which the bloodstock business is a peculiarly exciting form of gambling: the stakes are high, the competition open and public, and the game prolonged for two years or more.

The dual attraction which the horse has for members of the blood-

*A season is the right to have a mare serviced by a named stallion during a particular breeding season. In Britain this right is usually known as a nomination.

stock world creates a tension between money and sentiment. One of the themes of this book will be to examine the way this tension has fluctuated, and to show how at times any equilibrium between the pulls of money and sentiment has been lost. The horse is desired for what it is, and yet the horse is also a means of making money, in some cases the source of spectacular financial gains. If it is the pull of money that threatens to disrupt the equilibrium, then there will be a temptation to abuse the horse for the sake of the riches it can provide. However, here the need for horseracing to entertain outsiders acts as a stabilizing influence. The bloodstock business relies absolutely on there being people who will pay to attend racemeetings and will gamble on the result of races. For many of this public, the horse is as much of an attraction as the gamble.

Horseracing is concerned with both horses and gambling, for it is more than merely a lottery. If the racehorse is to maintain this hold upon man's imagination it must be seen as an exalted animal worthy of a degree of reverence, and those who succumb to the temptation are indirectly jeopardizing their own livelihood. This duality in the way in which the racehorse is seen, and the similarities between the motivations of the players in the bloodstock market and those of the gambler, gives the market an inherent instability and makes any attempt to predict its future course hazardous.

The bloodstock market is founded upon a central uncertainty. Nobody knows what a good racehorse is, or rather what exactly it is which enables one racehorse to run faster than another. Equally nobody knows how to set about producing a superior racehorse, or how to select one from a mass of relatively similar yearlings. Every participant formulates his own ideas or theories in the knowledge that they will never guarantee success, nor will any two different theories necessarily be mutually exclusive. This uncertainty is hidden by the myths and rituals of the bloodstock world. For if the business is to be a business its gambling aspect must be hidden and legitimized. Success must appear to be due to skill and superior judgement, not chance alone. The bloodstock market is formed by the play of information and misinformation which both shrouds and illuminates this uncertainty.

Information plays a vital role in all aspects of horseracing. The spectacle of a horserace is of little interest unless the observer has access to some information about the competitors in advance. Once the observer knows the horses' names, or has an idea of the personalities of their owners, trainers and jockeys, the race becomes potentially interesting. Unless the observer is able to differentiate between the runners in some way or other he will not be in a position to express a preference about the order in which they finish. If the result is of no importance then the race itself will be dull. The pleasure of the game of racing lies in acquiring this information and then sifting through it. One discards what appears to be irrelevant and selects what seems important before making a decision and then being proved right or wrong. The same could be said of breeding or selecting a yearling at an auction. There is a sense in which both endeavours are an attempt to control or predict the uncontrollable and the unpredictable. However, decisions must be made, and once again they are based upon the accumulation and grading of information. The game of the bloodstock market is a more complicated one, for in each transaction there will be two or more interested parties, each of whom will have an incentive to withhold and convey different aspects of the information. The bloodstock market exists in its present form because its participants believe it is possible to make a rational prediction of a young horse's racing ability on the basis of information about its pedigree and physique. The play is still there, for nobody is able to describe the perfect pedigree, or the ideal physique, and the experts would agree that an evaluation of these criteria can produce misinformation as well as information. These two touchstones and the information and opinions which are available about them provide the basis for prediction, and the justification for investments and gambles.

Without information about thoroughbreds' pedigrees and the achievements of their ancestors and relations thoroughbred breeding and the bloodstock sales would be uninteresting lotteries. Their fascination lies in the multitude of different interpretations and equally valid predictions which can be made on the basis of the same information. If a definitive method of breeding the Derby winner were discovered, or a foolproof manner of selecting the best racehorse from a collection of yearlings, then both the commercial possibilities and the attraction of the bloodstock market would be destroyed. The bloodstock business thrives because each decision maker, whether planning a coupling or selecting a yearling, is able to believe in the possibility of a consequent success. As long as there is a chance of securing a champion, however eccentric or unfashionable the criteria which are considered before the choice is made, then the decision-maker will be able to forget the likelihood of failure, for a time at least.

The aim of this book is to examine the causes and effects of the boom in the bloodstock market which took place between the mid 1970s and the mid 1980s. This will be done bearing in mind two distinctive features of the thoroughbred business. First, it is a business which attracts both gamblers and horsemen. It is not always easy to distinguish between these two types, because everybody within the business is regularly faced by this conflict between the power of sentiment and the lure of money. The second distinctive feature of the industry is this repeated game of information, misinformation and disinformation. There is a sense in which the bloodstock industry is like a game in which all the players are blindfolded before setting out to find the same object. The only ways in which each player can gain information are by feeling and touching on their own, or by asking one of their rivals to share their opinions and discoveries.

The first step will be to look at the horse and its heredity in order to illuminate this central uncertainty. During the years of the boom buyers at yearling auctions came to see the pedigree, and in particular the name of the sire, as an accurate indicator of a yearling's potential racing ability. Particular attention will be paid to examining the validity of the claims which were made on behalf of the stallion and of pedigree research as a whole. The question of the appropriate environment in which to raise young thoroughbreds will also be examined, first in order to give examples of this conflict between money and sentiment, but also to highlight the manner in which the management of stud farms has been affected by the rise in the value of bloodstock. Having begun in Part 1 by considering the horse, Part 2 will set out the basic features of the business: first, in order to set the stage for the boom, the similarities and differences in the pattern of racing, and in the way in which bloodstock is taxed in the United States, Great Britain and Ireland will be described; then the boom itself will be considered and the question of how it came about and what, rather than who, caused it will be discussed.

In Part 3 the personalities who have been involved in the business will be described in greater detail. The effect the boom had upon the activities and practices in each of the three major sites of the industry, the stud farm, the auction and the stallion farm, will be described. In addition the international divergence of these effects will be highlighted. Such an upheaval was bound to create pressures which encouraged unwarranted behaviour, which will be discussed in general terms. However, the author wishes to make completely clear that none of the individuals whom he names was in any way connected with any dubious practices, to which others might have succumbed, and which may be the subject of criticism here.

Finally by way of a conclusion there will be an attempt to look to the future. The policies and aspirations of the major buyers of blood-stock such as the Maktoum family, Prince Khalid Abdullah, Robert Sangster and Wayne Lucas will be considered. Then, to show the way in which the boom has transformed the industry, new institutions like the Breeders Cup Ltd and the European Breeders Fund will be described, in addition to the new developments in marketing and attracting sponsorship to horseracing. Finally, against this optimistic background, the disasters which could befall the industry will be considered, the introduction of artificial insemination for thorough-breds and the withdrawal from the market of the Arab buyers. It is hoped to show that although some of those within the industry would be hurt by either eventuality, neither would in fact precipitate a crisis.

Part One

═══ One ═══
What Makes a Racehorse?

Anybody interested in horseracing must sometimes wonder what it is that enables one horse to run faster than another. This question has a mysteriousness which may not be immediately apparent. The problem arises when one considers the similarities between young horses, rather than the differences between them which emerge later when they are tested on the racecourse. All racehorses are bred to be athletes and reared and trained with a view to maximizing their athletic ability. Yet by the time they are three years old their racing prowess will be widely differentiated. There is a gulf between the distinguished Derby winner and the sort of horse that wins minor handicaps at the major meetings, or other small races. However, this gulf is neither readily observable nor easily explained. To all but the most learned of judges the physical similarities between these two horses will be more obvious than any distinguishing features, and even those wise and experienced judges will probably pick upon different features to illuminate the difference in the horses' abilities. Indeed this might lead one to suppose that racehorses were remarkably similar and the results of races dependent as much upon chance as anything else, but this is clearly not the case.

If these two horses were to run against each other over a mile and a half carrying the same weight, and were both to perform at their best, the Derby winner would win by about twenty five lengths. For those who prefer to evaluate horses with a stop-watch, this difference is the approximate equivalent of three and a third seconds. The performances of racehorses is even more distinct than this, as the freak or great horse would probably defeat the average Derby winner by six lengths if they were to compete when both were at their peak. Asked to explain or account for this phenomenon, most people would begin by rephrasing the question.

This discrepancy between horses' deeds on the racecourse and the similarity of their genetic and functional background is usually explained in an evasive manner by reference to such abstract qualities as spirit, the will to win, or, most often in America, "heart". The racehorse has developed from a species which would run, and run fast, when threatened by danger. Today, when their only predators are little men with whips, a great number of horses just do not bother. So, the argument goes, many racehorses are physically capable of running a great deal faster than they ever choose to reveal. Those that win the big races are the ones that respond to their rider's urges, are naturally competitive and desire to win. This explanation tallies well with the notorious unreliability of racetimes when it comes to evaluating the comparative ability of two racehorses. The lesser horse may record similar or faster racetimes, but when faced with its more determined rival in a head-to-head struggle it may not be able to reproduce its earlier efforts. However, the problem is to distinguish between young horses and this spirit is not particularly helpful in this; it is generally considered to be ineffable. Nobody has worked out how it is produced or even how it can be detected before it is revealed on the racecourse.

Few attempts at a practical description of this concept of "heart" are any more dogmatic than the Italian breeder Federico Tesio's comment that he had seen great horses winning with different expressions in their eyes, but never with a stupid look.* There cannot be many people who have been close enough to a great horse at the moment of victory to be able to determine with any confidence whether or not they were looking sagacious, even if equine intelligence was a clearly defined concept itself. The problem of explaining horses' racecourse performances by a competitive urge is thus clearly illustrated; it leads swiftly to anthropomorphism. This is, of course, also the attraction of the hypothesis. Almost any animal which man has relied upon or come into close contact with soon acquires human characteristics and human powers of perception, at least in the eyes of the particular animal's keeper. Many breeders, trainers and grooms will look upon their charges as individuals and seek to discover their tastes and aberrations. Once the horse has acquired character and perception it is but a short step to expressing the felt need for the great racehorse to be both morally and intellectually, as well as physically, superior to its contemporaries. To be nominated a great horse is the highest accolade a thoroughbred can hope to achieve, so it should not

*Franco, Varola, *The Tesio Myth*. London: J. A. Allen, 1984.

be surprising that the great racehorse is accredited with those qualities its keeper most admires in his own species.

Many of those who have been fortunate enough to breed an excellent racehorse will tell tales of how it revealed unusual promise or spirit at an early age. One such story, typical in its charm and inconclusiveness, is told by Alice Chandler of Sir Ivor, the Derby winner she bred, raised and then sold to Raymond Guest as a yearling. Alice Chandler believes she recognized Sir Ivor's abnormal qualities while he was still a yearling. One night she was awoken during a fierce Kentucky thunderstorm by the sound of Sir Ivor neighing wildly and charging up and down his paddock. She wrapped a mackintosh about her and went out to try and catch him before he hurt himself. However, as soon as he heard her voice the colt rushed up to her and stood still waiting to be led in. This was, she reasoned, an extraordinary display of rationality in the face of such wild elements. Most horses in a similar state of panic would have been quite unsusceptible to human aid and would only have continued in their futile attempt to flee from danger. Alice Chandler herself ends her story on a disappointing note by adding that three or four other horses have given her a similar feel since that propitious night, but none of them turned out to be particularly distinguished racehorses.

We are no nearer being able to predict which of two young horses will be the better racehorse even if it has been established that their respective temperaments will play a part in determining this. These breeders' tales express much of the pleasure of breeding thoroughbreds, but they should be seen as fantasy fulfilment rather than an objective criterion for selecting racehorses. Part of the joy of breeding is to lean on a gate and imagine you are watching a Derby winner frolicking in your own paddock, but it would prove expensive in the long run to invest upon such whims.

Another aspect of the horses's temperament which undoubtedly affects its racing performance is its ability to learn and respond to man's dictates. No one is in a position to determine whether or not horses enjoy racing, let alone whether they savour victory, but a horse is not in a position to display these talents until it has been taught and trained by man. A good racehorse must be able to learn and be phlegmatic enough to cope with the stress of travelling and of the racecourse itself. Any animal will have a state of generalized emotional arousal in which it performs best, and unless the horse's can coincide with the environment in which man chooses to test it, then its racing ability will never be revealed. Some Derby favourites have been serenaded with brass bands on the days leading up to their ordeal in order to familiarize them with the peculiar atmosphere of Derby Day, but there are other horses which are unable to cope with the stress posed by the last race at Hamilton Park, or even of a journey in a horse box.

The psychology of the horse and the tension between its instinctive urges and desires and those which man requires of it must be central to any explanation of why one horse runs faster than another on the racecourse. The difficulty of determining and identifying the desired temperament becomes obvious when it is considered that man's knowledge of his own nervous system is only rudimentary. The supposedly curative discoveries of a psychoanalyst founded only upon his patient's utterances are inconclusive enough to highlight the problems of analysing an animal which has no language. The cynic would state that mental attributes are only imparted to those horses which are physically capable of feats which man considers to be worthy of analysis. Those with a more mundane, or at least less emotional, approach to horseracing will categorically maintain that one horse runs faster than another because it is put together in a mechanically more efficient manner. The physical structure or conformation of a racehorse must affect its racing ability and any study of equine conformation soon reveals the same tension between the horse's natural aptitudes and the demands which man makes of it.

Racehorses reach full physical maturity at about five years of age, by which time all superior specimens are exempted from any exercise more strenuous than copulation or giving birth. The most important tests for thoroughbreds are restricted to three year olds and take place in May or June. This means that none of the contestants in these races are more than three years and five months old, as all thoroughbreds have their birthday on January 1st. The decision, which the Jockey Club took in 1833, to make this date the day on which horses changed their age has had many implications for the breeding process; in addition it has led to the racehorse being subjected to its supreme test when it is still immature. Horses are able to run fast because their legs are long in relation to their body and weight, but this same attribute places particular strain on their bone ligaments, tendons and joints. Many racehorses suffer leg injuries of one type or another whilst being prepared for the racecourse, and young, immature horses are particularly prone to such injuries. As a result only a third of the foals born in Great Britain and Ireland are able to go into training as two year olds. Clearly the successful racehorse must stand on clean, sound and tough limbs.

The speed at which a racehorse is able to propel itself depends upon the efficiency of its limbs, the balance of its body, and its ability to draw in oxygen and pass it through its body. All experts of conformation will have their own idea of what the efficiently formed racehorse looks like when it is standing still or walking. All of them will place different emphasis on such features as the slope of the shoulder and the pastern, the size of the head, the length of the neck and the back, but these considerations are means of predicting what a yearling will look like when it is three years old and galloping on a racecourse with a jockey on its back. Once a horse has proved itself on the racecourse, what it looks like standing still is largely irrelevant. However, the correspondence between a horse's conformation and the way in which it runs is uncertain, for the manner in which a successful racehorse moves and how it differs in this respect from a less successful one still remains something of a mystery.

Nobody was able to visualize the movement of a horse's limbs while it was galloping before the advent of photography. The equestrian artists of the 18th and 19th centuries, even men like Stubbs who had an intimate knowledge of the horse's anatomy, were unable to solve the problem of the horse's gait. Modern gait analysis, which is based upon computerized experiments, is equally unable to make firm predictions. A succession of photographs is taken with a high speed camera at about six hundred frames a second while a horse is galloping; the timing and placement of each foot as it touches the ground is then analysed. Secretariat was found to possess an extraordinary gait, but unfortunately he shares this particular oddity with some rather moderate and slow horses. The manner in which a horse breathes must also affect its racing ability, since the ability to overcome exhaustion and to continue exertion depends upon the lungs and the supply of red blood cells to carry oxygen about the body. A yearling's lungs can be examined with an endoscope, but what then confronts the veterinarian's eye is only a matter for subjective analysis. The colt who was to be named Huntingdale was rejected by his purchasers at Tattersalls' Highflyer Sales on the grounds of a veterinary examination which expressed the opinion that the colt was unsound in the wind, the racing terminology for a breathing defect. The colt was returned to his breeders only to be nominated the champion two-year-old in Europe a year later.

The simple fact is that nobody knows what enables one horse to run faster than another. There are factors which obviously influence a horse's accomplishments on the racecourse, ranging from the will to win, the degree of responsiveness to man, to the shape and strength of a horse's legs and the efficiency of its lungs. It is difficult, however, to order these factors in a ranking, let alone work out how they are to be produced or how one can quantify their influence on a young horse. Once a racehorse has shown itself to be a "smasher" it is equally impossible to analyse what has enabled it to so distinguish itself. Prince

Khalid Abdullah's colt Dancing Brave offers an example. Dancing Brave was an exceptional racehorse. He dominated his contemporaries in Europe from April until October of his three-year-old career over all distances between a mile and a mile and a half and on going which ranged from heavy to firm. Dancing Brave's pedigree is not exceptional. His sire, Lyphard, had not, at the time of Dancing Brave's birth, produced a brilliant racehorse since being exported from France to Kentucky. The colt's dam, Navajo Princess, had had two previous foals neither of whom won even one race, although she was a winner of sixteen races herself and came from a family of useful but not brilliant winners. Lyphard covered several mares in 1982 who came from a more distinguished background than Navajo Princess, and it would be safe to say that on paper many of Dancing Brave's contemporaries appeared to have more potential than he did.

Dancing Brave was a unprepossessing young horse. He was turned down by Keeneland, who did not think he was up to the standard of their Select July Sale, and sold instead at Fasig Tipton's July Sale in Kentucky. When James Delahooke agreed to pay 200,000 dollars for him on Prince Khalid Abdullah's behalf his breeders, Glen Oak Farm and Gainesway, reached for the champagne, for this, they thought, was an event to celebrate. They did not believe this gangling, backward, almost overgrown horse was worth 200,000 dollars. At his prime Dancing Brave was not a beautiful horse. Indeed, he could almost be described as coarse, though he was undoubtedly powerful and strong. Those who have discovered some distinguished racehorses among Dancing Brave's American antecedents to explain his brilliance are fooling themselves, for there is nothing peculiar to Dancing Brave which sets him apart from thousands of his contemporaries, other than his ability on the racecourse.

For racing people the impossibility of determining or predicting a horse's ability is the source of the thoroughbred's fascination. The thoroughbred business thrives because it is possible to make a rational case for any number of matings, and for the selection of any number of yearlings, but no particular criteria will ever prove to be exclusively correct or conclusive. The inherent uncertainty on which the business is founded lures gamblers to place their bets on the racecourse or to try their luck in the auction ring. For the breeder this dichotomy between rationality and chance is the challenge of his trade or hobby. It is a familiar one for the biologist. For those who study evolution and inheritance the problem has always been to account for the variation of species and the manner in which variation is passed from one generation to the next.

The breeder of thoroughbreds attempts to produce successful racehorses. The only means by which a breeder can influence the quality of his product are by selecting appropriate mates for his mares and by structuring the environment in which the products of these unions are raised. There is a vast library of case histories and myths, as well as the canon of genetic science, to help the breeder select couplings. When choosing a suitable environment the breeder relies upon his knowledge of past practices, the natural habitat of horses and the horse's mental and physical requirements. To understand breeding as a business it is necessary to be aware of the nature of breeding itself. Once the various dilemmas of breeding and the theories which are used to help their resolution have been reviewed it may be possible to discern which are the most important factors, and to illuminate the breeders' role in determining which racehorse is able to run faster than another.

The odds against a breeder succeeding in his endeavour with any particular mating are overwhelming. Each year about 75,000 thorough-bred mares are covered* by a stallion in the United States, Britain and Ireland. Yet only a few hundred racehorses are acknowledged to show peculiar merit each racing season. Most breeders never produce a horse who gains election to this elite, some succeed occasionally and a few manage to do so regularly. This incidence seems to suggest the possibility of rationally explaining the success of the few. However, it seems unlikely that the answer lies in breeders' skill in selecting couplings. The findings of genetic science have led us to expect wide differentiation between the products of the same sexual union.

If the problem is considered at the simplest of levels and the concept of the gene is used almost as a metaphor, the element of chance in selecting matings becomes clear. If it is assumed there are ten alleles, or pairs of genes, which influence a horse's racing ability, and two parents are selected for mating both of whom carry the recessive and the dominant gene in each pair, then there are 1024 possible different types of offspring. Type here refers only to the offspring's physical appearance and not to the genetic material which it may later pass on. In reality the outcome of a particular sexual union depends upon more than the random combination of ten characteristics. So if there is a stallion whose genetic material is such that his union with a particular mare could produce a Derby winner, then even if the mare's owner chooses this stallion from the hundreds of possibilities available the chances of this one union producing a Derby winner are slim indeed.

This conclusion almost pre-empts the discussion. However, in exam-ining the relationship between genetics and thoroughbred breeding it

*When a stallion copulates with a mare he is said to be covering her: the usage of this word derives from the way a stallion mounts a mare and covers her back during copulation.

will be illuminating to look at breeders' own reflections on the subject and the various myths which they hold in high regard. Thoroughbred breeders have for years believed it is possible to improve the performance of racehorses through judicious selection of breeding specimens. From the time the four famous Arabian stallions were imported into Britain in the 18th century up to the beginning of the 20th century there is little doubt that for one reason or another the performances of racehorses did indeed improve. For the years since that date the proposition of steady improvement is more controversial, owing to such anomalies as the lasting nature of the record times at some major racecourses. This need not affect the argument, for some would see the greater specialization and conformity of the thoroughbred this century as a result of selection. If the thoroughbred population is conceived of as a pyramid, not only is the pyramid vastly greater in size but the top has been sliced off it. There are no longer outstanding individuals who stand at the peak. Instead there is a group who are all equally worthy of this position and who each spend a week or a month at the peak before being usurped by one of their rivals. If this were the case then the value and efficacy of selection would not be in doubt. Most breeders believe judicious selection increases their chances of producing a Derby winner and whether or not this individual is superior to a Derby winner of ten years ago is irrelevant, or only of anecdotal interest. Nobody would dispute this modest claim, but one would have more faith in the efficacy of pedigree research if it could be proved that the performance of racehorses had improved in some way or other over the last eighty years.*

There is a sense in which breeders classify their own activities within the field of eugenics. Positive eugenics is the attempt to improve the population of a species by selecting only its exalted members for the purposes of breeding. The term was first used by Sir Francis Galton in the years following Darwin's death, when it was widely believed that it would be possible to speed up the process of evolution to the great benefit of mankind. Here was an opportunity of raising the moral and physical performance of man in a way which would be more efficient and lasting than any programme of education. The study of eugenics in relation to man fell into disrepute because of the impossibility of agreeing upon the goals of any selection programme. Even if it were possible to formulate acceptable aims the optimism of early

---

*The author is not any sort of biologist and anyone who is interested is advised to read a basic biology text book complemented by way of the specialist works on the subject, for example, William E. Jones. *Genetics and Horse Breeding*, Philadelphia: Lea & Febiger, 1982, or Sir Rhys Llewellyn, *Breeding to Race*. London: J. A. Allen, 1964.

eugenics failed to take account of the uncertainty which surrounds the genetic influence upon mental and temperamental characteristics. The failure to conceive of evolution as being governed by probability working within environmental constraints led these early idealists to expect swift and decisive results. These same misconceptions or problems readily explain why breeding theories or programmes have been uniformly unsuccessful, or at least inconclusive. Exceptions to the rules of thoroughbred breeding are as common as individuals whose performances conform with the expected pattern. This is not surprising when such confusion exists about which physical and temperamental characteristics are desirable and to what extent they are genetically determined. However, it is more difficult to understand why breeders have come to place such an overwhelming emphasis upon the role of the stallion.

Many individuals and cultures have believed that the male and female contribution to inheritance is quantitatively and qualitatively different. One school of thought, which has been given the label ovist, arose from the observation of the enormous size of the ovum in comparison with the spermatozoon which fertilizes it. It seemed extraordinary that two bodies of such differing bulk should have a similar influence upon the product of their union. The spermatozoon, the ovists decided, supplies only the spark of life which upon union sets the ovum's regenerative powers in motion. There have been breeders who considered the mare to be of paramount importance, most notably Bruce Lowe and the Aga Khan III and his adviser Colonel Vuillier. It is unfortunate that there have been so few of a similar frame of mind, for in the field of thoroughbred breeding the ovist has probability working in his favour. A more common conception of the role of the sexes in inheritance was perhaps most clearly propounded by Aristotle.

When considering the means of inheritance Aristotle likened the role of the male to a carpenter and the female to a piece of wood. The female provides the substance of the produce of a sexual union, whilst it is the male who shapes and forms this material. Aristotle also considers the problem almost as a struggle between the various competing influences. If the mother wins this contest the offspring will be female, if the father is dominant it will be male. Further, if any of the grandparents are particularly potent then they will be the determining influence. This idea of an individual passing on almost a bundle of his own individuality which may then appear in subsequent generations frequently appears in breeding articles. In the case of a colt like the Derby winner Shirley Heights we are told that the influence of his sire Mill Reef was able to overcome the plebian attributes of his dam Hardiemma. The implication is of a powerful individual who is able to exert an influence over his family, without of course ever coming into physical contact with them. The gene becomes a conveyor of personality rather than of information, and a dictate rather than a code. Northern Dancer as the pre-eminent stallion is referred to in tones worthy of a magician among carpenters.

Another fallacy which has influenced thoroughbred breeding is the idea of acquired characteristics being passed on in the sexual union. Among horse breeders the most widespread applications of these principles have concerned the age of stallions. It is widely believed, without any particular explanation, that the standard of the progeny of some stallions deteriorates as the stallion becomes elderly. This characteristic is itself held to be inheritable as it is sometimes imputed to a whole line of stallions rather than a particular individual. Similar reasoning is often used to explain the divergence between the racing abilities of different crops of the same stallion. It is absurd to expect the progeny of any stallion to conform to any exact pattern, but if a year passes without any of the offspring of a reputable stallion making a mark on the racecourse there is a felt need for an explanation. This usually consists of remarks about the stallion's health and the environment in which it is being kept. Environmental influences are also sometimes used to account for a change in a stallion's performance following exportation to a different climate. A change in climate and handlers may well make a stallion more or less tractable but it will not affect its genetic material or the genotype of his offspring to the slightest degree.

These and the many other possible examples of an unstated belief in the inheritance of acquired characteristics can be placed in two categories. The various theories of the effect a horse's health and environment have upon its performance as a progenitor can be placed within the idea of soft inheritance. Federico Tesio's writings adamantly state his belief in soft inheritance. This is revealed by the value he placed upon the energy created by the act of copulation itself and by his theory that fillies should not be strenuously raced as this would deplete their scarce reserves of nervous energy. The other category, which can be termed theories of use and disuse, includes those which imply that a horse is able to pass on talents and characteristics which it adopted or was taught during its lifetime. An example of one of these arises from the observation that yearlings today are less perturbed by aeroplanes and the strain of being transported by air than their parents and grandparents were. There are many possible explanations for this, but none should include the idea of this aptitude being passed down from one generation to the next. After all, horses have been trained to wear a bridle and a bit for centuries, but this does not remove the necessity of breaking every young horse in its turn.

The ideas of soft inheritance and of the inheritance of characteristics acquired by use and disuse are ancient and have been subscribed to by many biologists, philosophers and animal breeders. The persistent hold these ideas have on the human imagination, despite the findings of genetic science, can probably be explained by misinterpretations of the phrase "the survival of the fittest" and a failure to understand, or an unwillingness to accept, the role chance plays in inheritance. If a particular skill or adaptation enhances a man's or a horse's ability to survive and excel, it seems logical that this should then be passed on to future generations. However, it has been proved deductively that an organism's genetic material cannot change during its lifetime and during the 1950s this was shown to be chemically impossible.

The means of inheritance are genes, and genes are only discrete particles which convey information and when assembled on chromosomes provide a programme for the development of an organism. Genetic science was able to develop rapidly once Mendel's work was rediscovered in 1900, for Mendel's experiments with peas showed that what have since been called genes are the only means by which attributes of characteristics are passed from one generation to the next as a result of a sexual union. As far as the potential for any such traits are present in a fertilized ovum they are conveyed by genes and by genes alone, and further the same chromosomes are present in every cell of the body. An organism's physical and mental attributes, its phenotype, are influenced by the environment in which it is reared and many other factors, but its genotype, which is fixed at the moment of fertilization, is only the result of its genetic inheritance.

Most erroneous ideas about inheritance are based upon a failure to understand this concept. People who have taken on the idea of the gene then abuse it by envisaging genes blending to produce an influence, urge, or a spirit of an ancestor: inheritance is thus seen in terms of personalities, aptitudes or other pneuma. There is, as has been said, a resistance to acknowledging the role probability plays in inheritance. The variation which can be observed in the individuals of any species is the result of the random way in which the genotype of an individual is formed from the chromosomes of its parents. In the case of a domestic animal like the thoroughbred the species is improved if the phenotype which results from a particular genotype is considered to be desirable, and this individual is then selected for breeding. By the laws of probability this individual is more likely to produce offspring with the desired phenotype than either of its parents were. As long as the same criteria are used for selection, then with each succeeding

13

generation the chances of obtaining the desired result will increase. However, as the thoroughbred breeder has only a vague notion of the phenotype he desires such a selection process is almost impossible. A brief exposition of the complexities of the gene will show that even if the breeder knew which mental and physical attributes he desired any lasting improvements could only be achieved gradually.

The irony of genetic science is that what began as a search for an explanation of the observed wonder of variation has led to the incidence of similarity being wondrous itself. This may only be the reaction of a layman not versed in the lore of biochemistry, but once the multifarious ways in which a genotype may be fixed and the connection between this genotype and the phenotype have been considered, it no longer seems surprising that the last eighty years of intensive selection of racehorses has not brought about a marked improvement in their performance. Indeed it seems almost extraordinary that any predictions about the aptitudes and abilities of a prospective mating are proved to be correct, beyond the one which says the produce will be a racehorse. One is left feeling like the beginner at a bloodstock auction who cannot understand why everyone pays so much attention to the pedigrees printed in the catalogue. If this cross or that broodmare has already produced a classic winner the chances of such a swift repetition must be slim indeed, the beginner reasons.

Everyone is in some degree aware of the Mendelian characteristics of a dominant/recessive relationship between genes. If an organism with a single pair of genes is considered, it has three possible genotypes: two dominant genes, one dominant and one recessive, or two recessive genes. The organism will only express the recessive gene in its phenotype if it has received two recessive genes, one from each of its parents. The individual with two recessive genes or with two dominant genes is called a homozygote, whilst the individual with both a dominant and a recessive gene is called a heterozygote. This relationship between genes is, as will be seen, only the most simple of many possibilities. Mendel purposely ignored any variations in the peas which he was breeding whose inheritance did not conform to this pattern. This enabled him to predict the probability of obtaining a ratio of three to one between the dominant and recessive phenotypes among individuals that were the produce of the mating of two heterozygotes. The incidence of this ratio proved that the means of inheritance are discrete but interrelating particles.

In reality an organism like the horse has numerous different genes* which can be located in thousands of different loci on the chromosomes

*William E. Jones, op. cit. rather unhelpfully suggests that a good guess would be between 20,000 and 60,000.

and whose relationship is expressed in several different modes. Some genes with a clear dominant/recessive relationship lead to the expression of different phenotypes in each sex. Some again are only semi-dominant, which means that a heterozygote will express a characteristic which is intermediate between the two homozygous characteristics. Other genes are epistatic, which means their presence will mask the influence of an untold number of other genes on the phenotype. Others again have a low penetrance, which means that an individual may hold them in the homozygous state but not express them in its phenotype. It is a mistake to conceive that there is necessarily a correspondence between a pair of genes and an observed characteristic, for in many cases several genes will together influence a single characteristic, a trait which is labelled polygeny.

Genes are both nuclear and discrete, but their locus on the chromosomes also affects the information which they convey. A collection of genes will impart a code but if they are at different loci on the same chromosome, or on different chromosomes altogether, this code may be entirely dissimilar. This concept of the placement of genes in relation to each other affecting inheritance is known as linkage. These various different relationships between genes which affect the information they impart increase the element of chance involved with any successful prediction of the attributes of a mating. However, the truly random nature of inheritance lies in the process of meiosis by which the gametes are formed.

A horse has thirty-two pairs of chromosomes in each and every cell of its body. Thirty-one of these pairs are similar in structure and position, the thirty-second pair consists of the sex chromosomes. There are two types of sex chromosomes, the X and the Y. The X chromosome was observed under a microscope and seen to be in the shape of a X long before it was linked with sex differentiation, which accounts for these labels. A male horse will have both an X and a Y chromosome, whereas a female horse has two X chromosomes. The X chromosome can be seen to be relatively large and it has been estimated that it carries 5 per cent of the total genetic material. As the X chromosome is exclusively derived from the feminine, a colt will inherit an X chromosome from its dam while a filly will inherit one from its dam and one from the dam of its sire; it is probable that the female plays the decisive role in the inheritance of racing ability in thoroughbreds. This probability must not be overstated; it is only the result of a proportion and a marginal ratio favouring the feminine. As the number of chromosomes in the horse, or any other organism, is constant, the gametes, that is in the horse the spermatozoa and the ova, must have fewer chromosomes than any other cell. In fact the process of meiosis

15

reduces these chromosomes in the diploid or paired condition to the haploid state, where each spermatozoon or ovum has exactly half the number of chromosomes of the other cells.

As the meiosis begins the diploid chromosomes are drawn close together. Three consecutive cell divisions then take place. In the first the number of chromosomes doubles and in the following two it is halved. The result is either three spermatozoa each with thirty-two chromosomes or one ovum with thirty-two chromosomes, as in the female three polar bodies are produced which do not affect inheritance. The chromosomes split lengthways, so the loci of the various alleles is not necessarily altered; however during the process a chromosome may break and cross over, joining on to another so as to change these locations. When fertilization occurs the diploid condition is restored and a highly specific code for development has been produced. It should not be surprising that the almost haphazard process of inheritance, a process of deconstruction, reconstruction, dominance and correspondance should allow for an infinite capacity for variation between individuals of the same species.

The obvious question to ask, once the means of inheritance has been understood, is whether or not the various theories of thoroughbred breeding correspond with these concepts.* One which certainly does is the theory of hybrid vigour. A cross between two unrelated individuals may well produce an offspring which is superior to both because most harmful genes are recessive. However, hybrid vigour is usually associated with matings of individuals from different species or within the same species as in the case of crossing a thoroughbred with an Arabian horse. In the case of man or the thoroughbred when mating is confined to members of the same variety, hybrid vigour is of limited significance.

The discussion of the significance of the sex chromosomes in thoroughbred breeding will have illuminated the earlier statement that the ovist has probability working in his favour in this field. Bruce Lowe's theories did at least take account of this fact and in some sense he was an ovist. Lowe traced back the pedigrees of countless horses to the hundred or so original mares in the English stud book. He then deduced that certain families (by a family he meant all horses who could be traced back from their dam to her dam et cetera to one of the original broodmares) were particularly distinguished as runners

*It is not intended to describe these theories in detail. This has been done endlessly elsewhere. Those who are interested should see William E. Jones op. cit.; Sir Charles Leicester, *Bloodstock Breeding*, London: J. A. Allen, 1983; Abram S. Hewitt, *The Great Breeders and Their Methods*, Lexington: Thoroughbred Publishers, Inc., 1982.

and others as stallions or progenitors. His findings have since been disproved on statistical grounds and anyway it is only possible to postulate a mare in the fifth generation as a determining influence on a horse's ability as a runner or a sire by discarding the collected knowledge of genetics. However, Lowe was not alone in believing the influence of the mare to be paramount. The Bedouin who bred the original Arabian horse, which at its time was more fleet and versatile than any other, valued a stallion only as the son of a prized broodmare. Another who was of a similar opinion was Colonel Vuillier, who advised the Aga Khan III on his breeding policy and whose success in that capacity popularized his own dosage theory of breeding. Unfortunately anyone who wishes to account for the phenomenal success of the Aga Khan's breeding operation must look for an explanation somewhere other than in Colonel Vuillier's dosage theory, for this does once again contradict the canon of genetics.

Dosage theories of inheritance are based upon Sir Francis Galton's law of ancestral heredity. Galton believed an individual received about one half of its heredity from each of its parents. He followed up on this reasonable supposition by saying that therefore it received about one quarter of its heredity from each of its grandparents, one eighth from each of its great grandparents, and so on. Galton based his stamina index on these beliefs and Vuillier built his dosage theory about them. Sir Francis Galton explained his stamina index as follows:

"If one half of the average distance of the races won by the sire and the dam, excluding two-year-old races, is added to one quarter of the similar averages for the four grandparents and one eighth for the eight grandparents, plus one eighth for the sixteen sires and dams of the previous generation, a stamina index can be obtained which will serve as an approximate guide to the potential distance up to which any particular horse can be expected to win races."*

The predictive powers of this index are probably as great as any other which is based upon the analysis of pedigrees alone. Vuillier studied many pedigrees and noted the recurrence of the names of particular stallions in the pedigrees of leading winners. He then used Galton's law to work out the average proportion of heredity certain particularly famous names contributed to leading contemporary winners. The next step was to arrange matings with a view to reproducing these proportions in the offspring. The fallacy of dosage theories is their conception of heredity as bundles of personality or ingredients

*Cited in the *Economist*, December 1985.

17

which are mixed together to form the offspring's genotype. Once this idea of genetic material being able to blend is accepted, then the possibility of a recessive trait appearing after some generations is precluded. Galton was attempting to explain the similarity of a species population and the manner in which hereditary traits tend towards the average in the population as a whole. In doing so, however, he simplified the means of inheritance and failed to allow for the infinite variety of individuals.

The two aspects of breeders' thoughts about their own endeavour which deserve the closest scrutiny are, first, the idea that a knowledge of pedigrees or pedigree research has some predictive efficacy, and secondly, the dominant role which has been ascribed to stallions. If it is assumed these are both valid approaches it must be asked whether or not it is possible to explain this validity in the terms of genetic science. A breeding programme for any domestic animal is unlikely to succeed until a breeder has a clear idea of which traits he desires. Those traits whose inheritance is relatively simple can be selected for and the herd or population which is controlled will display a degree of homozygosis within a few generations. If those individuals who display an unwanted recessive trait are excluded from the breeding programme the corresponding gene will slowly be eradicated from the controlled population. Eventually all its members will be homozygotes with respect to this particular allele. For the horse such traits include coat colouring and blood grouping. The problem facing the thoroughbred breeder is how to define his aims more specifically than simply to produce a good racehorse. As long as breeders' intentions are so nebulous there is a temptation to conceive of inheritance in terms of personality.

A horse's genetic material is only a code which gives it the potential to develop certain physical traits and to an unknown extent temperamental characteristics as well. It is misleading to speak of the genes which affect racing ability, for genes can only affect such an aptitude indirectly. The correspondence between a horse's genotype and its racecourse performance will only begin to be understood when the mental and physical factors which determine that performance are understood. These factors cannot be influenced to a significant extent by alleles with the simple dominant/recessive interaction. Breeding analysis usually assumes "the racing genes" are dominant and uses this to explain what is seen as the prepotency of the exalted stallion. At other times they are held to be recessive in order to account for the ability of a horse whose parents were only moderate, but whose grandparents or more removed ancestors were excellent racehorses.

Recessive they cannot be, for recessive traits are the easiest to produce by selection. For an individual to display a recessive trait it must be homozygous, therefore a mating between two individuals with the trait will produce offspring who are all homozygous in this respect. If "the racing genes" were recessive one would only have to mate two classic winners to be sure of producing a potential classic winner. Pure dominance alone is an equally unlikely explanation of racing ability due to the complete absence of any semblance of a ratio in incidences of repeated matings or attempts to follow the pattern of a successful mating. This result appears to be logical, for it would be extraordinary if the long list of mental and physical characteristics which affect a horse's racecourse performances were all determined by a few alleles and a dominant/recessive relationship. Inasmuch as they exist, "the racing genes" must be polygenic and this accounts for the wide and infinite variation in horses' performances despite centuries of selected breeding.

The idea of the prepotent stallion has fascinated thoroughbred breeders. Everyone involved with the bloodstock business seeks to discover or produce an excellent stallion and those held to have succeeded are inundated with riches and glory. This obsession with stallions has some rational foundations, that most often cited being the superior knowledge of the stallion's genotype which emerges by dint of the number of his offspring. A broodmare will only produce ten or fifteen foals, so, it is argued, by the time her ability as a progenitor is beginning to be revealed her fertile life will be nearing its end. This knowledge is, however, only marginal, for even the most hard worked and long living of stallions will sire only some one thousand foals* and few fashionable stallions sire more than five hundred. When one considers the multiplicity of the genetic material and the manner in which it is assembled, five hundred is as small and insignificant a number as fifteen. At the present time horses who are produced by artificial insemination are not allowed to run at any recognized thoroughbred racemeeting. The irony of this prohibition is that the widespread use of artifical insemination would enable breeders to gain significant information about a stallion's genotype. However, the introduction of artificial insemination is fiercely resisted by breeders and stallion owners alike for they have no interest in acquiring such information unless possession of it guarantees them fantastic financial rewards. The attraction of the stallion lies in its uniqueness and exclusivity. The mythological properties attributed to the stallion would appear incongruous if each were not unique, and without exclusivity the

*The notable exception to this are Irish National Hunt stallions, particularly those standing at the Coolmore Stud. Deep Run used to and Le Moss still does cover about two hundred mares every year.

stallion's owners would lose out on both the riches and the glory which they receive at present.

Knowledge of a stallion's physical and temperamental characteristics probably constitutes as good a guide as any to explaining a horse's merit once it has been displayed upon the racecourse, but the *ex ante* predictive powers of this knowledge seem to be generally overestimated. This confusion between rudimentary analysis and prediction is exacerbated by the statistics used to evaluate a stallion's ability and to place it within a ranking. The amount of prize-money and the number of races won by a stallion's progeny may well be impressive, but the most noticeable feature of the progeny record of any stallion is its unevenness. Approximately 30 per cent of the progeny of all stallions never appear on the racecourse, and although in the United States some of the more fashionable stallions produce 60 per cent winners, in Europe, where there is less but more competitive racing, this figure is rarely more than 40 per cent. When it is considered that the majority of these winners are only of average or less than average ability, it becomes clear that all stallions produce more slow or unsound horses than fast ones. In addition, the performances of even the most praised stallions fluctuates markedly from one year to the next, a fact which is hard to explain without resorting to ideas of soft inheritance if these horses are assumed to be prepotent. The idea of prepotency becomes even less valid when the numerous advantages the offspring of such prized stallions receive in terms of the environment in which they are raised and trained is taken into account. The offspring of these stallions will receive the greatest possible care from the moment they are born. They will be sent to the best trainers and will be ridden by the best jockeys, yet in Europe at least 60 per cent of them will never even win a race.

Another proof of the prepotency of select stallions is said to be the way in which they stamp their stock, the racing jargon for producing horses with a marked physical resemblance. In some cases this is indeed true as a ratio and does constitute a prepotency of sorts. However, a preponderance of this sort is only to be expected for those traits like coat colouring and blood grouping which have been shown to conform to a dominant/recessive relationship. If it were not possible to isolate such traits and select for them it would not be possible to breed beef cattle that fatten quickly or advantageously shorter strains of corn. This fact will not verify any prepotency with regard to "the racing genes" unless it is proved that such traits correspond closely with racing ability. By way of a comparison with stallions, the consistency of the quality of the produce of the best broodmares is remarkable. A broodmare like Lady Tavistock's Mrs Moss, who has to date produced nine foals all of whom have won and four of whom were up to competing in races of the highest standard, has a more even record than any stallion. This phenomenon need not have a genetic explanation, for a foal lives inside or beside its mother for two years.

The belief in the efficacy of pedigree research and the prepotent stallion stems from attempts to rationalize a racehorse's exceptional ability after the event. If they are to be used as an ad hoc explanation they have some validity, but their dubious nature is revealed when they are used to predict ability and to justify substantial financial gambles. Invariably these beliefs are founded upon the idea of the inheritance of personality rather than the concept of heredity as the random collection of genes working within the constraints of probability and selection. There is a sense in which pedigree research is founded upon the uncanny recurrence of certain names in the pedigrees of leading winners. The uncanny recurrence occurs at that moment chance takes on the character of fate. Fate, unlike chance, lends itself to analysis and rationalization and the oracle which possesses knowledge of fate will be accredited with prophetic powers. An exceptional racehorse like Dancing Brave is the product of chance rather than fate; in effect, the superior racehorse is a freak. Dancing Brave is unlikely to sire a horse better than, or as good as, he was on the racecourse, not because of any blending of hereditary influences or tendency to regress towards the "normal" but simply because freaks by their very nature are unusual occurrences. The probability of Dancing Brave producing a freak is greater than for most unproven stallions simply because he was one himself; whether this probability is such to warrant a stud fee of £120,000 is something which will be returned to later.

The pursuit of the knowledge of the pedigrees of horses is an entirely innocuous pastime or hobby whose rewards are similar to those gained by the study of crosswords or sporting almanacs like Wisden. The only reason for pointing out the fallacy of its foundation is to illuminate the bloodstock auction, and the role of the breeding expert and the bloodstock agent in the determination of prices and values. Again and again in the bloodstock world one comes across chance masquerading as fate and the totem of the pedigree is but one of the best examples of this. The breeder who arranges a mating with the specific purpose of inbreeding to Nasrullah in the fourth generation, or who mates the winner of the Dewhurst Stakes with the winner of the Cheveley Park Stakes, may well produce a good winner by chance, but he is unlikely to initiate a programme which improves the quality of his stock in this manner. To devise such a programme it is necessary to know which traits and characteristics you desire and which you are lacking. In order to achieve this the breeder must be aware of the physical faults and temperamental quirks of his stock and seek to find mates which will increase the probability of eradicating these defects. A controlled breeding programme is often a process of elimination rather than supplementation. Part of the breeder's activity is to chose appropriate couplings and his best guides for this are a rigorous and consistent selection procedure and close observation of his animals. With such techniques it is possible to affect a long term improvement in the quality of his stock.

Whether heredity or environment plays the more important role in determining a racehorse's ability is irrelevant to the breeder. A horse's heredity is largely a matter of chance and although the breeder may be able to swing probability in his favour to some marginal extent, until he is allowed to use artificial insemination, cloning and other techniques from the field of cybernetics the successful selection of matings will remain a matter of luck. The breeder does, however, have complete control over the environment in which his horses are reared and it is in this field that he is able to play a decisive role in determining a horse's racecourse ability. The dramatic increase in the value of racehorses and the financial rewards of successful breeding has not directly affected the manner in which couplings are selected, but it has had a correspondingly dramatic affect on the environment in which horses are reared.

══ Two ══
Environment and Management

Successful and efficient stud management has been transformed over the last twenty years. Traditional precepts and practices which horsemen were once happy to rely upon have been examined in a new light and any changes which might marginally improve the horse's performance have been eagerly adopted by those breeders who are determined to be competitive. The vet and the equine ecologist have come to play a major role in determining the environment in which the thoroughbred is kept and in the daily decisions of an efficient stud farm. It has become accepted that the manner in which a horse is raised is the decisive influence both upon its future racing ability and its short term commercial value. There has been an attempt to reconcile the horse's instinctive needs with the demands man makes of it. In particular close attention is now paid to fulfilling the horse's nutritional requirements and making the stable routine as natural as is possible without unecessarily increasing the risks of injury. The process of selecting matings has, in contrast, changed only insofar as the computer has enabled breeders to collect more statistics and search through more pedigrees in order to justify very similar decisions.

This progressive trend is only a response to new commercial incentives. For this reason it is more readily apparent in the care and management of foals and yearlings than of other categories of bloodstock. For the stallion and the broodmare the sentimental and commercial imperatives are not so easily reconciled. In their management there is a clear conflict between the horse's instinctual needs and man's commercial ends. A brief description of the routine on a modern stallion farm will serve as an example of this conflict and the tension induced by man's attraction to both the horse and to money. However, the first step is to look at the care and management of foals and yearlings.

The thoroughbred is able to adapt to the most varied climatic conditions. Racehorses who are able to compete in the highest international class have been raised in South America, Australasia, South Africa, Italy, West Germany, Florida and California as well as in those places like Kentucky, Ireland, Northern France and England which have traditionally produced the finest racehorses. Indeed, it would be possible to raise a superior racehorse wherever there is sufficient pasture, grain, water and salt to provide for the horse's basic nutritional needs. However, among the areas which satisfy these minimal requirements there is a wide variation of actual performance and the breeder is no longer willing to rely upon trial and error to determine the location of his operation or his choice of feeds. The equine nutritionist has discovered not only that either inadequate nutrition or a mineral imbalance can cause limb defects and other unwanted physical traits in the horse, but it has also been determined what the performance horse's requirements are and how they are best provided for.

On the modern thoroughbred farm the horses are given a controlled diet designed to provide them with the appropriate quantities of energy, protein, calcium, phosphorus and Vitamin A. If the suitability of a particular paddock for young horses is in doubt, then rather than giving a list of the famous horses who romped in the very same paddock when they were babies, the modern breeder will collect soil samples and send them to a laboratory for analysis. Horsemen have always considered the feeding of horses to be something of a mysterious art, but now there is so much money at stake the unconfident breeder is bewildered by an abundance of scientific analysis rather than mythical practices. What horses are given to eat has not changed that dramatically for, after much analysis and testing of feed supplements and additives, the present consensus among equine nutritionists is that horses are most suited to a diet of high quality hay, grain and water. This statement of the obvious does not belittle nutritionists, for they have defined high quality in a rigorous and falsifiable manner.

The breeding of thoroughbreds is essentially a farming activity, and like any other agricultural enterprise breeding has benefited from the findings of biochemistry and ecology. The successful breeder must know how to select or grow high quality hay and grain and particularly how to maintain the quality of his pasture. Horses are especially prone to parasitic infection and a young horse affected by worms may suffer irreparable damage. The usual method of containing this problem is to graze cattle or sheep on horse paddocks during the winter, or in some other rotation, the idea being that worms who thrive inside horses are not able to survive in the alimentary tract of cattle or sheep. For this reason the Lexington area of Kentucky is an important centre for both the horse and cattle breeding industries. Some of the large Kentucky farms like Claiborne have their own herd of cattle, while others like Taylor Made Farm let their paddocks free of charge to a nearby cattle farmer. The only alternatives to some form of mixed grazing are to give horse paddocks regular and protracted rests and to pick up manually all the dung deposited in a paddock. Neither of these alternatives is likely to allure the commercial breeder; the first means not using a valuable asset for two or three years, the second will involve paying his staff to perform a task which will take a long time and which they are unlikely to enjoy.

A new development in the management of horse pastures is the fashion for actively seeking out land which has never been grazed over by horses before, or at least not for some decades. In part this fad can be explained by the desire to minimize the menace of worms, but its proponents consider the use of fresh land to have a more encompassing significance. The desire to use fresh land is an inversion of the traditional practice of favouring farms or paddocks on which superior racehorses have already been raised. It does not have a clear economic explanation, for any saving achieved through purchasing run down agricultural land, rather than an established stud farm, will probably be outweighed by the cost of constructing appropriate facilities. Incidentally, for the benefit of those English readers who have never seen a run down farm, the Blue Grass area of Kentucky is almost entirely surrounded by smallholdings or tobacco farms in various states of disrepair. A more likely explanation for this new practice is the trope familiar to all amateur evolutionists which expresses the benefits of using virgin land. If a species is introduced to a virgin environment, or at least one in which the particular species is completely new, then for a time the species will thrive unnaturally. The most often cited illustration of this principle is the carp of monstrous dimensions which can be produced simply by introducing ordinary carp to a fresh pond. This trope is also a justification for the nomadic existence. Since horses are instinctively nomadic, this may itself be a sound reason for applying the principle to thoroughbred breeding.

This idea is most popular in Kentucky, where there is plenty of run down farm land available, but it is concurrent in England as well. Breeders like Lady Tavistock and Kirsten Rausing enthuse about the benefits of fresh land. Before Lady Tavistock started the Bloomsbury Stud, racehorses had not been raised at Woburn for two hundred years, whilst Kirsten Rausing bought an arable farm near Newmarket on which to establish her private stud, which had not been grazed over by horses since being ploughed up during the Second World War. In Kentucky Robert Clay is one of those who have put this principle into practice. He established his Three Chimneys Farm on what was a tobacco farm near Midway on the north western edge of the Blue Grass area. Every year he purchases some fresh land, buying up some of the run down agricultual land on the perimeter of the stud. He has entertained the idea of eventually selling the land he bought at the beginning, in which case the farm itself would gradually migrate westwards.

Another tradition of horsemanship which has been re-examined is the practice of keeping horses shut up on their own in stalls. Again, although innovations in this field are not exclusively American, much of the impetus for change has been derived from the new Kentucky stud farms. The herd instinct is strong in horses and not only will a horse always wish to associate with other horses, but it will have marked likes or dislikes for each individual. A hierarchy soon emerges within any herd of horses and an order of precedence will be respected by each of its members. The traditional stable routine thwarts the horse's social aspirations and can also harm it physically. When kept in a stable a horse is subject to draughts and will move from one extreme temperature to another each time it is turned out during the winter. A stable is often both dusty and dark. The first of these characteristics may cause respiratory problems whilst the second can be disconcerting, as the horse's eyes respond only gradually to changes in light. The modern American barn, which can be observed on farms like Lane's End or Taylor Made, bears a closer resemblance to a cubicled dormitory than to the rows of prison cells which constitute the traditional stable. The yearling barns at Taylor Made Farm have high ceilings, skylights in the roof and large overhead fans at either end. The boxes are all open so the yearlings can hear and see each other and each one opens both onto the central corridor and outside. There is an additional skylight above the outside door which provides yet more light. Those boxes which are built in the traditional English fashion now tend to be larger and lighter and to have efficient ventilation. The humidity of the Kentucky summer places a greater premium upon ventilation than is the case in Newmarket or Yorkshire, but all breeders are now aware of the benefits of keeping horses in a clean, light and dust free environment and allowing them to fraternize with each other.

This re-examination of the stable routine has affected not only the design of stables, but also the amount of time horses are kept inside them. It is now generally accepted that so long as a horse is not sick or particularly weak then it is better off outside than in a stable, except when it is being trained for racing or being prepared for a sale. Mares and foals are now often turned out together in groups for the entire first eight months of the foal's life. In those places like Florida or California with a temperate climate some mares are allowed to foal outside. In colder climates it is not possible to leave foals outside until spring is well advanced, and in any event most people with a valuable broodmare would be nervous about letting her foal without human supervision. Thoroughbred foals are usually weaned from their dams between the age of six to eight months. On some Kentucky farms the weanlings are segregated by sex, in order to eliminate the possibility of a precocious pregnancy, and then turned out together for the duration of the winter. They are only brought in again when it is time to prepare them for the sales. There does indeed seem to be some truth to the maxim that horses do not mind extreme heat or extreme cold, as long as the temperature is relatively constant.

One final trend in stud management worthy of mention is the Australian and American belief that the larger the paddock in which horses are turned out, the better. Some Australian farms have one thousand acre paddocks reserved for this purpose. In Europe people seem to be more wary of the possibility of injuries and there is a tendency towards maintaining the ability to supervise the young horse's activities. This nervousness about injury is the chief restraining influence on the need felt to allow young racehorses to develop outside, and in the company of their contemporaries. The outside life is held to be both healthy and educative, and its proponents claim that through romping freely together and competing for food young racehorses learn the benefits of competition and perseverance. As will be seen when the business of breeding is considered in detail breeders only produce the type of yearlings which are demanded at the yearling sales. If people are prepared to pay extravagant sums for sleek, fat and pampered yearlings, then breeders will be only too happy to provide them. However, this trend towards naturalness and an appreciation of the robust horse, even if it does have some scars and other exterior blemishes, is readily noticeable among both buyers and sellers at the major yearling auctions. If this means that young racehorses will be allowed to develop at a more considerate pace and in a less contrived environment, then it is difficult to see how this could be construed as anything but an advance.

This trend for raising horses outside without unnecessary supervision or cosseting is motivated by a calculated economic risk. The valuation of a young horse is determined by its potential to perform an arduous task. Therefore any preparation or training which is likely to help the horse stand up to this burden of work is likely to increase its value. "Is likely" rather than "will", because, as will be seen, the yearling market is not always so logical. If a breeder loses a foal or a yearling after an injury incurred in a paddock or because of an illness which went undetected because the horse was not kept under constant surveillance, then his loss is unquantifiable. For the small breeder with only one or two broodmares such a loss will have serious economic consequences, as the foal or yearling may represent his only chance of gaining a return on his investment in broodmares and stallion nominations in a particular year. On the other hand for the large breeder with a herd of broodmares the loss of a young horse is a predictable consequence of a policy which also yields compensating financial gains in the short term. The horse that dies or suffers a severe injury before being sold or tested on the racecourse might have become a great champion, but however fashionable its pedigree or marked its physical promise, it was more likely to have been just another disappointing racehorse. To compensate for the occasional loss the breeder has the knowledge that by allowing his horses to develop in comparative freedom he is enhancing their potential as racehorses.

The broodmare and the stallion present a different commercial proposition. The breeder is only interested in their reproductive capacity, and economically at least any other attributes they may have are purely incidental. The management of broodmares and stallions does therefore offer a clear example of the conflict between the horse's instinctual needs and man's commercial ends in the bloodstock business. That there is a conflict should not be surprising, for when the entire evolutionary history of the horse is considered the minor role which man has played in its development soon becomes obvious. Man's interest in the horse, and in recent times more particularly the thoroughbred, stems from the horse's ability to combine both speed and physical endurance. As was stated earlier the horse has peculiarly long legs in proportion to its body size and weight which enables it to run fast, and incidentally to carry man on its back. The horse is among the least fierce of animals and when faced with danger it will instinctively flee. Its natural speed is therefore probably the result of the premature death at the hands of predators of the less swift members of the species. The combination of speed and grace which has given the horse such utilitarian, aesthetic and symbolic importance in man's eyes is only an adaptation to the environment in which the horse lived before it was domesticated. Since domestication man has bred the horse selectively and developed numerous different varieties of horses to suit his own particular purposes. However, this physical differentiation and the aptitudes and habitats which the horse is trained to adopt are only a veneer which obscures its instinctive urges and desires.

For centuries the horse and horsemanship were particularly valued for the central role they played in warfare. An adequate supply of suitable horses and horsemen was considered to be vital for the well being of the state both by Aristotle in the fourth century B.C. and by the English Jockey Club at the beginning of the twentieth century. Those very qualities which made the horse so useful to man in his pursuit of war are the direct result of the horse's instinctive wish to avoid combat. It is indeed ironic that an animal which is peaceable by nature should have become a symbol of power and bellicosity. Federico Tesio was one thoroughbred breeder who was well aware of the ironic uses to which the horse has been put by man and he said of the cavalry horse:

"... The only reason why the horse charges into the enemy in battle is that he is short sighted and therefore cannot see him, and, being peaceful by nature, even less can he suspect that the enemy is going to shoot him."*

The broodmare's reproductive capacity is too wide a term to express the breeder's interest in it, for in fact the breeder is only interested in his idea of the mare's genotype. The mare is a capital asset, and in order to be efficient this asset must produce a foal every year. A broodmare's value depreciates annually, as a mare is only fertile for a limited period; some would generalize and say that the possibility of a mare producing a decent racehorse after the age of fifteen is small. A year without a foal is thus a year in which the asset depreciates, with no compensating source of income. The opportunity cost incurred by a breeder whose broodmare is barren is substantial. His asset has depreciated, he may well have paid a large fee for a stallion's services without obtaining any guarantee of a live foal. And then there is the mysterious cost of what might have been; this foal which was aborted, or which never even existed, might have been the million-dollar yearling or classic winner which is the peak of his aspirations and the object of his fantasies. The thoroughbred breeder and the stallion owner are therefore much concerned with the problem of infertility.

This concern is not sufficient to determine the selection procedure. Some physical types of broodmares are more fecund than others, specifically those with a wide pelvis and well developed mammary glands. But these qualities will not have much influence upon the value of a potential broodmare. No breeder searches for broodmares who

*Franco, Varola, *The Tesio Myth*, op. cit.

find foaling an arduous process, or who are not able to supply their foal with sufficient nutrition during the period before it is able to digest solid food, but then nor are they preoccupied with avoiding such difficulties. A potential broodmare's value will be determined by its record as a racemare and whether or not its pedigree is considered to be fashionable. If a mare is considered worthy of selection by these criteria then the question of its natural fecundity will be deferred until later. Once a broodmare has become a capital asset she is well on the way to being thought of as a machine for producing foals, and if this machine does not function efficiently then it is up to the vet to remedy the situation.

There can be little doubt that fertility or fecundity is to some extent determined hereditarily. On one level breeding from individuals with an inappropriate physiognomy increases the probability of perpetuating these problems by increasing the percentage of the population who are prone to them. In addition abortion can be caused genetically, and persisting to breed from infertile individuals may, even when a foal results, simply increase the proportion of the population who carry these harmful genes in the recessive state. There are recessive genes which can cause the death of an embryo, as well as genes which can cause endocrine disturbances particularly of the pituitary and thyroid glands which influence body growth, the development of the sex organs and the individual's metabolism. If an infertile mare produces a foal the breeder will see this as a cause for rejoicing, but the foal is likely to display the same characteristic infertility, or at least pass the trait on to its offspring. The colt born from a subfertile mare may well turn out to be a relatively infertile stallion as it may have inherited a harmful recessive gene. These traits are hard to eradicate as all homozygous individuals are likely to die while still embryonic, or in the case of gland disturbances the breeder may not be aware of the hereditary cause once the foal displays the symptoms.

This determination to have fertile stock without selecting purposefully for this characteristic has led to the vet playing an all important role in thoroughbred breeding. There was a time when the traditional horseman was wary of the vet and his scientific jargon and practices. Now no one will take a decision concerning a valuable broodmare without first consulting a vet. All valuable broodmares are continually being swabbed or having their ovaries felt through the wall of the rectum to determine when they should be covered, whether they are pregnant or whether they are infected in some way which might affect their fertility. Organizations like the British Thoroughbred Breeders Association spend a large proportion of their research funds on inquiries into the causes of infertility and veterinary research centres in Newmarket and Kentucky alike are mainly concerned with these and related questions. In the long run thoroughbred breeders may well resort to cybernetics or specifically to embryo transfer in order to avoid the selection dilemma.

The techniques of embryo transfer were perfected in America and Japan, although they have also been successfully put into practice at the Equine Fertility Unit in Cambridge. It is now relatively simple to flush an eight or nine day old embryo from a donor mare and place it, after a period in an incubator, in a foster mare who will bear the foal and mother it until it is weaned. The American Quarter Horse Association recently approved the registration of produce of embryo transfer as long as the donor mare had proved to be subfertile, or if the donor mare was more than fifteen years of age. Subfertile was defined as having failed to produce a live foal after bona fide attempts to achieve pregnancy during three consecutive calendar years. The various thoroughbred registries will no doubt initially approve embryo transfer on similar grounds. Once it has been allowed embryo transfer will of course dramatically change the typology of the racehorse. One can imagine there being a sharp division between breeding individuals and racing individuals with the only contact between the two being mediated by a test tube. Certainly those mares who are held to have a desirable genotype will be considered too valuable to be put through the hazardous process of actually giving birth. They may be too busy racing anyway, for a donor mare need only take a week or two off from the racetrack in order to be covered and flushed. Perhaps people will begin to breed mares specifically for the purpose of carrying and giving birth to foals; such mares need not of course be thoroughbred mares. There might be a problem, as nobody particularly wants colts with wide pelvises, but then the problem could be dealt with at the incubator phase.

To put the problem of infertility in a proper perspective it is worth pointing out that the fertility of thoroughbreds has improved dramatically over the last sixty years. In the 1920s the average conception rate of English thoroughbred mares was 33 per cent*; today the figure is around 70 per cent. This means the owner of a valuable broodmare is faced with a probability of 4/5 rather than 1/3 of obtaining a foal from his asset in any particular year. In America the national average is for only 55 per cent of matings to produce a live foal, but all serious commercial farms will record a conception rate of around 70 per cent. In the light of these figures the whole question of infertility takes on a slightly absurd air, particularly when all participants in the business

*Vamplew Wray, *The Turf: a social and economic history of horseracing*, London: Allen Lane, 1976.

believe there is an international problem of overproduction of thoroughbreds. There seems to be an epidemic illogicality whereby all participants agree that there are too many thoroughbreds, whilst simultaneously making strenuous efforts to produce the maximum number of foals from each of their own broodmares.

Another aspect of the problem which seems to be universally ignored is whether or not it is desirable, suitable or beneficial for thoroughbred mares to spend their entire lives in the pregnant state. The average pregnancy of a thoroughbred mare lasts for 342 days and scientific research has shown the "best" time for a mare to be covered is when she first comes on heat after foaling, usually some ten days later. "Best" here means only the time when the mare is most likely to conceive again. If a mare does not conceive after being covered during the foaling heat there is a period of about twenty days before she is once more in a oestrus state and is willing to accept a stallion. So a healthy thoroughbred mare will be pregnant except for a period of between ten and thirty days each year, and on average one year out of every five when she will fail to conceive at all.

Once the expedience of perpetual pregnancy is accepted the unsuitability of January 1st as the day on which all thoroughbreds' age advances becomes clear. All thoroughbreds, whatever their actual date of birth, become yearlings on the January 1st following the year in which they were foaled. Racehorses are, as has already been said, tested when they are still young and immature and in the spring of their three year old career there is a marked difference between the June foal and the January foal, who has had an additional five months in which to grow and develop. Thoroughbred foals grow extremely quickly, as is often the case with animals which are by instinct part of a nomadic herd. It has been estimated that the gains in a foal's height and girth measurement during the first three months of its life are only slightly less than the total increase in the following nine months. The competitive pressure on the thoroughbred to develop quickly is such that some breeders believe a foal who is abnormally small at birth, who weighs less than a certain amount, has no chance of catching up with its more precocious contemporaries in time to distinguish itself on the racecourse. All breeders would therefore like their foals to be born early in the breeding season, both to give the foal the advantage of relative maturity, and to enable them to get the mare in foal again in time to avoid having a late foal the following year. Unfortunately the optimum time for conception under this schedule does not coincide with the natural breeding season.

A foal who was born in the wild during January and February would have little chance of surviving in any but the most temperate climates. In England, Ireland and Kentucky the foal's nutritional requirements will not be provided for naturally until late April or May, when spring is well advanced. So mares will not normally begin to cycle in these environments until April, which does of course make the struggle to achieve an early pregnancy that much more arduous. The natural breeding season ends in August, though of course no thoroughbred breeder would want an August foal, and horses are not sexually active at any other time of the year. The most efficient solution to the problem was discovered by Dr Wendell Cooper in the early 1970s, when he realised that the broodmare's oestrus cycle responded to the number of hours of daylight. The solution was to place both broodmares and stallions, for the quantity of spermatozoa also fluctuates seasonally, under lights from December onwards to fool their metabolisms into believing spring had already arrived. A similar technique is widely used on battery hens in order to maximize the quantity of eggs they produce.

It is impossible not to wonder whether a more sensible solution would not have been to change the January 1st registration date to March 1st, or even revert to the original date of June 1st. The Jockey Club were moved to change the date in 1833 by the inconvenience of having horses changing their age in the middle of the flat racing season. This objection is now irrelevant, when in the United States at least there is flat racing all the year round. The solution which takes the greatest account of the horse's physiognomy would be to make March 1st the registration date and to discontinue the practice of racing horses as two-year-olds. The classic races would then be confined to four-year-old horses and the thoroughbred population as a whole would no longer be subjected to such physical and mental stress during its immaturity. The advantages of such a change would seem to be overwhelming and more than sufficient to overcome the prerogative of tradition. However, such a sensible transformation would be economically inconvenient.

The bloodstock business thrives upon gambling. One of the joys of gambling on bloodstock rather than upon the result of a particular horserace is the prolonged period of anticipation and anxiety between the placing of the bet and the resolution of the game. In the game of bloodstock the bet is placed when a mating is decided upon, or a yearling is purchased, and the resolution takes place either in the sale ring or when the horse's racing ability is evaluated. This period of tension, like most of man's satisfactions or desires, is subject to the law of diminishing marginal utility. Under the present system two years separate the beginning of the game and its termination with the handing out of prizes, both for the breeder and the owner. If the game is prolonged in some cases it is only because the possibility of the jackpot has already disappeared. Two years does therefore seem to be the optimum duration for this period of pleasure and pain. If young horses were generally sold as two-year-olds and the best racehorses were syndicated at the end of their four-year-old careers, then the game would be that much longer and more expensive. The rewards reaped by the owner and breeder of the successful racehorse would be the same, but they would have to wait another year for the harvest. The failures would become that much more expensive, as they would have to be looked after for an additional year before being given the opportunity to fail. However many sound reasons there might be for such a transformation they will always be overridden by the mental and economic incapacity to wait any longer than two years. So, racehorses are raced when they are immature and bred outside the natural season.

This conflict between the man and the horse is even more obvious in the case of the stallion. At the present time the stallion is simply too valuable to be treated like an ordinary horse. Broodmares, foals and yearlings are also valuable but their value lies in what they might become or might produce. The stallion's valuation rests upon what he has already achieved on the racecourse and on what he is. The stallion has already completed its task. Once a stallion returns to the stud farm after a brief sojourn on the racetrack or in a racing stable the only physical demands which will be made of it will be to copulate with about fifty broodmares a year. As long as the stallion is able to cover mares his financial value will be untarnished, even if he is only up to hobbling out of his box and scrambling on top of a mare in the corridor outside. In the long run of course the stallion's owners would like him to live as long as possible, but only a few stallions remain fashionable enough in their dotage to maintain their position at the select end of the market. For anyone who invests in a stallion the time of reckoning is the first five years of the horse's new career at stud, and for the duration of this time at least the stallion represents too large an investment to be exposed to any avoidable risk.

Some young stallions will always die whatever precautions are taken. In recent years three English Derby winners have come to an untimely end; Troy died of a twisted gut, Shergar was assassinated and Golden Fleece died of cancer, and of course Swale collapsed and died before he even had a chance to return to Claiborne. If Golden Fleece is the only racehorse who is known to have died of cancer it is because few other horses have been the centre of such protracted medical care and analysis which was able to pinpoint the cause of his illness. The cost of insuring a stallion against both infertility and death is prohibitive

34

and an early death is almost certain to bring with it financial losses for the horse's shareholders. An approximate estimate for such a premium would be 5 per cent of the stallion's total value each year. The insurance company will sometimes reduce its own risk by reserving the right to demand an independent valuation of a horse after an accident and to be obligated by this ex post figure rather than the initial valuation. The justification for this practice is that the valuation of a stallion is as whimsical as the tastes and opinions of bloodstock breeders and buyers. This practice adds yet another argument to the overwhelming case in favour of cosseting stallions.

Stallions are at risk from themselves, from other stallions on those farms which keep more than one, and most dangerously from mares during the act of copulation. The traditional method of overcoming, or at least diminishing, the first two of these risks was to keep stallions securely in their boxes for as much of the time as was feasible. Stallions were released when it was time for them to perform in the breeding shed, and occasionally they were turned out in paddocks for the purpose of exercise. Stallion paddocks were always small so they would not be able to gallop about or overexert themselves in any other way, and they were often surrounded by high fences to prevent one stallion from seeing another. In effect stallions were kept in solitary confinement and deprived of any visual or social distractions, except when they were presented with a mare. To resort briefly to anthropomorphism, it should not be surprising that when kept under such conditions stallions were often vicious, frustrated and liable to be violent with any men or horses they came into contact with.

In the wild a stallion will run together with a herd of broodmares, other stallions, foals and young horses. A mare will only accept a stallion's sexual advances when she is in the oestrus state; at any other time she will reject the stallion peremptorily or, if he persists, even violently. Thoroughbreds are segregated by sex from the age of about six months and thereafter a male horse will only come into fleeting contact with the opposite sex on the racecourse, until it is either castrated or retired to stud. This segregation of the sexes places the onus of determining whether or not a mare is in the oestrus state upon man. This diagnosis is deemed to be one of the most important aspects of stud management and as such the decision is often delegated to the vet and his scientific devices. The diagnosis is doubly important; if a mare is falsely designated as oestrus she may injure both herself and the stallion before the mistake is revealed, whilst if a mare is falsely designated as deoestrus she may inadvertently forgo her chance of conceiving.

All stallion farms rely upon the process of teasing to facilitate this prognostication. There are many ways of teasing a mare, but the most common is to lead a mare past a stallion and to observe her reaction. A stallion farm will keep an undistinguished but entire horse specifically for this purpose and the operation will take place at a teasing board. The teasing board is simply a padded wooden structure and the teaser is held on one side, whilst the mare is led past on the other. Teasing is a delicate procedure, but an experienced observer will usually be able to make a correct analysis of the mare's state after observing her behaviour on successive days. The act of copulation still presents a risk because of the possibility of an incorrect diagnosis and as a result of both horses' unfamiliarity with the opposite sex. The very unnaturalness of the environment in which teasing takes place can lead mares to behave in a deceptive manner and mistakes will be made on any stud farm.

When presented with a mare an inexperienced stallion can behave in a manner which is guaranteed to perturb all but the most placid of broodmares. Some stallions will stand on their hind legs and walk towards the mare squealing with their front legs flailing. Thoroughbreds have been hand bred for centuries and the practice will continue until such time as artificial insemination is accepted by all thoroughbred registries. There is no alternative method of breeding horses which does not both increase the chances of either the stallion or the mare being injured, and reduce the probability of a swift conception. To any studhand both the practice and the spectacle of hand breeding is normal and familiar, it is only a naive outsider who is likely to share the mare's perturbation. The final control on the act of breeding which is intended to reduce the risks of injury is to restrain both the mare and the stallion. Both will wear head collars and be held on a long rein, the mare's tail will be bandaged and held to one side and the mare will frequently be twitched as well. A twitch is a loop of cord which is used to control the mare by drawing it tight about her upper lip. Felt boots are often put on a mare's hind legs to soften any blow she might give the stallion and on some farms, or in the case of an awkward mare, hobbles will be put on her hind legs, or alternatively one of her forelegs will be held up. Occasionally the mare will be blindfolded as well.

The stallion farm is a clear illustration of the central tensions in the thoroughbred business. As is the case with any other domestic breed, the thoroughbred is reared in a contrived environment which masks but does not remove the tension between the horse's instinctual desires and the demands man makes of it. The equilibrium which has been formed by centuries of inter-relation between the horse and man can be upset when man becomes preoccupied with money, and sees the horse only as a potential source of income. If many of those who own shares in stallions cease to glorify, revere or even care for the horse except as a means of procuring golden eggs, then the horse will be debilitated. The third side of the triangle can restore the equilibrium, for even if the bloodstock business is preoccupied with money it will always rely upon the horse's ability to entertain, and a degree of sanctity is a prerequisite if the horse is to retain its hold upon man's imagination.

The stallion's lot has generally improved in recent years on the grounds of economic efficiency. A stallion who is unruly or vicious is more difficult and time-consuming to manage than a more contented one, and will obviously amplify the problems of hand held breeding. Stallions are now exercised more rigorously. Those who are habitually slow breeders will be lunged regularly during the breeding season, especially shortly before they are due to perform in the breeding shed. On those farms with sufficient staff all stallions will be turned out, lunged or given some form of exercise during the breeding season. Those stallions whose services are in great demand will be strenuously taxed in any case.

In the northern hemisphere the breeding season lasts for 155 days from February 10th to July 15th, with most activity taking place in the middle of this period as only a few mares are ready to be covered in early February and no breeder chooses to have a June or July foal. A mare will be given two or three chances before she is turned away barren, but the more efficient farms with the more fertile stallions will achieve an average number of coverings per conception of less than two. Even so the popular English stallion will be asked to perform about one hundred times a year, the Kentucky stallion probably more often and those Irish stallions who are asked to cover ninety or one hundred mares a year really have their work cut out for them. The practical difficulty of asking a stallion to cover so many mares soon becomes apparent if a slight illness confines the stallion to his box for a few weeks. The horse may then have to perform two or three times a day if he is to complete his task before July 15th. Such prodigious feats of virility can only be expected from a young stallion. The older horse is both less energetic and less fertile and so will usually have to cover a mare more frequently to achieve conception than was the case in his youth.

Stallions are still generally turned out in small paddocks and no one is likely to encourage them to display their athletic prowess, but few are still confined by high railings. Most breeders find the prospect of turning stallions out at night too alarming to contemplate, for if something does go wrong they do not want to rely upon the night watchman being both alert and able to cope with the crisis on his own. Instead, during the off season, most stallions are turned out for five or six hours in daylight and brought in every afternoon. On the large Kentucky stallion farms each horse will have its own particular paddock from amongst those ranged alongside each other about the stallion complex. This can cause problems. At Walmac International in Kentucky the two star stallions, Alleged and Nureyev, have the two adjacent paddocks nearest the stallion boxes, where their activities can easily be supervised. Alleged is a large and powerful horse who has been known to rip the shirt off a groom's back; in contrast Nureyev is a small gentle beast. Unfortunately Alleged's temper and disliking for Nureyev is such that they can never be turned out at the same time lest something untoward should happen to Nureyev. Nureyev has other problems besides Alleged, for he is not the most libidinous of horses and his spermatozoa have an unusually short life. If a mare who has been booked to Nureyev comes into season, whatever the time of day or night she will be rushed to the breeding shed at Walmac International. This is when the difficulties start, for Nureyev has been known to loiter for more than an hour before consenting to do the deed.

The luckiest stallions are those like Electric at the Whitsbury Manor Stud in Hampshire and Diesis at the Mill Ridge Stud in Kentucky who have large boxes which open directly on to their own paddocks. Diesis is particularly fortunate as his purpose-built box opens on to a four-acre paddock situated right in the middle of Mill Ridge Farm. He can observe everything which is going on on the farm and he is thus unlikely to feel starved of distractions. In Kentucky stallions, like all other horses, live in barns. On the more traditional farms like Claiborne or Greentree the stallion barns are simply two rows of tall roomy boxes facing on to the same corridor. Greentree's stallion barn is a tall wooden structure, freshly painted white, dark green and light green; with its spires and huge sliding doors it has an air of grandeur about it. Claiborne, with the exception of the Hancocks' imposing neo-classical residence, is an altogether more mundane place. The barn which houses such stallions as Nijinsky, Sir Ivor, Secretariat and Spectacular Bid has a dingy faded feel to it, although the farm would probably describe it as merely practical.

The more modern farms tend to group their stallions together in small separate units. The stallion barns at Gainesway were designed by Theodore M. Ceraldi and on their completion in 1984 won an award from the American Institute of Architecture. The citation described the new Gainesway as ". . . a masterly example of the great beauty and elegance that can result from simple design done well". It is a judgment which most visitors would agree with, for the barns are finely executed down to their paved stone floors and wrought iron grilles and fittings. Each of the barns holds four stallions and, grouped together in a park, they look like chalets or hotel cabins which would not look out of place at the Gazelle d'Or. Three Chimneys' stallions Seattle Slew, Slew O'Gold, Chiefs Crown, Shahrastani and Nodouble are housed in a single round building with a conical roof; their boxes are both large and open so the stallions are always able to see and hear each other. Unusually, the breeding shed is exactly adjacent to the barn, but none of the stallions are apparently perturbed at being able to overhear their colleagues' performances.

Robert Clay's Three Chimneys Farm is also unusual in that all of its younger stallions are ridden for two miles every day during the off season. This riding is nothing too dramatic for they are only walked along a narrow path between railings, but Three Chimneys' stallions do appear to be in a better condition and more relaxed than those on farms where the stallions are expected to exercise themselves in their small paddocks. On all farms the stallions are given some form of exercise in the months before the beginning of the breeding season, either by being lunged or walked outside on a lead shank. Despite what can only be seen as a progressive trend in stallion management, the physical and temperamental condition of stallions varies widely from one farm to another. On some farms the older stallions look bowed, buckled and stiff, on others they are obese and flabby. The temperamental differences between stallions is even more marked, particularly when it is remembered that horses are not by nature fierce or vicious. Chris Harper, the owner of the Whitsbury Manor Stud, is quite happy to walk into Known Fact's box and pat him gently on the head while the stallion is completely untethered. There are many stallions in Kentucky whom no one would dare approach under similar circumstances for fear of spending the following few days in hospital. These differentials must be in part the result of the environment in which the stallions are kept. In England the responsibility for wayward behaviour is usually assigned to the quality of the staff who look after the stallion. An eight- or nine-year-old stallion is a creature of awesome power, quite capable of seriously injuring a man with a playful gesture. Only the most experienced horseman is able to assert his authority over a stallion while maintaining the horse's sympathy.

There is a shortage of skilled and experienced staff in all of the centres of the bloodstock industry, except for Ireland. The Irish place a peculiarly high value upon the horse and the relative financial rewards and social prestige of horsemanship are higher in Ireland than anywhere else. To some extent the bloodstock business is kept going in

Newmarket, Normandy and Kentucky by migrant Irish labour. In Kentucky many farms rely upon young and mainly European people who work there for a limited period to gain experience before returning home to manage a stud or hold other exalted positions in the industry. Anthony Stroud, Sheikh Mohammed's racing manager, worked on Darby Dan Farm and Henry Cecil spent some time at Greentree, and both are now involved with bloodstock on a grander level. Greentree's manager Perry Alexander remembers Henry Cecil pulling blocks of ice out of a water trough with both arms, despite the fact that it was 15 degrees below freezing and the sleeves of his smart fawn jacket were frozen solid. However, there are many jobs which offer greater and more comfortable rewards than the meagre ones given to stud hands, and in Kentucky permanent posts seem to attract the disadvantaged. There is certainly a disproportionate number of blacks and Mexicans working on Kentucky farms. For those without a vocational calling the stud routine must be wearisome and at times alarming.

There are certainly instances of astounding negligence. When a stallion returns to stud after its racing career it is likely to be over-exuberant at first and to take some time to recondition to the more sedate pace of life. However, it hardly seems sensible to ease this transition by cutting back the stallion's feet to such an extent that even walking becomes a painful process, although a stallion in this condition is of course unlikely to charge about its paddock in an alarming manner. Then there is the case of the internationally famous young stallion who was partially blinded because someone decided to spray the fencing of his paddock without taking adequate precautions. Nonetheless the real cause of the abuse of stallions lies not with those who look after them from day to day but with the economic imperatives of the business.

When it is possible to charge as much as 500,000 dollars for the right to breed a mare to a stallion, it is not surprising that some farms believe it to be in their best interests to cover as many different mares with as many different stallions as is possible within the statutory 155 days. It is easy to become sentimental about a horse like Nijinsky, but one is less likely to be swayed by sentiment if one has gambled 600,000 dollars on his being able to perform the act of copulation. The sight of Nijinsky hobbling painfully on infected and inflamed legs is indeed pitiful. At the same time, at an auction of nominations, people were still prepared to gamble hundreds of thousands of dollars on him being able to cover mares the following year. However, the efficient and successful breeder is unlikely to have the same order of priorities as the untutored and financially unaffected observer.

The practice of walking mares in to a stallion farm when they are ready to be covered, rather than boarding them on the farm for some weeks or months, is undoubtably efficient. For the stallion owner "walking in" is efficient because it reduces the amount of land and labour needed to run a stallion farm. The farm which boards the mares who are to be covered by its resident stallion is responsible for supervising the mares foaling and looking after the mares and their foals for three or four weeks. In order to do this a farm requires at least sixty acres and three men for each of its stallions. A stallion farm to which the mares are walked in needs only enough land to provide its stallions with paddocks and enough labour to conduct the mating process safely. The difference between the two systems is made clear by comparing a traditional English stallion farm like the Aston Park Stud in Oxfordshire with the Gainesway Farm near Lexington in Kentucky. The Aston Park Studs stands two stallions, Elegant Air and Dominion; it has a permanent staff of seven and comprises some 140 acres, which makes some people wonder whether it has quite enough land. Gainesway Farm houses more than forty stallions. Yet it has only twenty-five stallion men and its five hundred acres are sufficient for the farm to board twenty or thirty mares as well as its stallions. For a traditional English farm to be able to stand forty stallions it would need to have at least 2,500 acres of pasture and a permanent staff or more than a hundred, a daunting prospect indeed for any manager or stallion entrepreneur.

Many breeders also prefer to "walk in" their mares; this enables them to oversee their mare's foaling and the first few weeks of the foal's life. In Kentucky, where walking in is the standard practice, the large breeders have their own farms on which their mares, foals and yearlings are kept and raised. Those whose operation is on a less grand scale will board their mares on a public stud. In either case the mare will only leave the farm on two or three days a year when she is vanned to a nearby stallion farm to be covered. It can be seen that "walking in" leads to centralization, for once a large stallion farm has been established it will attract a cluster of private and public broodmare farms about it. If, as seems likely, the practice becomes more common in both the Newmarket area and County Kildare, then both will exert an even greater pull on new investors than they do today. One can envisage there being a few stallion farms in Newmarket with the outlying farms, which at present stand their own stallions, turned into private or public broodmare farms.

The problem with "walking in" or more particularly with farms with thirty or more stallions is the practical one of carrying out the mating itself. If a farm is going to be able to mate some 1,500 or 2,000 mares in only 155 days it will have to be efficient. Consider for a moment a typical morning during the mating season at Gainesway Farm. Lest anyone should think Gainesway is being criticized, it is worth pointing out the farm's extraordinary efficiency. In any breeding season around 2,100 mares are covered at Gainesway and on average 80 per cent of this total will conceive, an admirable figure compared with the American national average of 55 per cent. If 2,100 mares are booked to be covered by Gainesway's stallions, then at least 4,000 actual matings will take place, or about twenty-five every day. In fact there will be more than twenty-five per day during the middle of the breeding season and fewer during the season's opening and closing weeks. On a morning which is not typical but rather successful, thirty mares will be covered in Gainesway's two breeding sheds in a two-hour session.

The two breeding sheds at Gainesway are adjacent and are both overlooked by the same glass-plated control box. This control room is similar to those which look on to the stage in a theatre, or on to the performers in a recording studio. In the theatre this room is the seat of the stage manager or lighting director; it will be discreetly hidden, enabling the director to see but not be seen and to control the lighting and stage effects and during rehearsals to give out admonishments over the loud speaker system. In the breeding shed there is no audience, only the human and equine performers concerned in the act of copulation, and the director, who at Gainesway is the resident veterinarian, Norman Umphenour. Norman Umphenour sits in his glass box looking down on to the scene of breeding, directing and giving instructions through his microphones.

The breeding sheds are large barns with high ceilings, soft floors and padded surfaces. They have few sources of outside light and are illuminated artificially. At one end there are large sliding doors through which the stallions enter and exit and the mares leave once the deed has been done. The mares arrive in horseboxes and are unloaded on a series of ramps just outside the breeding complex. The mares will be given staggered arrival times, but a proper order of appearance is not feasible as no one is prepared to wait for a mare who arrives late. Once a mare has been unloaded she will be led into the back of the complex in order to be teased. The teaser stallion is kept in a stall with grilles rather than closed walls on either side. The mares are placed in turn in the adjacent stalls, where they are able to see and smell the teaser. Their behaviour is observed in order to confirm that they are in the oestrus state.

Those deemed to be ready for covering are led on to the next stage of the procedure, where their genitals are washed and felt boots are placed on their hind legs. Additional precautions are taken for mares known to be difficult or shy breeders. The mare is then led into one of the four padded booths at the back of the breeding sheds to await her turn. At any particular moment there will be ten mares inside the complex, two performing in the sheds, four waiting in the booths, which look like equine latrines, two being washed down and two being teased. In addition there will be mares being unloaded and loaded up again outside. On a good morning a mare will spend only forty minutes at Gainesway. When the mares are waiting in their booths the stallions who have been selected as their mates will be prepared in their nearby chalets. At the appropriate moment the stallion will be led into one of the sheds, his genitals will be washed and he will be presented with his mare, at first to sniff her and then to mount her.

When things are running smoothly the stallion will spend less than eight minutes inside the shed. For two hours there will be a procession of mares proceeding through the complex in a circular fashion and of stallions being led to and from the breeding sheds. There will be about thirty men involved with holding, washing, leading and supervising on the floor, together with those who have come to drop off and collect the mares, and then there will be Norman Umphenour and his assistants directing the action in the glass box.

Inevitably things go wrong sometimes. In rare instances a mare is covered by a stallion other than the one her owner has paid for. To guard against this or any other incident which may result in the farm being accused of negligence, there are video cameras in both sheds. Occasionally a mare will take fright or otherwise reject the stallion, causing more immediate pandemonium. The stallion will sometimes cause the problems by lurching at the mare or being in some other way overkeen. In the words of one of Gainesway's stallion men, "... sometimes they go beserk and start trying to climb up the walls". When the problems of hand held breeding and the ease with which horses can be hurt in the process is considered, the extraordinary nature of the Gainesway phenomenon becomes clear. One may question whether this is a sensible or humane method of breeding racehorses, but one cannot fail to be filled with admiration for the calm poise of Norman Umphenour and the Gainesway staff. Not only do they manage to conduct four thousand or so separate couplings in one hundred and fifty five days, but only rarely do either the mares, the stallions or the men suffer a serious injury in the process.

The stud farm has for a long time been a symbol of tranquillity. Whether Stubbs's painting of a group of mares and foals or the more sentimental images which are used to sell chocolates are considered, the association of mares and foals with a sense of serenity is the same.

43

Unlike the majority of the English countryside the stud farm remains an evocation of the pastoral, for whereas Stubbs's cornfields with their stooks, scythes and wagons have long since disappeared, stud farms still have post and rail fences and paddocks separated by hedges or trees. Indeed, as anyone who has driven from London to Newmarket will know, the area has become an oasis surrounded by prairies. Even Kentucky farms retain an air of tranquillity once the freeways and the horrors of the New Circle Road have been left behind.

This symbolic import is much played upon. Advertisements for stallions or for farms themselves often feature pictures of the joyous horse in the green paddock. American equine advertisers are overtly sentimental and are particularly fond of photographs of the horse and barn silhouetted against the rising or setting sun. One can only presume this sentimentality is demonstrative of financial sophistication. Perhaps American farms realize that the new investor is drawn to bloodstock by the prospect of a rich gamble, but justify this lure with visions of cute horses in paddocks. So to attract clients the farm presents both statistical evidence of its economic efficiency and a suitably alluring visual image. Whatever its justification, this sentimental advertising is affectation, or at least nostalgia, for of all stud farms the leading American ones are most particularly places of business rather than of beauty.

The appearance and atmosphere of the stud farm is designed to attract and comfort the client as much as to benefit its equine inmates. The stud farm must appear to be appropriate for its specific function. As one stallion farm owner said, if your stallion's fee is more than £5,000 you should employ someone to mow the lawn, if it's more than £10,000 then you need rosebeds and other flowers as well, so you ought to take on a gardener. By the same chain of reasoning one can justify the red and white palace of Calumet, or the castellation of North Ridge. Man houses his domestic animals in buildings which befit his image of them, rather than those which would suit their needs. It should surprise no one that some Kentucky farms have built splendid shrines in which to house their stallions, or that the mangers at the Ashford Stud are lined with silver, for these are true reflections of the esteem in which their owners hold the stallion. If the stallion is to be venerated as the source of untold riches, then it is fitting that he should be surrounded by vulgarity and ostentation.

There are many thoroughbred breeders who would scorn such vanity and daintiness. The rural breeder sees his horses only as animals, and treats them in the same utilitarian manner as his other stock. The rural breeder is happy for his horses to grow up in a scruffy field in the company of sheep or cattle. He is not right or wrong, although he may

44

be less affected than his more sophisticated colleagues. Besides the ostentatious and the utilitarian there are other stud farms which could be labelled as traditional, notably Claiborne and the Aga Khan's Ballymany Stud in Ireland. There seems to be nothing new at Claiborne except for the stones in the graveyard. The breeding shed appears to be rickety, whilst the wood around the teasing stall is as worn as the tops of the desks which are supposed to have been used by Shelley. The mares' looseboxes at the Ballymany Stud are the same wooden boxes in which Aly Khan would have boarded his mares, and they do not appear to have been painted since his death. One feels that if Shergar had not been kidnapped the Ballymany Stud would have remained unchanged for decades more, but then the design is practical and a horse is not interested in whether or not its box has been painted recently.

The point is not to pass judgment on one type of stud farm in comparison with another, but only to describe the variety of different places in which racehorses are raised. The best of modern stud farm architecture, as at Gainesway or Lane's End Farm in Kentucky, is eminently successful. The staff on a stud farm are affected by its architecture as well as the horses, the clients and the owner, and the contentment and purposeful atmosphere of Lane's End Farm must be in some degree due to the resonance of its buildings. The foaling barns with their rubberized floors and walls and laboratorial air, and the staff bungalows in good post-modernist reds and browns, with sloping roofs and porches supported by classical columns, are particularly impressive.

Thoroughbred breeders are in the business of raising successful racehorses. All breeders, whatever their circumstances and financial resources are faced with two central problems: the sheer difficulty of succeeding in breeding a distinguished racehorse, and the unavoidable expense incurred in the attempt. No one really knows what enables one racehorse to run faster than another, or whether the attributes of a racehorse are determined genetically or by the environment in which it was raised. Even to make a guess at a ratio between the two influences would be absurd, for it could only be an arbitrary one. Perhaps the only certainty is that whereas the means of inheritance of racing ability remains a mystery and beyond man's control, the environment in which a horse is raised is wholly determined by man.

Similar reasoning, coupled with the new values assigned to blood-stock, has led the industry's members to look upon the young horse in a new light. The young horse is seen as being in need of analysis and encouragement, rather than instruction alone. The motivation for this change lies in commercial incentives alone, and, as yet, there has not been any parallel move towards showing stallions the same consideration. However, as will be seen later, the days of heedless mass production in the breeding industry have passed. If the emphasis of the demand for thoroughbreds is for physical quality and potential, then breeders will be encouraged to show consideration to all their stock. In order to understand breeding as a business it is necessary first to look at the causes of the boom in bloodstock values and the established differences between the industry in Europe and the United States which helped to mould the boom's affects on both continents. The most important of these established differences were the manner in which bloodstock was taxed and the pattern of racing on the two continents, and it is these differences which must be considered next.

Part Two

═══ Three ═══
The Impact of Taxation

When seeking to account for the differences between the British and American bloodstock industries, taxation may not be the most obvious answer. Nonetheless taxation policies have had a seminal influence upon the two branches of the industry and it is therefore worth examining these policies in some detail.

Thoroughbred breeding, and in the United States racing as well, has flourished because for a sizeable number of wealthy people the marginal utility of a racehorse is greater than the marginal utility of taxed income. If this is not immediately clear, then consider this statement from an advisory booklet on taxation and the thoroughbred: "... if the breeder pays tax on other income at 60% then the net cost of the breeding loss to him is only 40% after tax relief."* the figures of 60 per cent and 40 per cent show this to be a work of British origin, but the principal would be the same if they were 30 per cent and 70 per cent instead. Consider the man whose last £100,000 of income would, if he retained it for consumption, be split between the exchequer and himself on the basis of a 3:2 ratio. If instead of keeping this £40,000 to consume the man spent or invested £100,000 in a breeding operation then although he might receive no financial return or dividend, the total sum of pleasure and satisfaction which he derives from this £100,000 might be greater than he would be able to obtain by con-

*Guide to Taxation of the Bloodstock Industry. London: The Horseracing Advisory Council, 1987. Other reference works in this field include: Principles of Bloodstock Taxation. Dublin: Haughey Boland & Co, 1987. The Horse Owners and Breeders Tax Manual, Washington D.C.: The American Horse Council, Annual.

suming £40,000. The whole concept of tax shelters is of course derived from similar differences of marginal utilities and the singularly low marginal utility which many wealthy people assign to the prospect of paying an extra unit of tax.

The American judge who declared that: "... as long as tax rates are less than 100%, there is no 'benefit' in losing money"* was in one sense speaking the truth, but it is a literal statement which assumes money and utility are synonyms. American breeding has flourished primarily because lots of wealthy people receive many benefits from losing money on thoroughbred horses. Any decision to spend money is the result of a comparison between two marginal utilities; the question asked is whether one more unit of good A, or one more unit of good B, would give greater satisfaction. The incidence of tax shelters and tax avoidance has clearly shown that when good A is tax or payments to the government most people will choose good B, whatever it is, and even if it leaves them financially worse off. For the breeder to be faced with this choice rather than the choice between spending on horses and spending it on clothes, food, cars or something else more satisfying than tax, he must run his breeding operation in a businesslike manner. The Inland Revenue and the I.R.S.† will only allow a breeder to write off his breeding expenses against tax if they consider his breeding to be a business, rather than a hobby. Without this ruling the thoroughbred business would not be viable, and indeed the relative prosperity of the American thoroughbred business is in part due to the I.R.S. allowing the cost of training and racing horses to be set off against tax, if it is done in a businesslike manner.

The provisions of the taxation code which are related to bloodstock in Britain and the United States are easily summarized. In Britain a stud farm which is run on commercial lines is considered to be a taxable farming business, whilst the activity of racing is generally held to be a hobby. The proceeds of the sale of any bloodstock are therefore part of the stud's or its owner's taxable income. However, the commercial stud farm, like any other business, is allowed to set off against tax the cost of purchasing stock, that is broodmares and stallion shares. The expense of acquiring a stud farm is not tax deductible, but any improvements can be subsidized by up to 30 per cent tax relief. The commercial farm's losses can be set off against income from other sources for at least five years. After five years of consecutive trading losses the Inland Revenue may begin to wonder quite how commercial the farm is and only agree to maintain the business distinction if

*Jack Lohman & Arnold Kirkpatrick. *Successful Thoroughbred Investment in a Changing Market*. Lexington: Thoroughbred Publisher, Inc, 1984.
†Internal Revenue Service.

profits are expected in the near future. Clearly a breeding operation's classification as either a business or a hobby will affect its viability, for the expenses of a hobby are not tax deductible. The Inland Revenue does it seems attempt to tax all profitable activities while preventing those who indulge in loss-making activities from deducting their expenses from their taxable income.

The ownership of racehorses is considered to be an activity which is generally loss-making, and so the expenses of training and racing cannot be deducted from taxable income. This ruling has further implications for VAT for in Britain, unlike in Ireland, VAT must be paid on transactions of bloodstock. A business which is trading with a view to profit is allowed to recover the VAT it pays, but as owners in Britain are not held to be in business they are unable to do so. However, because racing is a hobby, any prize money a horse wins is exempt from tax, and if a horse's market value increases during its racing career this increment is free of tax as well. The ownership of racehorses is therefore one of the few hobbies from which it is possible to make millions of pounds tax free.

In the United States on the other hand racing and breeding alike are both considered to be taxable business activities. As regards breeding, the accepted practices are similar to those in Britain, except that horses or stock are depreciated more swiftly, and thus more generously, and tax relief is also accorded more generously. The major difference in the way in which bloodstock is taxed in the two countries is that in the United States training fees and other expenses of racing are tax deductible, and the cost of all horses which have been in training and are held for more than two years can be depreciated as an ordinary business expense. The reverse side of this ruling brings purse money and any change in the market value of the horse whilst it is in training within the definition of taxable income. In short, in the United States profits from a business like racing operation are taxed as capital gains, rather than as ordinary income, and any expenses can be written off as business expenses. There seems no point in quoting figures or percentages, as the American taxation system is at present undergoing a transformation, but formerly capital gains were taxed at a lower rate than ordinary income. Informed opinion suggests that President Reagan's tax reforms will not greatly affect the benefits racing receives from its guise as a tax shelter, although it is unclear whether this is the result of a desire to maintain a flourishing bloodstock industry, or to give favours to the collection of wealthy and successful Americans who patronize the auction ring and the racetrack.

In both countries the tax administrators are called upon to decide whether or not any individual's racing activities are a hobby or a business. This creates problems and anomalies, for there is no clear distinction between a racing operation which is a hobby and one which is a business. In Britain a breeder is unlikely to be granted business status unless he owns his own stud farm, and unless this stud looks like making a profit in the near future once it has been established for five years. The Inland Revenue tends to avoid any court cases upon such issues in order to maintain its right of discretion and freedom from any potentially binding precedents. As a result of these provisions nearly all large breeders who pay British taxes breed through a public limited company set up for the purpose. A company will not be regarded as a hobby and has the additional benefit of being liable for corporation tax, whose maximum rate is 35 per cent rather than income tax which can be as much as 60 per cent.

The American horseman's activities are likely to be deemed a business if they register a profit in two out of every seven years. This provision is only a guide-line and the I.R.S. has other precepts to help it distinguish between the two in the thoroughbred business. For example, only in a business will the taxpayer and his advisors possess expertise, and only a businessman will be successful in business. This distinction is necessarily arbitrary, for it is an attempt to judge intentions which can only be founded upon objective analysis of balance sheets or business methods.

The reasoning of both countries' tax administrators seems to define a hobby as an activity which uses capital in an inefficient manner. Taken to its extreme this reasoning would lead to an economic dictatorship whereby the inefficient capitalist could be bankrupted overnight by a decree which changed the definition of his activity from a business to a hobby. The inefficient manufacturer who had not made a profit for five years would be ruined immediately if the company was not allowed to deduct the cost of labour, parts or land from its taxable income. The problem is of course that both breeding and racing thoroughbreds are activities which are traditionally hobbies, yet which have, in many instances, become businesses. The dilemma is not so much how to distinguish between a business and a hobby, as to decide what the purpose of breeding and racing thoroughbreds is. If the owning of racehorses is only the pastime of the wealthy then there seems no reason why it should not be taxed like other luxuries. If, on the other hand, the owner is running a business which provides entertainment, employment and through exporting earns foreign currency, then why should his activities not be treated as a business? For most participants in the bloodstock business their activities are both their hobby and their business, and there is no obvious way of classifying them in one camp or the other.

To return to more general questions raised by taxation policies, the British system has numerous debilitating affects on the thoroughbred business. Firstly it encourages breeders to sell their products as yearlings, rather than retaining them and racing them themselves. When a home bred yearling is transferred from the stud to the racing stable its market value must be assessed and if the stud could have made a profit by selling the horse, then this estimated profit becomes part of the stud's taxable income. So the British owner breeder must pay for the conception and rearing of his horse, pay tax on a hypothetical profit and then meet the costs of training before even being in a position to receive a return of prize money, or to realize an increase in the horse's capital value. For a breeder to retain his produce as racehorses is a risk under any tax regime, but by treating the ownership of racehorses always as consumption and never as investment, and by taxing breeders when a horse is transferred from the stud to the racing stable, the Inland Revenue ensures that this risk is greater. The result is that fewer horses are raced by their breeders than would otherwise be the case. Whereas in the United States only one fifth of the annual foal crop are sold as yearlings, in Britain the figure is more like one third.

In addition the British system restricts the scope of ownership. If it was possible to treat the ownership of racehorses as an investment there would obviously be more owners, just as if running a pub was deemed to be a hobby there would be fewer publicans. In particular the American experience has shown that many individuals who would be unable to participate in racing under the British system are happy to become shareholders in partnerships, limited partnerships and corporations which invest in racehorses. There are some collective ownership schemes in Britain already, but their scope is severely limited, as the only return they can offer to prospective participants is one of pleasure and excitement. In America, thanks to the benign tax stance, limited bloodstock partnerships can entice shareholders with the prospect of a financial return as well. Although there have been examples of inept or even fraudulent management of bloodstock partnerships and corporations in the United States, such behaviour is less likely when the astute and responsible manager is able to make money both for himself and his shareholders legitimately. This principle is illustrated by the difference between the bloodstock operations set up in Britain under the auspices of the Business Expansion Scheme and the schemes of collective ownership.

The Business Expansion Scheme was initiated by Britain's Conservative government in order to encourage investment in new British businesses which are involved in a speculative trade. Investors in qualifying companies are allowed to claim income tax relief, which is given as a deduction of the amount invested from the investor's income before it is assessed for tax. Once bloodstock breeding was accepted as a qualifying trade various companies were set up with the intention of attracting high income earners with the prospect of a tax efficient capital gain. In many cases the subscribers turned out to be enthusiasts instead, but because these were companies which were set up in order to make money they attracted directors and managers of a high calibre. Owning racehorses is of course a hobby and so B.E.S. companies are unable to race their own stock, and collective ownership schemes cannot qualify for the B.E.S. Some of these bloodstock B.E.S. companies have impressive lists of directors. Newmarket Thoroughbred Breeders plc's directors include Robert Sangster, David Gibson, William Gredley and Barry Ryan, whilst Bloodstock Breeders plc's include Robert McCreery and James Wigan. These are some of the more successful people in the bloodstock business and no British collective ownership schemes are managed by people of a similar standing.

In the United States owning a racehorse is not an unduly risky enterprise for the wealthy. The costs of purchasing and training the animal can be written off against tax, and the possible rewards of purse money and capital gains are substantial even after they have been taxed. In Britain owning a racehorse is a gamble, but a gamble which offers a spectacular jackpot, indeed an unparalleled jackpot. There can be few legitimate ways for a British taxpayer to make £10 million tax free except by selling a potential international stallion. The lure of this jackpot is itself debilitating, for the tax-free capital gain dwarfs any other possible rewards of ownership. To race a horse beyond the stage where its capital values has been established is therefore expensive. Numerous stallions have been retired to stud after but one or two prestigious wins. However the effect of the tax-free jackpot is more pervasive still, for even the owner of a well bred but comparatively slow filly stands to lose a considerable amount by asking her to race after she has won a small race. Indeed, the understandable desire to realize any capital gain explains the timid and uncompetitive policies of many British owners and their trainers. Once a filly has won the smallest of races she will only increase her capital value by winning or being placed in a stakes race. If her trainer considers this to be an unlikely eventuality, then it is prudent to retire the filly forthwith so that she can go up to the sales without any further blemishes upon her race record. This is but one example; the same reasoning will apply to the racing career of any horse that has a resale value.

In contrast the American system of taxing the bloodstock industry has few similarly deleterious features. Breeders are encouraged to retain and race their own products, for racehorses are not eligible for capital gains treatment until they have been in training and have been held for more than twenty-four months. As was said earlier capital gains are taxed at a lower rate than income and therefore the owner of any sort of thoroughbred is encouraged to retain it for at least two years, which does of course preclude selling their own foals as yearlings. The domestic market for all types of bloodstock is remarkably strong, with many partnerships, limited partnerships and corporations both buying and selling. The incentive to make a profit in at least two out of every seven years also encourages the market by forcing those who have not made a profit by other means to sell some of their own stock. The bloodstock industry in the United States has flourished over the last twenty years and this cannot be entirely unconnected with the way on which it has been taxed.

To many British observers the American system of taxing the bloodstock industry seems extraordinary. Indeed, many of those who have reaped the benefits of it feel it is too good to be true, and others within the American industry feel it is almost indecent. Why should the American taxpayer subsidize the breeding operations of rich men so that they can afford to send their mares to Alydar and Danzig? It has often been said that the American bloodstock market is artificially steamed up by these unnatural tax breaks, and therefore its reckless expansion can only be a transitory phase. These and other similar opinions illustrate how difficult many observers and participants find it to recognize the commerciality of the thoroughbred world. The American system for taxing bloodstock has a certain logic, besides any political benefits it might have. The American bloodstock industry is certainly larger than it would be if it was taxed in the British manner. If economic activity is a good, then it might well be sensible to encourage as many participants as possible and to tax only those who are successful. The bloodstock industry benefits unequivocally, and it is possible that it contributes more to public funds than it would do under a British system. The American system encourages increases in purse money and the capital value of thoroughbreds, and defines both as being part of an individual's taxable income. The I.R.S. has helped to create a flourishing industry which is the world's leader in its field, while retaining a share in all the purse money offered to thoroughbreds, all stallion syndications, and all sales of yearlings and broodmares.

There are many economic, geographical and social factors which can be held to account for the differences between the British and American bloodstock industries, but it is hoped that the preceding discussion has made clear the primary influence of the taxation system in the two countries.

═══ Four ═══
The Pattern of Racing

The demand for various types of racehorse is largely determined by the pattern of racing. The pattern of racing in any country is nothing more than the overall emphasis of the conditions of each individual race. If a large proportion of races are run over distances of less than a mile, then breeders will try to produce horses who will excel in such contests, for these will be the type of horse demanded in the greatest quantities. Some owners will attempt to buy those horses who will have the most opportunities of winning, others will be concerned with securing the winners of the most valuable and prestigious races. What sort of races these will be, and thus what sort of horse is likely to win them, will also be determined by the pattern of racing. In Europe between the wars the most competitive races were run over distances of a mile and a half or more, whereas by the 1970s a new pattern had developed which gave greater rewards to speed and precociousness, although a handful of the most prestigious races were still run over a mile and a half. In America a similar quickening of the pace of racing was taking place although the continent's most competitive classic race the Kentucky Derby had always been run over a mile and a quarter on dirt. The pattern of racing in any country will gradually change in response to the wishes of those who own racehorses and the economic constraints upon their choice. However, it is interesting to compare the pattern of racing, the way in which this pattern is set and in which it appears to be changing in the United States and Britain. The differences and similarities in the two countries influence not only the demand for thoroughbreds in each, but also the interrelation between them.

The Pattern of Racing

The pattern of racing in the United States is fluid. The racing secretary at each racetrack is given discretion to put on whatever races he considers to be suitable. The conditions and timing of the major races are decided in advance, but even in this field there is no central authority which is able to dictate to the scattered, disparate and competing racetracks. If a racing secretary decides to attract some top horses to his meeting he will put on a race with as large a purse as is possible and then start talking to and cajoling the owners and trainers connected with the horses he wants. From day to day during a meeting the racing secretary will frame the coming races after talking to the trainers whose horses are stabled at the racetrack. His aim will be to keep the trainers and their owners content, and to put on competitive races which will attract a crowd to the racetrack.

To the outsider used to European racing the extraordinary feature of American racing is its uniformity. To sit underneath a satellite dish in Kentucky on a Saturday and watch live transmissions of racing from Atlantic City to Del Mar is exceedingly boring for all but the most dedicated of gamblers. One can gain an idea of the enormity of the United States and of its climatic variety, for after breakfast you are in the pouring rain in Atlantic City, whilst by tea time the scene has shifted to the shirt sleeves and sun of California. The races themselves are virtually indistinguishable. It is in some degree comforting that even the commentators do not try to baffle you with a stream of names, restricting themselves instead to utterances about the number six horse, or the number two horse. The numbing quality of the transmission is derived from the fact that all these multitudinous races are run in the same direction on nearly uniform tracks, and they are nearly all run over a distance of between seven and ten furlongs.

This is itself a relatively new development, for it was only recently that a race like the Jockey Club Gold Cup ceased to be run over two miles. However, over the last fifteen years the pattern of racing in the United States has been transformed by the increasing popularity of racing on grass rather than dirt. At the end of every year a collection of turf writers takes a vote to decide which is the horse of the year and which are the champions in various categories specificially; two-year-old colt or gelding, two-year-old filly, three-year-old colt or gelding, three-year-old filly, older male and older female. Unlike any equivalent polls in Europe, this vote, and the Eclipse Awards which are subsequently given out are generally regarded as having the utmost significance. It was only in 1967 that the turf writers first bothered to decide upon the name of the grass champion and it was not until 1979 that they nominated a female grass champion as well. Since 1967 such major races as the Turf Classic in New York, the Budweiser Arlington

Million in Chicago and the Hollywood Invitational Handicap, the Oak Tree Stakes and the Yellow Ribbon Stakes in California have all been founded to be run on grass. The Breeders Cup was in part designed to boost this trend, for besides the Breeders Cup Turf, the Breeders Cup Mile was one of the first major mile races in North America to be run on grass. Grass racing was given an even larger boost by the all-American hero John Henry who had a particular penchant for grass, and who won thirty of his fifty starts on the surface.

The dirt horse, with the exception of a few remarkable specimens, has little international appeal, for America is the only major racing nation which chooses to race its thoroughbreds on dirt. The horse which excels when racing on dirt will have different qualities to the excellent turf runner. These differences may or may not be primarily the result of training, but the aptitude for one surface or the other has some physical basis as dirt exerts different strains upon the horse's frame. The horse who is to stay sound whilst racing on dirt will have to have tough limbs. Racing on dirt is in many ways a form of prolonged sprinting. There are two reasons for this, the first being the disadvantage of being behind another horse during the race run on dirt. The follower is likely to have dirt or, what is worse on a sloppy track, mud thrown in its face by the leader. For this reason there is an advantage to be gained by breaking quickly from the stalls and running the race from in front. This style of running does not suit every horse, but when not in front in a dirt race it often pays to be wide or clear of other horses. The other reason for races on dirt being run at a furious pace from beginning to end is that American racetracks are, by European standards, extremely tight. Tight here means they are almost invariably oval in shape with straights, or stretches, which are two furlongs or less long. The typical American racetrack is just over a mile in circumference. A horse is not able to stretch itself while running round a tight bend and therefore it is far less of a test of stamina to run around a mile circuit than it is to run a straight mile. Speed is vitally important for the American racehorse, as it will need to break quickly from the starting stalls if it is not to be crowded out at the first bend, and American races are run at a great pace which would be unsustainable over a European course without the bends on which to relax.

The mile and a half turf course at Santa Anita, over which Manilla scored his greatest triumph in the Breeders Cup Turf, will serve as an example of the American racetrack. The course starts on a shute, which after a short straight followed by a 180 degree turn joins the main circuit at the beginning of the home stretch. To complete the mile and a half it is necessary to run around the circuit and then once more up the finishing stretch to the wire. This obviously constitutes a very different test from, for example, the mile and a half course at Newmarket, where rather than having to negotiate three 180 degree turns in a mile and a half, there are simply two straights joined by one gentle corner. A horse like Manilla who excels at Santa Anita may well not have sufficient stamina to last out more than a mile and a quarter at Newmarket. To the outsider used to American racing the extraordinary feature of racecourses like Newmarket is that the racegoers are expected to pay to watch races the majority of which take place a mile or more away and out of sight of the grandstands.

Racing on dirt rather than grass is only a response to the size of the United States, although in part the design of American racetracks must be due to the fact that since the Civil War horseracing has been a predominantly urban sport. A dirt racetrack requires careful attention and management, for if it is not watered and harrowed correctly it will become dangerous, but its advantage over a turf course lies in its durability. A dirt track can be raced over eight times a day for three weeks or more without deteriorating. The distances between training centres and racetracks obviously precludes the European system of trainers and their horses travelling from a permanent base to a different racecourse and back every day. American trainers are therefore itinerants, constantly on the move with their band of followers from one temporary base to the next. A trainer will take his charges to a meeting and remain there for its duration, stabling them at the racetrack and working them on the racetrack's training ground every morning. An alternative which is favoured by a few is for the trainer to stable his horses at two or three different racetracks spread across the country, and then commute between them himself in a private aeroplane. Either way the American horse is spared the stress of journeying from home to the racecourse on the morning of a race, whilst the American trainer suffers from the anxiety of the nomad.

One stress which the American racehorse is peculiarly susceptible to is that induced by medication, although some would say medication was usually a palliative. The question of medication is relevant here for medication affects the pattern of American racing, the demand for different types of thoroughbreds, and of course the thoroughbred itself. Some degree of medication is allowed in thirty-six of the thirty-seven states in which racing is held. The thirty-seventh state is New York, where the rules concerning medication are similar to those in European racing countries. This distinction often leads horsemen based in New York to be dismissive of racing elsewhere. In New York the capacities of racehorses are tested, in the other states the vet's and the trainer's skill at administering drugs is put to the test as well, for a perspicacious course of drugs can temporarily hold together a horse who is unsound mentally or physically. If a horse has a hard race, in order to get it back on the track as soon as possible the vet will be called to "jug" some fluids into it. Horses are regularly given vitamins, analgesics, and tonics, and those prone to burst blood vessels are given preventative drugs. Indeed in many ways the United States is a vet's paradise, for his services are always in demand and his scope is almost unlimited. Some of these drugs are used in Europe and New York as well, but once they have been administered the horse must be rested until all traces of the drug have disappeared. As a result they are administered less frequently and only when there is no alternative to a rest from the racecourse.

New York horsemen are not only proud of their rules concerning medication, but until recently they were equally proud of the New York State Testing Laboratory at Cornell University. Thanks to the facilities at Cornell, they said, New York is the only place which is able to enforce strict rules about medication. However, the Lashkari case has put paid to such pretensions. The Aga Khan's colt Lashkari finished fourth in the 1985 Breeders Cup Turf at Aqueduct. A routine drug test at the Cornell University revealed traces of etorphine, a drug which in large doses can knock out an elephant and which in small doses acts as a stimulant. So the horse was disqualified and his French trainer Alain Royer-Dupré was banned from American racetracks. The Aga Khan appealed against the decision and Royer-Dupré filed a suit alleging "unjustified defamation of character". Ten months later, after laboratories in Chicago, Florida, Colorado and Manchester had failed to find traces of etorphine in Lashkari's urine sample, the decision was reversed and the reputations of the horse, Royer-Dupré and the Aga Khan were officially restored. Those New Yorkers who had been inclined to be priggish about the efficiency of Cornell University were made to appear foolish. Nonetheless, however embarrassing the Lashkari case may have been, it will not affect the argument about medication in the long run.

There are those who believe medication is a bogus issue. As Johnny Jones, the manager of Walmac International, has said; "If you get a cough you take cough medicine, why shouldn't a horse?" Those who argue in favour of medication will say that no amount of drug taking will enable a horse to run faster than its frame will allow it to. However, medication will help a horse recover from minor illnesses and strains. Most medication is, after all, given to bad racehorses who are unable to run fast whatever stimulants or tonics they are given. Steroids, everyone would concede, are a different matter, for steroids can in the short run dramatically improve a horse's performance particularly over sprint distances. With the exception of steroids, then, medication can, when used judiciously, aid the trainer, the owner and the horse, and when it is abused or misused medication is of no benefit to anyone. These arguments have some validity, for the majority of prominent American racehorses perform as well in New York as they do elsewhere. In addition the combination of their sedentary life and the help of medication enables American racehorses to perform frequently on the racetrack, and some would see this as a positive effect of medication. However, even when taken together these points do not constitute a sound defence of the practice.

The misuse of medication may not benefit anyone but it will surely harm the horse which is its object. The racing industry will not attract customers by abusing the thoroughbred. Nor will racing attract gamblers if drugs are seen to be the decisive influence upon the result of races. The way in which medication reduces the international standing of American racing and debilitates the American thoroughbred is a more immediate concern for the bloodstock business. Many European horsemen feel the success and marked improvement displayed by so many ex-European horses in California can be explained by the laxity of the rules concerning drugs there. By similar reasoning the international standing of an American potential stallion is enhanced by a fine performance in New York, and a potential stallion who avoids New York will undoubtedly be considered to be rather dubious abroad. The American thoroughbred will gradually be enfeebled if horses are selected for breeding on the basis of peformances which were induced by medication. Whatever faults a horse may have which leave it reliant upon medication, it is likely to pass them on to some of its offspring, and the probability of any young horse needing the assistance of drugs to perform at its peak will gradually increase. American racing would benefit if medication was slowly phased out.

Medication affects the pattern of racing in America because it is in many ways a response to that pattern. Medication allows racehorses to run more frequently than would otherwise be the case, and this is an attribute demanded by the long duration of racemeetings. If a racehorse is stabled at the same racetrack for three or four weeks it might as well compete as often as is possible. The demand for thoroughbreds is affected by medication, which allows owners and trainers to circumvent some of their horses' faults which in New York or Europe might be critical ones. Medication is not the only feature of the traditional pattern of American racing which has become controversial. Indeed, the whole system is under some strain, particularly on the East Coast.

The major problem facing the system is the lack of stalls available at the racetracks. There are now so many thoroughbreds in the United States that there is simply not enough room to accommodate all the trainers and horses who would like to attend a meeting at Saratoga, or to be based at another East Coast track. Competition for stalls is intense and if a horse is injured, or for some other reason needs to return to its owner's farm for a rest, its trainer will have to fill its stall immediately, even if that means buying a new horse just for this purpose. A stall left empty for even a short space of time may be allocated to someone else, for every trainer is given fewer stalls than he applied for at the beginning of the meeting. The competition for stalls does of course explain some of the demand for medication.

In recent years the problem of stabling has been made more acute by a series of racetrack fires at Arlington, Belmont and in South Carolina. The resultant nervousness of insurance companies has led to an increase in the racetracks' overheads. New York racetracks, incidentally like York racecourse, are owned by private companies which are non-profit-making, but whose directors are personally liable for all losses. Whereas it was once possible to insure against liabilities of up to 150 million dollars with a premium of two or three million dollars, since the fires racetracks have been asked to pay seven million dollars for a cover of only thirty million dollars. As a result Saratoga racetrack, which used to take on some 800 horses for the spring, has declined to stable any two-year-olds or older horses returning from a rest from April 1st.

Of more immediate concern here, however, is the manner in which dirt racing and the uniformity of its structure has affected the American bloodstock market. The typology of the American thoroughbred population is almost egalitarian. There is little differentiation by type, as all breeders are concerned with speed. Great American champions like Seattle Slew, Spectacular Bid and Spend a Buck have come from the most unexalted of backgrounds, and yet have been accepted as fashionable stallions the moment they left the racetrack. On every Breeders Cup day one or two horses will triumph whose immediate ancestors are unknown to Europeans and obscure for American horsemen. This egalitarianism is reflected by the fact that there were as many as three hundred and seventeen stallions whose progeny earned more than half a million dollars on American racetracks in 1985. Of this collection of stallions there are of course some whose progeny generally fetch prices above the average. However, for an American stallion to achieve star status, and for his progeny to gain entry to any select sale by virtue of their sire's name alone, there has to be European interest in his offspring. The split in the American bloodstock market is not between sprinters and stayers, or even between East Coast horses and West Coast horses, but between the domestic and the international market. The domestic market is characterized by fluidity between particular types and pedigrees, whilst the international market is more faddish, less stable and thus more attractive to gamblers.

In comparison the pattern of racing in Europe is rigid, as it is imposed upon the racecourses from above. In Britain the Jockey Club does not dictate the conditions of each and every race, but the conditions of new races have to be submitted to a committee for approval. There are restrictions on the amount of prize money which is allowed to be added to each category of race; handicaps for instance are only allowed to be worth a certain amount. The system of centralized handicapping places further restrictions upon each racecourse's freedom to construct its own programme. The Jockey Club's panel of handicappers assign a figure to each horse in training as a gauge of their respective abilities. These figures are updated regularly and a horse who shows improved form will be given a higher one, whilst a horse which is thought to be deteriorating will be given a reduced figure. Once a horse has been awarded a handicap rating, this figure will determine which races it is eligible to run in. Stakes races are open to any horse whatever its rating, but in Britain the majority of races for horses more than two years old are handicaps rather than allowance or claiming races. Handicaps are restricted to horses with a rating above a certain figure, below a certain figure, or between two figures.

In the United States each racetrack has its own handicapper, whose job is to frame races which will attract both an audience and sufficient runners. If a racetrack decides to try and lure a famous horse to its meeting the handicapper might frame a race whose weight allotments favour above-average horses. In Britain the handicapper's task is simply to give as fair an assessment of horse's respective merits as is possible. The British system may well be admirable and provide every horse whatever its ability, or its lack of it, an opportunity to win a race of some sort, but it limits the scope of racecourse management. A British racecourse is told on which days it is to hold meetings and what time of day the meeting is to start; the amount of prize money it is allowed to put up for any race is limited, and on small racecourses the majority of races will be restricted to horses of average or below average ability.

The intention here is not to explain why any enterprising British racecourse manager is likely to be disappointed and frustrated, but simply to point out the effect of the decisions of the Jockey Club's race planning committee and the Horserace Betting Levy Board* has upon

*The Horserace Betting Levy Board is the body which collects and hands out the horseracing industry's share of the government's take in betting tax.

the thoroughbred business. In deciding upon the pattern of racing these bodies also determine which categories of the thoroughbred are the most sought after. A striking illustration of this power is provided by the Jockey Club's decision in the autumn of 1986 to increase the allowance given to two-year-old fillies when racing against males from 3lb to 5lb. Now a difference of 2lb may seem to be insignificant, but over the distances which two-year-olds are asked to compete it is the equivalent of approximately one length or 0.13 seconds. This may still appear to be a trivial amount; however, in the future two-year-old fillies will find it that much easier to defeat their male contemporaries. This change was justified on the grounds of fairness. Geoffrey Gibbs, the Jockey Club's handicapper of two-year-olds, produced statistical evidence of the discriminating nature of the old allowance.

The announcement of this change caused a furore within the blood-stock industry. The constitutional conservatism of the industry's members is pronounced enough for the announcement of any change to provoke a critical retort; in this instance criticism was directed chiefly at Geoffrey Gibbs' statistical evidence. Gibbs' conclusions were indeed surprising at a time when the casual observer of racing results was able to discern evidence of some sort of sexual revolution on the racecourse. Until recently members of the female sex were considered to be frail, temperamental, and less athletic than their male contemporaries. In recent years there has been a profusion of fillies and mares who were quite capable of beating their male contemporaries in Europe's best races with the assistance of a 3lb allowance. The female seems to be particularly resurgent in France, and it has become rare for a male to win one of France's four most important two-year-old races, and in addition France's premier race, the Prix de l'Arc de Triomphe, was won by females on five consecutive occasions between 1979 and 1983.

It is hard to conceive of a plausible explanation for such a phenomenon. Is it because owners and trainers have only recently begun to take their females seriously and to give them the opportunity to develop into distinguished racemares? Or alternatively is the male thoroughbred declining into fragility or simply being shielded from unnecessary competition? Perhaps Geoffrey Gibbs' figures are correct after all and no such revolution has taken place. Whatever position one chooses to take on these and similar questions is irrelevant, for they have no bearing upon the real effect of this change. If two-year-old fillies are now more likely to win races, then more people will want to own one. Fillies sold as yearlings or foals will fetch higher prices than would otherwise have been the case, and perhaps some breeders will decide to retain their fillies and race them themselves whilst they still have this new advantage. If these are desirable incentives then the change will be a beneficial one.

The Jockey Club, in common perhaps with other old British institutions, is desperately concerned with appearing to be fair. Fairness does not, however, have a role to play in the determination of the pattern of racing. If the Jockey Club is to retain the power to impose a pattern on the racecourses from above it should pause to consider which commercial trends it wishes to encourage. Consider as an example the trend for high class racehorses to be retired to stud at the end of, or in the middle of, their three year old career. The Jockey Club could encourage the owners of such horses to keep them in training as four-year-olds by tampering with the weight for age scale. The weight for age scale used in 1986 was, with one or two marginal alterations, the same as the one drawn up by Admiral Rous in the 19th century, when horseracing was thought to be about improving the thoroughbred and entertaining those who owned them. There seems to be no logical reason why this scale should not be adapted to suit the new commercial imperatives which govern horseracing today.

Britain's major race which is open to horses of all ages is the King George VI and Queen Elizabeth Diamond Stakes, run over a mile and a half at Ascot in July. In the years between 1976 and 1986 this race was won by seven three-year-olds and four four-year-olds. During this period the weight for age scale decreed that four-year-olds should carry 13lb more than three-year-olds in the race, in order to take account of their superior maturity. If this allowance had been 9lb rather than 13lb then only two of the three-year-olds, Ile de Bourbon and Shergar, would certainly have been able to defeat their elders. A change of this type would surely provide a powerful incentive to keep a high class horse in training as a four-year-old, for victory in a race like the "King George" guarantees a place at stud for any colt.

Another imposition or administrative idea which has had a significant effect on the bloodstock market is the pattern race system. The pattern race system was an initiative of the early 1970s, and in part a response to the new international outlook on horseracing. The idea was to construct a series of races which fairly tested the different attributes of the racehorse, and provided an objective means of evaluating horses' performances. The aim of the system was to define and reward equine excellence. Each racing country drew up a list of their major races and those of a championship status were designated as Group 1s, and the others were labelled as Group 2 or Group 3 depending upon the quality of horses they usually attracted. In Europe Group races are exclusively non-handicap races, which means that all entries are set to carry the same weight, or when they are open to horses of different ages, weight for age. In America the equivalent races are called Graded races and in keeping with the traditional pattern of racing many of them are handicaps.

When the bloodstock business was confined by national boundaries the participants in each country were able to judge the respective merits of horses without the assistance of any such objective standards. At a bloodstock auction the buyers would have been familiar with the relations and antecedents of the horses on sale. If they had not witnessed them on the racecourse themselves, they would be well aware of the traditional standard of the races in which they performed. In an era of international racing this is no longer possible as the relations of a horse sold at Newmarket may well have distinguished themselves in Australia or California. The pattern race system was a means to overcome this problem of information, for a horse who wins a Group 3 race in Melbourne should in theory be of similar merit to a horse who wins a Grade 3 race at Santa Anita. The system was also supposed to encourage competition. If Group 1 races were championship tests then any aspiring champions would have to compete with the best of their contemporaries in Group 1 races. The pattern was to be imposed after international consultations to ensure continuity, stability and fairness.

The pattern race system has achieved permanency, but it has only been a qualified success. The Group or Graded races are widely used as an objective means of valuation rather than of ability. By winning or being placed in a Group or Graded race a racehorse does increase in value, particularly in the case of a filly. Unfortunately it is simply not true to say that all Group or Graded races are of a similar standard. One of the effects of the pattern race system has been to encourage those in an area with competitive racing to send their horses elsewhere to race. In Europe those Group races which are run in Italy or Germany are easier to win than their equivalents in Paris or England. So many French and English trainers send horses to race abroad in the hope that to a Californian a Group 2 race is a Group 2 race, whether it is run at San Siro or Longchamp. There is a sense therefore in which the pattern race system provides misinformation rather than information.

The pattern race system has not in the event encouraged competition either. If by winning a Group 1 race a horse acquires prestige and capital value, then a commercially minded trainer will always seek to avoid competition. There is no point in competing in a Group 1 race at Longchamp unless the horse has a real chance of winning. If the horse would only be an outsider it is more sensible not to take on the cracks but to wait for a Group 3 race the following week, or go to Italy for a Group 1 the next weekend. Many trainers obviously reason in a similar manner for there are a multitude of richly endowed Group or Graded races which attract fields of only four or five horses, three of which have a chance of winning, and two of which are hoping one of the others will fall over so they can get a place in a Group race. The pattern race system has changed the way in which horses' programmes are planned. The commercially minded will seek not to display their horse's ability, but to mask it, and to gain as many Group or Graded wins and places as is possible. In Britain of course the astute owner is scheming for that tax free capital gain. For all but a handful of outstanding racehorses such an aim will entail avoiding any unnecessary competition.

For a pattern race system to succeed in its own terms the selection of races to which these labels were applied would have to be rigorous. At the moment there are simply far too many races of each category. But even if local and national pride was overcome and the whole system was cut back, its basic fault would still remain. Any system of rigid objective standards will be open to abuse in a sport where value and performance are relative and can only be determined through competition.

In Britain the pattern race system is assigned an additional task, which is to preserve the continuity and stability of the means by which the best racehorses are identified. To this end the power of the capital value of success in Group races is reinforced by linking the amount of prize money available to these labels. A Group 3 race is not allowed to be worth more than a certain amount, and a Group 2 race to have more than a certain greater figure added to it. Once again these regulations only serve to deaden any enterprise in racecourse management. The same end could be achieved by abolishing the whole pattern race system. Without these unnecessary labels the most valuable horses would be those who revealed the greatest ability, and the most prestigious races would be those which were well established and whose names were known throughout the bloodstock world. A racecourse, with the help of a sponsor, could put on a new and valuable event which attracted runners from more traditional contests, but without continuity and a reputation such races would be of only national significance.

The most famous example of such short-sighted decision making was the occasion when the Jockey Club prevented Robert Sangster and York racecourse from putting on a £100,000 added race in June, on the grounds that it would interfere with and detract from the traditional contests at Royal Ascot, and the Derby at Epsom. A more sensible course of action would have been to let Robert Sangster have his way and then to open up Royal Ascot to commercial sponsorship in order for the meeting to be able to compete. However, as we have seen, the pattern race system has achieved a permanence and it is now the object of conservative sentiment, so it will maintain its determining influence upon the bloodstock market. This influence is so decisive because the bloodstock market is an international one. All Europeans are relatively ignorant of American racing and most Americans are completely ignorant of European racing, therefore information concerning horses' respective abilities is both important and valuable. The pattern race system appears to provide such information in a manner which is both cheap and easily accessible.

In the catalogue for a bloodstock auction each horse is given a page on which its pedigree is set out, going back three generations. Below this the racing performances of the horse's first three dams and their descendants is printed. There is now an international convention whereby all of those relations who won Group or Graded races have their names printed in capital letters and in bold type. The names of those who were placed in a Group or Graded event are also printed in bold type, but usually in lower case letters. This bold or black type has become part of racing's vernacular. A horse will be sent to run in Italy in order to gain some "black type". The more "black type" which appears in a yearling's catalogue entry, the more valuable the horse is likely to be. Unfortunately this profusion of "black type" is as likely to misinform a buyer as it is to enlighten him, for the pattern race system is clearly not the objective guide it purports to be. However, the scarcity of information and the perceived importance of "black type" leads the demand for particular types of racehorses to follow the vagaries of the race system.

These first four chapters have set out the background to the thoroughbred business. The first step was to consider what the ideal racehorse is, and then to examine how it is affected by its heredity and the environment in which it is reared. The last two chapters have looked at the differences in the organization of the American and British bloodstock industries, and in particular at the way in which they are taxed and the differences in the pattern of racing in the two countries. It is now time to bring these different aspects of the business together in order to explain what it was that caused the boom in bloodstock values between the mid 1970s and the mid 1980s.

═══ Five ═══
The Bloodstock Boom

Economic activity at bloodstock auctions has been on an unprecedented scale since 1976. Indeed, many participants in the business had become so accustomed to a bull market that when, in 1985, there were signs of a falling off in prices there was alarm and financial embarrassment. In 1974 the value of every category of bloodstock fell. Over the next ten years values rose continuously. The four leading auctions in England and Ireland are Tattersalls' Highflyer and October Sales in Newmarket, the Doncaster St Leger Sales and Goffs Bloodstock Sales at Kill near Dublin. In 1974 the combined average price at these sales was 3,000 guineas. By 1984 this figure had risen to 33,000 guineas, while in 1986 it fell to 26,000 guineas. The combined aggregate of these sales has displayed the same trend rising from 5,700,000 guineas in 1974 to 68,000,000 guineas in 1984, and then falling to 55,000,000 guineas in 1986. Tattersalls' Highflyer Sales are the best yearling sales in Europe and whereas the average price at the equivalent sale in 1974 was 5,200 guineas, in 1984 it peaked at 93,000 guineas. In 1986 the average price at the Highflyer Sales was 77,000 guineas.

The Keeneland Association's Select July Sale is the leading yearling auction in the United States. In 1974 the average price there was $53,000. In 1984 the average price peaked at $600,000 and by 1986 it had fallen to $410,000. At the Saratoga yearling sale the average price rose from $37,000 in 1974 to $260,000 in 1985 before falling to $190,000 in 1986. If the four major yearling sales in the United States (Keeneland Select, Keeneland Wednesday, Fasig-Tipton Kentucky and Saratoga) are taken together their aggregate peaked in 1984 at $260,000,000 before falling to $180,000,000 in 1986, and their average price peaked

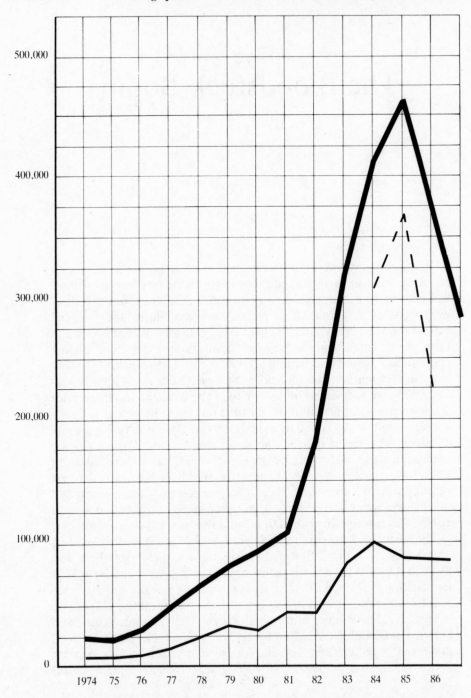

£s STERLING

━━ **Average price at Tattersall's Houghton/Highflier sales.**

── **Average price at Keeneland select sale.***

--- **Average price at Keeneland select & Wednesday sales combined***

500,000

400,000

300,000

200,000

100,000

0

1974 75 76 77 78 79 80 81 82 83 84 85 86

* The prices at the Keeneland sales have been converted into £ sterling
using the Jockey Club's recommended exchange rate for each year.

The result of the four major British & Irish yearling sales combined. (Tattersalls' highflyer & October sales, Doncaster St. Leger sales, Goffs premier Irish yearling sales.)

GUINEAS STERLING

▬▬▬ **UPPER QUARTILE** ——— **MEDIAN** ——— **LOWER QUARTILE**

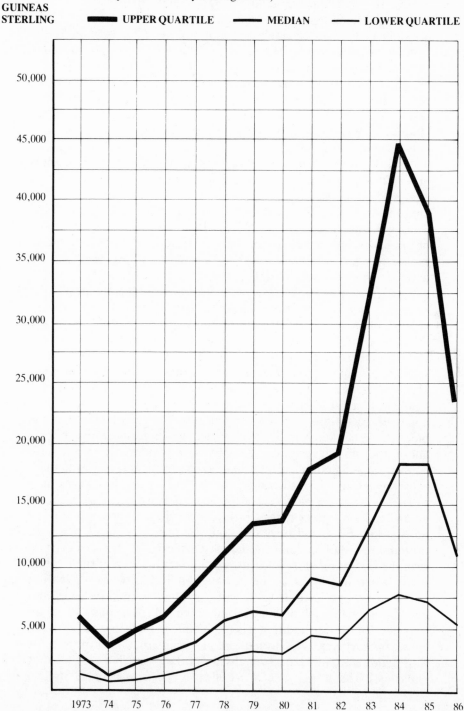

in 1984 at $280,000 before falling to $210,000 in 1986.

It is not only bloodstock auctions which have thrived: thoroughbred breeding as a whole has flourished as it has never done before. In the United States the size of the annual foal crop has doubled from 25,000 to 50,000 in the last decade; the world's thoroughbred population is now probably more than a million, whereas at the beginning of the 1960s it numbered about 300,000. These figures, and there are countless others of a similar vein which could be quoted, clearly reveal why the bloodstock business and bloodstock auctions have ceased to interest only a handful of insiders.

A broad outline of the events and landmarks passed in the business during this period will be familiar to anyone with the vaguest of interests in horseracing. The appearance of the 13 million dollar yearling and the 40 million dollar stallion were events which attracted widespread attention. The problem is, therefore, not to describe such phenomenon but to account for their occurrence. Most attempts at an explanation have been unsatisfactory because they have been founded upon a list or a description of a series of human and equine personalities. The names which have been cited most frequently are Robert Sangster, Northern Dancer and Secretariat; an Englishman, a Canadian stallion and an American racehorse. However, the proportions and spread of the boom dwarf the activities of any one individual. How could one man or one horse possibly influence a multitude of separate economic choices made in California, Newmarket and many places on between? To lay the credit at the feet of a stallion is particularly fanciful for though there have been many stallions who appeared to eclipse their contemporaries, the recent boom in the bloodstock market was unprecedented. To understand this bubble and outpouring of resources it is necessary temporarily to put aside curiosity about individual players and the attraction of outstanding achievements,and instead examine the business in an abstract manner.

There seem to be two facets of the boom which particularly demand an explanation if the changes in the thoroughbred business are to be understood. First, and obviously, the rise in the values of yearlings, broodmares, stallions and indeed all categories of bloodstock, and then the formation of an international market for each of these categories. When one looks at the thoroughbred industry over a period of ten years one is confronted with countless events, statistics and conflicting trends all of which cannot be taken account of in an overview like this. In addition it is often difficult to distinguish between causes and effects. The formation of an international market for thoroughbreds could have brought about the boom, but then again it could easily have been one of its effects. The term boom is itself a nebulous one and it will not be defined further except in the course of the discussion. What follows are therefore only generalizations based upon simplification.

If the boom is conceived of as a speculative blaze, then the sparks which set it off were various developments extraneous to the bloodstock world, and the wood with which it was fuelled was the nature of the bloodstock market and the uncertainty upon which it is founded. Of the extraneous developments the most important were the American taxation practices described in Chapter 3. The dramatic affect of turning the thoroughbred business into a tax shelter is most clearly illustrated by the explosion in the thoroughbred population in the United States. More racehorses were demanded by many more people, corporations and partnerships. Most of this new demand was satisfied by domestic breeders from Kentucky to Florida to Illinois; nonetheless at the same time the United States began to import more than just the odd excellent stallion. Besides the importation of breeding stock Americans began to buy thoroughbreds from Central and South America, and Europe as racehorses. Another fiscal development whose affect on the bloodstock market was not insignificant was the abolition of exchange controls in Britain in 1979.

The idea of exchange controls is to prohibit individual taxpayers and corporations from buying overseas assets without first obtaining government permission. In effect the aim is to limit overseas spending of any sort to what is deemed to be in the national interest. Once the controls had been lifted, British breeders were able to buy shares in stallions who were based in Kentucky, Florida or Waitotara. The ownership of a stallion share secures access to the stallion, so once they had bought shares it became sensible for British based breeders to buy nearby stud farms on which to board their mares and raise their foals. Exchange controls did not only have a negative affect on the thoroughbred business. E. P. Taylor was only able to buy the nomination to Nearco which he used to produce Northern Dancer's sire Nearctic because Nearco's owner Martin Benson wished to circumvent the controls by persuading Taylor to pay him in Florida rather than in England. Before 1979 it would have been difficult for a British commercial farm to sell a yearling at Newmarket whose sire was based in Kentucky. This is still an infrequent occurrence, but many British-based breeders now race horses whom they bred themselves in the United States. Exchange controls are now an anachronism. A system that enabled a government to oversee all the foreign currency transactions of its citizens would have to be of dictatorial proportions, when it is possible to obtain cash with a piece of plastic throughout the capitalist world. Such technical advances provide stability themselves and allow the enterprising dealer to build up an operation which is based upon trade between national bloodstock markets, which were until recently separated. So the American taxation laws could be said to have created an international demand for bloodstock and the abolition of British exchange controls enabled British breeders to take advantage of this demand. However, there was still a prominent feature of an internatonal market missing, which was of course information.

Consider two abstract countries each of which has its own bloodstock market functioning independently. Suddenly a method is discovered of cheaply transporting horses from one country to the other, and the governments of both countries make no attempt to intervene in any trading of bloodstock. Will international trade begin immediately? The answer is that it will not, for the potential buyers in both countries will be completely ignorant of the horses in the other country. Thoroughbreds have only a comparative value, and without information it is impossible to make any sort of a comparison.

The American breeders who bought English Derby winners in the 1930s were not taking an extravagant risk, even if they had been ignorant of the nuances of British racing. The Derby is after all the world's most famous horserace. Anyone who wants to buy a British racehorse as a stallion is playing safe if they decide to buy the Derby winner. At that time, moreover, British bloodstock still had an unsurpassed reputation for excellence. Any breeder throughout the world who wanted to improve the quality of his stock would look to British bloodstock as the catalyst. As a result breeders in New Zealand, Italy and Kentucky alike were prepared to pay for and to take time collating information about British racing and breeding. There was, however, no such incentive for British breeders to follow developments in the American bloodstock world. There came a time when these developments were sufficient for Americans to lose interest in all but the very best European racehorses.

Yearling sales are usually, or at least traditionally, parochial affairs because the outsider is unable to differentiate between one horse and another. If the most famous and feted of bloodstock agents were suddenly taken up and flown to Santiago and asked to choose between a collection of yearlings he would be perplexed. The names of their ancestors would only bewilder him, and the list of races won by their relations would be equally useless to him as he would never had heard of their titles. Indeed he would be quite unable to judge which of their relations had been superior racehorses. Even the yearlings' physical appearance would be of limited value, for the agent would be ignorant of the manner in which they had been trained and prepared, and the mode in which they were presented would appear foreign. Without information and specialized knowledge a horse is just a horse, and more particularly a yearling is just a yearling. Then again even that is not certain, for if someone whose knowledge of horses was entirely gained in Poland were to be whisked to Kentucky in July and shown a sales yearling, he would probably swear he was looking at a two-year-old.

When America became the repository for the world's best thoroughbreds the first European buyers to appear at Keeneland or Saratoga must have felt as confused as the agent in Santiago. Similarly any American who attended Tattersalls' Houghton Sales in 1970, or who wanted to buy a tested racehorse which was not among the best of its age, would not have known where to begin. Until information was disseminated internationally there could not be an international bloodstock market. This information gradually began to appear because those who collected it were in a position to make money. Enterprising Europeans went to the United States to buy yearlings, raced them in Europe and then sold them back to the Americans as potential stallions. These entrepreneurs were taking advantage of the superiority of the American thoroughbred, their knowledge of the pattern of European racing and the American demand for exalted breeding stock. The success of these enterprises changed the nature of the market by disseminating information about these three things. The Europeans became aware of the superiority of the American thoroughbred and of the American demand for proven racehorses, while the Americans became interested in the European pattern of racing. Kentucky stallion farms began buying stallions which had raced in Europe, not because they hoped to sell their offspring on the domestic market, but in order to sell them to the Europeans as yearlings. The information dam had been breached on both sides and what had been a trickle became a torrent of facts, statistics, results and pedigrees.

The flood of information was of course swelled by extraneous developments in information technology. The breeding statistics which are thought to be the most important are the various tables which compare the peformances of the offspring of different stallions. These tables are now produced every week in the greatest detail by trade publications in the United States and Britain. This would not be possible unless the results of races were computerized daily, indeed many of the indices which are now taken for granted would be impossible to devise without the help of a computer. Consider the Sire Production Index which is, according to *The Thoroughbred Record*, ". . . based on the cumulative Standard Starts Indexes (average earnings per start, calculated separately for colts and fillies to account for differences in earnings by sex) for all of a sire's progeny. These are combined in a weighted average that provides a lifetime S.P.I. for a stallion as a measure of his performance versus other North American based sires." Clearly this index was not formulated by a man with a pen and a pile of books containing the results of past races. If these tables are available then so are the results of races. After every European Group race the order of finish and the pedigrees of the horses who were placed will be sent to Kentucky by telex or facsimile within the hour. And it is not only the results of races which create such an interest for the prices attained at bloodstock auctions; the average price fetched by the offspring of one stallion, the median price of the lower quartile, are all transmitted across oceans post haste.

More recently than its directors would probably like to admit, the British Bloodstock Agency would delegate their new recruits to the vital task of copying out in long hand the names of the winners of Group and Graded races and cataloguing them under the names of their sires. Today any large bloodstock agency or stud farm will keep such information on floppy discs and employ secretaries to feed their machine on a daily basis. A proportion of these statistics and facts can only be of therapeutic value, but they are important not least because they are perceived as being so. Decisions are easier to make if they can be justified by reference to figures and tables, and the more sophisticated these appear to be the more gravitas their beholders acquire. There was a time when the British breeder felt he was well informed if he read one of the national racing papers every morning. Now the same man will feel he needs to know the results of the major races and bloodstock auctions in North America, Australasia and all the major European racing countries, as well as the pedigrees of the prominent racehorses and stallions in these countries. If American horsemen are generally less concerned with events abroad, then the size of their own industry is now such as to necessitate the use of sophisticated hardware to acquire and store the required information. Supplying bloodstock information is a trade which has expanded rapidly in recent years. There are now specialist agencies in the United States and Britain; indeed in London alone there are two companies whose main business is to collect information about overseas racing and breeding, and distribute it to newspapers and private clients. The trade publications in both countries are uniformly international in their outlook. It would be stretching the point too far to say that the advances in information technology caused the bloodstock boom, but it is hard to see how it could have taken place without the help of the telex, the facsimile and the floppy disc. There is a sense in which the boom depended upon there being enough information for people to believe they were informed about foreign events, and too much for any individual to be able

Inside the Keeneland Association's Sale Pavillion.

Kentucky stallion 'dealers': Johnny Jones II of Walmac International (right), Robert N. Clay of Three Chimneys (below).

Kentucky stallion barns: Gainesway (above), Walmac International (below).

Chief's Crown, America's champion two-year-old in 1984, is led away from the stallion barn at Three Chimneys.

Inside Tattersalls' Newmarket salering.

Michael Goodbody and Omar Assi inspect a yearling, held by David Cecil of the Cliff Stud, outside on the saleground.

Tattersalls' Irish auctioneer David Pim during a performance.

Alan Lillingston of the Mount Coote Stud talks with Arturo Brambilla of BBA Italia at the sales.

Faces at Tattersalls' Newmarket Sales: Major W.R. Hern, the Queen's trainer, talks to Robert McCreery (above). Bloodstock agents Rhydian Morgan-Jones (below left) and Sir Philip Payne-Gallwey Bt (below right), compare the horses with the catalogue.

Anthony Stroud,
Sheikh Mohammed's
racing manager.

Newmarket bloodstock agent David Minton at home.

to master all of it. Once there was a demand for racehorses, unfettered capital movements and the required information the next step towards the boom was to facilitate the international movement of thoroughbreds.

Horses do not find aeroplanes alarming. Indeed many are less perturbed by a long flight than by a short journey in a horsebox, when they will have to negotiate sharp corners, roundabouts and traffic jams. The Curragh Bloodstock Agency, who organize flights for some 4,000 horses every year, say that fewer than one horse in a hundred needs to be tranquillized for a long distance flight. The fear of flying is it seems a rational emotion, which is perhaps derived from the knowledge of past aeroplane disasters and from the feeling of helplessness induced by entrusting one's life to the skill and alertness of the pilot and the crew. Horses are unconcerned by such considerations and most are only worried by the noise, which may be loud but is at least constant. Pilots experienced at flying horses will taxi on to the runway and take off without stopping first and then roaring the engines, which is the usual practice for transporting humans. When flying people most airlines are concerned with economy rather than comfort and the sooner an airliner reaches it cruising height the less fuel it will use on the flight. Those who charter areoplanes for racehorses are prepared to pay for a more gradual and less alarming ascent.

The only drawback of transporting thoroughbreds internationally is the expense of aeroplanes. The cheapest Boeing 707 will cost around £4 million and in addition its owner will have to pay the variable costs of a crew and regular servicing. Robert Sangster is the only European horseman who owns an aeroplane large enough to enable him to carry his horses about with him. Robert Sangster's plane is a Skyvan, known in the trade as "the bread van", for it is not even large enough to accommodate an outsized racehorse. So racehorses are transported on charter flights, which are in their turn expensive unless the costs are shared. A small trainer sending a runner from Cambridge airport to Italy will be happy to share with any sheep, pigs or goats which happen to be going to Italy on the same day. Those with a more exalted opinion of their horse's value tend to be less tolerant of such lowly travelling companions. The facility with which thoroughbreds are flown between Europe and the United States cannot therefore be seen as a cause of the boom for it is not due to any technical advance, but only to increased demand. The Curragh Bloodstock Agency alone take two flights of broodmares a week from England to Kentucky during the breeding season, and a one way ticket for a broodmare costs a mere £2,000. The emergence of an international market for thoroughbreds led to a fall in the costs of flying horses, however, the consolidation of this market is beginning to have a negative effect instead.

Of this figure of £2,000 for transporting a broodmare from England to Kentucky, half is sufficient to cover the freight charges; the remainder is to pay for the administrative work which is necessary before a thoroughbred can be exported to the United States. As the number of thoroughbreds crossing national boundaries has increased there has been a corresponding proliferation of rules and regulations which seek to minimize the risk of disease. The bloodstock boom promoted international promiscuity and as a result there have been international epidemics of equine venereal diseases. First, in 1977, there was an outbreak of Contagious Equine Metritis in Britain. Metritis is the condition of an inflamed womb which can cause abortion. The bloodstock business's main concern has been with the link between venereal diseases and unwanted abortions, or loss of fertility in some other way. In reaction to this outbreak of C.E.M. in 1977 the United States placed restrictions on the importation of bloodstock. These unwanted abortions and the temporary suspension of international trade made breeders in both Europe and the United States aware of the need of a strict code of practice to limit the chances of another epidemic. Both broodmares and stallions are now swabbed before being allowed to mate, and any bloodstock importations are kept in isolation until they have been cleared by bacteriological tests.

In 1984 there was an outbreak of Equine Viral Arteritis in Kentucky. It was generally believed that E.V.A. could cause broodmares to abort, so, on the morning on which Kentucky's July yearling sales began, it was announced that all thoroughbreds moving from Kentucky to Britain would have to spend thirty days in isolation outside Kentucky before they would be allowed to enter Britain. This decision and its timing caused some inconvenience to those British based buyers who had been planning to import some sixty yearlings from Kentucky at the end of the following week. The administrative problems caused by E.V.A. were the result of the different British and American reactions to the disease. The British tried to exclude all thoroughbreds who showed any trace of E.V.A., while in Kentucky all stallions were given a live E.V.A. virus as a preventative measure. So every stallion that was in Kentucky in 1984 will never be allowed to enter Great Britain. These epidemics and regulations have increased the costs of participating in international bloodstock trade.

Some idea of these additional costs can be given by considering the conditions under which thoroughbreds are imported into the United States. A horse imported for the purposes of breeding must have two clear swabs taken at least seven days apart before leaving England. On arrival in the United States it will be kept in isolation for thirty days before being allowed to proceed to its destination. So the process of moving a broodmare from a Newmarket stud farm to one in Kentucky will take at least forty days. A horse temporarily imported for the purpose of racing will be given a waiver certificate to avoid the isolation, although it must have the clear swabs. Instead of being isolated the horse will spend two days in full quarantine, during which time it can only be approached in protective clothing. For the remainder of its stay in the United States the horse will be kept apart from other thoroughbreds. Throughout Bold Arrangement's stay in Kentucky in 1986, when he ran in the Blue Grass Stakes and the Kentucky Derby, he was accompanied by a guard for twenty-four hours every day, and was moved around in a van which was sealed by the U.S.D.A. to prevent anything larger than a slim man slipping in and out of it without their knowledge. However, despite the escalating costs and bureaucratic difficulties, there is now an international market for bloodstock which is of an unparallelled size and range.

The major European racing countries have traditionally exported tested racehorses as breeding stock. There are famous stallions throughout the world who proved themselves on the racecourses of England, Ireland and France. Or rather, in the case of those which are not in the United States, they nearly proved themselves, for on the whole Europeans exported the bloodstock they did not want to keep themselves. For years much of this export trade took place at Tattersalls' December Sales, where breeders and owners sold the broodmares and horses out of training which they no longer wished to retain. Trade with the United States has always been different, and from the 1930s American breeders have taken their pick of Europe's stallions. So there has always been international trade in bloodstock, but until recently it was limited to breeding stock and the United States imported bloodstock while Britain was content to export. Those American thoroughbreds who came to race in Europe were generally brought over by American owners and, with a few notable exceptions, they returned to American studs when their racecourse careers were over.

Today the pattern of bloodstock trade is different, for it embraces every type of bloodstock and the United States, England, Ireland and France are all involved in both importing and exporting thoroughbreds. Numerous thoroughbreds are now imported to the United States as racehorses. These are not usually among the best of their age group, but hundreds of horses of varying abilities; some of them can be seen running at obscure racetracks some five or six years later. A two-year-old who has performed well in Britain but who seems to be just behind the best of its generation, or an older horse who is sound and speedy but whom no one wants as a stallion, these are both types that are now likely to be exported to the United States. Indeed any Grade I race for older horses in California is likely to have two or three of such types among its contestants.

It is now common for European based horses to compete for major prizes in North America. Until recently these challenges were confined to the autumn races, which are run on turf and are specifically designed to attract international competition, but there have recently been attempts to win races in the spring and even the American Classic races, which are run on dirt. In 1986 A. P. Richards' Bold Arrangement ran third in the Blue Grass Stakes and second in the Kentucky Derby, an achievement which others are sure to try to emulate. The top international horses compete against each other with sufficient regularity for the Jockey Club to consider including American based horses in their International Classification, and for European horses like All Along and Pebbles to have been given Eclipse awards for outstanding performances in the United States.

The movement of breeding stock is different as well. It is common for European based broodmares to be flown to Kentucky to be covered, and the leading European racing concerns own farms in the Lexington area at which to board their mares during the covering season. The leading American commercial farms send fillies to race in Europe, with the intention of having them covered by European based stallions before returning them to the United States. American stallion farms buy shares in stallions which are based in Europe, and compete against each other to purchase those who are for sale in their entirety. Similarly English and Irish stallion farms buy proven American racehorses as stallions. If it had not been for the E.V.A. vaccinations some established American stallions would probably have been exported permanently or temporarily. Stallions have been traded between Europe and Australasia, and some such as Godswalk, Palace Music and Dahar, have spent different covering seasons on each continent. European stud farms like Airlie and Coolmore own and manage stallions who are based in Australia or New Zealand.

Perhaps the most dramatic change of all has been the creation of an international market for yearlings. Every year four or five hundred American bred yearlings are imported into Great Britain alone. This may be a small number from a foal crop of 50,000, but it is a significant proportion of the 3,000 two-year-olds that go into training in Britain each year, and the 500 tend to come from the top of the American market. Selling yearlings has become an international business as well as buying them, for a few Europeans have sold yearlings in the United States, and many more Americans have sold yearlings in Europe. The transformation of the thoroughbred business which these facts illustrate can be clearly shown by considering the effects of the exportation of the English Derby winner to the United States as a stallion.

When the Aga Khan III sold his Derby winners Mahmoud and Blenheim to the United States in the 1930s they might as well have gone to the moon for all the chance British breeders had of ever using their services again. In 1986 his grandson the Aga Khan IV sold his Derby winner Shahrastani to the United States as a stallion. However, Shahrastani was born and raised on the Claiborne Farm in Kentucky, and the majority of the syndicate who now own him are based in Europe themselves. Some of Shahrastani's offspring are sure to be sold at Newmarket, and the majority of them will race in Europe. Another clear indication of the extent of this international integration is the similarity between the lists of the leading stallions in the United States, and in Great Britain and Ireland. In 1986 the Kentucky based stallions Lyphard and Nijinsky were among the leading three stallions in the tables based upon the prize money won by stallions' progeny both in the United States and in Great Britain and Ireland. So, for a time at least, the facility with which horses are transported internationally has completed the four features which can together be said to explain the origins of the bloodstock boom—the fiscally inspired surge in the American demand for racehorses, the freedom and security of international capital movements, the dissemination of information about bloodstock, and finally the ease with which horses, agents and owners are flown around the world. If these account for the boom's beginning, then the next step is to look at the bloodstock market to explain its scale.

The bloodstock market is characterized by an elastic demand for, and an inelastic supply of, thoroughbreds. If this is not immediately clear, then consider first the demand side of the market. The demand for thoroughbreds can be conceived of in two categories. There are those who wish to own racehorses for social reasons, and there are those who own them for financial reasons. Alternatively, one could say that people are motivated to buy racehorses by greed, social aspirations and the desire for entertainment. All three of these demands will be elastic with respect to their alternatives, simply because there are many of them. Those who seek financial gain could equally well invest in a traded option, a commodity future, or any number of other financial assets, whilst an aeroplane or a piece of "fine art" can be a social symbol equally potent as a racehorse. In order to analyse these demands further, it is necessary to generalize. One would expect changes in the social demand for racehorses to correlate with movements in their price, and in some indicator of general economic prosperity. For example if a particular type of horse becomes more expensive then the demand motivated by enjoyment will switch to another category; if the price of all bloodstock rises then perhaps the pleasure seeker will be forced to withdraw from the market altogether. Similarly, during times of general economic prosperity, there will be more people who feel able to indulge their social aspirations and their desire for enjoyment, so that one would expect the social demand for racehorses to increase.

This is a simplification because the social demand for racehorses is fragmented internationally. Some nations and individuals will be enjoying periods of prosperity while others are not, and the social demand for racehorses will reflect this disparity. Some would say that there are individuals whose demand for racehorses is completely inelastic with respect to price, meaning that they will buy the horses they want whatever price they have to pay. This is a dubious proposition. The financial or speculative demand for racehorses will also correlate with these two indicators, but in precisely the opposite direction.

The speculative demand for racehorses will rise in times of economic uncertainty and high inflation. When the financial and industrial sectors of the world's economy are performing poorly prosperous individuals are led to invest in such commodities as racehorses, gold or "fine art", whose value need not be affected by the wider level of economic activity. Robert Sangster, who was for years the most prominent of the bloodstock gamblers, certainly used to justify his activities by comparing the rise in the average price recorded at Keeneland's July Yearling Sale with the performance of the Dow Jones Index. The speculative demand for racehorses will also rise as the value of bloodstock rises. The more valuable bloodstock is, the greater will be the capital appreciation of the successful racehorse, and the greater therefore will be the attraction of the horse in the eyes of the gambler. It is not only the gambler who will be lured by the possibility of spectacular financial gains, for the existence of such opportunities will also affect the social demand for racehorses. An activity which is accompanied by large sums of money will attract publicity, and in a society fascinated by Mammon a degree of glamour, which appeals to those with social aspirations, will follow close behind. In addition there is the lure of the jackpot and, however remote the possibility, everyone who buys a yearling colt must secretly hope it will grow into an Alydar of the future.

The demand side of the bloodstock market is made up of two parts. One, which can readily be seen as a gamble, is unstable and almost inverted, inasmuch as when the value of racehorses increases the gambler's demand is likely to rise correspondingly. The other can be seen as a market for enjoyment whose strength will vary inversely with fluctuations in the value of racehorses. Both of these demands are elastic with respect to price, which is why, incidentally, one of the effects of the bloodstock boom has been the squeezing out of the social demand for thoroughbreds, and the blurring of the distinction between that part of it which remains and the speculative demand. On the other hand the supply of bloodstock is inelastic with respect to price. This is because of the time lag between the decision to produce, and the moment when the product is in a proper condition for sale. Once a breeder has planned a mating he will have to wait at least two years before he is able to sell its product as a yearling. So even the established breeder is unable to respond to sudden changes in the level of demand for thoroughbreds. In addition, as will be seen when the business of breeding is considered, there are formidable barriers of capital, experience and knowledge which prevent any newcomer from satisfying a sudden rise in demand. If the demand for bloodstock in general rises the breeder will not be able to respond for at least two years, and the same is true of a particular type of bloodstock. This inelasticity of supply is the cause of the financial insecurity of many breeders, but it also guarantees all breeders the possibility of securing abnormal profits. If a particular family, or pedigree, or type of thoroughbred suddenly bcomes fashionable then those breeders who already possess bloodstock with the appropriate credentials will be able to dominate the supply of fashionable racehorses for at least two years. Indeed this inelasticity has attracted gamblers to breeding by holding out the possibility of controlling, if not the means of producing successful racehorses, at least the means of producing fashionable yearlings. In short the inelastic nature of the supply side of the bloodstock market raises the possibility of being able to manipulate the market, and of being in a position to ration supply and discriminate between buyers.

These abstractions will become clearer when the business of breeding and the management of stallions are discussed in greater detail. Here it is intended to account for the boom in bloodstock values. The value of bloodstock is determined by the interaction of demand and supply in the bloodstock market, and to understand this interaction is to understand the bloodstock boom. Any attempt to account for the value of bloodstock without recourse to these concepts can only come to nebulous conclusions. One approach is to say that a racehorse's value will always be comparative. All the attributes for which the horse is marketed—speed, stamina, beauty, fertility—are relative concepts of which there is no ideal. The owner's satisfaction will depend upon the result of a contest, so the horse's value can only be estimated by comparing it with its exact or near contemporaries. For instance a good racehorse who happens to be born amidst moderate ones will appear excellent, and will therefore reward its owners with more money and pleasure than would have been the case if it had been born in a year in which there were numerous champions to outshine it. However, knowledge of the comparative nature of horse's value does not put its holder in a position to predict or justify the figures given for lots at bloodstock auctions.

An alternative approach is to look at the yearling market. Most thoroughbreds are more valuable when they are yearlings than at any other time of their lives. The yearling's value lies in its potential and in what it might achieve on the racecourse during the next two years of its life. In most cases once a horse appears on the racecourse it begins to disappoint its owners, and with each succeeding failure the attraction of its potential is tarnished and its value diminished. Or one could say that the yearling has no real value, possessing instead one of hope and expectation. To acquire a real value the young horse must win significant races, for the million dollar yearling that never appears on the racecourse will depreciate in value as swiftly as the one that appears only to be regularly defeated. There is no avoiding the connotation of a qualitative difference in the use of such terms as real and unreal value, however this is simply a diversion for no such abstract distinction is justified. There is nothing more or less sensible about spending hundreds of thousands of pounds on an equine embodiment of hope and expectation, than in spending the same amount upon a proven and tested racehorse. To say a horse has a real value of x million pounds is as absurd as saying the real value of a painting by Braque is £6,600,000, for neither paintings nor racehorses possess such a thing.

The same could be said of almost any good or service which is exchanged, for what value a commodity has is derived from the process of exchange rather than from an abstract guide or objective Torah. However, this feature is particularly true of those commodities like paintings, sculpture or racehorses whose value or utility is more symbolic than practical. Neither the painter nor the breeder can have much affect upon the worth which the society in which he works assigns to the products of his trade. The painter and the breeder can only hope to outshine their contemporary competitors. The worth which any society ascribes to such symbolic goods depends only upon fads, fashions and whims. The value of racehorses is determined solely by the demand for them. To clarify this it is necessary to look again at the supply side of the bloodstock market.

The rewards of the owner of a broodmare or a stallion are almost entirely made up of economic rent. Economic rent is the income earned by a factor of production above that amount which is necessary to prevent it from transferring to another activity. A stallion like Alydar commands an economic rent of something in the region of 15 million dollars every year. This is an extraordinary figure, for it makes Alydar more valuable than any man. The highest paid executive in the City of London is said to earn a million pounds a year, of which probably half is a reward on top of what is necessary to prevent him from transferring to another activity. So this pre-eminent executive receives an economic rent which is but a twentieth of that showered upon the excellent stallion. The figure is extraordinary, for a twelve-year-old stallion like Alydar has few, if any, alternative uses. Indeed, excluding any sentimental urges, the horse's owners are faced with the choice of charging mare owners for Alydar's services as a stallion, or of having the horse put down. Alydar's owners would therefore be prepared to sell his services for almost any sum, as long as the revenue they received paid for the horse's keep, yet there are mare owners who are willing to pay about 15 million dollars between them for Alydar's services each year. In other words Alydar's owners have no control over his value whatsoever, for it is determined solely by the demand for his services. The same is true of the broodmare, for its owner can only use it to produce racehorses, or keep it as a pet. The bloodstock market will be dominated by the demand side, for neither the stallion nor the broodmare has any attributes which can be marketed, other than their ability to mate.

In this sense at least the bloodstock market is similar to the market for "fine art". Values in both are determined by a demand which is elastic and which can be motivated by a desire to enjoy, or to speculate. In addition the supply in both markets is inelastic. The gallery which takes control of an artist's work can be compared to the stallion owner, for both are trying to control and ration the supply of a particular type of desired object. In the terms of this comparison the artist is of course the horse. A final similarity can be seen in the role of the dealer and the man who controls, rather than produces, the supply. In both worlds the dealer attempts to capitalize upon the inelasticity of supply by creating a market and educating and directing the taste of those who have the money to spend. In the bloodstock world this is done with the help of the pedigree and the labels supplied by the pattern race system, which should perhaps both be seen as the equivalents of the work of art historians or critics.

The bloodstock boom began with a surge in the demand for thoroughbreds in the United States. At first shrewd dealers made money from buying yearlings in the United States, racing them in Europe and then selling them back to the United States. However, it soon became clear that the big money was being made by the leading American stallion farms. The most lucrative opportunity the boom presented was the possibility of controlling the supply of fashionable yearlings. The stallion farm prospered more spectacularly than the commercial breeding farm only because a stallion can have up to one hundred offspring a year, whilst the broodmare can have but one. If this control was to bring such a return then the demand for a stallion's services had to be manipulated or educated so as to become inelastic. This was achieved temporarily with the help of the cult of the stallion and the pedigree, which was used to split young horses into four categories which then determined their valuation. The offspring of a stallion who belonged to the top category were valuable, almost regardless of what they actually looked like. For a time bloodstock auctions were trading not physical and mental types of thoroughbred, but horses' personalities, or more accurately the spirit of their ancestors. In the meantime the boom reached one new peak after another. However, sooner rather than later, the bubble burst and the cult was seen as fallible, even if it has yet to be rejected.

These categories are distinctions of purpose or of intentions, rather than of achievements or results. The buyer of a yearling has only its present appearance and its pedigree as guides in his attempt to envisage its presence and achievements in two years' time. In making his choice the buyer will examine only his narrowest private interest and his own conceptions, yet at the same time the decision will be determined by the instincts of the mass of buyers. For the observer bloodstock auctions are generally the least surprising of events. To predict prices successfully may be difficult, but to split a catalogue of yearlings into these four categories is relatively simple. The grading of prices within a category will be determined by the decisions of individual buyers, but the mass of buyers will be in agreement about each yearling's place in the hierarchy.

At the bottom of the scale are those horses who are said to be bred for sprinting. One of the effects of the pattern race system has been to elevate the status of the older sprinter in Britain. Of the races which were designated as Group 1 in 1986 those which quite clearly would not have been awarded such importance in 1966 are those which are run over five or six furlongs, and are open to horses which are more than two years old. There are therefore many more horses born into this category in Europe than was once the case. However, the commercial possibilities of sprint bred horses are still limited for there is no international market for this type of horse. In France there is one important race for older sprinters which is won year in and year out by horses trained in England or Ireland. In the United States sprint racing may be becoming slightly more prestigious under the influence of the Breeders Cup Sprint. Nonetheless the connections of Smile, the winner of the 1986 renewal, felt the need to announce that their horse was more than just a mere sprinter.

Sprinters are popular among those who buy racehorses for pleasure, for they offer the possibility of a quick return and without the attention of the gamblers they are relatively cheap. Sprint bred horses are thought to be precocious and they are often trained to win early two year old races, giving their owners a swift return. The absence of an international market reduces the possibility of a substantial capital gain, so sprinters are usually expected to race frequently and over a number of years, both of which are features which appeal to the buyer for pleasure.

The next category is the one which used to be the most sought after but whose appreciation has declined, the mile and a half horse or the stayer. Again the explanation lies in the lack of an international market. Some of Europe's most valuable and reputed races are still run over a mile and a half, so the yearlings deemed to be at the top of this bracket still offer large commercial rewards. However, for the breeder this type of horse presents the greatest risk for those not considered to be potential winners of these top races have as little value as the sprinter. The pattern race system rewards the excellent stayer, but offers nothing for the average one. At the top of this category the demand is international but largely confined to Europe, Japan and Australasia. The pattern of American racing offers few opportunities to the classical European stayer, so the largest market for bloodstock excludes the stayer, considerably reducing the type's commercial appeal. Those famous classic-stout stallions such as Alleged and Vaguely Noble who stand on American stallion farms are there only to cater for the export market, and the majority of their offspring will actually race in Europe.

The most important category of bloodstock in terms of numbers are those who are thought likely to excel over distances of between seven and ten furlongs. This is the type of horse which is demanded in the United States and which is increasingly favoured by the European pattern race system. This definition embraces the winners of the most prestigious two-year-old races which are run over seven furlongs or a mile, as well as the older milers and middle distance horses. When there were select sales in Europe they were generally filled with this type of horse. These are the sort of horses which attract the attention of gamblers for those which live up to their labels will be readily marketable anywhere in the bloodstock world.

The final category is the international horse. This is the sort of horse that appears at first to belong to the seven to ten furlong category, yet who might also be capable of winning Europe's top races over a mile and a half—in effect the horse that would be equally suited to American and European racing. The stallion Northern Dancer and his sons seemed to hold a temporary monopoly right to this accolade, which does of course account for their international fame, although stallions like Alydar, Seattle Slew and Blushing Groom have been allowed to usurp their position to some degree. These are the sort of horses which fill America's select yearling sales, for the majority of stallions and broodmares who are considered to belong to this category are American bred horses who spent their racing careers in Europe, and who are now domiciled in Kentucky. Their counterparts who remained in America were rarely given the chance to prove themselves under European conditions, so it has proved harder to establish their right to belong to this equine elite. Some prominent American stallions like Danzig, Chief's Crown, Slew O'Gold, and Conquistador Cielo may secure their places in the future. Equally it is possible that some stallions who were not re-exported to the United States after their racing careers may eventually join this elite, the possible candidates being Sadler's Wells, Lomond, Shareef Dance, and of course Dancing Brave. Finally there is one European bred and raced stallion who can aspire to the same heights, Lord Howard de Walden's Kris.

These categories may appear to be self-evident and not really of any interest except to those who are active buyers and sellers in the world's bloodstock markets. Their interest lies in their ad hoc nature. The pedigree expert would probably consider it to be reasonable and logical to distinguish between thoroughbreds on the basis of their pedigrees alone. Any expert would, if presented with a list of stallions or of broodmares, be willing to position each name within one of these categories. Indeed those pedigree experts who publish their own magazines or journals carry out a similar exercise at regular intervals, and sell the results to their subscribers. However, a perusal of some of these journals, or a conversation with more than two pedigree experts, will soon make it clear that each will hold fundamentally different views. If these lists were given to twenty renowned individuals twenty very different results would be obtained. Each expert would be able to produce reams of facts and statistics to support his case, and none which could prove their opponents to be mistaken. The market's selection is far more stable and is based upon a more rigorous logic.

For a time, at the peak of the boom years, the cult of the pedigree and of the stallion achieved the status of infallibility. Each year, or every two years, a particular type of pedigree or stallion was elevated into the elite and every yearling who conformed with the new pattern was eagerly competed for in the sales ring. If the expected, or hoped for, results were not forthcoming on the racecourse then, rather than wondering if the principle of selection was sensible, instead a new hero would be found and deified in the first one's place. This is the logic of revolutionary politics: appoint the first man who shouts the dictator, give him absolute powers and when he fails to achieve what the people desire, behead him and find a new one. The office of dictator is not fallible, only the man who holds it.

The cult was able to acquire such credence because the process of simplification is a natural preliminary to any complicated decision or choice. When choosing a yearling there are, as the first chapters of this book pointed out, countless different factors to be considered, and without some degree of elimination a choice would simply never be made. The cult of the pedigree should be seen in this light. The pedigree is a simple means of differentiating between thousands of similar young horses. In different circumstances the length of horses' canon bones might have been used as a touchstone instead, but the pedigree has a logicality and an attraction which has yet to be surpassed. A major part of this attraction was that there was a time when the pedigree was a valid means of categorizing young horses. When there were many fewer thoroughbreds, all confined within a small geographic area, a horse's pedigree was an accurate guide to the limits of the possibilities of its performance.

The pedigree and the possibility of controlling the means of inheritance have always had a powerful hold on the human imagination. Just as Sir Francis Galton hoped to improve mankind with the judicious selection of breeding specimens, so thoroughbred breeders have fondly believed in a similar possibility within their own field. The research into thoroughbred pedigrees is almost considered to be an intellectual pursuit, and it has lent respectability, rationality and a sense of permanence to a favoured form of gambling. The pedigree allows the appearance of a superior racehorse to be construed as fate rather than chance, and thus the purchase of a yearling can be seen as an investment rather than a gamble. The pedigree was raised to the status of a totem at a time when the recent integration of national bloodstock markets led the prospective purchaser to be inundated with a surfeit of information. Some form of simplification was obviously necessary, and what was false was not so much the distinctions themselves as the predictive powers assigned to them.

One would expect the prices fetched by yearlings at auctions to reflect in some way the ease or likelihood of accurately predicting their performances on the racecourse. If the probability of an accurate prediction is small, then one would expect the range of prices which yearlings fetch to be correspondingly small. During the years of the bloodstock boom the prices thoroughbreds brought at public auctions ceased to correlate in any manner whatsoever with racecourse performances. The bloodstock business was for a time concerned with producing and acquiring desired objects, rather than racehorses. The horse became a convenient currency, rather like the gambling chips in a casino. A chip is an almost worthless object, but by convention its holder is allowed to exchange it for cash on leaving the casino. The casino which the bloodstock world became was, like many others of its kind, frequented by shrewd professionals and by rich fools. The prices in the bloodstock market were inflated higher and held up for longer than would otherwise have been the case, because many of its prominent players had other sources of income, looked upon the business as a sport and relied upon the regulars to provide them with expertise.

For those who had been in the business for a long time the boom must have appeared as a most extraordinary bonanza. The vet, the breeder, the trainer, the bloodstock auctioneer and the bloodstock agent, these are all trades to which people were once attracted by their love of horses and an outside way of life. Over a few years the rewards offered by such callings increased immeasurably. As a result numerous new people were attracted to the business, many of whom had spurned it before on account of the meagre financial rewards it offered. A legion of auxiliaries were enlisted to supplement the few who were already established as specialist transporters, bankers, advertising agencies, insurers, journalists, accountants and lawyers. There can be little doubt that the boom has irrevocably transformed the thoroughbred business.

In order to examine this transformation in greater detail the next step is to look at the three prime sites of economic activity within the business. First the stud farm, for it is the breeder who must decide which type of thoroughbreds to produce and how many of them, then the bloodstock auction where the buyer and seller interact, and finally the stallion farm where the big money is, or was.

Part Three

Six
The Stud Farm

The business arrangements of the stud farm have been, in comparison with the stallion farm, relatively unaffected by the bloodstock boom. Indeed the major changes in stud farm management which have taken place over the last twenty years are those which were described in Chapter 2. The thoroughbred breeder now takes account of the findings of the agronomist and the equine ecologist in his daily decisions, and accords the vet the respect his science deserves. These changes are obviously to some extent the result of the boom, and this must be particularly true of the primary concern of infertility. The larger the financial investment the broodmare comprises, the more important it becomes to receive an annual return from her. However, the business of breeding remains largely unchanged because, despite these technical and managerial advances, it remains a hazardous commercial proposition.

Thoroughbred breeding requires skilled labour and prime agricultural land in abundance. If money were no object the breeder would like to have at least ten acres of pasture for each of his broodmares to graze over with their foal. But with the price of suitable land in the Newmarket area, for example, being about £10,000 per acre, only a few are able to afford such a luxury. The stud farm requires the services of the vet, the blacksmith, the groom and the others who deal with the horse itself, as well as a considerable amount of administration. The breeder needs to cope with the paperwork which is necessary to comply with the VAT regulations in Britain, and to inform the Inland Revenue or the Internal Revenue Service. In addition breeding has its own sizeable bureaucracy; for example, in Britain a breeder is required to fill in twenty-six forms on a foal's behalf from the time it is born until it enters a training stable. The breeder must also acquire information. He must know about his market and which types or categories of horse are demanded, about the performance and physical attributes of stallions, where they stand and how much their services cost. He must maintain the commercial viability of his stock by culling those broodmares who are no longer suitable and tracing and purchasing appropriate replacements. All these activities take time, and can only be performed successfully by those with experience. Stud farming obviously uses land and labour intensively, besides which it also requires sizeable capital investments which offer only the prospect of a return in the long run.

When a breeder buys a broodmare he will have to wait for a year at the very least before obtaining any sort of return. If he buys a broodmare who is already in foal at one of the breeding stock sales in November or December he will have to wait for eighteen months before the first opportunity to sell her offspring as a yearling, and in the mean time he will have paid to have her covered twice more. If a maiden mare is purchased straight out of training instead, there will be a period of six years before the first two of her produce have been able to perform on the racecourse as three-year-olds, and the mare's buyer is able to judge whether or not she constituted a sound investment. Buying a broodmare is clearly a risky and long term investment, and the same could be said of a stallion season. The breeder knows when he pays for a broodmare to be covered that there is at least a 25 per cent probability she will either fail to conceive, or her foal will be born with a disability or acquire one from an accident or disease, before it can be sold.

The only way of limiting these risks is to breed on a large scale, an option which does of course increase the initial capital investment and which is therefore beyond the means of most breeders. The cost of raising ten foals is only slightly smaller than ten times the cost of raising one. However, breeding is a business in which there are considerable economies of scale, for scale is the only means of minimizing the risks which are an inherent part of the business. The majority of the breeder's products will be failures; to be commercially successful the breeder must either sell them before their ability is revealed, or produce enough for him to be able to have at least one major success a year. The Aga Khan's breeding operation is a good example of the potential economies of scale in the business, for he is Europe's most successful breeder. The Aga Khan owns about one hundred and eighty broodmares from whom he probably expects to obtain some one hundred and forty foals every year, of whom around ninety will go into training

96

as two-year-olds. In recent years at least two or three of these have proved successful enough on the racecourse to be syndicated as stallions, thus paying for the whole operation. These figures and percentages give some idea of the difficulty of making money by breeding from one or two mares.

These financial requirements, together with the considerable expertise, knowledge and experience which are the breeder's prerequisites, serve as a formidable obstacle for any newcomer who wishes to enter the business of breeding. The abnormal profits some breeders were able to make during the boom years encouraged some to attempt to emulate them. However, the risk and size of the capital investment and the long wait for any return deterred many, who chose to gamble on stallions instead. For this reason only a handful of newcomers were able to establish themselves at the top of the trade during the boom years, and on the whole the business side of breeding is unchanged. As the Arab owners who have invested in strings of stud farms and swarms of mares will discover, breeding thoroughbreds is a trade in which managerial skill and experience can bring success in the long run, but in which there is no necessary correlation between the sums of money spent and the results achieved. To clarify these preliminary points, it is necessary to amplify and detail the sheer expense of raising thoroughbreds.

The simplest method of approximating the cost of raising a racehorse is to consider the charges of a reputable public stud farm.* On this basis the cost of raising a yearling to sell is £7,300 in England and 14,600 dollars or £9,700 (at $1.5 = £1) in Kentucky. This figure presumes a mare in foal is bought at one of the breeding stock sales. It takes into account the keep of the mare until she foals, the keep of the mare and her foal until it is weaned from her, and finally the keep of the foal until it is sold the following year. This figure takes no account of any depreciation in the mare's value or the cost of any insurance for either the mare or her foal. At an English stud farm the expense can be broken down as follows:

Buy mare in foal in December, four months board on her own at £8.75 a day	= £ 980
Mare with foal at foot kept for seven months at £11.25 a day	= £2,205
Foal kept from weaning until beginning of sales preparation, nine months at £8.75 a day	= £2,205

*All figures given are for 1986, and the English charges are those of the Aston Park Stud farm in Oxfordshire.

Cost of the sale (entry fee, groom's wages) = £ 400
Veterinary and blacksmith charges = £ 900
Total cost of raising and selling a yearling = £7,300

The purchase of a thoroughbred mare is just the beginning of a long term investment. A mare's potential as a progenitor, or as a source of income, will not be clearly revealed until her first foal has completed its three-year-old career. In the case of a maiden mare this will be five years after she has taken up residence on a stud farm, during which time she will have been covered five times and have given birth to four foals. A clearer idea of the risk breeders habitually take is given by laying out the expenses incurred by one mare and her offspring from the time the mare retires to stud until her first foal completes its three-year-old career.

Life cycle of the mare:-

Year 1,	November	leaves training
Year 2,	April	covered for first time
Year 3,	March/April	foals and covered again
	November	first foal weaned from mare
Year 4,	April	foals and covered again
	November	second foal weaned from mare
Year 5,	April/May	foals and covered again
	November	third foal weaned from mare
Year 6,	May	foals and covered again
	November	fourth foal weaned from mare

So in these five years the breeder has paid five nomination fees in order to have his mare covered. He has sold three of the mare's offspring as yearlings, one has just been weaned and one is due to be born the following May. His total outlay will have been something like this;

Twenty-seven months in which mare is kept on her
own at £8.75 a day = £6,615
Twenty-eight months in which mare is kept with foal
at foot, at £11.25 a day = £8,820

Life cycle of foal:-

| Year 1, | March/May | born |
| | November | weaned |

Year 2, August   sales preparation begins
         October   sold

Three offspring sold as yearlings:

Nine months from weaning to sales preparation at £8.75 a day	$= 3 \times £2,205 =$	£ 6,615
Last eight weeks to sale at £11.00 a day	$= 3 \times £$ 616 $=$	£ 1,848
Cost of sale (entry fee, grooms wages)	$= 3 \times £$ 400 $=$	£ 1,200
Veterinary care during covering and foaling	$= 5 \times £$ 300 $=$	£ 1,500
General veterinary care and blacksmith's charges		$= £$ 2,500
Total outlay over five years		$= £30,000$

These figures do not take account of the nomination fees, which for most breeders will make up the largest single expenditure each year. In Kentucky the outlay would be more, because public farms charge more per day than they do in England. A permanent boarder on her own will cost about $18 a day, whilst a mare with a foal at foot will cost around $23 a day. Americans take sales preparation seriously and a good farm will charge $25 a day during the final few weeks before a sale. Using these figures, and presuming the yearlings are sold in September and not July, an equivalent total outlay in Kentucky would be $57,000 or £38,000.

The breeding of thoroughbreds can clearly no longer be considered to be a pleasant and absorbing hobby, like breeding labradors or old roses. When the cost of raising a racehorse and keeping it in training for two years is nearly £30,000, breeding becomes a hobby beyond the financial reach of all but a few potentates. An operation which kept ten broodmares and raced their offspring for two or three seasons would probably cost £400,000 a year to run, without including the purchase of stock and stallion nominations. There are of course splendid possible rewards in yearling sales, prize money and stallion syndications, but any stud farm will produce many more slow and unsound racehorses than successful ones, and both cost the same amount to raise and train. All breeders are aware therefore that their endeavour is either a business, a gamble or a combination of the two.

The boom brought out the gambler in some breeders, and encouraged some gamblers to become breeders. In other words the boom, and particularly the prices attained at yearling sales, encouraged breeders to take a short term perspective of their trade. Every breeder must decide whether his overriding aim is to produce a successful racehorse or a fashionable yearling. Both ideals are beyond the reach of the mass of breeders, for it is almost as difficult to predict the fads of the yearling market in advance as it is to raise a successful racehorse. From the commercial viewpoint, however, the former ideal is one which involves waiting, whilst the latter brings its reward swiftly. The farm with a long term policy which raises a Derby winner will receive its bonanza, even if it sold the horse itself cheaply as a yearling, as long as it has retained the horse's mother, sister, cousin or aunt. Victory in a Derby will take a horse and his family to the top of either the middle distance or staying category, and thus ensure fashionableness for any near relations who are sold in the following years. However, the farm will have waited for at least three years for the horse to prove himself on the racecourse, and in the meantime it may have sold a gem like his half sister or even his dam herself before it was aware of their true value. The short-term breeder is not prepared to take such risks, nor to wait so long for a return. The farm with a short-term policy would of course like to raise a similar crack or champion, but it will not be prepared to rely solely on such an unlikely event to produce a profit. Instead, the short term breeder is concerned only with the yearling sale. To his mind the results of past bloodstock sales are as interesting as the results of any race, and the knack of correctly valuing a yearling as impressive as the selection of a winner. The differences between the short-term and long-term breeder were greatly amplified by the bloodstock boom, and for a time their methods of selecting and rearing horses were quite distinct.

The long-term breeder can be either a private or a commercial breeder. This distinction is widely used, although it is often a misnomer. The breeder who intends to sell his produce as foals or yearlings is usually described as a commercial breeder, in contrast to the breeder who retains and races his own horses, who is called a private breeder. Some private breeders, like the Aga Khan, make a great deal of money and as we shall see many commercial breeders lose much of theirs. However, these names serve as useful labels. The short-term breeder will always be a commercial breeder. His aim will be to produce yearlings whose pedigree will lead to their being placed in the most sought-after category by the mass of buyers, and indeed in the most valued section of the category. At first sight this seems to be a simple way of making money. If it is as easy as has been claimed to place yearlings in categories, then surely it is possible to do so in advance when the coupling is planned or selected. The problem is of course the time lag between planning and selling. Once again it is the inelasticity of the supply of the thoroughbred. The short-term breeder must make his choice two to three years in advance of the day when the wheel comes to rest on his game. Clearly it is problematic for the producer to attempt to respond to or catch the vagaries and fads of bloodstock fashion.

When the reward for success in short-term breeding was the million-dollar yearling many were prepared to give the game a go. For a time they introduced new criteria for the selection of breeding stock, new methods of preparing yearlings for sale, and, for the bloodstock world at least, unparalleled attempts to market and sell their product. Some of these introductions and innovations are best labelled as excesses and have disappeared; others have achieved a degree of permanence. It is as well to bear in mind again the pressing conflict between money and sentiment in the heads and eyes of those who try to make a living in the thoroughbred world.

This is not an appropriate place to consider in detail how best to select a broodmare and, subsequently, an appropriate mate for her. As we saw in Chapter One, the wise long-term breeder will decide upon a rigorous selection criteria and then obey its imperatives in the hope of gradually improving the standard and quality of his stock or herd. The short-term breeder has no time for such pedantry. His concern will be for what will appear on his yearling's page of the sales catalogue. As long as the yearling looks correct on the day of sale its mental and physical attributes are the buyer's concern and of no interest to the breeder. There are only two factors which are important for an impressive entry in the sales catalogue: the name of the yearling's sire and the amount of black type which has been accumulated by its relations. The breeder is trying to forecast types and place his horses within them, and he knows the mass of buyers will be swayed by these two factors alone.

So when the short-term breeder is looking for a broodmare, above all else he is searching for black type. The preferred solution is for the mare herself to have earned the right to carry black type, or at least to have earned upper case letters by winning even the smallest of races. For this reason a mare's value is disproportionately increased by the least meritorious of victories, or by placing in the most unexciting of pattern races, for fourth place in a field of four is enough to secure the precious black type. Besides the mare herself there must be plenty of other black type on the yearling's page, and the closer it is to the top of the page the better. The breeder would rather buy a mare whose brothers and sisters had earned black type, rather than having to rely upon the appeal of aunts and uncles. Black type is of course expensive, but then the breeder with limited resources can use a winner of the Cleveland Oaks or the Preis de Jahrlingsanktion to colour his page rather than a winner of the Kentucky Derby. The only other criterion to be considered when selecting a broodmare is the consistency of the record of her own progeny if she is of an age to have been represented on the racetrack. In Britain the mare's produce record is important because it must be printed in full in the catalogue, but in the United States it is only a marginal matter, for you only need to advertise the good news. "Dam of two horses to race, and two winners," the catalogue will announce, when a mare has had ten foals eight of whom were not physically capable of racing.

Once he has selected a broodmare by some means or other, the breeder must find her a mate. The choice of a stallion is the decisive one for the short-term breeder, for its sire's name will all but determine a yearling's category. There are two ways of going about this decision. The first is to repeat the pattern of those matings within the family which have already produced the winners of black type races. For example, if the mare's half brother by stallion X won a Group 2 race, then you send the mare to X or to a son of X and announce the yearling as being bred upon similar lines to the winner of a Group 2 race. This repetition of patterns or crosses which have already produced black type winners can be carried to further removes. One can mate a granddaughter of Buckpasser with a son of Northern Dancer in order to obtain a yearling which exhibits "the famous Northern Dancer–Buckpasser cross", or alternatively one can arrange a mating so that the offspring will be inbred to Nasrullah in the third generation, "like the famous black type winners alpha, beta and gamma". The other method is to bank on the stallion's reputation. The safest bet here is to go for the stallion young enough for none of his progeny yet to have appeared on the racetrack. In this case you will be selling the spirits of its ancestors and not incidence of their reincarnation in its offspring. The most hazardous choice is a stallion whose progeny have yet to race, but who will have done by the time your yearling is sold. If there is no sign of the next Dalai Lama in a stallion's first two crops then its reputation will evaporate, however confident the earlier predictions of an imminent second coming. An established fashionable stallion presents a similar risk, for it will be particularly expensive, and by its very nature no fad can last for ever. Every stallion who lives too long will at times fall from favour, and the breeder does not want this humiliation to coincide with his mare's bearing of the stallion's foal.

The permutations of selection are endless. The short-term breeder will study the results of past auctions, the prices of nominations, listen to gossip and talk to prospective buyers, in an attempt to gain a vision of tomorrow's categories. There is no need to share the agony of each if and every but, for the essential features of short-term criteria are simple. Each selection of a mate, or of the mare herself, is a discrete and unrelated decision. A breeder with ten mares may follow a different hunch with each of them, and then the following year change his mind and start again from scratch. In effect each coupling and its result is a purely random selection, although the breeder is unlikely to see it in this way. By some means or other the decision will be made and the coupling carried out. The next stage is to ensure the yearling looks the part on the day of the sale.

The commercial breeder's income depends upon the appearance of his yearlings on three or four specified days each year. Therefore it makes sense for him to aim to present his products looking at their very best on these days. The problem is to decide what the best yearlings look like. Yearlings are, of course, sold as potential racehorses, so it would seem foolish to prepare them for sale in a manner which impairs their racing potential. However, at any yearling sale there will be hundreds of young racehorses all of whom look relatively similar, and for one particular horse to sell well it will have to stand out from the crowd. The more closely a yearling resembles a racehorse, rather than an immature baby of a horse, the more likely it is someone will be prepared to pay a lot of money for it. As a result there is a temptation for any commercial breeder to force his sale's yearlings to develop at an unnatural pace.

A horse retained and raced by its breeder will probably be left outside, running in a paddock, until the autumn of the year in which it is a yearling. During the autumn it will be trained to accept and respond to a bit and a rider, and then at the end of the year it will leave the stud farm to join a trainer. In contrast the yearling who is to be sold at one of the July sales in Kentucky will be brought in and begin to undergo intensive training in April, while the autumn sales horse's preparation will start in July or August. There need not be a gulf between the two regimes, for some private breeders will begin to exercise their yearlings in the spring to prevent them from putting on excess weight, but nobody would have their yearlings as forward as a July Sale's yearling unless they were planning to sell them.

A sale is an ordeal for any horse and the sale's yearling must be prepared mentally and physically. Once it has arrived at the saleground the yearling will be kept for anything up to six days in an unfamiliar box, and surrounded by strange people, noises and horses. At any moment it may be displayed to prospective purchasers, asked to walk up and down and then to stand still while it is prodded and felt all over. After six days of examination in intense humid heat any horse will be exhausted. At the end of the 1986 Keeneland July Sale Charles Dingwall went to take a last look at a filly by Smarten he had bought on behalf of Prince Ahmed Salman. He cooed at her, petted her and whispered to advise her to prepare for a long flight, for she was off to join Henry Cecil. Unfortunately she was too tired to even lift her head to acknowledge such solicitations. The Keeneland Sales that year were held in especially oppressive conditions, but a yearling must be exercised to ensure its fitness before any sale. The yearling who stands out will also have been taught to stand and display itself. When a prospective buyer inspects a yearling he expects it to stand straight and still and the horse who plays up, jumps in the air or backs away violently will appear overexcitable and nervous in comparison with its more stolid competitors. A yearling can only be taught to present itself by a patient groom who spends hours cajoling it and making it respond to the voice and the leading rein.

Although there is nothing illegitimate per se about preparing a yearling for a sale, there will always be some conflict in the breeder's mind between the desire to maximize a horse's commercial potential and the wish to allow it to fulfil itself on the racetrack later. For the short-term breeder the sale will always come first. The benefits of raising horses in company and, for as long as is feasible, outside were outlined in Chapter Two. In contradiction of those precepts, many sales yearlings have been unnaturally cossetted and pampered. The unfortunate Kentucky yearling is kept apart from its siblings once it has been weaned in order to reduce the risks of an injury or slight blemish which might detract from its appearance at the sale. From the beginning of spring it will be kept inside during the day, for sun-bleached coats are thought to be unsightly.

The more unscrupulous short-term breeders are prepared to resort to drugs and surgery to safeguard their return. Some yearlings have been given anabolic steroids to boost their growth and development, and in the United States it is possible to pay for elaborate surgical operations which mask the effects of injuries or disabilities. Foals born back at the knee can be operated on and made to appear forward at the knee.* In one infamous case the same vet was asked by a vendor to patch up a yearling's foot before it was sold, and then a few days later asked by its purchasers to discover what was wrong with their expensive yearling's foot. There can be little doubt that many yearlings have been ruined mentally or physically, and have had their capacity to race destroyed, by the preparation they were put through before being sold. A sales yearling will often deflate visibly in the weeks following its ordeal. Indeed, transporting American sales yearlings back to Europe can be a thankless task. For by the time they arrive

*A "good" yearling's forelegs will be perfectly straight and not form an angle at the knee. For fuller explanation of equine conformation see William E. Jones, op. cit., pp. 379–405.

some will look very different from the sleek fat beasts their new owners paid millions of dollars for a few weeks before, and the transporters are sometimes held to blame.

The more lasting innovations, which will survive the era of short-term commercial breeding, are first, the mechanical labour-saving devices and, in addition, the commercial breeder's concern with presentation and marketing. The use of these machines and the practice of salesmanship are both more advanced in the United States than in Europe. This is in part because the size of the American market makes it difficult for a farm to acquire a distinct identity, but then American breeders generally display a greater concern for and knowledge of the balance sheet than their English counterparts. Yearlings on most American commercial farms are now exercised on a treadmill. An equine treadmill is simply a short section of a travelator, like those commonly used at airports, on a slight incline with padded sides. Once a yearling has become accustomed to a stationary machine it will be switched on in reverse whilst the horse is standing quietly. To keep its poise and balance on the machine the horse will have to walk slowly. In the weeks leading up to a sale a yearling will be exercised on the treadmill daily, and throughout the period the machine's speed and the time the horse spends on it will be increased. By the last weeks any man who takes the yearling's place on the machine will have to work to keep up with its pace.

A treadmill dramatically reduces the number of man hours required to prepare a yearling for sale. For instance, with the help of a hotwalker two men can exercise eight yearlings on a morning without doing anything more strenuous themselves than walking from the yearling barn to the exercise barn and back eight times. A hotwalker consists of a central pole with several arms or spokes extending from it which rotate at a gentle walking pace. A yearling's rein is looped over an arm above its head, and when the machine is started the horses who are attached to it walk in a circle, meekly and quietly. A hotwalker seems to have a mesmerising affect upon young horses; it is a frail contraption which they could easily stop, yet they comply with its orders in silent docility. Perhaps it is only lethargy induced by the Kentucky summer.

Despite their many advantages there are many breeders, particularly British ones, who disdain to use a treadmill or a hotwalker. Some consider them to be dangerous, although those who have actually used them know they are no more dangerous than any other method of exercising young horses. The clearest reason for not using a machine is the separation of the man and the horse it effects. A yearling walked by hand or lunged will have to respond to the man's movements and voice throughout the period of exercise. For the yearling on the machine exercise is only part of a monotonous daily pattern. However, the traditional method of preparing yearlings for sale is time consuming and expensive, for if it is to be done properly then no groom can be responsible for more than two yearlings. At present conservatism and high prices ensure its continuation, but with a prosaic market many farms will be forced to consider reducing their labour costs.

Whether the market becomes more prosaic or not, commercial breeders have come to realize the rewards of preparing their customers as well as their horses. For the commercial breeder there are two phases of marketing; one is advertising the farm's name, its successes and its products, the other is the mode of presentation on the day of the sale itself. Salesmanship in both areas has become more sophisticated. The large commercial farms regularly take advertisements in the trade's magazines and newspapers in order to keep the farm's name in the minds of potential customers, and especially to give publicity to a major victory of a horse the farm raised. In the weeks prior to an important sale the magazines are full of advertisements for particular yearlings which are due to come under the hammer. More diverse forms of advertising are problematic because of the need to target for a specific audience. Needless to say Lexington is the only place where horses are advertised on television and billboards. During the Kentucky sales one television channel broadcasts interviews with various bloodstock pundits interspersed with advertisements for yearlings, farms and stallions, and as you drive away from Lexington's Blue Grass airport the billboards on either side of the highway proclaim the virtues of farms and stallions, rather than cigarette brands or automobiles.

This copious advertising is more common in America than in Europe, where the market is smaller and many vendors feel they can rely upon personal contacts alone. Breeders feel they can push their products adequately by going racing and making a point of being charming to and interested in those who have already, or might yet, buy their horses. A major racemeeting, particularly those at Newmarket during the sales weeks, is a business convention or seminar and those who take their job seriously are seriously concerned with talking to the right people for the right amount of time. An exception to this European distrust of advertising is the vogue for previews of major yearling sales, which are filmed and sold as videos. Whether there was originally any foundation for it or not, it became accepted that the major Arab buyers liked to see video pictures of yearlings charging about in paddocks before deciding which of them to purchase. As a result equine video is now a thriving business. Most farms simply show the yearling in the field with a background sales talk, although some vendors appear in person with their yearlings explaining forcefully why they are likely to be excellent racehorses.

The amount of advertising in the bloodstock world has increased but the advertisements themselves remain conventional and unimaginative. The advertisements for sales yearlings are especially unremarkable; indeed they often simply repeat the information which will be printed in the sales catalogue. There are the occasional exceptions; for instance one advertisement for Lady Tavistock's stallion Precocious consisted of a large colour picture of an even larger hippopotamus announcing that she too wanted to be covered by Precocious. The auctioneers Goffs have done some imaginative advertising as well, although they tend to favour obscure photographs of Irish bars or moustachioed waiters bearing oysters, whose connection with bloodstock is uncertain. Bloodstock advertising tends to be dull because bloodstock advertising agencies tend to be staffed with recruits from the world of bloodstock, rather than the world of advertising. The agencies would claim their market is conservative and therefore their advertisements are tailored to suit its members—a specious argument, for the briefest of looks at the crowd who throng Keeneland during sales weeks is enough to demonstrate that people who buy bloodstock are not that conservative.

Presentation on the days of the sale counts, for every farm or vendor wants to attract the wealthy bidders and their agents from this throng. At Keeneland each vendor is allotted boxes in one of the forty barns which are spread out down the hill away from the racetrack and the training track. The vendor will leave his individual mark on his barn or row of boxes by hanging up flowers, signs and logotypes, and setting out chairs emblazoned with the farm's name. Should you go up and ask to look at lots 92, 132 and 238, the farm's owner or manager will get up to talk to you and try to ascertain how much money you and your client have, without asking for information in case he ought to know who you are. Moments later a waiter will appear with a tray of juleps and cocktails straight from the deep freeze. The glasses will be printed with the farm's racing colours and among the crushed ice inside will be a swizzle stick also carrying the appropriate colours. Meanwhile three or four usually young people dressed in the farm's livery and baseball caps will have scurried away inside the boxes to brush and prepare the yearlings for your appraisal.* They will emerge in turn and present each yearling and walk it around the striped marquee top which provides shade between the barns, while the owner withdraws to let you scribble learned notes on your catalogue in privacy.

*Most of the grooms are permanent employees, but there are professional sales handlers who spend the year migrating from Kentucky to Saratoga to Louisiana and wherever else bloodstock auctions are held.

Personal contacts matter at Keeneland as well, and if you are observed talking in a friendly manner to Anthony Stroud or one of the other agents who buy on behalf of the leading Arab owners, you will be treated with due deference thereafter. Indeed, there can be few places in America where an English accent is more of an advantage than at a select yearling sale. If you sound English and can talk intelligently, or at least knowingly, about pasterns, then everyone will presume you work for one of the English-based Arab owners. The Arabs' main agents themselves are courted assiduously, and if one of them is moved to comment on a yearling then its owner and groom will begin to tremble, for if he should decide to bid for it then perhaps their Danzig colt will fetch a million dollars after all.

By comparison presentation at bloodstock sales in Europe remains understated. At Newmarket some farms place a board with the yearling's pedigree and lot number on the door of its stall, but others do not bother. There will be a groom about to show the yearling for you, but the animal is as likely to jig around excitedly as it is to walk up and down sensibly, and many display an inconvenient reluctance to return to their stalls. The people who are most disconcerted by the British tradition of letting the horse sell itself are their owners, the commercial breeders. Everybody enjoys buying at auctions. Each successful bid is a victory in itself, and the joy and excitement usually shine out from the purchaser's face as he leaves the sale ring after signing the sales chit. Selling is not so much fun. The breeder will sit in the bar knowing there is nothing more he can do to persuade people to bid for his horses, though he will not be able to resist going out quickly to ask his groom if everything is all right and to discover how many people have been to inspect his yearlings. If you are looking at a yearling at Newmarket its owner is probably the man or woman hovering nervously on one side, not knowing whether to talk to you, to keep quiet or to go and hide somewhere until it is all over.

The mass of the newcomers to the business of breeding in the years after 1975 were attracted by the gamble and the thought of the million dollar jackpot rather than any long-term financial plan. The daily decisions, choices and activities of the majority of breeders have been relatively unaffected by the boom and the money which it has brought with it. There are more thoroughbred breeders than ever before, but for the majority this wealth, although it may shape their dreams and fantasies, has only a marginal affect upon their activities. Most of all the yearlings and foals who are sold at public auctions fetch a price which is less than the cost of producing them,* and most racehorses

*In 1985 60 per cent of yearlings sold in North America fetched less than $10,000.

are either slow, unsound or both. There must be a great number of breeders who consistently lose money year after year. Some of this number are unsuccessful businesses, but the majority look upon breeding as a mixture of a hobby and a gamble. Due to the conventions of taxation this is particularly true in Britain and in the early 1980s the Thoroughbred Breeders Association estimated that of the 6,400 broodmares in Great Britain 4,100 were owned by people who had but the one mare, and a further 1,000 were owned by people who had two. Only a fool relies upon one or two broodmares for his daily bread.

The small breeder is faced with the conundrum of having to sell all or some of the horses he produces as yearlings, and yet not being able to afford to buy fashionable stock or nominations to fashionable stallions. The man with one or two mares is therefore likely to lose money steadily, but he will reason that one win alone will cancel out years of losses. There are three ways in which he can win: by breeding a good horse himself, by winning on his choice of stallions, or on the offspring of his broodmare's family. For if one of his mare's relatives produces a good racehorse the whole of her family will rise in status behind her. The small breeder is like the alchemist, striving to effect a transmutation of his base stock. He is also indulging in a gamble with diminishing returns, for the more players there are the more horses there are, and the wider the gap becomes between the cost of production and the average prices realized at the lower end of the market. The gamble encourages overproduction, and the resulting low prices force the small breeder to risk more each season.

In the United States there were more newcomers to the game, who generally had more money to spend on stock and stallion seasons because of the benign tax stance. In Great Britain a breeding operation will not be accepted as a business by the Inland Revenue unless it owns its own stud farm. On the other hand in the United States a breeder who owns no land at all and who boards his mares on a public farm ought to be able to convince the Internal Revenue Service that he is in business.* As a result of this ruling many rich American businessmen decided in the 1980s to buy broodmares in order to make money. Many were advised to get into the business by their accountants, and few were prepared to go to the time and expense of setting up their own farms. Instead they sent their mares to public studs or to one of

*This ruling is the result of the size of the United States and the widespread practice of walking in mares to stallion farms. A commercial breeder who aims to sell at the top of the market will have to board his mares near where the fashionable stallions are, regardless of where he resides himself and of where the fashionable stallions were two years ago.

the farms which specialize in preparing yearlings for America's most important sales. Some of these new investors were limited partnerships, others were plain businessmen, and Ed Sczesny can serve as an example of one of the latter.

Ed Sczesny is the president of a company which develops new technologies for the glass industry. In 1983 he was persuaded by his friend and business partner R. D. Hubbard to get into the horse business. At the time he knew little or nothing about horses. He got lucky straight away for the first horse he sold was a weanling (foal) by Alydar. Alydar's offspring were just beginning to appear on the racetrack, and that year one of them, Althea, was nominated the champion two-year-old filly in the United States. The weanling fetched $750,000, which was at the time a world record price for a weanling. Fired by this success he bought a mare who was in foal to Northern Dancer. Unfortunately the market decided that his mare was not worthy of Northern Dancer and when her foal was sold he found he had lost money on the deal. Ed Sczesny was not put off. Indeed he decided to stop boarding his mares at Walmac International and buy his own farm instead. In April 1985 he bought a corn and soya bean farm near Paris, Kentucky, in partnership with R. D. Hubbard. By October the farm was called Crystal Springs and had two yearling barns and 235 acres of railed paddocks. When Crystal Springs sold its first yearlings at Keeneland in July 1986 it was among the sale's top fifteen consignors. Ed Sczesny now owns six broodmares and has purchased seasons to such elite stallions as Nijinsky and Danzig.

Ed Sczesny has been more successful than most newcomers to breeding, but he can also serve as an example of the benefits of the American organization of the breeding business. By allowing new-comers to breeding to deduct their expenses from their taxable income even before they owned a farm, the Internal Revenue Service has encouraged a multitude of Sczesnys to try their hand at commercial breeding. In addition a large number of breeders and farms have established themselves and accumulated enough capital to expand by boarding and selling other people's horses. These public farms charge for the keep of boarders and their foals, but they make their money as a percentage of the prices the yearlings they prepare fetch at the sales. When taken together these two factors account for the com-paratively swift turnover in the prominent names in the American bloodstock business. The drawback of the American system is of course that many of these newcomers are purely short-term commercial breeders whose future prospects in the industry are likely to be as emphemeral as their outlook. However, the deleterious influences will be examined later, once the favourable aspects have been reviewed.

Some of these public farms are exclusively concerned with looking after the bloodstock interests of those who board their mares with them; the best known of these are Eaton-Williams and the Taylor Made Farm. The Taylor Made Farm was set up in 1976 by the three sons of Joe Taylor, who has long been the general manager of Gainesway Farm. At the time they were in their early twenties. The family has a marked physical resemblance and the brothers are equally large, quiet and reserved. Their farm is among the least ostentatious and most practical of Kentucky farms. One almost expects to see that characteristic saying of Duncan Taylor's, "there's nobody who spends money as carefully as the man it belongs to ...," written on a plaque and hanging in the farm's office. Instead there is a picture of Dancing Brave who, along with Manilla, was among the yearlings they consigned to the sales in 1984. The brothers look after one hundred and fifty broodmares for other people, and to keep these distant owners involved they send them a new photograph of their mare and her offspring every month. A simple task, one thinks, before adding up the number of mares, foals and yearlings and realizing that they must employ their own photographer.

In addition to preparing the horses they have raised from birth, the brothers take on numerous more yearlings from between three months and a few weeks before they are due to be sold. This is another beneficial feature of the American system, for a small breeder can send his yearling on a short intensive training course which will cost less than $1,000, and then sell it under the auspices of an internationally known farm. The Taylors are not dogmatic in their selection of yearlings and they will never turn one away who is not a cripple, for they would not want to refuse the next Dancing Brave or his breeder. The cost of all this sevice is open to negotiation; they charge a different percentage depending upon the client and the price his horse fetches. Other farms like Walmac International and Three Chimneys have boarded mares for commercial beeders as a means of accumulating capital, and both are now leading stallion farms; like Taylor Made Farm both had gained a place among the leaders in their field within ten years of being set up.

Walmac International was founded, near the Lexington end of the Paris Pike, in time for Alleged to retire to stud there in 1978. Three Chimneys is younger still, although the farm's owner Robert Clay has had a farm near Midway, Kentucky, since the mid 1970s. Johnny Jones Junior has managed Walmac International since the beginning and he has shared ownership of it with a succession of different partners; originally Robert Sangster and Marvin Warner, then William Farish and finally since 1985 Alec Head and Roland de Chambure of the

Haras d'Etreham. Johnny Jones Junior would be proud to describe himself as a Texan horse dealer, but he rarely takes his cigar from his mouth for long enough to be able to say much more than "Correct" or "That's it". He does, however, claim to be impoverished and quite unable to buy shares in the stallions which he stands. This is almost certainly equivocation, for he owns an enormous farm and training ground which is waiting in Texas for racing to be legalized there, and Walmac itself is flourishing. The striking feature of Johnny Jones and Walmac International is that both have established themselves by reinvesting profit derived from the thoroughbred business. Walmac has always had Alleged, but a proportion of the funds have come from commercial breeding. Jones himself owned thirty mares in 1986 and he boarded around one hundred and thirty for other people.

Robert Clay only came into the thoroughbred business because he got a job working at night in Spendthrift's foaling barn while he was a student. He says he worked at night, slept in the morning and went to lectures in the afternoon. His only responsibility at night was to prod the foaling manager to make sure he was awake, but he decided he enjoyed thoroughbreds. After leaving the navy he settled near Lexington to work for a fertilizer company. He bought his first mare when she was in foal to a cheap stallion for $26,000, and boarded her in a tobacco barn. When he sold the foal, who subsequently won Graded races in California, for $35,000 he became a commercial breeder. His first client and his mentor was Peter Burrell who had been the Director of the English National Stud. For some years Robert Clay's trade was raising yearlings and selling them on a commission basis; within ten years he was in a position to syndicate a champion like Slew O'Gold. In 1986 Robert Clay's Three Chimneys farm owned twenty broodmares and boarded a further ninety.

If Walmac International and Three Chimneys are among America's leading stud farms, then another newcomer who has joined their number is William S. Farish III's Lane's End Farm. There are about one hundred mares permanently on Lane's End Farm and the only boarders belong either to the Queen or Daniel Wildenstein, so William Farish is a breeder who takes advantage of the economies of scale. Lane's End is of course an extraordinary size for such a new farm, but then William Farish had established himself in other fields before he came into the thoroughbred business. Johnny Jones enjoys saying that the difference between Farish and himself is that he has only his horses to fall back on, whereas Wil has chunks of I.B.M. These three farms have been able to join the established elite of North America's commercial breeding farms during the years of the boom. Of this elite two of the most vibrant are Charles Taylor's Windfields Farm and Warner

L. Jones Junior's* Hermitage Farm, both of which were founded in the 1930s. Windfields Farm, which is now divided between Maryland and Ontario, was founded by E. P. Taylor, who bred such horses as Northern Dancer and Nijinsky. The farm owns about one hundred mares, and boards a further two hundred. The Hermitage Farm, which was the vendor of the world record priced yearling, is in north Kentucky near Louisville.

These farms are not going to suddenly disappear. During the boom years they were able to consolidate their position at the top of the industry and they now have advantages of capital and reputation which any newcomer will find hard to compete with. Indeed, without the help of abnormal profits it is hard to imagine anyone creating a major farm like Three Chimneys in only ten years. It is not only the appropriate broodmares and facilities which take time to acquire, for in the new commercial climate a reputation is just as important. To succeed at the top of the market a commercial breeder must attract the bids of the agents who work for the Maktoum family, Prince Khalid Abdullah and Robert Sangster and his partners. Tom Gentry, who used to be among America's leading commercial breeders, noticeably failed to sell a single horse to one of these concerns at the 1986 Kentucky Summer Sales.

The structure of the breeding business in Europe is in comparison rigid. There are relatively few businessmen who have established themselves as commercial breeders, and even fewer who have set up completely new stud farms. In Britain this absence of new commercial breeders can be explained by the conventions of taxation, for only a handful of newcomers are prepared to purchase their own farm, particularly as until the mid 1980s the price of agricultural land was absurdly inflated. One way to circumvent this barrier to entry into the breeding business is for the agent who manages his clients' bloodstock interests to bring their mares to his own farm during the crucial period preceding and following covering, conception and foaling. The Newmarket agent David Minton favours this system, for it allows his clients to have their mares and foals at home for the majority of the year without their having to be experts in stud management; he can personally supervise the first months of their foals' lives and the last few weeks before they are sold.

Another feature of the American breeding business which is absent in Europe is the large commercial farm on the scale of Windfields or Hermitage. Some of those which approach this size are Peter Goulandris' Hesmonds Stud in Sussex, Sonia Rogers's Airlie Stud near

* In 1987 Warner Jones announced his intention to retire.

Dublin, and the Haras d'Etreham and Paul de Moussac's Haras du Mézeray in Normandy. However, the European yearling market is simply not large enough for any one farm to sell fifty or more yearlings annually, even if any European breeder had the capital to buy a hundred fashionable broodmares. The large stud farms in Europe are private farms, and indeed the operations of the Aga Khan, the Maktoum family and Prince Khalid Abdullah are on a greater scale than Kentucky's last three grand private studs, the Whitneys' Greentree Farm and John W. Galbreath's Darby Dan Farm and J. T. Lundy's Calumet Farm. If one had to generalize one could say that Europe's successful commercial breeders tend to be horsemen who have been in the business for twenty years or more, whose entrepreneurial skills enabled them to prosper during the boom. Other examples would be Lord Porchester's Highclere Stud and James Delahooke's Adstock Manor Stud. A slightly different type is Gerald Leigh's Eydon Hall Farm. Gerald Leigh is a comparative newcomer and with a small group of mares he aims to sell internationally, regularly consigning yearlings to Keeneland's July Sales and selling American bred yearlings at Newmarket. Perhaps the most successful European commercial farm in the 1980s has been Alan Lillingston's Mount Coote Stud, near Kilmallock in the south-western corner of Ireland.

Alan Lillingston began running his family's farm in 1958 when he was still in his early twenties. For some years he combined running it with riding, first as an amateur jockey in jump races and then as part of Ireland's Three Day Event team. His victories included a Champion Hurdle and a Gold Medal in the European Three Day Event Championships. Mount Coote's commercial policy changed in 1981 as a result of the death of John Hay Whitney, who had for some years boarded all his European based mares at Mount Coote. When the Whitney mares were disbanded the farm needed to find some new clients. Alan Lillingston went to Australia and the United States in search of customers and attracted William Farish, Warner Jones, the Kinderhill Corporation and Robert Holmes A Court, who, unlike Mr Whitney, were commercial breeders. Alan Lillingston is a pragmatic breeder. He is more interested in how his horses are raised than in who their third dam happens to be. He is also a man of forceful authority. At the Newmarket sales he will stand with his upright poise next to the boxes in which his yearlings are stabled and make a point of speaking to every potential customer who passes. Indeed he goes out of his way to impose his personality upon Mount Coote. He appears in person on the farm's sales preview videos, he stands prominently by the ringside while they are sold, and when he comes to England to attend the major racemeetings he will pay his respects and compliments to his present and possible future clients. His personality and the racecourse performances of Mount Coote's produce maintain the farm's commercial momentum.

A successful commercial farm with a more recent origin is Kirsten Rausing's Lanwades Stud near Newmarket. In her first season at Lanwades Kirsten Rausing sold five yearlings who included Kala Dancer, Europe's champion two-year-old in 1984, and Petoski, whose victories included the King George VI and Queen Elizabeth Diamond Stakes. Kala Dancer's ability was unheralded, but Petoski had always seemed to be out of the ordinary. Doug Smith, the ex-champion jockey who is now a bloodstock agent, came to look at the yearlings at Lanwades in the summer of 1983. He was so entranced by Petoski that he returned every morning for a week just to gaze at the Niniski colt running in his paddock. He assured Kirsten Rausing that the colt would win the Derby, but when it came to be sold Smith was outbid by Robin Hastings of the British Bloodstock Agency, who bought Petoski on behalf of Lady Beaverbrook. Kirsten Rausing is, however, no newcomer to the breeding world, for 1986 was the twenty-second consecutive breeding season in which she had managed a farm. She began her career managing a stallion farm with a hundred visiting mares even before she had entered university at Stockholm. She is an unusual breeder, not least because of her sex for only a handful of women run their own breeding operation, but also because she began her career at Simontorp in a remote part of Sweden which is near Gdansk and only a forty-five minute flight from Leningrad. She came west permanently after a fortuitous meeting with Captain Tim Rogers of the Airlie Stud.

A young Kirsten arrived at the Airlie Stud with some mares from Simontorp who were due to be covered there. A smart looking man in a suit watched her unloading them from a horsebox, and asked her admiringly where such good looking mares came from. On hearing the word Sweden the man began to shout and look for an explanation. Apparently he did not relish the idea of having mares from bloody Siberia on his stud farm. The mutual respect this contretemps engendered led to Kirsten Rausing managing one of the Airlie farms, first the Baroda Stud and subsequently the Grangewilliam Stud. Kirsten Rausing only finally left Ireland because at the time when she bought Lanwades it was considerably cheaper than an equivalent farm in County Kildare.

Kirsten Rausing is also unusual among breeders in repeatedly questioning the value of her activities. She appears to have a conscience about spending her life absorbed in a process which fascinates her.

Indeed she seems still to share her family's original misgivings about her choice of a livelihood. Her family had no connection with racing, although her father had been a reserve in Sweden's Olympic Three Day Event team and had taught her how to jump fences with a glass of water in one hand. In many ways she lives up to her own dictum that the Swedes are a race which see things in black and white. For Kirsten Rausing the pedigree is very white, and many of the features of short-term commercial breeding are particularly black. Her belief in the pedigree is such that she flew from Sweden to Ireland to buy Petoski's dam on the strength of the information in the sales catalogue, and the fact that Sushila turned out to have a crooked leg and to have produced four foals who had not won a race between them did not weaken her resolve in any way. Kirsten Rausing is a lady with a forthright presence and extraordinary green eyes.

Robert McCreery can serve as a final example of the successful commercial breeder. Like Alan Lillingston he was a distinguished jump jockey and was the champion amateur in Britain on two occasions. When he retired from the saddle Bob McCreery was set up as a commercial breeder by Sir John Astor and John Hay Whitney, who both sold him a mare for a nominal sum. He was successful fairly quickly, for one of the first yearlings he sold at the Houghton Sales was the Classic winner and Classic stallion High Top. High Top's sale illustrates the fortuitous nature of the business, for he was one of the first ten lots to be sold on the first morning of the sale. The Newmarket fog that morning was so dense that almost no one arrived on time and High Top was led from the ring unsold. Sir John Thorn arrived at Newmarket some hours too late and inquired about purchasing the colt privately; he only finally agreed to do so when Bob McCreery offered to retain a half share in the colt. Sir John Thorn reasoned that if the horse's breeder wanted to retain a half share, then it was worth his while purchasing the colt outright.

Bob McCreery is perhaps best described as an urbane man, and one whose views are respected but which are only given when asked for. He has now moved from his original base to the family home at Stowell Hill in Somerset. He is keen to innovate and has experimented by weighing his foals and testing their blood regularly. He specializes in selling internationally and in preparing American yearlings for European sales, and as will be seen later Bob McCreery has been a prominent buyer of stallions. These three breeders, together with their counterparts in the United States, share a combination of aptitudes which have hitherto been unusual in the thoroughbred business, for they display equally an expert knowledge of horsemanship and an entrepreneurial flair.

Another group within the thoroughbred business whose numbers were temporarily swelled by the bloodstock boom are those dealers who are known as pinhookers. The pinhooker either buys foals with the intention of selling them as yearlings, or yearlings with the intention of selling them on as two-year-olds. The latter course of action is only really viable in the United States, for two-year-old in training sales have never been popular with either buyers or sellers in Europe. There is a two-year-old in training sale at Doncaster in March, but it is not of the same quality as the leading American ones held in Florida and California in March and by Fasig Tipton in May. These American sales cater mainly for the strong local market for horses ready to race, although Robert Sangster bought his first piece of Alleged at the Californian Thoroughbred Breeders Association two-year-old sale at Hollywood Park. On the whole, though, pinhookers gamble on foals.

To the uninitiated the foal sale is a peculiar spectacle. A yearling sale will always appear to be sensible, for yearlings do look like young racehorses. However, a collection of eight-month-old foals are an incongruous sight in a large walking ring. Few of them will be taller than their groom's waist and many appear to be startled. They look up and about themselves in amazement and trepidation. Foals are generally cheaper than yearlings because judging a foal's racing potential is so problematic; in addition, the foal has an extra year in which to injure itself or go wrong in some other way before it enters a training stable. Those farms which sell their produce as foals usually do so in response to a cash flow problem, or because they do not have the facilities to prepare them for the yearling sales. In contrast to yearlings, foals do not need to be vigorously prepared for sale, and they often appear in the sale ring woolly and muddy in their winter coats. Most foals are bought by farms which have the staff and the facilities to prepare yearlings for sale, but which for one reason or another lack a sufficient number of horses to utilize them fully. A few are bought as cheap racehorses, though not many owners will be in a position to look after the foal until it goes into training, and some are bought by the dealers.

The most renowned specialist dealers in Europe are Tim Hyde of the Camas Park Stud in Tipperary and Hamish Alexander of the Partridge Close Stud in Durham. Tim Hyde's largest coup was buying a colt foal by Shergar out of Galletto from Robert Sangster for 325,000 Irish guineas. Eleven months later he sold the colt to Sheikh Mohammed for 3,100,000 Irish guineas, and as a three-year-old, by which time it had been named Authaal, the colt won the Irish St Leger. These dealers gain an advantage from their specialization, for many bloodstock agents and trainers are not able to distinguish between foals and do not buy at foal sales. For a time therefore foal sales were a buyer's market, where the expert could secure a bargain. However, the spectacular profits of a few attracted many newcomers to the trade and, like commercial breeding, pinhooking is now a business in which the number of profit-making participants is declining. The pinhooker takes the same gamble as the commercial breeder but he does not have to worry about barren broodmares, slipped foals or difficult births, and he has only a year to wait for the wheel to come to rest. Those experts with a reputation are backed by others with the money but not the skill to participate in such a gamble. A new problem these syndicates face in their quest for a quick pay off is that some purchasers are wary of buying from dealers. Nonetheless successful pinhookers are given great respect within the business and are often featured in the racing press—a clear demonstration of the way those in the business admire the pure gambler.

Whether or not they were respected, the bloodstock gambler's time, or his halcyon period, has passed. The success of those suppliers in the bloodstock market with a short-term outlook depended upon a market which was expanding in size, and one in which the general level of prices was rising. The man who buys an expensive yearling which has been given steroids, or which has been operated upon in order to hide a physical disability, will soon discover that he has wasted his money. If the duped purchaser ever goes to a yearling sale again he is most unlikely to buy another yearling from the same stud farm. In an autarkic bloodstock market such legal but unethical behaviour is less likely to take place, for the buyers and sellers at bloodstock auctions will be known to each other, and will probably live in close proximity. If a consignor sells horses which are most unlikely to succeed on the racecourse, he will soon acquire a dubious reputation and will find it difficult to sell his horses. In an international market, particularly in one which is rapidly expanding, the unethical seller need not suffer in the short run, and when his rewards can be in millions of dollars the short run may provide him with an adequate return. The short-term breeder might be in Florida, his disgruntled client in Newmarket and his next customer in Milan. This dispersion of participants reduces the import of a dubious reputation. There is therefore a sense in which short-term commercial breeding exploits the absence of information or experience. However, by the mid 1980s the leading buyers at the top of the international yearling market had acquired at least five years experience, and they simply ceased to buy from those consignors whom they did not trust.

If a lack of information allows the short term breeder to exploit the buyer, then a generally rising price level allows him to overcome the difficulty of the time lag between the planning of a mating and the selling of the produce. The short-term breeder could afford to misjudge the swings of fashion, for the general rise in bloodstock prices would often supply him with a profit in any event. Of course competitive short-term breeding did for a time fuel this inflation of prices itself. Agents and gamblers were forever exhorting each other and potential newcomers "to get in at the top", for it was apparently only possible to make money by dealing at the top of the market. For a time at least there were so many people trying to compete at the top that together they succeeded in pushing up the top even higher. A speculative demand can have a cumulative affect; those trying to reach the top will be prepared to pay extravagant sums for fashionable broodmares and stallion nominations. In its turn this will make yearlings more valuable, for those who are still faddish when they retire to stud will be able to command similar prices. In its turn this will make commercial breeders even more determined to reach the top.

During the years of the bloodstock boom the bloodstock market was dominated by gamblers with this speculative mentality, and it was therefore unstable even during the peak years. In a market which is largely formed by such dealers the level of demand will respond positively to changes in the level of prices. For example when a stallion became fashionable the short-term breeders would compete for its services, thereby increasing the price of the stallion's seasons. However, this rise in price would attract rather than deter breeders, and the more expensive a stallion's advertised fee, the more breeders wanted to use it. This same inverse relationship between demand and changes in the level of prices could be observed in the market for yearlings and broodmares, as well as for stallion shares and seasons. The inverse nature of this relationship was revealed most purely when the market was falling. If a stallion fell from favour the fall in the value of its seasons and progeny would be swift and in most cases final. As a result of this instability many commercial breeders found themselves in financial difficulties even at the best of times. If a stallion's stock plummets then the commercial breeder who holds yearlings or foals by the horse will see the commercial value of his assets simply evaporate. The speculative mentality creates a market with negative feedback, which means that the foolish or unlucky speculator will be able to lose his money rapidly.

On one level the short-term breeder is bound to lose eventually for the man who buys the dud yearling will realize his mistake and not only refuse to buy from the same farm, but will also become wary of buying a yearling at all. This is what happened in the mid 1980s on a broader scale. As a result the bloodstock market is more honest, even if its participants are no more or less moral. Those who buy expensive yearlings are wiser; even if they are largely the same people they are now better informed, and therefore those who sell them must produce a different product if they are to remain successful. This new found wisdom is illustrated by the more normal relationship between changes in prices and in the level of the demand in the bloodstock market. In effect the buyers became concerned with the long term and with buying potential racehorses rather than desired objects. As a result the name of its sire no longer safeguards a yearling's commercial value. Indeed the name of a yearling's dam, the manner in which it was reared and its physical appearance are factors which will now influence the decision to purchase to the same extent as the name of its sire. The recognition of the primacy of the broodmare and the environment in which a horse is raised will encourage the private breeder, and may well lead to a decline in the relative importance of the yearling market.

The private breeder has of course been affected by the escalation of bloodstock prices. The manner in which he chooses couplings and raises his horses may well be completely unchanged, but the rewards for success are considerably greater. The private breeder receives a return on his investment through prize money, by selling those fillies out of training or broodmares which he does not want to breed from and by selling his colts as stallions or for further use as racehorses. For the British private breeder such rewards are of course tax free, and with the strength of the American demand for proven racehorses as an additional incentive some commercial breeders like Robert McCreery believe it is possible to make a living by breeding to race. In the case of an established breeder such an endeavour would be easier if the Inland Revenue were to accept that his business was in fact a hobby. The same proposition must also be true in the United States, where the private breeder is compensated for having to pay tax on his capital gains by the high level of purse money and by being able to write off his expenses against tax.

One possible development would be an increase in the size of the market for proven racehorses who are two or three years old. The proven racehorse will appeal to the buyer who is seeking entertainment as it will constitute a small risk. When buying a three-year-old horse the purchaser is able to evaluate its form on the racecourse as well as its physical appearance and pedigree. The demand for the proven racehorse is stronger in the United States than it is in Europe because the pattern of racing offers lucrative opportunities to the older horse with its many well endowed handicaps which are open to horses of four years of age and more. In addition the strain the American pattern of racing places upon young horses leads many of them to break down and be forced to retire from the racetrack before the end of their three-year-old careers.

There is undoubtedly the potential for an international market for two- and three-year-old horses. The private breeder could supply this market by developing his horses at a considerate pace and racing them only as a means of advertising their ability and future prospects. The Matchmaker Corporation had this potential in mind when they organised an auction of proven racehorses in California in the autumn of 1986. The auction was a failure, with only a few of the lots sold to anyone other than the staff or directors of the Matchmaker Corporation, but it demonstrated that the only barrier to an international market is a lack of information. The Californian buyer is unlikely to be aware of the nuances of European two-year-old form and therefore may not feel comfortable bidding at an auction with only a sales catalogue as a guide. Most of the numerous sales of proven European racehorses to the United States are organized by or facilitated by specialist agents who are unlikely to support auctions while they are able to earn more than a 5 per cent commission when working independently. This superior margin is available mainly because of the ignorance of the seller, the horse's European owner, as well as the ignorance of the American buyer. If this market were to expand, then the information about comparative values and performances would be more readily available. In addition, the private breeder specializing in such a trade is likely to be more informed than the lucky owner in search of a bonanza. Moreover there seems no reason why this should be purely a transatlantic trade, for Australian and South African owners have also shown an interest in purchasing European tested racehorses. This shift towards viewing breeding and racing thoroughbreds in a long-term perspective can only be encouraged by the massive operations of the European based private breeders.

The bloodstock boom did of course coincide with the new Arab involvement in the business and in the years to come, aside from the Aga Khan's, the most influential private studs will be those belonging to Prince Khalid Abdullah, Mahmoud Fustok, Sheikh Mohammed bin Rashid al Maktoum and his brothers Sheikh Maktoum and Hamdan Al Maktoum. It is now clear that the effects of these large private studs on the yearling market will not be as drastic as some had predicted. As long as they wish to be sure of racing leading horses from each generation then these operators will continue to buy at the international yearling sales. In 1986, for instance, Sheikh Mohammed bought more yearlings than he had in any previous years, despite having raised more of his own than ever before.

However, breeding operations of this size (Khalid Abdullah is planning to have between one hundred and one hundred and fifty broodmares and the Maktoums already own many more) which continue to purchase yearlings are bound to sell many horses which they do not wish to keep themselves once their racing ability has been established. The VAT regulations in Great Britain require the owner of a horse imported into the country to pay VAT on the animal's purchase price, unless it is re-exported within two years. For this reason the surplus colts and fillies who were purchased in the United States as yearlings are likely to be sold at the end of their three-year-old careers. If the young horses rejected by the Maktoums and Khalid Abdullah were sold at European breeding stock sales, those sales would become among the most important in the world. The overseas interest in them would increase, for many of such rejects would be demanded as both racing and breeding prospects. Of course it remains to be seen how many of these horses will be sent to race abroad or will be sold privately rather than at public auctions, but the British Bloodstock Agency at least is looking forward to a boost in the business at Tattersalls' December Sales.

The established commercial breeders will not be affected, although it will be increasingly difficult for any newcomer to join their ranks. These leading commercial farms will become more international in their scope; indeed, it may be only a matter of time before a successful Kentucky farm sets up a branch in the Newmarket area or in County Kildare. Already Three Chimneys Farm owns shares in Dancing Brave and Shareef Dancer, who stand at the Dalham Hall Stud in Newmarket, and Gainesway and Taylor Made Farms own shares in Kris, who stands at the Thornton Stud in Yorkshire, while prominent American breeders like Robert Clay, William Farish and Alice Chandler send horses to race in Britain. One can envisage the bloodstock market being split broadly into two tiers. On one, private breeders, speculators and a few wealthy owners compete for the classic horse or the international horse; whilst on the other, those who seek only entertainment will buy two- or three-year-old racehorses. There cannot be much of a future for a business like short-term commercial breeding in which the majority of producers consistently lose money.

Finally, it is interesting to recall a sentence Franco Varola wrote in 1974: "More specifically, the Thoroughbred is sociologically significant because ... it is a microcosm of man and repeats man's motives and trends in the various areas and times."* In the twelve years following the publication of Varola's views on the subject there has been a marked change in attitudes towards the female thoroughbred and there

*Franco Varola. *The Typology of the Racehorse*. London: J. A. Allen, 1974.

is evidence of a sexual revolution on the racecourse. In addition, as a result of international promiscuity, there have been epidemics of venereal diseases among thoroughbreds. A last parallel between the world of the thoroughbred and that of man will be the revelation of the dubious practices in the bloodstock market which were encouraged by a speculative boom following upon the integration of national markets which were formerly separated. As far as the bloodstock world is concerned, these revelations will demonstrate once more the speculator or the gambler's propensity for overreaching himself, taking unnecessary risks and eventually bringing about his own downfall.

=== Seven ===
The Bloodstock Auction

Racehorses have traditionally been sold at public auctions. At times, when the number of horses sold annually was relatively small, individual stud farms were able to attract buyers to their own private auctions. Some of these private sales were not conducted as auctions; instead the farm would produce a list of horses for sale and the prices they would accept and then, for their own convenience, invite buyers to come and inspect the horses on the same day. Today, when nearly ten thousand yearlings are sold in the United States each year and about three thousand in Great Britain and Ireland, the bloodstock market is formed by a few large auctioneering companies. These companies attract large numbers of buyers and sellers to their sale rings at the same time by advertising and establishing a good reputation. The auction is an appropriate method of selling racehorses, as it reflects the competitive nature of racing. The auction also facilitates the selection of yearlings by gathering together a large number in one place, inviting buyers to inspect them, and imposing a time limit on their ruminations.

The criticisms of potential abuses of bloodstock auctions which will be discussed in this chapter do not apply to any individuals who are named in this book.

Bloodstock auctioneering is an eminently monopolistic business. In Europe there are three major companies; Robert J. Goff & Co, Tattersalls and the Agence Française de Vente du Pur Sang. The Agence Française de Vente du pur Sang sells yearlings over nine days in August at Deauville during the major racemeeting there. Robert J. Goff & Co has three subsidiaries; Goff's Bloodstock Sales, Goff's France and

Goff's Espagna. They hold yearling sales on one day in Paris, two days in Madrid and the company's major yearling sale at Kill in County Kildare near Dublin over four days in early October. Tattersalls, which began life as an exclusive gaming club on Hyde Park Corner in 1766,* has both an Irish and English division. The English division is now based in Newmarket, where there are two major yearling sales, the Highflyer in late September or early October, and the October in mid October. The Irish division, which is moving to a new permanent base at Fairyhouse, north-west of Dublin, in 1988, holds a two-day yearling sale in mid September

Tattersalls remains Europe's leading bloodstock auctioneers, with an annual turnover in the region of £80 million. The firm is still privately owned, so its accounts are not published, but like all auctioneers its return comes from the fees charged for entry to a sale, the commission it takes on the sale of each lot and the auction fee which is charged for accepting a reserve on a lot. In 1986 Tattersalls' commission was 5 per cent for up to 400,000 guineas and $2\frac{1}{2}$ per cent thereafter, of each lot sold. There is no auction fee for reserves of up to 10,000 guineas, between 10,000 and 100,000 the fee is 2 per cent of the reserve and then 1 per cent thereafter. Tattersalls will in addition charge a commission on any private sales which take place between the publication of the catalogue and seven days after the sale. One of the services any auctioneer offers its clients is to advertise their products, and they all expect to be paid for any transactions which their advertising induces.

Under the forceful management of Jonathan Irwin, Goffs considerably increased their share of the European market during the years of the bloodstock boom. By the standards of European horsemen they are extraordinarily keen on public relations and will take care of prospective purchasers' travel arrangements. On one occasion, when there was a strike of petrol distributors during the yearling sales, Goffs commandeered their own tanker in order to supply their clients' needs. For years there were rumours that Goffs were about to set up an auction ring in Newmarket, to compete directly with Tattersalls, in conjunction with an American firm. Nothing has happened but for more rumouring, and with Tattersalls deciding to build a new sale ring at Fairyhouse it will be Goffs whose position is challenged by new competition. Anybody who has dealings with Tattersalls will soon learn that the firm's characteristic stance is one of inordinate conservatism; behind this, and they would no doubt say because of it, the firm has an unsurpassed reputation for integrity. To the

*See V. Orchard. *Tattersalls*. London: Hutchinson, 1953.

annoyance of Goffs, and a few British breeders, Tattersalls now sell the horses of many of Ireland's leading commercial breeders. There are those who believe that Goffs' position is compromised by having Robert Sangster among its directors, and it is certainly unusual for an auctioneer to have one of the leading buyers in its market among its directors.

In 1987 Goffs instituted the Million Sale in the hope of attracting new customers. The new sale is based upon an idea which has been conspicuously successful in Australia. On the first three evenings of the Irish National Yearling Sale in 1987 Goffs will sell a maximum of 250 yearlings. On 1 October 1988 there will be a race over seven furlongs at the Phoenix Park racecourse in Dublin for which only these 250 horses can qualify. This race will have £1 million of prizemoney, of which £500,000 will be given to the winning owner. The money will be raised by the vendors, both as entry fees for the sale and a percentage of the prices attained by yearlings, and by the buyers who will have to pay additional sums to nominate and run their horses in the race. The race will be the richest two-year-old event ever.

The Australian experience suggests that the sale will attract new buyers who will be prepared to pay a premium for the opportunity of competing for the Million. The concept was first put into practice in Perth in 1979 and as a result the sale's popularity and the average price attained there soared. In 1987 Elders Pastoral and William Inglis & Sons, who are traditionally Australia's leading bloodstock auctioneers, both held similar sales. The English Jockey Club attempted to block Jonathan Irwin's idea on the grounds that it would interfere with the pattern race system. Goffs hope that their sale will boost the European bloodstock market and that they will be able to put on similar events in England or France in the near future.

In the United States there are two major bloodstock auctioneers. For many years the Fasig-Tipton Company was unrivalled and its premier sale at Saratoga Springs in New York State was America's finest. In 1985 however the Fasig-Tipton Companies handled only 27 per cent of the aggregate of America's bloodstock sales, although they conducted thirty auctions at eleven different sites in the United States and Canada. Fasig-Tipton's subsidiaries and associates sell yearlings in New York, Kentucky, California, Florida, Lousiana, Maryland and Toronto. Fasig-Tipton's supremacy was challenged fortuitously in 1944, as the Kentucky breeders were unable to transport their blood-stock to New York that year on account of the war, and two auctions were held in 1944 at the Keeneland racetrack near Lexington in central Kentucky. The Keeneland Association's auctions had a turnover of $385 million in 1985, which is 60 per cent of the total American market.

The Association holds a three day yearling sale in July and a seven day one in September.

The Keeneland Association, which runs both the racetrack and the auctions, is a non-profit making charitable organization. In 1985 the Association handed out about $3,500,000 to local charities and institutions, ranging from the Blue Grass Boys Ranch to the University of Kentucky. The Association's directors are drawn from America's leading breeders and those who regularly sell at Keeneland including Alice H. Chandler, William S. Farish III, John R. Gaines, A. B. Hancock III, Seth Hancock, Warner L. Jones Jr and Charles Taylor. Any new auctioneering firm which sought to compete with Keeneland at the top of the market would have to attract the custom of some of these breeders, so Keeneland's pre-eminent position is secure. Some would argue that this security and the lack of a commercial incentive has led Keeneland to be unduly complacent and would cite as evidence for the Association's unwillingness to innovate the fact that Fasig-Tipton have been able to set up a rival auction on the outskirts of Lexington. If Keeneland had increased the number of days of their July sale it would have been difficult for Fasig-Tipton to establish another yearling auction in the Lexington area only a week earlier.

Before considering in detail the conditions and practices of auctions at Tattersalls and Keeneland, so as to compare the European and American methods of selling yearlings, it will be interesting to give some idea of the size of the international market. The major international yearling sales are in North America; Keeneland's July and September Sales, Fasig-Tipton's August Sale at Saratoga, Fasig-Tipton Kentucky's July and September Sales and the Woodbine Sale in Toronto, Canada. At these sales in 1986 3,669 yearlings were reported as sold for a total of $280 million. In Europe the international yearling sales are: Agence Française Invitation and Select Sales at Deauville, Goffs Irish National Invitation, Premier and Open Sales at Kill, and Tattersalls' Highflyer and October Sales at Newmarket. At these sales in 1986, 1,951 yearlings were sold for a total of $97,000,000.* When combined together these figures give a total of 5,620 yearlings sold for $355 million. To put these figures in a proper perspective, 1986 was two years after the bloodstock market had reached its peak, and prices had declined by about 25 per cent. To give some idea of the international nature of these sales, about 40 per cent of the aggregate at the North American sales was spent by foreign interests, and finally to give some idea of the dominance of the Maktoum family some 17

*Computed at £1 = $1.5.

per cent of the North American aggregate can be accounted for by them alone. Yearling sales are obviously a major part of the thoroughbred business, and it is in the interests of all the industry's members for bloodstock auctions to be well conducted.

The two contentious issues raised by bloodstock auctions are, first the question of whether or not yearlings should be sold with any warranties, and secondly the fairness of certain bidding conventions. At the present time yearlings are sold with only the minimum of warranties. Tattersalls' conditions of sale state: "Purchasers are advised to inspect each lot prior to purchase. Each lot is sold as it stands and there is no term implied in any sale that any lot is of merchantable quality or is fit for any particular purpose." In fact Tattersalls accept that a purchaser can return a yearling if it turns out not to be a thoroughbred. In addition a yearling which is a whistler or a roarer and is not so described at the time of sale is returnable, as long as it has not been removed from Tattersalls' premises and the purchaser demanded a re-examination in writing within twenty-four hours of the fall of the hammer. A whistler or roarer is defined as "a horse which can be heard to make a characteristic abnormal inspiratory sound when actively exercised and which has Laryngeal Hemiplegia when examined on the endoscope." A horse with such a disability is most unlikely to be successful on the racecourse.

The warranties with which yearlings are sold at Keeneland can be summed up even more succinctly: "Unless otherwise expressly announced at time of sale, there is no guarantee of any kind as to the soundness or condition or other quality of any animal sold in this sale except animals which are unsound of eyes, or possess any deviation from the norm in the eyes ... or are cribbers,* must be so announced at the time of sale. In the case of horses less than three years of age there is no guarantee as to soundness of wind." In addition neither Tattersalls nor the Keeneland Association accept responsibility for any errors contained in their sales catalogues. Indeed it is only recently that Tattersalls began testing the identification of the yearlings in their sales. However, now thoroughbred identification is recorded on the basis of blood typing, the chances of a fraudulent or accidental mis-identification have been reduced. There have been examples of mis-taken identity, and one prominent English private stud accidentally confused two filly foals and the error was not revealed until they were both six years old and one had been sold to Australia.

At first sight this seems to be an extraordinary manner in which to

*A cribber is a horse which is in the habit of grasping fixed objects with its teeth and at the same time noisily drawing in breath. This is often a sign of a nervous disposition or of unsoundness in the wind, or both.

conduct an auctioneering business. A warranty serves both to curb the seller and to reassure the buyer. In a market which so conspicuously lacks such safeguards it is only the seller's conscience which restrains his unethical side, while the newcomer can only rely upon the advice of some unfamiliar expert. The auctioneer forms a market by providing information and stability, but it would seem that in the bloodstock market the auctioneer is determined to avoid vouching for any more than the minimum of information. This is obviously a happy situation for auctioneers, as the fewer guarantees they offer the smaller their risks are. The bloodstock auctioneer is never faced with the problems which arise from misattributions at auctions of fine art. Sotheby's conditions of sale disarm objections by stating that:

"Any representation or statement by Sotheby's, in any catalogue as to authorship, attribution, genuineness, origin, date, age, provenance, condition or estimated selling price is a statement of opinion only. Every person interested should exercise and rely on his own judgement as to such matters and neither Sotheby's nor its servants or agents are responsible for the correctness of such opinions."

However Sotheby's, like other fine art auctioneers, are happy to sell their opinions to their clients and indeed to a large extent their commercial success and reputation relies upon the esteem which is generally accorded to their experts' opinions. The extraordinary feature of bloodstock auctioneering is that no one is even prepared to give an opinion. No auctioneer will want to give warranties; for example, if a bloodstock auctioneer announced that he would only sell those yearlings which he considered to be sound of wind and limb, he would soon be inundated with law suits. Those breeders whose year-lings were rejected might consider they had been defamed, while buyers whose yearlings did not turn out to be physically capable of racing would feel they had been cheated. A Californian company which offered yearlings under similar conditions was forced to withdraw them in the face of law suits of the latter variety. However, it would be possible to offer more precise information without having to take responsibility for any definitive statements.

Robert S. Miller, a Lexington lawyer, has proposed that every yearling which is entered for sale should be examined by a panel of vets at the auctioneer's expense. This is a solution which would bring bloodstock auctioneers into line with their counterparts in the fine art world. The panel would produce a report on each yearling which anyone who was interested would be able to purchase. The report need not contain any definite statements: indeed in many cases it would probably express dissenting opinions. However, any prospective buyer, whatever his experience and knowledge of horses and the bloodstock business, would be able to purchase for a small sum precise information about the physical condition of the animal he is considering purchasing. At present a buyer is able to pay a vet to examine a yearling on his behalf with its vendor's consent, but the new or inexperienced buyer is unlikely to be in a position to judge the skill and honesty of any available vet. Under the present system such a buyer is undoubtably at a disadvantage, for he can only rely upon informed opinion, without necessarily being able to decide which opinion is more or less informed. Unfortunately such a beneficial change is unlikely to be implemented for the majority of buyers and sellers are as happy as the auctioneers with the traditional system of caveat emptor.

This traditional system is obviously derived from the time when bloodstock was sold only in localized markets. In such a market information is likely to be freely available and widely distributed, for it is not in anyone's interests to withhold it dishonestly. In an international market with a multitude of buyers and horses the potential rewards for discreet silence on the part of short-term commercial breeders are obvious.

There have been some cases of expensive yearlings who were discovered to have a serious disability. The most expensive lot at the 1984 Highflyer Sale was a filly, subsequently named Whitethroat, which Robert Sangster bought from the Airlie Stud. The filly was promptly returned to her vendors the next day when she was found to be what Tattersalls define as a whistler or a roarer. The most infamous case took place in the same year when Robert Sangster purchased a colt by Northern Dancer from the Windfields Farm for $8.25 million at Keeneland's July Sale. The colt was X-rayed and found to have a problem with a foot, whereupon it was rumoured that Sangster was threatening to sue or withhold payment unless Windfields Farm struck a new deal. A new arrangement was made and Windfields retained part ownership in the colt. The following year it was revealed that the Maktoum family had been involved as well, for when the colt, now called Imperial Falcon, appeared on the racecourse he carried the colours of Sheikh Mohammed. By the end of his three-year-old career Imperial Falcon had made four starts in Ireland, winning three of them including a Group 2 race.

If Robert Sangster and Sheikh Mohammed with the assistance of the best available advice can buy a defective yearling then it is hard to see how any newcomer can approach a yearling sale with confidence. These incidences, and there are many others which could be quoted, are in part a consequence of the ritual of the sale itself. The usual practice at bloodstock auctions is for the animals which are due to be sold to arrive at the saleground two or three days before the sale itself commences. During these days a crowd of prospective buyers and onlookers examine in a more or less rigorous manner the people and horses on display. The buyers and their agents and trainers are restricted by the crowds, the number of possibilities and the prevalent customs. The agents and trainers are out stamping the ground from seven o'clock in the morning, before the place is cluttered up with owners and spectators. They move, often in small groups of confederates, from one barn to the next, or at Tattersalls from one yard to another. They pause by a stall and one yearling is presented before them. They will look at it from one side, and then walk around it and view it from the other. The expert will place one hand on the horse's withers, run his hand down its forelegs, and perhaps lift up a foot to examine. Then he or she will stand with head on one side and arm on hip while the yearling is walked away from him and then directly back towards him. A glance at the appropriate page in the catalogue and then a last look at the yearling. "Thank you very much. Could I look at lot 92 next please?" While walking to the next stall a few comments are scrawled on the by now dirty catalogue: small, light of bone, slack in pasterns, turns one foot out, or quality, well balanced, strides out well, scope for further improvement. There is not the time nor the room to do much more. After three hundred such inspections in three days the agent will decide how to spend his clients' millions.

In the United States there is a company which claims to examine yearlings in a scientific manner to determine whether or not they are structurally capable of being stakes winners. They are often derided by "proper" horsemen, usually because they take half an hour to look at each yearling. Some agents will use a stethoscope or even a tape measure, but most rely upon their eyes and hands. It would create a precedent if a buyer asked to X-ray a yearling's limbs and anyone who produced an endoscope would be viewed with suspicion. Peering through an endoscope is a far from infallible manner of detecting breathing disabilities, but the obvious alternative which is to exercise a horse vigorously and listen to its breathing is also ruled out at a sale. Yearlings are only expected to walk at the sales and those who break into a trot do so inadvertently. The tradition is not so much a dishonest one as one which avoids discovering truths which might be damaging.

Many racing people consider yearling auctions to be the most monotonous of occasions. Superficially there is nothing to observe at an auction but for a succession of yearlings being led through a sale ring. Indeed it is hard to see any obvious connection between this spectacle and the competitive drama of racing itself. The yearling auction is in many ways the most ephemeral of all racing's events. A five-year-old sales catalogue has about as much interest as a list of fictional charac-

ters in a novel which you have not read—a novel of Proustian proportions, for among the hundreds of characters there will be one or
two whose descriptions are familiar, but even the literati will be unable
to recount the characters' histories and the events in which they played
a part. Similarly even the bloodstock agent will struggle to connect
a five-year-old sales catalogue with names, races and events in the
intervening years. However, the thrill of the yearling auction lies not
so much in the sale itself, or in a retrospective analysis of the subsequent
achievements of the yearlings, but in the days before the auction begins,
when the yearlings are inspected, evaluated and selected.

The yearling auction is in a sense a game of hide and seek in which
the participants are metaphorically blindfolded. The excitement of the
game is heightened by the time limit imposed upon it, the competitive
nature of the search, and of course the possible rewards of success.
The possible rewards of later successes on the racecourse, however,
are almost incidental to the game which is in a sense self-enclosed. For
three days a collection of owners, agents and gamblers work their way
through hundreds of yearlings searching for the one or two who will
prove capable of laying golden eggs. Once the game is completed and
the yearlings have been sold, there will be a period of at least six
months before the long-term results begin to be revealed, and in the
meantime everyone who bought can believe in their own decision. For
the bloodstock agent to use a stethoscope and X-rays would be akin
to the priestesses of Delphi using economic models and systems analysis; their own role would be degraded and their devotees would become
customers. Without the screen and the mystery prophecy loses its
charm, and without the blindfolds the game would not be so absorbing.
The bloodstock agent thrives upon the game and perhaps more surprisingly some of the owners who gamble with their own money are
amongst its most enthusiastic players. It has often been said that Sheikh
Mohammed enjoys the meditation of breeding and the excitement of
victory, but that what appeals to him most about the thoroughbred
business is the thrill of the auction.

For the seller, the commercial breeder, the yearling auction is a more
mundane affair. The truths which the sellers would rather not disclose
do of course concern their animals. The dishonest few would be happy
to sell a cripple of a yearling if they could find someone fool enough
to buy it. The majority of breeders will not sell a yearling with an
obvious physical fault; nor on the other hand, will they be keen to put
their yearlings through any severe tests. If one is likely to break down
in training, or has lungs that are not suited to prolonged exertion, they
would much rather not know about it until it has actually happened.
Only a few commercial breeders will lunge their yearlings and retain

those who make an ominous noise.

This explains why there are so many horses in training which are patently lacking any aptitude for athletic performance. They are sold by breeders who do not want to discover that they are useless as racehorses, and once someone has bought a horse it may well take years for them to accept that it is useless. There is therefore a sense in which the yearling market is similar to the market for second-hand cars. However cheap a second-hand car is there will be someone who thinks it is a bargain, and if they subsequently realize they have been duped they will always be able to find someone else prepared to maintain or feign ignorance long enough to pass it on to yet another bargain hunter. The more one thinks about it, the more apt the metaphor appears, for no second-hand car dealer will allow a customer to do more than drive around the block before they commit themselves to paying up.

The agent or trainer who specializes in buying yearlings, like the garagist or trade buyer of motors, does rather well out of a tradition of caveat emptor. The specialist has more information and knowledge than any outsider could hope to acquire when he decides to buy a yearling. The successful agent will have a policy of building up contacts with grooms who work on the leading farms and establishing a friendly relationship with the farm's owner. The agent will know, or at least have a better idea than the outsider, which farms are honest and which raise their horses in a sensible manner. However, the bloodstock agent is fallible, for it has often been said that their obligation is fulfilled when a horse they purchased actually appears on the racecourse, yet every year they buy hundreds of horses between them who turn out to be physically incapable of running in a race let alone winning one.

Those within the industry would object to a system of inspection by a panel similar to the one outlined earlier because its introduction would deprive the yearling auction of its mystique. Bloodstock agents and commercial breeders alike jealously guard their right to be mis-informed. The play of information and disinformation is central to the thrill of the yearling market. The business's members would claim that, because it is impossible to predict which yearlings will be physically capable of racing, it would be misleading and simply confusing to sell the utterances of a panel of experts which newcomers might place great store by. If this prediction is not impossible then it is a matter of individual flair and tingles in the spine, rather than of objective analysis. These arguments do not detract from the case for a panel, as the experts' findings could be preceded by an announcement to the effect that they are only subjective opinions and lay no claim to definiteness.

Opposition to such a scheme might also come from the auctioneers.

The entries to select sales are already selected on the grounds of their pedigree and physical appearance and the difference between this examination and one by objective vets may not be immediately apparent. The sales companies select yearlings with a view to gathering together those with the greatest commercial potential. The vets would only suggest which yearlings are more or less likely to stand up to the physical stress of racing and training. No panel, whether it is comprised of wise men or fools, will be able to predict which yearling out of two or three hundred will be the best racehorse. Nevertheless a panel would be able to supply enough information to enable people to make an informed gamble or guess at the yearling sales. At present the international yearling auction offers a gamble which only a few can afford to indulge in. With the present high stakes it is a game which is turning sour even for the few. This disillusionment is the result not least of some of the prevalent conventions of bidding. It is necessary, then, to describe the methods of British and American auctioneers and the layout of their sale rings, for it is only against this background that such disputes as there are can be understood.

The sales pavilion at Keeneland is an enclosed building and on a summer's day comparatively dark inside. The seats are tiered in a semicircle facing the pedestal on which the auctioneers sit and the ring in which the horse being sold is stood by the same liveried groom. Inside it is calm, for the corridor behind the seats is sealed off by glass to allow the air conditioning or heating to work efficiently. Directly behind the auctioneer's pedestal, and linked to the sales pavilion by two small discreet doors, is the circular walking ring to which the yearlings are brought shortly before they are due to be sold. The walking ring is open to the air at one end and full of people leaning on the side of the ring, walking about and talking. The proceedings next door are relayed on loudspeakers and two of Keeneland's bid spotters sit on a platform at one end. This ring constitutes the most frightening part of the sale for the yearlings and they often boil over, kick the sides of the ring, charge across it backwards dragging their handler after them, or rear up and come down violently on whatever happens to be underneath them. Nevertheless there is always a crowd standing in the centre of the ring engrossed in conversation or catalogues, with their backs to the yearlings. When someone is kicked or narrowly escapes some flailing hooves the crowd thins out a little, but ten minutes later it will be as large and unconcerned as it was before.

Meanwhile, inside, the auctioneer sings, really sings in a steady rhythmic tone which is best described as lulling rather than monotonous. He calls out not the figure which has been attained but the number which the next bid will be for. So if someone has already bid

$500,000 the auctioneer will call out "Who'll give me six, six hundred thousand, six hundred thousand, I want six hundred thousand..." This is a drone with no precise diction, but the digital displays clearly show the size of the last bid. The bidder must catch the eye not of the auctioneer but of one of the bid spotters. There will probably be four of these standing at the bottom of the aisles in the sales pavilion, as well as the two outside in the walking ring. While the auctioneer is calling thus, the spotters will hold up six fingers and peer across the seats in front of them or over the crowd behind. If someone catches their eye and nods or moves a finger they yell out "Haarr!" and strike their sales catalogue vigorously against their leg. The ejaculations of the spotters outside are linked directly to the auctoneer's ear by a small speaker.

The auctioneer is impassive. If no bids are forthcoming the announcer at his side takes the microphone and makes some bland enticing comment: "Ladies and gentlemen, this good lookin' colt is a half brother to a winner at Newmarket last month, the sire's getting some good runners and I think he might be worth more than this." The auctioneer starts singing again and the performance starts once more. The spotters act out a dumb show of temptation, encouragement and reluctant thanks to those bidders who withdraw. They use their faces, arms and of course their catalogues. The auction is taken at a great pace and often the bidders themselves are not certain if it is their bid which is live. It is difficult to find out who you are bidding against, for if you are inside your opponent may be outside, and if you are outside you cannot see the audience at all.

The sales pavilion at Tattersalls is circular and surrounds a ring about which the horses being sold are led by their own groom. The horse enters through large double wooden doors on one side and is led away through similar doors on the other side after the event. Bloodstock sales companies have prospered in recent years and most of them have built new sales pavilions, which display a penchant for wood and are generally more attractive and less comfortable than most modern amphitheatres. This is especially true of Keeneland and Tattersalls rather than of Fasig-Tipton, Kentucky, or Goffs, where cars, metal and glass are more prominent features than any trees or grass; but then at Keeneland the trees are mature, whereas at Tattersalls some of the yards long predate the pavilion they encompass. Anybody who wishes can attend a Tattersalls sale, so there is more of an atmosphere of movement than at Keeneland where all the seats must be reserved in advance. The auctioneer stands distinctly visible to his audience on a platform overlooking the ring, and conducts the proceedings on his own.

A bidder must catch the auctioneer's attention himself. The auctioneer will turn slowly from one bidder to the next clearly distinguishing them in his speech. It is his role to cajole, and thank those bidders who are unsuccessful, as it is also to announce that this is a ridiculously low price for such a racy looking colt with a pedigree packed with winners. As a concession to modernity Tattersalls have recently introduced bid spotters; but Tattersalls' bid spotters are young ladies with their hand bags on the floor in front of them, who wave their arms hesitantly, nervous of being disregarded. Some bidders try to hide themselves by standing halfway down the stairs that lead to the seats at the top of the hall, but most regular buyers regularly buy from the same place. The representatives of the British Bloodstock Agency and the Curragh Bloodstock Agency, Britain's two leading agencies, usually stand to the left and right of the auctioneer respectively. The whole event is slow and by American standards almost pedantic, but it allows the auctioneer and the bidders time to discover who is participating in the contest for each lot.

Tattersalls' star is their Irish auctioneer David Pim. Clients of long standing are allowed to enter their horses for sale on the condition that Mr Pim is on the rostrum to sell them. David Pim has a presence, a dramatic awareness and a wit which make him an outstanding auctioneer. After ten lots he is red in the face and is throwing back his head to remove the wayward lock of hair from his eyes and reaching for a sip of water, with ever greater abandon. He uses his arms a great deal, gesturing towards each bidder and turning his hammer in circles when there are not enough bids forthcoming. He identifies each bidder with a wry comment and then moves on to entice and tease them. He will turn his back on one and pretend to ignore him and he will talk to them as if they were having a private conversation on a stage. He never shouts but he sometimes whispers; he never gabbles but is frequently brisk.

At any auction a vendor is affected by the time of day his lot is sold. No one wants to own the first lot in the morning or the last lot before lunch, but with the British system it matters far more which auctioneer is performing. For the purposes of clarifying the disputes about auctions, the distinction between the American and British methods of selling horses lies in the ease with which the participants are able to recognize each other.

The most widespread of the various dubious conventions at auctions is what is known as by bidding, that is bidding for your own lot. For an auction to be a fair means of exchange, each bidder must compete for a lot under the same terms. In a perfect market every bidder would have access to the same information and although practically this is impossible the closer the conditions of a sale approximate to this ideal the fairer it will be as a means of exchange and of establishing values. Someone who bids himself, or through an agent, for a lot which he already owns is quite obviously not competing on equal terms. Someone who makes a bid for his own lot does so secure in the knowledge that if it is successful they will only have to pay the auctioneer his commission. Any other successful bidder will have to pay the vendor the full sum signified by their bid. By bidding has a pernicious effect whether or not it is successful. If a vendor bids for his own lot but does not purchase it, then he has succeeded in extorting money by running up the purchaser on unequal terms. If the vendor bids for and purchases his own lot he has succeeded in establishing a deceptive valuation for his property. An auction is both a means of exchange and of valuation, for in any private sale of bloodstock the prices can only be set with reference to market prices.

At Tattersalls by bidding is expressly prohibited by the conditions of sale: "No vendor shall in any circumstances whatever bid or allow any agent or other person to bid on his behalf for any lot owned by such vendor whether individually in syndicate or in partnership save that this restriction shall not extend to Lots which are stated in the catalogue to be 'Partnership Property'." Unfortunately it is still a frequent occurrence, indeed it happens so often that some breeders would like to see the practice officially legitimized, since it seems impossible to restrict. This would surely be a retrograde step. The problem of prevention stems in part from the convention whereby the ownership of a lot need not be declared. Horses are sometimes sold as "the property of a gentleman" or more frequently as being "from" a certain stud. In America if a yearling is consigned by a farm acting as an agent then the catalogue will also declare the name of the horse's owner. Fasig-Tipton go one step further and print a list of the breeders of each yearling. If the owner or owners of each lot had to publicly declare their interest, those determined to by bid could only do so in a clandestine manner. However, the real problem with by bidding is that many of those within the business consider it to be a relatively harmless custom and fail to understand that it undermines the legitimacy of the auction.

Once again this short-sightedness is induced by the joy of the play of information and disinformation and the wish to retain the right to dupe the foolish. If someone buys a yearling for 400,000 guineas they must consider this a reasonable sum, for no one forced them to bid, and so if their only competitor from say 200,000 guineas onwards was an agent of the yearling's owner then those within the business would consider the owner to have been clever or cunning, but not fraudulent.

By bidding transforms the auction from a market place to a poker game. Placing a reserve upon a lot is a fairer means of protecting the vendor, for with a reserve there will be no deceit and bluffing. The reserve is fixed and set in advance of the sale and at Tattersalls the auctioneer will announce when the bidding has surpassed it.

Commercial breeders, and indeed the bloodstock world as a whole, are obsessed by the statistics of bloodstock sales. The average and median prices realized by each stallion's progeny, the average and median prices at each separate yearling sale and attained by each commercial farm, these and many other statistics are dutifully recorded. Many participants in the business plan their future actions on the basis of these entrails of past sales. Therefore many people by bid in order to slant these auguries in their favour. The owners of a young stallion will often have a policy of bidding for his progeny at auctions in order to boost their performance in the sale ring. This can be done in a more or less legitimate way. The less legitimate ways of boosting a stallion's sales averages involve hiding the true ownership of a lot. Sometimes this is done by the means of a private sale during the period after the catalogue has been printed; so a lot will be sold as it appears in the catalogue as the property of X, whereas in fact it will be the property of Y who will purchase it once more in the salering. Y's fee for this advertisement is the 5 per cent commission he must pay the auctioneers for having purchased his own horse. Needless to say, such behaviour is contrary to Tattersalls' conditions of sale.

Another favoured method is for the owners of a stallion to offer foal sharing agreements to impoverished owners of fashionable brood-mares. The agreement is usually along the following lines. The brood-mare is covered by the stallion without any charge and the resulting foal is owned in partnership by the stallion's owner and the mare's. When the foal is sold as a yearling the stallion's owner undertakes to bid for it and if necessary to buy it. The result is that the mare's owner receives half the figure for which the yearling is sold, the stallion receives publicity and the stallion's owner buys his own yearling. Sometimes this is done legitimately and the yearling is sold as the property of a partnership; sometimes it is not and the yearling is sold as the property of the mare's owner or as having come from another stud altogether. The mare's owner receives as much or more than he would have done in other circumstances, having taken a small risk and put up less capital.

If Tattersalls wish to withstand the pressure from those within the business and maintain their prohibition on by bidding, a sensible step would be to announce the ownership of each lot in their catalogues. In the case of a partnership property or a lot owned by a syndicate the names of all the partners should be listed. One of the reasons why some buyers are wary of purchasing yearlings who have been pinhooked is that such lots are often owned by a syndicate, so it is difficult for a bidder to be sure that he is not competing against one of the horse's owners. At Tattersalls it is relatively easy to identify the bidders during the course of an auction, so under these circumstances by bidding would be that much more difficult to conceal.

In the United States it is illegal to bid for your own lot at an auction unless the conditions of sale explicitly authorize the practice. Keeneland's conditions of sale do just this; "... the right to bid in this sale is reserved for all sellers, including their disclosed and undisclosed agents, unless otherwise announced at the time of sale." This is once again a left-over from the time when the majority of buyers and sellers were familiar with each other. By bidding is a common practice at American bloodstock auctions; one of the more famous examples involved the Northern Dancer colt who was later named Adjal. Sheikh Mohammed's agents were bidding for the colt sitting inside the sale pavilion, while their only competitor was standing outside by the walking ring. When the bidding was already in terms of millions of dollars the Sheikh's agents sent a runner outside to find out whom they were bidding against. When the runner returned having discovered their only opponent was the colt's owner Sheikh Mohammed promptly stopped bidding. He later bought the colt in a private sale.

At American bloodstock auctions it is difficult to identify the bidders while an auction is in progress. Besides the obfuscating speed of the auction, the bidders can be in two entirely separate chambers. In a competitive market this would be a beneficial feature, as any two bidders would be less likely to be able to collude and come to a private deal later which bypasses the vendor. However, the market at select yearling sales is no longer competitive and the present situation allows vendors to manipulate the market for their own ends.

Keeneland's conditions of sale also state that: "In the event that the consignor (or his agent) bids in his own animal, then Keeneland shall be notified within 30 minutes of conclusion of that sales session." At American select yearling sales generally somewhere between 15 and 20 per cent of the lots offered are officially reported as having failed to reach their reserve or having been bought in. However, Robert Miller has written that: "The industry understands that it cannot know whether the auction prices reveal the true sales price of at least one half of the animals auctioned."* This incidence of by bidding and the

*Robert S. Miller. *America Singing: The Role of Custom and Usage in the Thoroughbred Horse Business.* The Kentucky Law Journal, Volume 74, Number 4, 1985–86.

buying in of lots officially recorded as having been sold brings to mind the sale of Impressionist paintings at Christies, New York, in 1985. David Bathurst was forced to resign from his post at Christie's, New York, when he admitted having publicly announced some paintings had been sold, when they had in fact been bought in. When asked to justify his action David Bathurst claimed that had he announced that only one painting had been sold there would have been newspaper reports of a crash in the market for Impressionist paintings. Many in the bloodstock world would justify by bidding and concealed buying in on similar grounds. In all probability prices in the American yearling market were artificially inflated during the boom years by widespread by bidding, and since 1985, when the market began to decline, prices have been supported by undisclosed buying in. It is impossible to estimate what proportion of lots are affected by such actions, but some idea of the scale of the problem is given by a new Kentucky folk tale.

Many people in Kentucky believe that when Wayne Lukas made the second highest bid at any yearling auction in the world he was bidding on behalf of a partnership which already owned the colt who faced them in the sales pavilion. Now this is not true, for the colt in question was, as is generally recorded, sold by Warner L. Jones Jr. It is interesting however to elaborate on this folk story, for it clearly illustrates the attitudes of those within the business, even if in this case they were mistaken about the facts. The year was 1985 and the colt in question is by Nijinsky out of My Charmer, which makes him a half brother to the brilliant American champion Seattle Slew and the wayward Two Thousand Guineas winner Lomond. This was a yearling who was likely to appeal to both European and American buyers. The story goes that shortly before the day on which the colt, who had been widely admired since his arrival at Keeneland, was due to be auctioned Wayne Lukas bought him on behalf of a partnership which included Eugene V. Klein and C. R. French. When the colt was led into the sales ring the announcer described it as the property of Warner Jones. From seven million dollars onwards the bidding concerned solely Wayne Lukas, who was sitting in the sales pavilion one row in front of Eugene Klein and C. R. French, and Robert Sangster, who was with his partners outside by the walking ring. After Sangster had bid $12.5 million there was a long pause before Lukas jumped to $13 million, Sangster replied with a bid of $13.1 million, whereupon Lukas got up and walked out of the sales pavilion. Robert Sangster had bought a colt for the world record price of $13.1 million which he later named Seattle Dancer. The interesting feature of this story is the manner in which it is told, for the teller invariably speaks of Wayne Lukas with admiration and awe. The story is embellished with details about the sweating and shaking of Klein and French as they feared Lukas would push their luck too far and actually buy the colt. From seven million onwards they were hoping Lukas would decline and settle for a modest profit. Throughout the proceedings, so the legend goes, Lukas showed no sign of emotion. His dark glasses remained on his face, his neat grey parting remained unflicked and untouched, and his hands remained on his lap.

Only his finger moved until the end, when he got up and smiled. This, were it true, would have been the behaviour of a classical gambler, a mighty poker player, the sort of man revered by many racing people. Other interesting features of the story are, first, that it is Robert Sangster who is supposed to have been hoodwinked. This adds some irony for there are similar legends in which Robert Sangster plays the role of the hero villain taken here by Wayne Lukas. Secondly, this is a story which is implicitly believed in by many knowledgeable and well informed people. However widespread such practices are, or may have been, it seems extraordinary anyone should accept that such a thing happened at the sale of the world's most expensive yearling.

One last convention or custom of the bloodstock sale which is quite clearly undesirable concerns bloodstock agents and their rewards. In both the United States and England bloodstock agents usually take a commission of 5 per cent on the sales they arrange or otherwise carry out. In the United States bloodstock agents are usually paid by the seller. Someone who wants to sell a horse will ask an agent to find a buyer and agree to give him 5 per cent of the price he obtains. In England it is usually the buyer who pays an agent to find a suitable horse for him. This difference of traditions need not be of any concern, although a few agents have managed to take a commission from both the buyer and the seller without either party realizing that their agent is being overpaid. More serious incidents occur when an agent and a vendor collude before a bloodstock auction and agree to defraud the purchaser.

The procedure here is for the agent and the vendor to agree that beyond a certain figure they will split the money fetched by the vendor's horse. When the yearling in question is led into the ring to be sold the agent and an accomplice will bid against each other up to a figure which they consider to be plausible, before the accomplice drops out leaving the agent to purchase the horse on behalf of his client. The agent will then receive 5 per cent of the total figure from his client and 50 per cent of the difference between the agreed price and the one which was finally realized, from the vendor. The vendor will gain because his yearling will fetch far more than it would have done in other circumstances. Some would allege that at smaller yearling auctions a group of such agents have been able to form a ring to dominate the market, and have then refused to buy from those vendors who did not agree to deal with them.

There are always those who are prepared to believe any auction is rigged. Often these allegations are made by people who are unable to compete in the market on the scale which they would like to. As far as the bloodstock market is concerned these rumours are too widespread and too rarely satisfactorily confounded for them to be based upon fantasy, envy or malice alone. Nobody is in a position to express the proclivity towards these various more or less fraudulent practices as a percentage or proportion of the market as a whole, or to judge its effect. However, it is certain that these practices will have a more pernicious effect the less competitive the bloodstock market is. The market for select yearlings is far from being a competitive one, indeed it is more aptly characterised by the term monopsony. A monopsonistic market is one which is dominated by a few buyers.

In 1966 292 yearlings passed through the ring at Keeneland's July Select Sale and there were 164 different purchasers. In 1986 291 yearlings passed through the ring, but this time there were only 100 separate purchasers. This suggests that there are fewer buyers at the top of the yearling market than there once were, but the transformation has been a more dramatic one as a few statistics of more recent summer sales reveal. The summer sales are North America's three most important yearling sales: Keeneland and Fasig-Tipton, Kentucky, in July and Saratoga in August. If the years between 1980 and 1986 are taken together, of the total amount spent at the three summer sales 21 per cent was accounted for by the Maktoum family. In recent years the Maktoum family have increased their expenditure on yearlings and in 1986 they spent 30 per cent of the aggregate at the three sales. Besides the Maktoums the other major buyers at the select yearling sales in America are Prince Khalid Abdullah, Robert Sangster, Vincent O'Brien and partners, and the Americans Allen F. Paulson and D. Wayne Lukas. In 1986 this second group spent 21 per cent of the aggregate at the summer sales between them. There are others who have frequently bought from these sales, notably Alan Clore, Prince Fahd Salman, Ahmed Salman, Ted Sabarese, James P. Mills and W. T. Young, but these first five have dominated them since the late 1970s. The only other buyer who has ranked with them is Stavros Niarchos who was a leading purchaser for some years, at first on his own and then in partnership with Robert Sangster and Vincent O'Brien. However, since his split with Sangster and O'Brien in 1986 Stavros Niarchos seems to have withdrawn from the yearling market in order to concentrate on his breeding operation.

In Europe the position is even worse. At the end of the 1986 season both Goffs and Tattersalls decided to discontinue the practice of holding a one day session of specially selected yearlings. The market at these sales was derisory, as there were only three potential bidders for each lot, one of the Maktoum brothers, Prince Khalid Abdullah and Robert Sangster and partners. Once they declined to bid against each other these sales became a farce, with in many instances a lot attracting only one live bid. The auctioneer would take bids from the wall until the reserve was reached and he could sell the horse to whichever of the three was bidding for the lot in question. It would be an exaggeration to say that this happened on every lot, but it happened frequently enough for the sales companies, who had never been keen on selected sessions, and the breeders, who had enthusiastically requested them, to agree that they should be discontinued forthwith. Some breeders whispered darkly that the leading trainers declined to bid against the Arabs on whose patronage they rely. More likely explanations for the lack of competing bids at these select sessions were, first, that few other buyers in the European market can afford to spend such sums on yearlings, and secondly that other buyers presumed the yearlings in the select sessions would be beyond their means and therefore did not bother to consider and inspect them carefully in advance of the sale.

A monopsonistic market is easier to manipulate than a competitive one. This is particularly true if all the members of the monopsony purchase with differing intentions, and if for some of them the decision to purchase is taken with few financial constraints. The yearling market is the place where many newcomers to thoroughbred ownership begin and the whole industry is therefore damaged by questionable behaviour within it. The passing of the boom has led all participants in the business to keep a more careful control over their expenditure, lessening the scope for such behaviour, but the incentives remain the same.

The primary motive for fraudulent or unnecessarily sharp behaviour is of course greed. Greed rather than avarice, for the greedy tend to have a short-term and often short-sighted perspective. The level or incidence of greed within a population is presumably fairly stable, but the greater the potential rewards the stronger the full greed exerts upon its minions. In the case of the bloodstock business, its new wealth probably attracted newcomers with a predilection for money or wealth, rather than horses. A further incentive is the nature of the yearling market. The buyers in the yearling market are often newcomers with a naive approach both to bloodstock experts and the bloodstock business, and in today's international market they are widely separated and relatively poorly informed. For those tempted to deceive these features reduce the likelihood of detection and ease its consequences. In the bloodstock market at least there will always be enough fools to go round.

Fraud in the bloodstock market is often a crime which allows for an easy conscience, for there are rarely obvious victims. Market valuations may be distorted, but then few people would claim they were more than approximate anyway. The deceitful vendor may induce someone to pay more for his horse than they might otherwise have done, but nobody is forced to buy a horse. The agent who buys many excellent racehorses for a man who is prepared to spend extravagant sums to acquire them is unlikely to feel guilty when asking the vendor for a part in his share of this bonanza. Indeed the agent may feel he is doing the vendor a special favour when he buys his horse, and is therefore only charging for a service he has rendered. The bloodstock market has been widely abused because to many of its participants this abuse is only part of the game or gamble which they thrive upon. However, unless the market is more strictly regulated potential new investors will be scared away, and perhaps more dramatically some of the leading buyers will realize that it is in their interests to bypass the auction and buy those horses they desire in private sales. There are already signs of such a trend, for in 1986 Allen Paulson bought fifteen yearlings in February from the North Ridge Farm, and the top lot at the 1986 Highflyer Sales was bought on behalf of Sheikh Mohammed without passing through the ring or attracting any other bids.

However much you are prepared to spend, the yearling auctions do not offer an easy route to successful racehorse ownership. It has often been said that the thoroughbred population can be divided into an elite, those who run in and win "black" type races, and the rest, almost indistinguishably moderate. The proportions which are usually quoted are 3 per cent and 97 per cent respectively. If this were true one would have thought it would be simple to buy the better racehorses at yearling auctions, given sufficient money to compete at Keeneland and Saratoga. With the help of a little pedigree research and a swift inspection of the yearlings before the sale starts, it should not be too difficult to distinguish between this 3 per cent and obtain the odd brilliant racehorse. The bloodstock business exists on its present scale because this is quite clearly not the case. When thoroughbreds are four years old it may just be possible to divide them between an elite 3 per cent and the rest, but when they are yearlings the situation is different. For each horse destined to join the elite there will be at least nine others who appear to have as much or more physical potential and who have the right names on their page of the sales catalogue.

High priced yearlings are notoriously slow racehorses. Of the eleven yearlings who have been sold for more than $4 million at Keeneland's Select July Sale, Imperial Falcon has shown the most ability on the racecourse, and his achievements are relatively modest. The Keeneland Association are inordinately proud of the fact that 1.9 per cent of the horses sold at their July Sale in recent years have won either a Group 1 or a Grade 1 race, whereas the outsider might think this was a small figure for a sale at which in the years between 1980 and 1986 the average price was $400,000. But when we see how horses are reared for and selected and sold at these sales, this low rate of success in the highest class should not be surprising. Horses are unpredictable and anyone who categorizes young horses in order to predict their racing ability is likely to be made to appear foolish. Indeed the high prices realized at these auctions are more surprising than the paucity of outstanding athletic achievements recorded by their graduates. The leading yearling auctions offer an almost unparalleled opportunity to throw money away.

This is not, needless to say, how the leading buyers look upon the yearling sales. Men like D. Wayne Lukas, Allen Paulson, Robert Sangster and Prince Khalid Abdullah presumably believe their experience, knowledge and advisers should enable them to achieve results considerably better than the average. Until 1985 they probably all thought, even if they did not announce it, that the way not to achieve results at the yearling sales was to approach them in the manner of the Maktoums. From 1980, when the Maktoum brothers first showed an interest in the American summer sales, they have been the most lavish of yearling buyers. In the early years they seemed to select their horses either by consulting an ever expanding committee of advisers, or by asking their multitude of trainers to buy for them. These advisers and trainers amounted to such a number that a large aeroplane was chartered to fly them all over from England together. The advisers were unable to agree and so bought all the horses each of them liked in order to avoid unneccessary disputes. When given their heads some of the trainers became so keen that they would bid against each other on behalf of their patrons to make sure the horse they wanted came to their stable rather than going to one of their rivals. Each trainer was given a few million dollars and told to buy a certain number of horses for their stable. The result was barely hidden confusion and a bonanza for the vendors. During these years between 1980 and 1984 the Maktoum family between them bought 255 yearlings at the summer sales for $170 million.

Surprisingly, against this muddled background the results they achieved were just a little bit better than average. Of those yearlings, nine went on to win Group I races in England, Ireland or France. This is a proportion of $3\frac{1}{2}$ per cent, but then they cost more than the average at about $670,000 each. This is an approximate calculation and only worthy of mention as a rebuff to those who believe the Maktoums have squandered their money in the most reckless manner. They have of course wasted a great deal of money and bought some expensive duds, but that is something which nobody who buys a lot of expensive yearlings can hope to avoid. Since 1985 the brothers have exerted and implemented a more rigorous chain of control within their operations and there is every reason to expect them to be more successful in their selection of yearlings in the future as a consequence. The three brothers with major bloodstock interests, Sheikh Maktoum Al Maktoum, Sheikh Hamdan Al Maktoum and Sheikh Mohammed bin Rashid Al Maktoum all operate separately, with different managers, stud farms and trainers. They consult together only to ensure they do not bid against each other at auctions.

Maktoum Al Maktoum's activities are managed by Michael Goodbody and his purchases are made in the name of the Gainsborough Stud, Hamdan Al Maktoum's manager is Hubert de Burgh, who buys in the name of the Shadwell Estate Company, while Sheikh Mohammed's racing manager is Anthony Stroud, who uses the Darley Stud Management as his nom de guerre. Anthony Stroud is in many ways representative of the new bloodstock agent. He is young and has never worked outside the bloodstock business, and his knowledge and activities are international.

In Britain bloodstock agency was for years largely the pursuit of ex-army officers. Many of them became bloodstock agents after leaving the army because they had a love of horses and racing, but were unable to afford to participate in any other way. Bloodstock agency offered comfortable, if far from spectacular, financial rewards and a good life which revolved around racecourses and sale rings. Now, as with many other aspects of the thoroughbred business, bloodstock agency is both international and more obviously commercial and professional. Those who are successful receive the appropriate responsibilities and rewards whatever their age and wherever they spent their youth. However, when the British Bloodstock Agency was floated as a public limited company in 1984 six of the ten directors of its English division had served as regular officers in the armed forces.

Bloodstock agency remains a more reputable trade in Britain than it is in the United States, partly because it has long been considered to be an activity worthy of a "gentleman" in Britain, and the bloodstock world is a milieu where such distinctions are thought to be important. In the United States the bloodstock business has been more overtly commercial and those "gentlemen" within it have been either owner dealers or have made a living from stallions or commercial breeding. An additional factor, and probably a more important one than such nebulous social distinctions, is the lack of any form of regulation of bloodstock agents in the United States. The Federation of Bloodstock Agents GB Ltd was set up in 1978 to give buyers confidence when employing agents to help them purchase bloodstock and to investigate complaints about any of their members' activities. In the United States there is as yet no similar trade organization and anyone who wishes to can become a bloodstock agent overnight. There are reputable agencies in the United States like the Cromwell Bloodstock Agency and the Taylor Made Sales Agency as well as many smaller thoroughbred management corporations and thoroughbred consultancies, but none with the size, range of activities and renown of the large British and Irish agencies.

The British Bloodstock Agency and the Curragh Bloodstock Agency were established in 1911 amd 1948 respectively. Both are concerned with equine insurance, transport, the management and syndication of stallions and the purchasing of all categories of bloodstock at sales throughout the world. The C.B.A. are also estate agents specializing in the sale of stud farms, training stables and country properties. The C.B.A. has prospered in recent years as a result of its close ties with the Maktoum family, initially forged by Lieutenant Colonel Richard Warden, one of the firm's directors. The B.B.A. is probably the world's largest bloodstock agency, with an annual turnover in the region of £5 million and some seventy-five employees. Bloodstock agency is still mainly concerned with personal contacts and individual skills, but an agency the size of the B.B.A. has the advantage of contacts and representatives in every major racing country. The B.B.A. has been closely associated with Robert Sangster and his partners, particularly Joss Collins and Tom Cooper, the head of the firm's Irish division. Now Robert Sangster is no longer the force he once was within the industry the B.B.A. may well lose its ascendancy. However, the firm continues to hold a strong portfolio of stallions and to specialize in buying breeding stock for numerous international clients.

Anthony Stroud may be representative of the new bloodstock agent, but he has been unusually successful. Having no family background in the racing business, when he left school he worked as a groom on various stud farms in England, Ireland and the United States. After a time spent working on the Brownstown Stud farm in Ireland he joined the C.B.A. and within four years was one of its directors. In the spring of 1985, after some months of internal wrangling, he accepted the post of racing manager to Sheikh Mohammed. His job is to buy and manage the Sheikh's racehorses. The buying alone is practically a full time job, for Sheikh Mohammed purchases about one hundred yearlings annually to supplement the sixty he breeds himself.

Anthony Stroud takes his work immensely seriously. Racing is above all his business and the racecourse and the sale ring are his places of work, and there is a marked difference between his on and off duty demeanour. When he is representing Sheikh Mohammed there is an air of high seriousness about him. He appears to be reticent and withdrawn, absorbed in his task. He enjoys working on his own and has complete confidence in his own ability to judge a horse. He moves about the saleground on his own examining each and every yearling and making an exact evaluation of each, even if he is unable to communicate what he sees verbally. He is happier at American sales than at those in England and Ireland, where so many more people expect him to talk to them. He is always scrupulously polite, while maintaining his distance, and makes a point of thanking and talking to the groom holding and displaying each yearling. When he visits a farm in advance of the sales he will write and thank the farm's owner or manager for allowing him to inspect their horses, although it is of course the farm which gives thanks for his arrival, as they fervently hope he will decide to bid for their horses. He is also authoritative, both by dint of his example and his informal almost conspiratorial tone. This is important, for many of the trainers and others whom he deals with are not only older but have many more years of experience in the business. Sheikh Mohammed is both a patron and a friend and as capable as anyone of teasing him about his earnestness. During the 1986 Keeneland Sales Sheikh Mohammed's £3.1 million purchase Authaal made his first appearance on the racecourse in a modest maiden race. Sheikh Mohammed sent an emissary to Anthony Stroud telling him that Authaal had been beaten a short head and that he was not to mention it to "the boss" who was absolutely furious. When they met Anthony Stroud maintained his silence and a long face which was both appropriate and sincere, until he was informed that Authaal had in fact won the race by ten lengths.

Anthony Stroud begins working on the summer sales in May when he goes to Kentucky in order to visit the vendors' farms and inspect their sales yearlings. Many commercial breeders in England are loath to show their yearlings to anybody until they arrive on the sale ground, but in Kentucky these inspections are now an accepted practice. Agents like James Delahooke, Amanda Skiffington and George Blackwell make a tour of the Kentucky farms in the spring before the final sales gloss is added to the yearlings. This has affected the vendors' attitudes towards the importance of this gloss and makes one wonder why more private transactions are not completed which bypass the auctions. Stroud will return in July to look at every yearling again and see how they have developed and adapted to the new environment of the sales ground. When the sales begin Sheikh Mohammed arrives in Lexington, as do his trainers. The trainers look through the yearlings, selecting the ones they would like to buy and drawing up a short list to submit to Anthony Stroud. Some, like Michael Stoute and Henry Cecil, are accompanied by a bloodstock agent, David Minton and "Tote" Cherry Downes respectively; others rely on their own judgement or the advice of their wives and her friends. The final decision to buy is taken by Anthony Stroud after consulting with Sheikh Mohammed, who will have seen many of the yearlings himself. When the yearlings arrive in Europe in November they are divided among the trainers as far as is possible in accordance with their short lists. When more than one trainer puts the same yearling on his short list Anthony Stroud decides which of them will have the privilege of training it. There is still some play within this new system, for if a trainer particularly wants a yearling he may be able to persuade Sheikh Mohammed to buy it, and each trainer will try to persuade Anthony Stroud to buy the horses which have especially caught their eye. However, Anthony Stroud himself will have a major influence upon the future development of the European bloodstock business.

The relationship between a sole agent and his client is an interesting one. Some agents have been given almost unrestricted opportunities to select and purchase yearlings. The agent who works exclusively for one extremely wealthy client will not only have the time and the resources to visit every major yearling sale, but will also be able to go and inspect the yearlings which will be on offer on their vendor's farm in the preceding months. If the relationship between the agent and his patron is a confident one, in addition to being able to carry out extensive research the agent will be able to take risks at the sales. In this situation it is easier to justify expensive purchases than it is cheap ones. If the agent feels insecure he may only buy the obvious yearlings at the top of the market which everyone expects him to bid for, but if he is confident he will buy whichever yearlings appeal to him, whether or not his views are in line with the general opinion. The patron may have his own insecurities and wonder whether his agent is being thorough or simply buying the horses which belong to his friends or clients. The patron is after all paying and wants to feel that ultimately it is he who is in control.

In comparison most bloodstock agents are restricted. Those who are self-employed are only able to justify attending those sales for which they have been given definite orders. The young Newmarket bloodstock agent will not consider flying to Kentucky to attend the July sales, unless he is sure he will be able to purchase yearlings there on behalf of his established clients. Even if he is able to afford an earlier trip to inspect the yearlings on their farms, without a reputation he may not be allowed to do so. The smaller agent will probably be asked to buy one or two yearlings every season by each of his clients. In this position he is unable to take risks in selection, for one gamble which does not come off may permanently lose him a client. There can be little doubt that the agent with the sole patron has many advantages, so it is not surprising that the two most famous bloodstock agents, James Delahooke and Sir Philip Payne-Gallwey achieved their greatest success when employed in this manner.

In the four years between 1980 and 1983 Sir Philip Payne-Gallwey bought Stavros Niarchos ten Group 1 winners including the Classic winners Law Society, Melyno, L'Emigrant and Northern Trick, and Seattle Song and Procida who won major races in North America. In the years between 1982 and 1984 James Delahooke bought Prince Khalid Abdullah such major winners as Dancing Brave, Rainbow Quest and Rousillon as well as Alphabatim and Hatim who have won Grade 1 races in North America. James Delahooke's success does not quite fit this pattern, for before he worked for Prince Khalid Abdullah he had already bought Young Generation, Recitation, Kalaglow, Ela-Mana-Mou, To-Agori-Mou, Master Willie and Lear Fan for other people. The uncertainties of such relationships are revealed by the fact that both these agents have since parted company with their patrons. Sir Philip Payne-Gallwey has returned to the B.B.A., who had seconded him to Stavros Niarchos, and James Delahooke having abruptly parted with Prince Khalid Abdullah in the summer of 1985 is now working for Stavros Niarchos. Sir Philip Payne-Gallwey apparently no longer wished to be perpetually on call, whilst James Delahooke and Prince Khalid Abdullah are said to have fallen out over a transaction involving a broodmare from New York. The composition of Robert Sangster's coterie of advisers seems to have an unusual permanence for Vincent O'Brien, John Magnier, Tom Cooper and Joss Collins have all been involved with his purchasing decisions for ten years or more.

There are only about fifteen agents who work under these conditions, in a position to go where they want and buy what they want, and they are nearly all either English or Irish. This may explain why English and Irish bloodstock agents are considered to be the best in the world. It is not only the agents themselves who consider they are the best in the world, although they undoubtedly do, but many of the vendors at the American summer sales would agree with them. This may only be because over the period from 1976 to 1986 the European agents had more money to spend than any other individuals.

One American at least who has been as successful at the sales as anybody is D. Wayne Lukas. Wayne Lukas comes from Wisconsin and was for a time a basketball coach. For a long time after he had given up coaching people he was North America's most successful quarter horse trainer. In 1978 he first began training thoroughbreds and by 1986 he was conditioning six hundred horses who were spread from California to Chicago to New York, and was established as North America's perennial leading trainer. He finds time to get away from the racetrack long enough to select all the stable's horses at the yearling sales. He is reputed to buy the horses himself and then sell bits of them to his backers, prominent among whom are Eugene Klein and C. R. French. He favours big sprinting types who are going to go flat out from the gate to the wire, and he is as accomplished as Vincent O'Brien at creating and promoting stallions. When he first went to Keeneland in 1977 he was only able to buy one horse, and the one he chose was Terlingua, who won the Hollywood Juvenile the following year. Since then he has bought such horses as Landaluce, Althea, Codex, Tank's Prospect, Blush with Pride, Saratoga Six, Life's Magic, Lady's Secret and Capote.

These men and women are exceptional, particularly Wayne Lukas who has such extensive commitments away from the sale ring. Most of those who buy at yearling sales have neither the opportunity nor the talent to display such flair. Indeed most yearling selections are governed by an innate conservatism. If a half-brother to a good racehorse is sold it will be astonishing if the good horse's owner and trainer do not bid for its younger relation. Conformity may be a more apt description than conservatism; tastes and beliefs change, but they tend to move together following the statistical vagaries. It is impossible not to be slightly cynical about bloodstock agents in general and to wonder whether personal charm or an ability to distinguish between young horses is the more important attribute for an aspiring member of the profession. Perhaps as with many self employed pursuits business acumen is the only necessary requirement, the ability to sell yourself and manage your patrons. One cannot observe agents and trainers working over the yearling sales without wondering how many of them would be lost without their sales catalogues as a guide. Tingles in the spine and intuitive feelings are all very well but in many cases it must be what actually appears on paper that holds sway over both selection and valuation. Some agents are primarily concerned with a yearling's physical appearance and of these "Tote" Cherry Downes must be one, for he is fond of saying that " ... the only thing a pedigree tells you is how much a yearling is going to cost." However, for most the pedigree is the means for justifying their inclination and their clients' gamble.

The valuation of yearlings is a problematic question, for there is nothing with which a yearling's value is obviously linked. Alan Lillingston is one breeder who claims to have given up even attempting to predict what price his yearlings will fetch. In 1984 he sent two yearling colts by Shirley Heights to the Highflyer Sales, between which he found it difficult to distinguish, The market took a different view for one was sold for 100,000 guineas, while the other fetched 1,000,000 guineas. The million-pound yearling was a strange phenomenon itself. For a few years million-pound yearlings were infrequent but regular occurrences. It became accepted that the top lots at the Highflyer Sales would fetch a million pounds, as would one or two at Goffs, and then suddenly they disappeared. Agents and experts who a few years before had competed for million-pound yearlings were by 1986 able to state categorically that there would be no more million-pound yearlings. These refutations and denials were so adamant it seemed to the naive astonishing that anyone had ever been so foolish as to pay a million pounds for a yearling. Yet some perfectly sensible people like Robert Sangster, Major Richard Hern and "Tote" Chery Downes did, and it is hard to see what had changed in the meantime.

Those who buy expensive yearlings tend not to be overly concerned with valuations. Valuations are calculated in relation to the prices fetched by other yearlings rather than any objective standards or indices of possible returns. The most important consideration is to buy a good racehorse. There is a sense in which the demand for expensive yearlings is similar to the demand for expensive stallions. They are in both cases unique and separate animals which a few very rich people want to own at least a part of, just in case. If the expensive yearling turns out to be a champion those who were in a position to buy it but decided not to, probably feel varying degrees of annoyance. If they buy an expensive yearling which turns out to be useless they are probably irritated, but at least they have not missed an easy opportunity of buying a champion. When none of the million-pound yearlings and few of the multi-million dollar yearlings turned out to be champions perhaps the irritation became more irksome than the annoyance, and the very top of the market collapsed. In the United States the six million-dollar yearling became the two-million-dollar yearling, whereas in Europe by 1986 600,000 guineas seemed to have become the new maximum people were prepared to pay in order to avoid being annoyed. However, there seems no obvious reason why this should prove to be any more lasting or stable a figure than the million pounds which preceded it. If there is a more rational explanation for the disappearance of the million-pound yearling and the eight-million-dollar yearling, then it must lie in the market for stallions.

=== Eight ===
The Stallion Farm

For as long as there has been a competitive thoroughbred business the stallion has offered its greatest commercial opportunities. The stallion is valuable because each is unique and qualitatively different from every other one, and because its owners are able to control their price as well. In effect the stallion owner is a monopolist, in the unique position of being able to ration the supply of his product and to discriminate between different buyers in order to maximize his revenue. It is this capacity which distinguishes the stallion farm from the commercial breeding farm and which attracts businessmen and gamblers to the former rather than the latter. The commercial farm sells potential racehorses, but no farm can hope to monopolize the supply of potential champions. There will always be a distinction between the products of different farms, but no one farm will ever be the sole source of fashionable yearlings. A commercial farm will never be able to increase the value of its products by withholding them from the market. If, for example, one of the world's leading commercial farms like Warner Jones' Hermitage Farm decided not to sell any yearlings one season, this would have no effect whatsoever upon the demand for and the value of its yearlings the following season. Equally if Warner Jones sold only half the number of yearlings he usually does, the remaining half would be neither more nor less valuable as a result. Commercial breeding is a competitive business because each separate product is differentiated from every other one, and none will ever exclusively possess the desired attributes. The stallion farm on the other hand is selling only sperm or the means of conception, and the stallion owner has complete control over one particular type of sperm or method of achieving pregnancy.

If Warner Jones decides not to sell his yearlings, then those who might have bought them will simply buy other potential racehorses instead. But if the owners of Northern Dancer decided not to sell any seasons to their stallion, then no breeder would be able to have a mare covered by Northern Dancer. A covering by Northern Dancer is a unique, an exclusive thing. If instead Northern Dancer's owners decided to allow their horse to cover ten mares rather than the usual forty, then the market price of a Northern Dancer covering would increase as a result. The stallion owner is able to increase the demand for and the value of his product by rationing its supply. In addition, because each covering is identical (if Northern Dancer is to cover ten mares one season, none of the selected mares' owners is likely to mind whether their mare is covered third or sixth). The stallion's owner is able to discriminate between his buyers. In a way the stallion's owner sells its services by tender. If he decides to sell twenty seasons he will ask those breeders who are interested how much they would be prepared to pay for one season. Once he has all the offers in front of him he will simply choose the twenty highest. A breeder who is determined to use the stallion might offer $500,000 while the twentieth offer might be only £150,000. Price discrimination is the monopolist's privilege.

The stallion, then, is an unrivalled commercial proposition within the thoroughbred business because the supply of its services is completely under the control of its owner. But for this property to be of any commercial value the demand for the horse's services must be relatively unresponsive to changes in their price. If the demand for a stallion's services is elastic with respect to price, then if its owner restricts the number of mares it covers he will simply deny himself revenue, for he will sell fewer seasons at the same price. The risk of stallion ownership lies in the fact that the demand for stallions is generally elastic. If the stallion owner's monopoly is to be rewarded he will have to ensure the demand for its services is relatively inelastic. At the risk of being esoteric, it will be illuminating to illustrate this diagramatically in a simplified form.

In this model the stallion owner decides how many seasons he is prepared to sell and their value is determined by the decisions of the mass of breeders. Stallion A is an ordinary stallion and the demand for his services is perfectly elastic. Then its owner decides to reduce the number of seasons he sells each season, he finds to his disappointment that his revenue falls, for their value is unaffected by their comparative scarcity. In contrast stallion B is obviously tremendously fashionable, for when its owners reduces the number of seasons on offer, he finds breeders are prepared to pay more in order to secure their season, and his revenue increases dramatically.

The abstract appeal of the stallion for the businessman or speculator is clear, the problem is how to select and manage a stallion in order to ensure that the demand for its services is characterized by a similarly eudemonic upward slant. This abstraction shows why it is possible to make a great deal of money from a stallion; the practical details will reveal why a stallion will always constitute a hazardous investment or a gamble.

The usual procedure is for a colt to be syndicated into forty shares when it retires from the racecourse and takes up residence on a stallion farm, although sometimes there are as few as thirty-two shares. The colt's owner retains as many or as few of these shares as he wishes and sells the remainder at a fixed and stated price. The colt's original owner sells in order to realize some of his capital gain and therefore reduce the risks inherent in an investment in a stallion. Stallions are generally superior racehorses, members of the minority whose capital value appreciates during their racing career. So the stallion owner's original investment is likely to have appreciated dramatically already and he is unlikely to be willing to jeopardize all of his gain. A further reason for selling shares in a new stallion is to involve other persons financially in the outcome of the stallion's new venture. The shareholders will share the owner's desire to promote the stallion and further its prospects, for they will also profit from its success and lose by its failure.

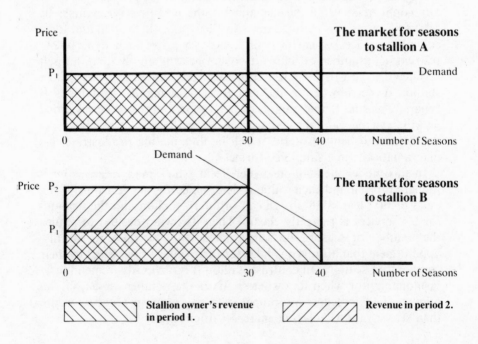

Price   **The market for seasons to stallion A**

P_1 Demand

0   30   40   Number of Seasons

Demand

Price P_2 **The market for seasons to stallion B**

P_1

0   30   40   Number of Seasons

Stallion owner's revenue in period 1.   Revenue in period 2.

The Stallion Farm

People buy shares in stallions first, if they are breeders, to secure access to the horse, and secondly whether or not they intend to use the stallion's services themselves in the hope of securing a capital gain. A stallion share gives its holder the right to use or sell one season to the horse every year. For the breeder the purchase of a share means that, however popular and expensive the stallion's seasons may become, he will always be able to send one of his mares to be covered by it without any additional payment. If the stallion does become popular and expensive, or if it was originally and becomes yet more so, the shareholders will profit either by selling their shares, or by selling their seasons at the new inflated value, or by selling the products of their seasons at auction. Movements in the price of a stallion's seasons tend, after an initial period, to follow movements in the prices attained by the stallion's offspring at yearling auctions. So if a horse's seasons are popular and expensive this will be either as a result of, or in anticipation of, his yearlings becoming popular and expensive as well. At the time of the original syndication the price of the horse's seasons is set at somewhere between a quarter and a third of the price of one share.

Shareholders sell their seasons when they decide they would rather have their annual income as cash, rather than in the form of a covered broodmare. Breeders buy nominations in an attempt to maximize, within their financial constraints, their chances of obtaining either a successful racehorse or a yearling which will fetch a high price at a public auction. The stallion market distributes two products, the share and the season. The supply of both is limited and controlled by the stallion's owners. The demand for a stallion's shares need not respond to the success of its offspring in the sale ring and on the racetrack, for it is governed by long-term considerations: whether or not the breeder wishes to secure access to the stallion in the future, and whether or not the stallion's seasons will still be eagerly sought after in three or four years' time. The level of demand for a share is obviously influenced by a stallion's age and general state of health. The level of demand for a season depends upon the expectation of the prices the horse's off-spring will fetch in two years time and the stallion's reputation as a progenitor of successful racehorses. The level of demand for a season will therefore tend to respond to the success of a horse's offspring in the sale ring and on the racetrack. One further deduction which needs to be emphasized is that there is no reason for the value of a season and of a share to be linked by a common multiple, even in the case of a young stallion. The demand for a share is determined by long-term factors, while the demand for a season is determined by related, but separate, short-term factors.

The stallion lures investors with the long-term prospect of a monopoly of the supply of a product which is demanded with only a scant regard for its price. But the stallion also offers tantalizing short term rewards, particularly to the sleeping partner who need not concern himself with the stallion's future. During the period of its first five years at stud a stallion's value is volatile, and volatility is a characteristic of markets which attracts speculators. The problem is to decide how valuable a young stallion is and the colt's owner and his agents must come up with an answer before the horse can be syndicated. A share price must be set before any have been offered for sale. A figure could be calculated on the basis of formal and informal questioning of potential buyers, but the usual procedure is for the owner and his agents to think of a figure and gamble upon it. The owner or his agent will categorize the stallion on the basis of its achievements on the racecourse, its pedigree, and less crucially its physical confirmation. They will decide whether the stallion is likely to be seen as a sire of potential sprinters, Classic horses, 7–10 furlong horses, or members of the international elite. Having categorized the horse they will fix its share price in relation to its immediate predecessors and select which breeders to invite to purchase shares. There are some breeders who are never interested in buying sprinters, some who cannot afford to buy potential international sires, and others whose reputation is such that any syndicate would like to have their support. Stallion shares appeal to speculators because these categories are unstable and a horse's placement depends upon nothing more objective than a tingle in the agent's spine.

A stallion will have completed five breeding seasons before his first crop of foals have completed their three-year-old careers. Once there has been some proof of a stallion's ability on the racecourse its category placing will be readjusted. Despite the firmly held beliefs of those who look upon the pedigree as a totem, the performances of stallions are most unpredictable. There are countless examples of horses who have moved from the bottom of a category to the top, or into a higher one. The most successful stallion based in England and Ireland in 1986 was the Irish National Stud's Ahonoora. When Ahonoora retired to stud in 1980 he had won but one pattern race, although he had been awarded another after a disqualification; his pedigree was distinctly unfashionable and he had never won a race over a distance of further than six furlongs. The best his owners could realistically hope for was a place in the middle ranks of sprinting stallions, an estimation which was reflected in his initial stud fee of £2,250. Now Ahonoora is among the leading dozen 7–10 furlong stallions in Europe with a stud fee of £20,000, and his original shareholders must have made a satisfactory capital gain. Ahonoora is not an exceptional case. There is a long list of stallions in Europe and the United States whose reputation and capital value have ascended with similar rapidity; among the more obvious examples are Kris, Shirley Heights, Niniski, Danzig and Halo. When Shirley Heights was syndicated in 1978 each share was sold for £40,000; in 1986, by which time he was middle aged, one of these shares was sold for $535,000. These rapid gains attract gamblers into stallion investment and encourage breeders to have a flutter on the stallions themselves.

The possibility of a substantial financial gain may encourage people to invest in stallions but the most likely outcome of any such investment is less alluring. Most stallions fail, or are at least unsuccessful commercially. A multitude of stallions succeed in siring one or two distinguished racehorses but relatively few have consistent enough records to maintain their place in the hierarchy. Once their first one or two crops have performed on the racecourse most stallions begin to slip down the rankings. This failure rate is illustrated by looking at stallion advertisements or select sale catalogues which are, say, five years old. They have a spectral feel to them; many of the names which are prominently displayed will have disappeared, banished to distant countries or anywhere which has no connection with the leading stallion farms that were once so proud of them. The failure of the majority need not deter investors, for there is this period of limbo before the market passes its final judgement on a stallion and before there is any evidence on the racecourse of a stallion's merit. This is the period when a stallion's fate is decided and when skilful management is of paramount importance.

Five years is often sufficient for the investors to recoup their original investment, or if things look bad to arrange a face-saving sale to a distant country which judges stallions by different criteria. During this time the stallion's owners must establish its rank and maintain it with judicious advertising and promotion. This is done with glossy advertisements in the trade press, making enticing videos, or even holding promotional parties to boost the stallion's name. The crucial period comes when the stallion's racecourse achievements are receding from the public memory and its progeny have yet to appear on the racecourse. Then all forms of persuasion are used to maintain the stallion's prestige and its place in the market. A stallion who is forgotten will be sent only a few mares and is therefore doomed to a cyclical record and only intermittent demand. The first indicators of a stallion's commercial standing are the number of mares it is asked to cover, the prices fetched at auction by mares who are carrying its foals, and then the prices fetched by its first foals and yearlings. The adroit stallion manager will present this information in a manner which encourages potential customers.

All young stallions are fully booked, for to admit otherwise would be to admit failure and unfashionableness. A stallion's owners will prefer to pass up some income rather than publicly announce a drop in their horse's nomination fee. When the stallion is tested by auction they may well be prepared to bid for its offspring in order to boost its sales performance and prove its fashionable appeal. During this period the stallion's owners are selling an image and a ranking which may well later be proved to have been false. For these reasons the stallion market thrives upon ignorance and misinformation. Stallion managers are wary of public auctions of seasons and shares, or any other means by which vital information is made public before they are able to compile it. Even if you are buying a season to a stallion yourself it will be difficult to find out how many mares are already booked to be covered by it and how much their owners have paid for this privilege. Once the five years are up and the stallion's progeny are running on the racetrack the die is cast and the imperative of secrecy is less pressing, but for a time a stallion's image must be carefully presented.

The legitimacy of this system of marketing stallions is, once more, derived from a time when the buyers and sellers in the stallion market were, because of their physical proximity and repeated personal contacts, relatively well informed. If you wanted to buy a stallion season you were probably in a position to wander round and ask the manager of the farm on which it stood how things were going. The bloodstock boom created new tensions in the stallion market and placed the traditional system under severe strain. The initial effect of the boom was to increase the level of demand for stallions. The quantity of stallions demanded increased, particularly in the United States where there was such a rapid growth in the thoroughbred population. In the early 1970s there were probably eight hundred stallions in the United States sufficiently popular to be kept busy throughout the breeding season; by the mid 1980s this figure would have doubled. In addition there was a shift in the demand for the fashionable elite of stallions. The higher the prices select yearlings fetched at Keeneland or Saratoga, the more commercial breeders were prepared to pay for the services of fashionable stallions. The value of seasons to the fashionable stallions rocketed upwards in stages which corresponded to the rises in the average prices attained at the select yearling sales. For those owners and brokers who were already established in the stallion business it was a time of unprecedented profits—abnormal profits, which changed the rules of the market and attracted new competitors to the business.

The Stallion Farm

The new demand for stallions was not only greater than ever before, it was also more volatile. If a stallion fell from favour, because it failed to produce a major winner in its first crop or on account of an inexplicable rumour or general feeling, then the demand for its services could evaporate within months. The short-term commercial breeder is concerned only with fashion and has no need to look more than two years in advance. For this reason he is unlikely to want to invest in stallion shares, but he will be prepared to pay extravagant sums for a season to the stallion of the moment. For a time the two aspects of the stallion market were curiously separated. Stallion shares were bought by brokers and speculators, many of whom did not own a broodmare, for the purpose of selling seasons at inflated prices to short-term commercial breeders. The stakes of the game were raised so high that both sides of the market became preoccupied with the short term.

Stallion broking became fiercely competitive and each individual or company was prepared to pay munificently for a potential stallion. As soon as a colt had revealed exceptional promise on the racetrack the leading stallion brokers would compete for the privilege of syndicating it. Their efforts were spurred on by the wish to pre-empt any further rise in status and to outwit their competitors. Whereas it was once usual for a horse to be syndicated as a four-year-old, colts like Devil's Bag and Chiefs Crown were syndicated as two-year-olds. Robert Clay sold twenty shares in the latter for $500,000 each before the horse had completed its two-year-old career. If a leading two-year-old was worth $20 million, then it appeared to be sensible for a top three-year-old to be worth $40 million. Those who bought the fashionable yearlings were of course mindful of these valuations. Indeed many colts had their entire racing careers planned with a view to maximizing their value as a potential stallion. Vincent O'Brien and Wayne Lukas were two particularly skilful proponents of such a policy. The categorization of potential stallions began much earlier, and once a horse had established a position at the top of the rankings there was little point in its continuing to race, when its status could only decline. Fashion could be created by one or two performances, and once made was far too valuable to be put at risk. Once the selection and valuation of stallions had become so whimsical, stallion management had to be concerned with short term objectives.

The volatility of this new demand for stallions encouraged the short term perspective as well, for it meant that the risks of stallion investment were as great as the possible rewards were magnificent. A short-term market demands sensations and is governed by fads. The majority of stallions will be commercial failures in any circumstances but in a market which is addicted to sensationalism the turnover of stallion "stars" will be that much more frantic. If the shareholders in a stallion are predominantly concerned with financial gains rather than with securing access to an excellent stallion, then the temptation to follow a short-term management policy is often overwhelming. This was proved to be particularly true when the cost of the shares was so high that only spectacular success could ensure an adequate return if a more long-term policy had been pursued.

The dictates of such a policy are firstly to set the stallion's stud fee as high as is possible without appearing ridiculous, but not to announce any figure publicly. The next step is to attract as many mares as possible, charging the full price when it is feasible, but offering deals to breeders. If the horse is fully booked at the high fee, this will create prestige. When mares carrying the stallion's foals and its first foals and yearlings appear at the sales, bid for them and if necessary buy them in order to promote the horse's commercial appeal. Throughout the five-year period maintain a vigorous and noticeable advertising campaign. At the end of five years the stallion will probably flop, but the shareholders will have collected enough in nomination fees to have made a clear profit anyway. In many cases a stallion's owner would follow such a policy without syndicating the horse initially. A few shares would be sold for exaggerated sums and then it would be publicly announced that the horse had been syndicated for x million dollars, when in fact only a small percentage of it would have changed hands. High syndication values help foster prestige and a fashionable image, whilst holding many shares increases the income from stallion nominations and the capital gain in the event of the horse actually proving to be a good stallion. One final precaution was to ask the stallion to cover anything up to one hundred mares a year in order to maximize the income received from sales of seasons, and in the hope that when they first appear on the racecourse the stallion's offspring will make a mark if only through outnumbering the offspring of their contemporaries.

These short term policies were a consequence of the new tensions created by the competition between the established and the new stallion brokers. In response to the new demand for stallion seasons brokers succeeded in bidding up the value of shares in potential stallions, thereby immeasurably increasing the risks of their own business. In addition the boom attracted new investors to the stallion market who were not familiar with its traditional precepts. Established personal contacts and relationships no longer formed a barrier against competition when the important investors were newcomers themselves. There were clearly opportunities for a new type of stallion broker who served the short-term investors and supplied them with the information they desired. The first company to fill this gap was the Matchmaker Breeders Exchange. Initially the company simply held auctions of stallion seasons and shares in Lexington hotels, but it expanded and developed a computerized weekly ask-and-bid market for both seasons and shares. Matchmaker will be considered in detail later, but its significance was that it began disseminating information about the value of seasons and shares which was traditionally withheld. Matchmaker was attempting to cash in on the cult of the stallion by facilitating transactions of seasons and shares, in the hope of attracting new investors and customers. Ironically the information Matchmaker supplied only helped to bring about the exposure of the falsity of the stallion market. Placed under spotlights, it became clear to all observers that the stallion emperor was not wearing any clothes.

The justification for the high valuation assigned to stallions was the decisive influence they were supposed to have upon their offsprings' racecourse performances. In the name of the prepotent stallion those who bought racehorses for pleasure were prepared to spend millions of dollars on the offspring of fashionable stallions. This led commercial breeders to pay hundreds of thousands of dollars for a season to a fashionable stallion, and stallion brokers to pay millions of dollars for potential fashionable stallions. The million-dollar stallion season and the four million dollar stallion share were both therefore direct consequences of the myth of the prepotent stallion. The market was of course supported by the activities of speculators and arbitrageurs, but sooner or later the absurdity of the myth had to be revealed. When the process of selection and valuation of yearlings became more sensible the short-term commercial breeder and stallion broker, who either believed in the myth for himself or had gambled on his customers continuing to do so, saw the value of his assets shrink and his income dwindle. There was an excess supply of both "fashionable" yearlings and stallions which had been encouraged by the volatility of demand and the magnificent possible rewards. The stallion broker, using the same reasoning as the commercial breeder, was prepared to try ten new stallions in the belief that one success would comfortably pay for nine failures. In the same way as in the field of breeding and the bloodstock auction, those who followed short term policies were able to earn abnormal profits from stallions for a brief period. But the more short sighted these policies became the more obvious it was that the stallion is not this decisive influence, or in Aristotelian terms the divine carpenter. Those within the thoroughbred business have yet publicly to admit that the myth of the stallion is ridiculous, but their actions clearly show they believe it to be so.

Since 1985 most potentially valuable stallions have been managed with a view to long-term objectives. The ruling idea of stallion management has become not maximizing the revenue obtained by selling seasons, but maximizing the horse's chance of actually producing distinguished racehorses. As the potency of the myth waned, the speculative demand for stallion shares fell, and as a result the syndication values of most stallions fell correspondingly. The exception has been those stallions held to be potential top international stallions. Sixteen shares in Dancing Brave were sold for $600,000 even before he had won the Prix de l'Arc de Triomphe, but the majority were bought by private breeders who wished to secure access for their broodmares to such an outstanding racehorse. The remainder were bought by leading commercial breeders like Windfields Farm and Three Chimneys Farm, who were also motivated by long-term considerations. The new emphasis in stallion management is on attracting and securing a supply of high class broodmares for the stallion during its formative years. The paradox of the stallion market is that those who own stallions can still secure a monopoly rent, yet those who manage them believe a horse's reputation and commercial prospects rest upon the quality of the broodmares it covers during its first five years at stud.

This overview is clearly a simplification and it will be interesting to look at the English, Irish and American stallion markets separately. The character and financial opportunities presented by each of these markets were shaped differently by their traditional structures, but in all of them the gamblers were able to win and lose millions.

In Ireland and the United States most stallions are syndicated and managed by the farms at which they stand. Stallion farms in Britain are not the large prosperous commercial enterprises they are in the United States because they are not encouraged by the central government's fiscal policy and because they are not able to stand numerous stallions. Due to various social, economic and geographic factors walking in has never been popular in Britain and stallion farms have traditionally looked after the mares sent to be covered by their stallions for three or four weeks. In Britain the role of the stallion farm is closer to the maternity hospital than the sperm bank, and the farm's profits are derived from the fees paid by the mares' owners rather than the sale of nominations. British syndication agreements allot one, or at the most two, nominations every year to the farm at which the stallion stands, whereas in the United States the figure is usually four. When taken together all these factors explain why British stallion farms do not have sufficient resources to buy and syndicate their own stallions. When they do buy a stallion it is an ordeal and the process and risk of syndication are handed over to a specialist agency as soon as possible.

The first time Bernice Cuthbert, the owner and manager of the Aston Park Stud, was involved with a stallion syndication was in 1985, when she bought the four-year-old colt Elegant Air from Paul Mellon. The whole process was an alarming one, at first because Aston Park had to compete with other farms in Ireland and New Zealand; then, after Mr Mellon had agreed to accept her offer, there was an agonizing period when the farm owned the horse outright. A farm like Aston Park cannot afford to invest a million pounds in anything and there was always a chance that it would prove impossible to sell shares in Elegant Air at £30,000 each. The syndication was organized by Simon Morley of the B.B.A. but even with the security of the B.B.A.'s reputation the wait for acceptances was frightening enough for Bernice Cuthbert sincerely to hope she does not have to go through it again for at least ten years. Bernice Cuthbert is a newcomer to the thoroughbred business, but she was lured to it almost by chance on account of her love for horses rather than by the prospect of an attractive commercial opportunity.

She and her husband were looking for a farm to buy in the area when the Aston Park Stud came on the market in 1980. After some months of meditation they gradually came round to a decision to purchase it. Once they had acquired the farm they were petitioned by the farm's staff and those who lived in the village in which it is situated, who wanted it to remain a commercial stallion farm. Despite her complete lack of experience in the field Bernice Cuthbert decided to maintain the farm for at least a trial period. She was encouraged by Bob McCreery, who manages the stallion Dominion, which had arrived at Aston Park in 1979 and was already proving to be a commercial success. Her only training was a one-day intensive course in stud management given to her by Chris Harper, the owner of the Whitsbury Manor Stud. As a type Bernice Cuthbert is far removed from the Kentucky stallion broker. Although she is a keen event rider and a horsewoman her interest in racing itself is marginal and confined at the moment mainly to following the exploits of Dominion's offspring. She attends a few major racemeetings but only in order to maintain contacts. On taking over the farm her first concern was to improve the facilities it offered to the mares which visited it. She renovated the farm's buildings and installed closed circuit television in the foaling boxes and a scanner to test for pregnancies. During the breeding season she is preoccupied with fertility and with those mares who prove difficult to get in foal or who return dirty swabs, for the farm's commercial success depends upon its reputation for efficiency and the condition of the mares who are boarded there. A smartly dressed woman with two white dogs, she gives the impression that Aston Park is only a hobby or a sideline, but her attention to detail and the farm's achievements show this is not the case. She is an astute manager rather than a shrewd dealer. The farm's success has convinced her to stay on and expand with the help of Elegant Air. A new stallion is a major step, not least because the horse must be promoted. In his first year at stud the advertising budget for Elegant Air was £50,000. In this field Bernice Cuthbert can always rely upon expert advice for her husband commutes daily to London to work for an advertising agency.

Thoroughbreds have always played a central role in Kirsten Rausing's life and she is happy to theorize and speculate about stallions and stallion management. However, in the same way, for six months of the year, she is preoccupied with the problems of infertility. As she has said herself, one cannot run a stallion farm and go to cocktail parties. Throughout the breeding season Kirsten Rausing only leaves the farm once a week to dash to Newmarket to buy provisions. It is a matter of pride to her that whilst she has been at Lanwades not a single mare has died while giving birth there. She bought her first stallion Niniski in 1980 in the middle of its four-year-old career. Unfortunately the colt's programme was interrupted when it was jarred up running on firm ground and it ran only twice subsequently, both times unplaced. The horse was syndicated by Simon Morley of the B.B.A., but it was not at first a fashionable stallion. In his first five years at stud Niniski produced only eighty-six foals and Kirsten Rausing was forced to sell guaranteed seasons to him for as little as £2,000. However, when Niniski's first crop was shown to include Petoski and Kala Dancer everything changed; the value of the horse's shares increased by eleven times in a few years and his stud fee soared to £40,000. Niniski will have relatively few winners in 1986 and 1987 because he will have so few representatives on the racecourse. By 1988 breeders may begin to forget about Petoski and Kala Dancer and pass over Niniski when selecting a mate for their mares, yet that will be the year when the horse's first full crop since his first will appear on the racecourse. One quiet year in the breeding shed can then start off a new cycle of popularity and comparative obscurity.

Bob McCreery comes closer to fulfilling the American role of a stallion dealer, even though he does not own or manage a stallion farm himself. He bought Dominion as a stallion as a result of a chance encounter with the horse at Gulfstream Park in Florida. He was so impressed by the colt's physical appearance that he found out its identity and subsequently decided to re-export Dominion back to

England. He syndicated Dominion himself and still manages the horse, keeping its stud fee low enough for the horse to be oversubscribed and for him to be able to select the mares he considers to be most appropriate. Bob McCreery is also involved with the management of two other stallions, Carwhite which he bought as a proven stallion in France and Electric which he bred and raced himself. In order to give Electric a chance of proving himself as a stallion McCreery bought some of his foals to supplement the ones he had bred himself, with the intention of sending them all to leading trainers. These are both managerial moves which are clearly designed to bring a reward only in the long run. When it is remembered that Bob McCreery also bred High Top it is clear that he has been a major influence on the English stallion market, but his activities are low key in comparison with his American counterparts. Nonetheless few British breeders are prepared to take such an active role in dealing with stallions; the majority like Bernice Cuthbert and Kirsten Rausing immediately delegate the responsibility to one of the specialist agencies.

Stallion management and syndication in Britain is largely conducted by three men: Simon Morley of the B.B.A., James Wigan of London Thoroughbred Services and Rhydian Morgan-Jones of Thoroughbred Management Services. The C.B.A. and the Newmarket firm Rustons & Lloyd also have fairly large portfolios, but the majority of the commercially successful stallions in Britain were syndicated by and are managed by one of these three men. This does not take account of those which are managed by the agents of Prince Khalid Abdullah or of one of the Maktoum brothers, but they will be considered separately. At the beginning of the 1987 covering season these three men managed sixty-eight stallions between them and of the fourteen English based stallions whose advertised fee was £20,000 or more Simon Morley controlled four, James Wigan three and Rhydian Morgan-Jones two. The remainder were the responsibility of one of the major Arab organizations. The B.B.A. have of course been syndicating and managing stallions for years, but the other two organizations are more recent creations.

James Wigan is the sort of Englishman who looks out of place in a hot climate. This is a characteristic he shares with another prominent English bloodstock agent David Minton, though in each case the unease has a different cause. Under the Kentucky sun David Minton is a small rotund figure which visibly melts despite the sun hat drawn tightly down on top of his head. In contrast James Wigan is tall, thin and pale as he stalks from one piece of shade to the next. Both appear to be more at ease when wearing a dark suit or a sweater at Newmarket in October. However, James Wigan always has a diffident and restless air. He comes from a particularly sound racing family and although he pondered over entering the art world, he decided instead to work for Keith Freeman's bloodstock agency. In 1976, when he was twenty-six, he left to set up his own London Thoroughbred Services whose elegant office is on the first floor of his house in Chelsea, overlooking one of those pubs which the local American bond dealers like to sit outside in the summer.

He initially made his reputation organizing the sale of stallions to Japan, Australia and the United States, but from 1980 he has syndicated and managed numerous leading stallions including Young Generation, Kris, Slip Anchor and Sharpo. By the time he was thirty he had owned and bred a prominent winner and this colt, Final Straw, was still one of his stallions eight years later. When James Wigan says he is never happier than when handling foals on his farm one is inclined to believe him, for despite his evident success he seems extraordinarily uncynical for someone who has been in the stallion business for so long. It is easier to envisage Rhydian Morgan-Jones happily handling a large cigar than a new foal, but then there is no reason why the first aptitude should not be as much of a help in his trade as the latter; after all, many of his clients probably smoke large cigars as well. He too worked in bloodstock agency before setting up Thoroughbred Management Services with Charles Rowe in 1984. This agency is also based in London, so it would appear that stallion managers follow their clients rather than their horses.

To the outsider the management policies of these three organizations appear to be relatively similar. If you are in the happy position of owning a potential stallion, which of the three you choose to turn to will probably depend upon your judgement of the personalities involved. The success and failure of stallion management depends upon personal contacts and personal powers of persuasion, rather than any sophisticated management techniques or philosophies. Once an agency has been selected, the first step in the syndication process is to set a price for the shares, and to draw up a syndication agreement. The three companies produce broadly similar agreements, for the management's interest in a stallion is unambiguous. To reassure the shareholders a limit is set on the number of mares a stallion will cover, often forty-five in its first year and fifty every season thereafter. As an additional safeguard for potential investors, it is normal for the horse's original owner to insure against the possibility of its proving to be infertile in its first season at stud. The majority of the agreement's stipulations, however, are for the benefit of the management rather than the individual shareholders. Stallions are formally managed by their syndicate's committee. The committee is made up of the colt's original owner, a representative of the farm at which the horse will stand, the agent who is handling the syndication, and two or three shareholders. A stallion's committee will often retain the right to veto any mares which it does not consider to be suitable mates for the horse and it will oversee the restrictions which are placed on the sale of seasons and shares.

These restrictions are essentially that no share or nomination can be sold by auction or advertised for sale at a price or in a manner which has not first been approved by the committee. The intention is of course to reinforce the committee's discretion to decide when to disclose vital information about the horse. The sale of a share at an auction publicly establishes a value which may be at odds with the one the committee is seeking to maintain. The question of auctions of seasons and shares highlights the central problem of stallion management.

If you ask one of these agents in whose interests they attempt to manage, they will probably reply the stallion's. This is avoiding the question, for the horse himself clearly has no say in the matter. There is a problem because people are motivated to buy stallion shares by both long and short term considerations, and in many instances the interests of both parties will not be compatible. There is likely to be tension between the two groups when the horse is performing particularly well or particularly badly. Take the example of a horse like Niniski: when the value of his shares increased by eleven times any short-term investor would have been tempted by the American auctions, while the long-term investors would have been looking forward to selling his offspring as yearlings, or congratulating themselves on securing access to an excellent stallion at a discount price. When things are going badly, or during the horse's third and fourth years at stud when the demand for every stallion tends to shift backwards, the management may be faced with a mutiny if they relax their authority. The first to be tempted by the auctions will be the straightforward investor who has nothing but the value of his share to lose. The next to go will be the commercial breeder, for although he may already have a foal and a broodmare who is carrying another, if the indicators are poor he may feel the best option is to cut his losses, rather than face the prospect of selling a succession of unfashionable yearlings. Once the value of a stallion's nominations and shares begin publicly to fall its reputation will be ruined, and may not recover until it has been sold cheaply for export.

The stallion agent will wish to avoid sales at auction under any circumstances. His interest in the stallion will always be a long-term one, for his managerial services will be rewarded by an annual fee. A mutiny or a forced sale will therefore deprive him of future income. In addition, if the call of the auction is withstood, the agent will be the primary broker of the stallion's nominations and will receive a commission on each transaction of a season or share he negotiates. The auction will generally make his life more difficult, for if one shareholder manages to sell a season at a Lexington hotel for $230,000 then many of the others will be on the telephone the next day asking why he sold their season for only £100,000. To avoid such awkward discussions and having to resort to the courts to uphold his authority, and of course to further the stallion's best long-term interests, the agent will seek to attract a homogeneous collection of shareholders. Specifically he will desire a syndicate made up of reputable, established breeders who wish to buy shares for long-term reasons. Whether or not he succeeds will depend upon his personal powers of persuasion and his contacts.

These details of stallion management may appear to be unnecessarily esoteric and of little interest to anyone who is not planning to buy a share in a stallion. However, they demonstrate the essential features of the British stallion market and the changes which have taken place within it during the years of the bloodstock boom. The manner of stallion management and the people involved with it have changed little if at all. The two new firms who play a prominent role in the market are both run by men with a traditional outlook, who look back longingly to the period before 1976. For them the purpose of stallion management is to moderate the swings of fashion and to forestall the market's judgement on a stallion until it has had at least one or two generations of representatives on the racecourse. The traditional system was upset by changes which took place elsewhere and by the broadening of the scope of the international stallion market. The stallion market was suddenly of interest not only to a handful of established private breeders but to outsiders, foreigners, and even investors with little knowledge of either stallions or the breeding of bloodstock.

In England the reaction to these developments was to maintain the old system by reinforcing it with new and more stringent restrictions. There was undoubtedly a commercial gap that could have been filled by a dealer or a stallion farm which was prepared to exploit the new stallion market, rather than attempting to exclude it or keep it at bay. This did not happen in England because the traditional system offered no short term incentives to the dealers, and the stallion farms were not wealthy enough to take the risks themselves. The people who possessed the appropriate knowledge and experience were either established as traditional bloodstock agents or aspired to that position, while no outsider or stallion farm had sufficient resources to overcome the traditional prejudices and take the necessary risks. In the United States and Ireland the situation was different.

In Ireland and the United States the leading stallion farms have traditionally been run by charismatic owner-managers who have selected, bought, syndicated and managed their own stallions without any help or interference from outside, for in both countries there have been farms large enough not to need to rely upon the services of intermediaries and specialist agencies. In both countries a stallion farm's achievements tend to reflect the personality and judgement of the man who runs it, for the owner-manager is clearly able to exert a more powerful influence upon his stallions' prospects than either the syndicating agent or the farm manager in England. An additional distinction between the stallion market in these countries and the market in England is that there can be no confusion over the question of in whose interests the stallion's career should be managed, for the owner-manager stands unequivocally to gain from a commercial outlook and a whole hearted pursuit of profit.

Irish stallion entrepreneurs, or those who are based in Ireland, do not yet have the advantages of the walking in system, but unlike their counterparts in England they are positively encouraged by the central government. Since 1969 income which is received from the sale of stallion seasons in Ireland has not been included as part of an individual's or a company's taxable income. This ruling, which was introduced by Charles Haughey, has undoubtably boosted the Irish stallion business, yet it has also damaged it by encouraging farms to concentrate on the short term and on maximizing that part of their income which is derived from the sale of stallion seasons. Nonetheless, with at least two hundred and fifty thoroughbred stallions, Ireland must have more per head of its population than any other country in the world. The three principle stallion farms in Ireland are the Coolmore and Airlie organizations and the Irish National Stud. The Irish National Stud is owned by the government and has always had training and research services to fulfil, and these two obligations together have meant that it has not had the commercial influence of the other two farms. For some years it was run by Michael Osborne, who has an unrivalled reputation among stud managers, and under his control the farm attracted stallions with the potential of Sallust, Tap On Wood and of course Ahonoora.

Coolmore, Castle Hyde and Associated Stud Farms are owned by a partnership whose members include its managing director John Magnier, Robert Sangster and Vincent O'Brien. Stavros Niarchos was another partner until 1986 when he withdrew, in order to concentrate on his own stallion farm, the Haras de Fresnay-le-Buffard in Normandy. The Coolmore partners were among those who were involved most prominently with the business of buying fashionable yearlings, turning them into potential stallions and then re-exporting them. They were helped by Vincent O'Brien's skill as a trainer, by the convenient combination of the uncompetitive standard of Irish racing at the time and by the pattern race system. Their excellent racehorses, like The Minstrel and Alleged, were campaigned in England and France as well as in Ireland, and then sold as stallions to America's leading stallion farms. The partners' horses whose athletic ability was not so exalted earned their "black type" in Ireland and were then sold to the less prosperous farms in the United States, or to Australia and South Africa. Coolmore has been a large stallion farm for a long time and as early as 1976 there were already sixteen stallions there. From around 1977, after the arrival of Robert Sangster and The Minstrel and Alleged who both carried his colours on the racecourse, the partners decided to turn Coolmore into an international stallion farm. Rather than selling the successful racehorses they had bought at the leading American yearling sales, they would retain them and stand them as stallions at Coolmore. In 1978 Be My Guest began covering at Coolmore; he is the son of a champion American racemare and was a record priced European yearling himself before a slightly disappointing racing career. The following year the Northern Dancer colt Try My Best, who had been Europe's champion two-year-old, arrived at Coolmore. These were both horses who could easily have been sold to American farms. Since those early years Coolmore has continued to expand and in 1982 it acquired a Kentucky annexe at the Ashford Stud, where another champion two-year-old Storm Bird took up stud duties. By the 1987 covering season the Coolmore partnership was responsible for twenty-four stallions, of whom three were at the Ashford Stud in Kentucky.

Coolmore's commercial success was founded upon its partners' keen awareness of the developments in the international thoroughbred business. It would not have been possible without their excellent record for selecting yearlings at auctions, but then nor would it have been possible without a strong market for the relative failures who won but the odd Irish pattern race. The racing careers of the parnership's colts, and they bought very few fillies, were carefully planned with a view to maximizing their commercial value as potential stallions. This was done meticulously, careful attention being paid to such small details as interviews with the press and the announcement of future plans for each colt. When they could the partners sold the winners of races at Royal Ascot, but when this was not possible they sold horses who would have run at Royal Ascot if they had not been injured, or which Vincent O'Brien had considered to be among his most promising two-year-olds. The stallions they retained were managed according to the dictates of the short-term perspective.

Coolmore's syndications have always been mysterious affairs, and there are few English breeders who will admit to owning a share in one of Coolmore's stallions. Their stud fees were considered to be less rigorously confidential and they were always high; Golden Fleece stood at £100,000, Caerleon at £80,000, Be My Guest at £75,000 and Kings Lake at £50,000. Figures this high were almost without precedent in Europe. Despite this, Coolmore's stallions covered unusually large numbers of mares; Kings Lake and Gorytus, for example, both covered more than seventy mares in their first season at stud. Many of this mass of mares were covered after their owners had come to some form of foal-sharing agreement with one or other of Coolmore's partners. For stallions with such high fees an unusually large proportion of their offspring were sold as yearlings. It is generally the case that the higher a stallion's stud fee, the fewer will be the number of his offspring who are sold as yearlings. The exceptions to this rule are those stallions based in Kentucky, yet whose offspring only appeal to European buyers, and all the stallions who stand at Coolmore. For instance the leading English stallions Kris and Shirley Heights rarely have more than ten, or a quarter of their crop, sold at yearling auctions every season. On the other hand in 1986 there were six Coolmore stallions who had more than twenty-five yearlings sold at auction, and both Kings Lake and Gorytus had more than thirty. Another distinctive feature of Coolmore's management policy is the prominence and lavishness of the farm's advertising.

Coolmore's international promotion was initially organised by Richard Craddock, but when he began to work for the Maktoum family as well the farm switched its allegiance to a Dublin-based firm instead. Coolmore evidently do not believe in low key advertising; even since Robert Sangster sold his interest in Pacemaker International to Michael Smurfitt the Coolmore Stud has continued to advertise on the first two pages of each of the magazine's issues. In the United States the farm maintains a steady campaign by invariably taking the back cover of each issue of *The Thoroughbred Record*. The farm's annual brochure is printed in full colour on each of its eighty pages and besides the horses and the selected quotations, the 1986 edition was endorsed by "J. R. Ewing" and "Sue Ellen" as well as Dr Patrick Hillery, the President of Ireland, and Mr Dick Spring, who was Ireland's Deputy Prime Minister. Piles of these Coolmore brochures are left lying around in the bars at Europe's sale rings in the hope that by brightening a breeder's drink they will persuade him to use Coolmore next year. Coolmore's promotion is successful in one way at least; it must be the only European stud farm whose name will be familiar to anyone who goes racing more than once or twice a year in Europe, and which is also widely recognized in the United States.

In the early 1980s the Coolmore partnership were extraordinarily successful on the racecourse, but the stud's record has been more ambiguous. Coolmore's major problem has been a lack of successful stallions, or least of one whose services are demanded inelastically in the long run. The only proven international stallion on the farm is Be My Guest, and because he was not initially fashionable the brilliant achievements of his first crop in 1981 and 1982 have been followed by three or four years of relative obscurity. The list of stallions who once stood at Coolmore but who proved to be commercial failures is, in comparison, long; Deep Diver, Gay Fandango, Green God, Home Guard, Mount Hagen, Rheingold, Thatch, Sun Prince, Red Alert, Saulingo, Arch Sculptor, Last Fandango, Crofter, Pas de Seul, and London Bells are among those horses whom the farm has promptly sold on. Indeed, Coolmore's only unambiguous success has been the champion jumping stallion Deep Run. The farm has also been afflicted with unavoidable natural problems, such as the early death of Golden Fleece and the severe difficulties with Try My Best's and El Gran Señor's fertility during their early years at stud. El Gran Señor was originally retired to the Windfields Farm at Maryland, but when he proved to be subfertile with only eighteen of the mares he covered in his first season conceiving, Windfields Farm sold its shares in the horse to its insurers and the horse was moved to the Ashford Stud.

In 1986 Coolmore faced a hiatus, for the farm's short-term policies were clearly not suited to the new commercial climate. The partners' response was considerably to reduce their stallions' nomination fees, and to buy the Breeders' Cup Mile winner Last Tycoon, their second major purchase in two years following the classic winner Commanche Run in 1985. The farm's stallions who are potentially the most lucrative propositions, like Sadler's Wells, Lomond, Law Society and Caerleon have yet to be represented on the racecourse, but the farm must be fearful that they, like Kings Lake, will suffer from the anachronistic nature of the policies pursued during their early years at stud. Kings Lake's commercial standing is in jeopardy as a result of the absence of any particularly successful racehorses, and the abundance of moderate ones, among his first few crops.

For Robert Sangster 1985 and 1986 cannot have been happy years, as far as his bloodstock interests were concerned. Besides the problem of bringing Coolmore into line with its competitors and the lack of successful racehorses in Vincent O'Brien's stable, his attempt to establish Michael Dickinson as his private trainer at Manton in England was a dismal failure. The cost of refurbishing the facilities at Manton were far higher than he had anticipated, and then Michael Dickinson failed to send out more than a handful of moderate winners.* He must long to convince the Arabs of the delights of the Australian summer, and racing at Melbourne and Sydney. Indeed there can be few people who took greater pleasure than Robert Sangster in watching Sheikh Hamdan Al Maktoum's colt At Talaq win the 1986 Melbourne Cup.

In contrast with Coolmore, the Airlie Stud has never tried to compete with the leading Kentucky stallion farms, but it has been consistently successful within the European market. The farm became prominent under the direction of Captain A. D. D. Rogers. Tim Rogers had a formidable reputation, though Kirsten Rausing says he used to enjoy shouting more for the sake of the relief it gave him than the fear it imparted to others. He secured Airlie's commercial future when he bought Habitat from Charles Englehard in 1969, for from 1975 until his death in 1987 Habitat was Europe's most successful sire of stakes winners, and in 1987 was still able to command a fee of 80,000 guineas. Following Captain Rogers' early death the management of Airlie was taken over by his widow Sonia Rogers, and in 1987 the farm was responsible for fourteen stallions, of whom two stood in England and three in New Zealand. By way of a comparison with Coolmore, in 1976 Airlie stood nine stallions, of whom Habitat and Tumble Wind were still there in 1987, and who also included Petingo, a commercial success until his early death. The Airlie farm has never had Coolmore's pretensions, but with the support of Habitat, who has been the perfect monopolist's stallion, the farm has maintained its standing throughout the years of the bloodstock boom.

Whereas Tim Rogers is often credited with having created a modern bloodstock industry in Ireland, in the United States stallions have long been seen as a commercial opportunity rather than a fortuitous bonanza. The centralized pattern of racing and breeding and the acceptance of the walking in system have enabled the large stallion farms in the United States to acquire a wealth and a prestige unrivalled by any other commercial organizations within the thoroughbred business. In the United States the farm on which a stallion stands is usually allotted four seasons a year, which means the farm is able to prosper

*In 1987, however, Robert Sangster's fortunes have revived to some degree. Barry Hills who took over the training of his horses at Manton, has been successful in Europe. Meanwhile his horses have continued to record important victories in Australia.

with the stallion's reputation even if it does not own shares in the horse as well. A farm with thirty or forty successful stallions will receive an enormous income from the sale of its one hundred and fifty seasons. The stallion market remains stronger and stallions' advertised fees remain higher in the United States than anywhere else in the world. Of the fifty-four stallions in England, Ireland and the United States whose advertised fee for the 1987 covering season was higher than £40,000, six were based in Ireland, five in England, two each in Florida and Maryland, one in Virginia and thirty-eight in Kentucky. These figures understate the relative prosperity of the American stallion business; there is an incentive to give an artificially low official figure for a stallion's fee as its owner must pay an equivalent sum in order to qualify the horse's offspring for the Breeders Cup races. Nonetheless, even based upon these figures, the leading stallion farms clearly have a vast turnover. In 1987 the Claiborne Farm stood thirty stallions, and its four seasons in only the ten most fashionable of these were worth about $6,500,000. The leading farms have no need for intermediaries to help them with the financial risks of syndication; instead they have actively competed with each other to buy the best racehorses and have then sold shares in them to their regular associates, and to each other by way of an insurance. For twenty years and more the best known names in the American thoroughbred business have been the Hancocks of Claiborne, the Taylors of Windfields and the Combs of Spendthrift.

At the beginning of the 1970s the American stallion market was dominated by these large established farms and John Gaines, Gainesway Farm, which was a relative newcomer. These farms would compete between themselves for the honour of syndicating the outstanding colts in both North America and Europe. But while the bloodstock boom increased their revenues, at the same time it placed their monopoly under threat. The large farms were able to defend their monopoly with the advantages conferred by their established size. In a market dominated by short-term expectations it is an advantage to be able to offer many products which are different, but obviously of the same type. This is the market strategy of the detergent giants who, when faced with new competititon, produce a whole range of new brands of soap themselves, in the hope of absorbing the market for novelty. Gainesway especially, and to some extent Spendthrift and Windfields as well, bought numerous top European racehorses to fill up their stallion barns. The idea was to sell both seasons and shares in these horses to American commercial breeders who aimed to sell their yearlings to the European-based buyers at the Keeneland and Saratoga yearling sales. John Gaines also bought some of Europe's most successful proven stallions like Lyphard, Riverman and Sharpen

Up, for he was able to make offers of a magnitude which no European shareholders could possibly afford to refuse. Claiborne has in contrast always concentrated on the domestic market, and the only European racehorses the farm has bought in recent years are Sir Ivor and Nijinsky. Although the farm may have bought predominantly horses whose reputation was made in races run on dirt, many of the offspring of its stallions are also in demand in Europe. Nevertheless, despite the boons of an international market, these farms were forced to take greater risks by the escalating costs of buying potential stallions and the volatility of the market, while at the same time their position was challenged by new competitors.

One challenge came from those private farms which succeeded in raising an excellent stallion themselves. One fashionable stallion was sufficient to transform a farm's commercial position, as was shown by Calumet and Alydar. The Calumet Farm had been in a state of genteel decline for years, but with the arrival of Alydar, whose seasons have traded for $400,000 or more each, the farm has become acquisitive, buying Affirmed, Mogambo and the English Derby winner Secreto to supplement its star. John Galbreath's Darby Dan Farm has also prospered during the boom years, having produced the English Derby winner and successful stallion Roberto and leading American winners like Proud Truth.

If a farm does not breed its own stallion it will have to buy one, and none is likely to be able to do so until it has accumulated reserves and a reputation, from commercial breeding. Johnny Jones' Walmac International, Robert Clay's Three Chimneys Farm and William Farish's Lanes End Farm all progressed towards becoming leading stallion farms in this way. Other prominent newcomers have been the Stone Farm, which is owned and run by Arthur B. Hancock III, the older brother of Seth Hancock who owns Claiborne, and the North Ridge Farm, which was set up by Franklin Groves who lured Michael Osborne from Ireland to run it for a while.

When the perspective of stallion management shifted from the short to the long run these smaller farms found themselves at an advantage. When there was excess demand in the stallion market size was an advantage, but when there is excess supply it is the small farm which is able carefully to manage and promote each of its stallions. A farm with forty stallions can only sell a type or a brand name, rather than personally approaching breeders to discuss the prospects of one stallion. In the words of one of the winners, factory farming thoroughbreds was no longer as popular as it had been.

The Spendthrift Farm has been one of the major casualties of the bloodstock boom. From the early 1980s it was clear that the farm was in serious financial difficulties. An attempt to go public in order to raise funds was disastrous; the farm found itself contesting seven law suits which alleged that there had been omissions and misrepresentations in the prospectus produced at the time of the abortive sale. The farm, which had been the leading consignor to Keeneland's Select July Sale for the years from 1949 to 1964, was forced to sell all its stock at a dispersal sale, and some of the farm's more fashionable stallions were removed from Spendthrift by their shareholders to stand at other less troubled farms.

Spendthrift was not the only major farm which had difficulty adapting to the new commercial climate, for when Charles Taylor took over the presidency of Windfields Farm it was clear that it too was struggling to maintain its position in the market. In 1987 Northern Dancer was twenty-six* and approaching the end of his life, and when he dies The Minstrel will be Windfields' only proven international stallion. The farm washed its hands of El Gran Señor and was forced to sell Halo, so its hope for the future is probably the Canadian champion Deputy Minister. Gainesway and Claiborne continue to control some of the world's most fashionable stallions, but by the mid 1980s neither was as aggressive commercially as it had been in the 1970s. Claiborne has profited from the success of its private clients, in particular Henryk de Kwiatkowski, who achieved the extraordinary feat of breeding Danzig and Conquistador Cielo, two of the world's most fashionable young stallions, in the space of three years. In fact Claiborne is in a better position to adapt than the other large American stallion farms, as its young stallions are supported by the private breeders who board their mares on the farm. Even so some of Claiborne's most famous horses like Damascus, Forli, Nijinsky and Sir Ivor are approaching the end of their lives. The change in the structure of the American stallion market was clearly demonstrated in 1986 when none of the large farms were even part of the contest to purchase the year's leading three-year-olds, Dancing Brave, Shahrastani, Bering and Manilla.

Robert Clay was one farm owner who perceived the new trend in the stallion market. In 1983 he decided to expand his commercial farm and purchase six potentially high class stallions. His idea was that with only six stallions he would be able to manage them closely and solicit the best available mares for them. The first colt which interested him was Slew O'Gold, a son of Seattle Slew and owned as he had been by Mickey Taylor and Jim Hill. After he had watched Slew O'Gold finish fourth in the Kentucky Derby Robert Clay telephoned them to say he

* In the spring of 1987 he was retired from covering duties.

was interested in syndicating the colt, only to be told it had already been arranged for Slew O'Gold to retire to a farm in New York. Clay heard nothing more until September the same year when he received a telephone call from Jim Hill while he was on holiday in Marbella. In 1983 there was still an excess demand for stallions and those who owned potential ones were able to name their own price in the knowledge that the farm they were dealing with would rather accept than risk being outbid by a competitor. Hill told Clay he wanted to sell a quarter of Slew O'Gold for $4,000,000. The same night Clay made a few discreet telephone calls and once he had received some provisional acceptances he got in touch with Jim Hill again and the deal went ahead. In fact fourteen shares, or 35 per cent of the horse, were sold for $400,000 each.

When Robert Clay returned to the United States he was told by John Gaines that he was a brave man to syndicate a horse with only one testicle for such a sum. However, Robert Clay had secured a bargain for as a four-year-old Slew O'Gold was a champion, meeting his only defeat when finishing a most unlucky third in the first Breeders Cup Classic. The colt retired to stud with total lifetime earnings of $3\frac{1}{2}$ million and a further eighteen shares in him were sold for $465,000 each. In his first season at stud Slew O'Gold put paid to any doubts about his virility by getting all fifty-four of the mares he covered in foal.

As a result of the success of the Slew O'Gold syndicate Robert Clay's career as a stallion broker blossomed. One of the syndicate's members introduced him to the owner of Chiefs Crown and he sold twenty shares in the colt shortly before it won the first Breeders Cup Juvenile. When he sold another ten shares in Chiefs Crown a year later the colt's achievements on the racetrack had been sufficient to push up the asking price from $500,000 to $750,000. The happy course of events continued, for the proven stallion Nodouble was lured from Florida and Mickey Taylor and Jim Hill decided that Seattle Slew would be better off at Three Chimneys as well, rather than remaining at Spendthrift. Leslie Combs fought hard to retain his farm's most valuable asset, but after an acrimonious campaign the owners of 33 of the 40 shares in Seattle Slew voted in favour of the move. In 1986 Robert Clay syndicated yet another leading racehorse after defeating William Farish in the contest for the Aga Khan's Derby winner Shahrastani. Clay had first approached the colt's trainer Michael Stoute after watching it win a race at York in May, and he finally completed the deal after the colt had defeated Dancing Brave in the Derby. At the time William Farish must have been very disappointed, yet by the end of the year Manilla, the colt he had bought instead, had gained an equally exalted reputation by defeating Theatrical, Estrapade and Dancing Brave in the Breeders Cup Turf.

Clearly the activities of a stallion broker and commercial breeder like Robert Clay are far removed from those of his English-based counterparts like Bernice Cuthbert and Kirsten Rausing. He receives six seasons to each of Three Chimney's stallions every year, for he owns two shares in each of them which supplement the four seasons he and his wife receive as the farm's owners. In 1987 these thirty seasons were worth about $3\frac{1}{2}$ million. His own role within the organization is now solely to select and attract stallions and deal with their share-holders. To do this he will travel to the major racemeetings in Europe and the United States to maintain his contacts and view the aspiring candidates. The farm is managed by Dan Rosenburg who, when he arrived, announced his intention of touching the horses, however as general manager he too rarely has time for such soothing activities. The farm's policy with its stallions is to forbid any shareholder to sell at Matchmaker's auctions and to accept only the more successful private breeders as shareholders. Robert Clay has complete control of the stallion's seasons and shares during its first five years at stud and his only objective is to lure the best broodmares to Three Chimneys. When a stallion is established and the demand for the small number of its seasons which come on the market is appropriately inelastic, then the farm and the horse's shareholders will enjoy their monopoly profits.

The most extraordinary thing about Three Chimneys is its youth. Robert Clay was just forty when he syndicated his first Derby winner and yet he had no experience or knowledge of racing or breeding at all until he wrote a thesis about the business of his native state while at college. There is a sense in which it is possible to gauge the character of a Kentucky farm from the atmosphere of its offices. For instance at Gainesway the visitor is greeted by two pretty girls sitting behind shiny wooden kiosks, who discuss privately the problems posed by the moral conservatism of Kentucky's landladies while resting their telephones on their shoulders. At Three Chimneys, on the other hand, the visitor is received in a well renovated house with stained broad beams, wide, open stone fireplaces and wooden floors. One is asked in a manner which has been perfected by the English National Trust to sign the visitor's book and wait on an elegantly uncomfortable wooden bench, before being led through a panelled room which dates from the eighteenth century to see Mr Clay. Robert Clay sits in an armchair in a "polo" shirt with his hands held together in front of him, and talks of his success with a carefully timed polite enthusiasm. On the mantelpiece behind him stands the most prized symbol of all Kentucky farms, the Christmas card from Her Majesty Queen Elizabeth II.

The office at Walmac International has a different feel, but in his own way Johnny Jones displays the power an American stallion dealer has even in a shrinking market. The office itself has a large enough desk and is lined with bookshelves, but in the adjoining antechamber the piles of papers, sales catalogues and brochures spill onto the floor and the secretaries maintain a sophisticated, disaffected air. While chewing on cigars, spitting into the waste paper basket and yelling defensively at his administrative assistant and the keeper of his stallion records, Johnny Jones syndicates the farm's latest acquisition, the French Derby winner Bering. He picks up the telephone and calls the first names which come to mind; Charles Taylor, Robert Sangster, Lester Piggott... "I'm no soothsayer but I kind of think he'll win the Arc ... that man Head knows how to win them." A pause and then he reels off the conditions, "$350,000 a share, 40,000 on signature, 70,000 on December 1st and the remainder in yearly instalments, Head keeps twenty shares, pays for the horse's importation and insures it against infertility." As a break between calls he rang a man in California and bought a couple of yearlings.

The shares in Bering were all sold within a week, and although he did not win the Arc he finished second to Dancing Brave in a race which was not run to suit him and in which he sustained an injury. Alec Head, who together with le comte Roland de Chambure is a partner in Walmac International, is one of Europe's most successful stallion dealers. Bering was bred by Alec Head, owned by his wife and trained by his daughter, but was the first of his horses to retire directly to an American stallion farm. Before 1986 Alec Head and Roland de Chambure had specialized in establishing stallions at their own studs, the Haras de Quesnay and the Haras d'Etreham, before selling them for export as proven stallions. Among the stallions they have sold are Lyphard, Riverman and Green Dancer.

Johnny Jones believes the essence of stallion management is to be flexible. If there is a good mare who needs to be covered in June, then there will always be a season available to a Walmac stallion. He is particularly dismissive of Matchmaker and the auctions of seasons and shares, saying they sell too few of each to have more than a marginal influence. He personally sells the majority of the shares and seasons of Walmac stallions which come on the market. Robert Clay, though clearly no admirer or supporter of Matchmaker, would disagree. He feels Matchmaker has an important influence on the American stallion market, despite the small number of tradings they organize. Matchmaker does, Robert Clay feels, act as a stock exchange in that it reflects trends and sets prices. Both men feel Matchmaker worthy of comment and the company has clearly influenced the market, if only by raising possibilities rather than realizing them. However, before examining Matchmaker, and as an antidote to these accounts of financial fixity, it will be interesting to tell the tale of Brian Sweeney and Erin's Isle. Brian Sweeney is one man who was moved by sentiment rather than greed or financial prudence to buy a potential stallion.

Brian Sweeney was working at Phoenix Park in Ireland for the O'Brien, Magnier conglomerate when he first saw Erin's Isle. Once he had watched the colt win the Ballymoss Stakes with Kings Lake and Critique trailing behind he decided he had to own the colt. The decisive factor was the unusually fast time in which the horse covered the final two furlongs of the ten furlong race. From that day onwards Brian Sweeney trailed Mr McCaffrey, who owned Erin's Isle. He went to watch the colt's every race, and on each occasion he made Mr McCaffrey another still higher offer, but each one was refused. When Erin's Isle came second in the Irish St Leger on his final start as a three-year-old the horse was still owned by Mr McCaffrey. That winter Brian Sweeney finally ran his man to ground in Australia and persuaded him to part with Erin's Isle. The price? Well it was so ridiculously high he was too embarrassed to admit the enormity of his folly to anyone. At the same time he had become disillusioned with the management at Phoenix Park, so Brian Sweeney collected Erin's Isle and took the horse with him to California.

Once in California the colt was entrusted to Charlie Whittingham and proceeded to show over the next two years that Brian Sweeney was no fool, for he won five Grade 1 races including the Hollywood Invitational and the San Juan Capistrano and $1,222,190 in purses. When Erin's Isle was retired to stud Brian Sweeney's affection for him was in no way diminished. Whenever he is in Kentucky he goes to visit the horse at the Greentree Stud and points out its kind head and big ears to any other visitors, and tells them how his little daughters used to ride the colt. As the farm's manager Perry Alexander says, if anyone loved a horse it is Sweeney and Erin's Isle. Unfortunately Erin's Isle is not a fashionable stallion, for he is bred to be a classical European stayer, and in fact he is just the type of horse whose commercial prospects could be ruined by stallion season and share auctions

The idea of auctions of stallion seasons and shares will not catch on in England in the foreseeable future because of the implacable opposition of the three stallion men, James Wigan, Rhydian Morgan-Jones and Simon Morley. Bloodstock agents in the United States probably object to the auctions just as strongly, but their opposition is of no importance, as they have no role to play in the syndication and management of stallions. Some stallion farm owners object to

Matchmaker's auctions, but those who have formed syndicates since 1983 have been able to prevent their shareholers recoursing to Matchmaker, and in any event no large successful farm will be seriously compromised by the company's activities. The difference being that no three men, not even Seth Hancock, John Gaines and Charles Taylor, have the proportionate influence on the American market of England's three stallion men. Without the compliance of their sixty-four syndicates and of the Arabs' agents, whose opposition is equally fierce, a Matchmaker sale in England is an impossibility.

Matchmaker's style is also peculiarly American. From the time of its conception in 1983 the Matchmaker Group has gone out of its way to attack and ridicule the received ideas and conventions of the thoroughbred business. As the company's president Barry Weisbord is fond of saying, Matchmaker only exists as a result of the incompetence which proceeded it: "If farm managers had been doing their stuff there would have been no Matchmaker." The company enjoys irritating the conventional on a more trivial level as well. When they held their first July sale, they commissioned the pop artist Peter Max to paint some garish red, green and yellow representations of a horse which were called Northern Dancer. When Charles Taylor was confronted with the pictures as he came up the escalator at the Radisson Plaza he began to froth at the mouth. While he yelled obscenities the hotel's security staff gathered nervously underneath the painting, for Charles Taylor is not a small man. However, the custodian of Northern Dancer's image was persuaded to leave rather than attack, which he did vowing never to return to a Matchmaker function.

The same auction was intended to cause other frictions, as it took place on the same night as the cocktail party the Keeneland Association traditionally give on the eve of their July sale. Keeneland's cocktail party is in its way a charmingly nostalgic occasion at which elderly couples dance to a sedate jazz band under a brocaded marquee. As the crowds began to file into the Radisson in downtown Lexington the company's directors were rejoicing in having wiped out that party in a tent. Matchmaker's auctions are carefully sumptious affairs, indeed they cost around $250,000 to put on. The Group's members and their guests are invited to arrive an hour before the auction begins in order to drink and begin their dinner before it is interrupted by the screams of some of the more flamboyant bid spotters. When the majority are seated and merry, and with around fourteen hundred people this takes some time, the sale itself begins. The auction is conducted in the same way as any American horse auction, with the spotters sporting tuxedos gesticulating between the tables. The company's officers, also in tuxedos, rush about carrying pieces of paper looking alternately anxious and exceedingly important. As a social occasion the auctions are inconclusive, but as commercial show business they are undoubtedly a success. The company holds three auctions annually and in the year ending in July 1986 236 seasons and 136 shares were sold at them for a total of $53 million.

Matchmaker exists because of the energy and determination of its president, Barry Weisbord. He combines charm and a quick wit with the ability smilingly to ignore the hostility his company arouses. He is impatient, restless, and never seems to be happy when sitting down— a rare occurrence, for he appears to work and travel continuously. For Barry Weisbord nothing is ever concluded, it is simply left until he sees a possible use or improvement; he tends to say upon parting, "Well ... Tomorrow's another day." Barry Weisbord dropped out of university in order to work on the racetrack. His father, Norman Weisbord, who was at the time enraged, is now a director of Matchmaker and follows in Barry's wake gazing at him adoringly. For a time Barry Weisbord worked as a hots walker, which means he walked horses while they cooled off after being exercised. He was apparently a "real good hots walker", the only one who could walk efficiently and read a novel at the same time. After a brief spell as a trainer he set up Executive Bloodstock Management Corporation in order to deal for himself and for his clients in all forms of bloodstock and anything connected with them.

His first major coup was with a broodmare called Veruschka, whom he bought cheaply and sold after one of her early offspring had won twenty-two races and over a million dollars in purses. He then began to deal in stallion shares, making a killing on Halo and Alleged, in whom he is now the largest shareholder, and losing some of his winnings on Monteverdi. Barry Weisbord is a natural dealer who delights in playing with margins and gambling. However, even his ebullience is not perpetual, for before the first July sale he was worried, quiet and fearful that, as everyone had told him, it would prove impossible to sell seasons without any guarantee a full seven months before the breeding season began. Afterwards he was his usual bullish self, claiming they had set values which would encourage trading on the exchange all through the summer.

All the seasons which Matchmaker trade are sold without any guarantee whatsoever. If the stallion to whom you have purchased a breeding right dies, or fails to get your mare in foal, you have simply wasted your money. Traditionally stallion seasons are sold on the basis of a split fee, half due before the mare is covered and the remainder some five months later, but only if the mare is believed to have conceived. Matchmaker feel it should be the mare's owner who takes the financial risk of infertility. The company's other precepts are to facilitate transactions by charging low commissions and by attracting many more potential buyers for each share and season than any individual agent could possibly contact. The company firmly believes a competitive market will allocate mares to a stallion more efficiently than any other system of selection or choice. The essential maxim is that a man who pays $400,000 for a season to Alydar is not going to gamble his money on an indifferent mare.

To put these ideas into practice Matchmaker held their first private auction in November 1983. In order to avoid the supervision of the securities commission, and to circumvent the restrictions in stallion syndication agreements which prohibit the sale of seasons and shares at public auctions, Matchmaker Marketing and the Matchmaker Breeders Exchange will only deal with the Group's members. In 1986 there were about 700 horsemen from the United States, England, Ireland, France, Canada and Australia who were prepared to pay $400 a year for the privilege. The success of Matchmaker Marketing led to the setting up of the Matchmaker Breeders Exchange which organizes on its computers two bid markets and one ask market each week. On the bid markets, those who wish to buy list the seasons and shares they are interested in and the prices they are prepared to pay. On the ask market the sellers list the seasons and shares they wish to sell and the prices they will accept. Buyers and sellers alike have two days to accept an offer, and draws are held in the case of multiple acceptances. In the year ending in July 1986 the Group's members traded 449 seasons and 136 shares for a total of £22 million on the exchange.

Matchmaker's failing is the company's apparent inability to appreciate the horse as an animal, rather than as a financial opportunity. The clearest instance of this is their determination to sell seasons without guarantees, for although this may well be eminently sensible from the businessman's point of view, it only acts as an incentive to abuse the stallion itself. The pathetic spectacle of Nijinsky at the end of his life should serve as a warning, for those who have gambled many thousands of dollars on the prospect of a future covering are not going to throw away their money on account of some minor ailment or physical incapacity. If there is any possibility of the horse covering a mare it will be made to do the deed.

In the main Matchmaker appeals to the naive short-term commercial breeder who is not interested in, or who is unaware of, the individual mental and physical characteristics of his mare and her prospective mate, for he is dealing only in symbols, prestige and "black type". Matchmaker wishes to treat stallion shares and seasons as stocks or securities, without pausing to consider the fundamental differences between financial assets and horses.

When someone decides to buy a computer they are not in any way influenced or interested in the fluctuations of the value of shares of computer manufacturers; but when a commercial breeder buys a season or a share in a stallion, its price, and whether it happens to be on an upward or downward trend, is the single most important determinant. The demand for the products which a stallion's owner sells is inexorably linked with the stallion's value and commercial standing. For this reason an exchange like Matchmaker's can completely ruin a stallion's commercial prospects. If, for example, shares and seasons in a stallion like Erin's Isle are traded on the exchange and their value is publicly revealed to be falling (any fact which is known by 700 horsemen will soon become common knowledge in the bloodstock world), then the horse's prestige and the demand for its services can evaporate within a few months, without any of the horse's progeny having performed poorly at an auction or on the racetrack. This has not happened to Erin's Isle, but it certainly did happen to the Windfields stallion Assert in 1986.

Matchmaker seeks to destroy the monopoly which a stallion's owners have over its seasons and shares and to deprive them of the opportunity to manage their values during the horse's early years at stud. Without these monopoly rights, however, it is impossible to establish any but the most obviously fashionable stallions, and in a system dominated by Matchmaker unlikely horses like Niniski and Ahonoora would never have achieved their status as stars. Matchmaker reduces the long term demand for such stallions' shares, for it ensures that if they turn out to be successful those who did not buy the original shares will be able to buy into them later when the risks are smaller. Matchmaker is founded upon a belief in the myth of the stallion and the efficacy of categorizing potential stallions on the basis of the whims of the bloodstock market.

Matchmaker has however had many positive effects as well as the deleterious one of making the stallion market even more fickle and divorced from the reality of practical breeding. By attacking those with a vested interest in maintaining a monopoly based upon personal contacts, it has attracted new investors to the business and forced those established within it to be more receptive to outsiders. Indeed the Matchmaker Group's activities are characterized by a paradoxical mixture of innovation and naivety. The Group has been perceptive in its wish to encourage newcomers and to regulate bloodstock auctions in a manner which would protect them from unnecessarily sharp behaviour, yet it has been short-sighted in inadvertently encouraging petty short-term abuses of the horse. The bloodstock market's retraction and the withdrawal of many short-term commercial breeders from the business will reduce Matchmaker's turnover, but it will continue to attract those successful commercial and private breeders who wish to gain access to fashionable stallions in whom they do not own a share. Eventually Matchmaker will probably decide not to trade seasons and shares in stallions until they have been at stud for five years and have been represented on the racetrack. A competitive market in the seasons and shares of established stallions will have few negative affects and by facilitating transactions will reward those who have invested in successful stallions and afford access to them for newcomers and those who declined the invitation at the time of their initial syndication. In any event Matchmaker itself continues to expand and the company intends to diversify further by participating in bloodstock advertising, insurance and transport, all of which are fields which could only benefit from a dose of brash innovation.

The bloodstock boom coincided with the entry into the thoroughbred business of the Arab owners and it is they and the successful private breeders who will shape the stallion market during the late 1980s. By the mid 1980s it was clear to all that the world's leading investors in bloodstock were Sheikh Maktoum Al Maktoum, Sheikh Hamdan Al Maktoum, Sheikh Mohammed bin Rashid Al Maktoum and Prince Khalid Abdullah. These four men are not the maniacal spendthrifts they have sometimes been portrayed as, for they wish their bloodstock operations to become self-financing; they have both the patience and the resources to plan for the long term. The only possible means by which an operation with a hundred broodmares and a hundred and fifty or more horses in training can begin to be self-financing is by producing or selecting, and marketing, stallions. After five years or more experience in the business these four men and their advisers came to realize their opportunity lay in creating a long term monopoly with a few elite stallions, rather than in seeking to emulate the short term policies of the Sangster, O'Brien and Magnier group.

The first indications of their new approach came in 1986 when Prince Kahlid Abdullah's Rainbow Quest and Sheikh Maktoum Al Maktoum's Shadeed retired to stud. These were both excellent racehorses, even if they fell short of being absolute cracks, and both boasted extremely fashionable pedigrees. In other hands they would both have been the subject of multi-million dollar syndications and would have started covering with a stud fee of around £100,000. Instead neither horse was syndicated and both began their stud careers with remarkably low fees, £25,000 for Rainbow Quest and $50,000 for Shadeed, who was temporarily boarded at Robert Clay's Three Chimneys Farm while Sheikh Maktoum Al Maktoum's Gainsborough Farm near Versailles, Kentucky, was completed. As a result both stallions were heavily oversubscribed and their owners' agents were able to select only the very best broodmares. In Shadeed's case forty-six were selected from the two hundred who applied, while one hundred and thirty mares were turned away from Rainbow Quest. The idea was to give the stallion every opportunity to succeed in the expectation of receiving a reward later by rationing the supply of seasons to a popular proven stallion.

The next example was Dancing Brave, who from the July of his three-year-old career was owned jointly by Prince Khalid Abdullah and Sheikh Mohammed. Sixteen shares in the horse were sold shortly before he was due to contest the Prix de l'Arc de Triomphe. A stallion who is not syndicated at all is difficult to manage, since there are no outside breeders who will gain by its success and by its third or fourth year at stud it may well prove difficult to sell twenty or thirty seasons a year to the horse each year, and even if its owner has one or two hundred mares he is unlikely to want to have more than twenty of them covered by the same stallion. The solution was to sell a limited number of shares to selected breeders who were known to possess outstanding broodmares. There are a few private breeders who possess such outstanding broodmares and whose proven record for raising excellent racehorses is remarkable enough for any stallion syndicate to welcome their support. In Europe the obvious names are the Aga Khan, Eric Moller, Daniel Wildenstein and Alec Head, while in the United States they are Paul Mellon, Henryk de Kwiatkowski and the Greentree and Darby Dan farms. When Dancing Brave was syndicated the intention was to attract as many of these farms as possible, together with a few leading commercial farms, all of whom would be sure to support the horse with some of their best mares during his first five years at stud. In addition the stallion's managers will be prepared to come to a satisfactory agreement with anyone who owns a particularly special broodmare.

The aim is for the horse to cover an outstanding collection of mares and for it only to be necessary to sell a few seasons each year. Even in the short run these seasons will be rare enough to be extremely valuable and for the demand for them to be relatively inelastic. In the case of the commercial prospects for a horse like Dancing Brave the trends and valuations of the yearling market are almost irrelevant, for there are enough private breeders willing to pay extravagant sums for his seasons and shares simply to avoid being left out. Nevertheless the chances are that when the first Dancing Brave yearlings appear at yearling auctions in 1989 the horse's managers will feel duty bound to bid for them, just to encourage commercial breeders to buy the few seasons which they will have to sell before Dancing Brave's offspring perform on the racecourse.

Since 1985 Sheikh Mohammed has clearly followed a commercial policy with his bloodstock. Eight years after he had won his first pattern race Sheikh Mohammed instituted obvious changes in his management policies. Anthony Stroud was given responsibility for selecting yearlings and planning his horses' racing careers, while Robert Acton manages the stallions and the breeding programme. As a result the selection of Sheikh Mohammed's yearlings is more rigorous, and he has fewer trainers, who are, without exception, among the best in their particular country. An increasing proportion of his horses are trained outside England, for it makes no sense for them to compete against each other, and Sheikh Mohammed now has trainers in Ireland, France, Italy and on the East and West coasts of the United States. His horses are sent to race where they are most likely to win important races, and if they are not likely to they are sold, many of them as three-year-olds.

When it comes to stallions Sheikh Mohammed's policy differs from his brothers', for both Sheikh Maktoum and Sheikh Hamdan now own farms in Kentucky, whereas his stallions stand in England, Ireland or France. The elite stallions, who in 1987 were Shareef Dancer and Top Ville in addition to Dancing Brave, stand under the management of Alec Notman at the Dalham Hall Stud in Newmarket, which is the central office of Sheikh Mohammed's bloodstock operations and where he has built himself a Newmarket residence. The elite stallions are managed by the dictates of what can be called the Dancing Brave policy of selling a carefully controlled supply of very expensive seasons and shares. The first division stallions are sent to the Kildangan Stud in County Kildare, Ireland, which is managed by Michael Osborne. They are more broadly syndicated, but the idea is to pursue a similar policy on a lower plane. The first of Sheikh Mohammed's stallions to go to Kildangan was Sure Blade, who was also one of the first stallions to be syndicated publicly with advertisements inviting applications being placed in the sporting press. The remainder of Sheikh Mohammed's stallions, of whom some are syndicated and some are not, are spread throughout England, Ireland and France on other people's stallion farms, where their services are sold relatively cheaply. The idea is to give them a chance to prove themselves, so that those who succeed can be promoted to Dalham Hall or Kildangan. The whole is a carefully orchestrated development plan on an enormous scale, clearly planned to come to fruition in ten or fifteen years time.

Prince Khalid Abdullah's plans may well be similar, but they are more obscure and any statements of policy are given with a deliberate guarded ambiguity. One feels that the Prince and his advisers are still smarting from the sudden split with James Delahooke in 1985, and as a result they are only interested in withstanding any attempts to intrude upon their privacy. Indeed, when they are asked direct questions Prince Khalid Abdullah's advisers only commit themselves to contradictions, so strenuous are their attempts at equivocation. If one of Sheikh Mohammed's employees is asked a question he would rather not answer he will reply smilingly with polite blandness; in the same circumstances Prince Khalid Abdullah's advisers tend to be rude and offhand and to treat their interlocuter as an intruder.

According to his advisers Prince Khalid Abdullah does not buy yearlings from the top of the American market because his bloodstock operation is not, like Robert Sangster's, a commercial one. On the other hand it is his intention to make money from his bloodstock activities. Prince Khalid Abdullah has no wish for his bloodstock activities to be compared with anyone else's, nor has he ever shown the slightest interest in becoming the leading owner or breeder in Britain, France or anywhere else. However Prince Khalid Abdullah's assistants are clearly proud of the fact that none of the Maktoum brothers have had horses as talented as Alphabatim and Hatim in training in the United States. Another oddity of the organization is the way the advertisements for its stallions never mention the horses they defeated on the racecourse, or even display a photograph of one horse competing with and defeating another. This desire to be seen as uncompetitive while so prominently engaging in such a competitive sport is difficult to fathom.

James Delahooke's successor as Prince Khalid Abdullah's racing manager was Tony Chapman, who had formerly been the Prince's solicitor and a private breeder on a small scale himself. His assistant, or supervisor, is Grant Pritchard-Gordon and together they receive visitors sitting in black leather chairs about a round table on the top floor of a house in Belgravia. Grant Pritchard-Gordon opens the proceedings by saying that as Tony Chapman has not been with them for very long he will probably not be able to help very much, and then whenever Tony Chapman shows signs of being helpful he intervenes and cuts him short. When the visitor is led away by the most authoritative of secretaries he is comforted to some degree by a wan smile from Tony Chapman. They can be seen together on racecourses and at bloodstock auctions, the one tall and almost dignified, the other wearing dark glasses, and they both often appear to be rather harassed. They are prepared to confirm that in 1986 Prince Khalid Abdullah had 120 horses in training in England, 70 in France and 30 in the

United States. In the future the Prince intends to rely upon those horses he breeds himself on the Juddmonte Farms in Berkshire, County Meath and Kentucky, for he believes the manner in which a thoroughbred is reared is an important influence upon its racing ability. In this field he admires the methods of Nelson Bunker Hunt and the Hancock brothers, and in general he has the greatest respect and admiration for the breeding operations of Daniel Wildenstein and the Aga Khan.

The beliefs and practices of men like Sheikh Mohammed and Prince Khalid Abdullah only reflect the general feeling and opinions of those within the thoroughbred business. Thankfully the era of the stallion and of the obsession with short-term commercial ends is over. There can be few people who wholeheartedly believe in the myth of the stallion any more, indeed in the next phase of development it seems the emphasis will be placed instead upon the role of the broodmare and of stud management. Decisions will be made not upon the prognostications of the pedigree expert and the stallion seer, but as a result of investigations into the horse's ecology and studies of its mental and physical characteristics. It is difficult to imagine a reason for not applauding such a trend. The stallion market itself seems likely to continue to be characterized by excess supply, if not saturation, although as long as there are thoroughbred breeders there will be a strong demand for the champion racehorse and the champion stallion.

═══ Nine ═══
Marketing and Sponsorship

The distaste engendered by some of the excesses of the boom years should not be allowed to obscure its positive effects and the manner in which it has transformed the thoroughbred business. The years of plenty ensured that the bloodstock business acquired a financial and marketing sophistication which it had previously lacked. The rewards of enterprising behaviour became sufficient to attract entrepreneurs. Although it is true that to some extent the Arab involvement in British racing is due to the personal contacts made by men like Colonel Warden and Tim Bulmer Long, such far-sighted behaviour was rare. The general feeling was that there would always be some foreign millionaire who wanted to waste money on racehorses. One wonders, for instance, how many British and American bloodstock agents are learning to speak Japanese and to court Asian millionaires.

The absence of a felt need to market the business was in part due to the difficulty racing people find in understanding that many outsiders find horseracing very dull. The need to explain the attraction of horseracing to outsiders is often not recognized by those for whom horses and racing have been a natural and lifelong obsession. The increased rewards for success in the bloodstock business attracted participants who would formerly have viewed racing as a hobby or pastime. As a result the business has become more competitive and more aggressive in its approach to outsiders. Men like Ron Muddle, Lord Porchester and John Sanderson, the managers of Lingfield Park, Newbury and York racecourses respectively, have highlighted the potential gains of management sophistication, and Michael Smurfitt, the Chairman of the Racing Board of Ireland, has set about transforming Irish racing. The most magnificent example of marketing in the thoroughbred business, however, is undoubtedly the Breeders' Cup, which was formulated as a response to a peculiarly American situation.

Sponsorship has only played a marginal role in American racing because both bookmakers and off course betting were banned fifty years ago. During the 1930s many States found themselves short of revenue and so looking to a gambling monopoly to ease the problem, instituted the Pari-Mutuel system. In most cases the profit from legal betting is divided between the racetrack and the State administration. The State's sole interest in racing is to maximize the amount of money wagered on the racetrack, or the handle as it is known. The racetrack's objectives are much the same for their income is derived mainly from their share of the daily handle. For example in New York 17 per cent is deducted from the handle and split between the interested bodies, the remainder being returned to the public as winning bets.

The consequences of this system were, first, to make the cost of admission to American racetracks very small, in order to encourage as many people as possible to come to the racetrack and gamble. Racetracks invested their revenue in purse money, rather than in improvements in their facilities; it was felt that as long as there was open and competitive racing people would come and gamble. Race-tracks only have an incentive to provide more than viewing and betting facilities if they are seeking to compete with other leisure activities, rather than other gambling opportunities. The traditional racetrack was designed exclusively for those with an interest in horses or betting, or both. On the other hand the racetrack which is trying to attract sponsorship and to entertain people other than dedicated racing fans is likely to be clean and comfortable as well.

Another consequence of this legalized monopoly was a frantic increase in the number of races run. Across the country racetracks put on more days racing and more races on each day. In New York the season which used to run from April 1st to November 1st became perennial, with the sole exception of Tuesdays, and there are now eight or nine events on each day's card. The more races there are, the more people will bet and the more revenue there will be for the racetrack and the State government. If the administration looks upon racing as a numbers game, then it is not surprising the audience eventually come to see it in the same light. Any system of organizing horseracing which encourages the racetracks, or in a more centralized industry like Britain's the administration as a whole, to have as its objective the maximization of betting turnover is certain to decline in the long run. A more short-sighted approach is hard to imagine, for if it is only possible to make racing profitable by marketing it as a lottery then the whole industry is an absurdity. If racing's only attraction to outsiders is as a gambling medium, then rather than investing time and money in raising horses it would be more sensible to run an electronic lottery instead.

The number of racing fans will steadily decline unless new and younger adherents are continually attracted to the sport. There are now numerous other gambling mediums which offer similar possibilities of financial gain, without requiring the same amount of effort and knowledge. So unless racing is marketed as a spectacle and an entertainment its popular support will gradually disappear. This is what has happened in the United States; whereas Belmont Park could once attract crowds of 80,000, by the mid 1980s 40,000 was an exceptional attendance figure. The American racetracks made the disastrous decision to discourage television coverage as they feared it would encourage illegal off-course betting. The result was that millions of potential racegoers who watched sport on television had no idea whatsoever of the spectacle and atmosphere of a racetrack. Other sports gained widespread media coverage and a national following, their stars became national figures whilst names like Shoemaker, Whittingham and Stephens were unknown except to convinced racing fans.

In Britain racing only avoided the same fate because of the incompetence and hesitation of those who believed in a state run gambling monopoly when they had a real chance of implementing their dream in the early 1960s. The bookmakers with their need to be constantly producing betting innovations ensure that horseracing remains unsurpassed as a popular gambling medium. In England every town and many villages have their own betting shops, and this, together with extensive television coverage, ensures that every national newspaper prints each day's card in full. As 75 per cent of the British population read a national newspaper every day and as many as 100,000 read one of racing's specialist daily newspapers, it is not surprising that racing's stars are among the best known men and women in the country. The presence of a top horse or a top jockey at a small country racecourse will double or treble the attendance, something that until recently would not have happened in the United States. British racing has many problems and is beset by many other administrative follies, but it is safe to say that things would have been disastrously worse if a betting monopoly had been legally instituted.

Any statements of decline in American racing are of course generalizations. Some racetracks and States adapted to the new economic conditions more readily than others. Santa Anita, and Californian racetracks as a whole, have a reputation for "hugging the customer", the owner, and the young newcomer. However a report* on the racing industry in the United States published in 1986 concluded that racetracks would have to improve their general cleanliness, seating facilities, food services and parking arrangements if they are to attract new customers. The report, based upon interviews with 949 persons who lived near a racetrack, also found that among the various possible reasons cited for deciding to attend a racemeeting the quality of the horses on display came well down the list. This is not surprising in the American context, for the sport has been managed as if it were a lottery for fifty years and as a result a large proportion of its audience look upon racing only as a socialized gamble. In addition to the wider sample, sixty persons who were currently working in the media were asked for their views on the sport. It was found that they were even less aware than the general public both of racing's attractions and of the actual size of its public following. The original decision to discourage television coverage has clearly continued to harm the racing industry ever since, for not only have many potential fans never been exposed to the spectacle of horseracing, but there now seems to be a bias against racing within the media itself.

The report highlighted the distinctive features of the peculiar situation of the American racing industry at the beginning of the 1980s. The bloodstock side of the industry was reaching the end of an unparalleled period of expansion. There were more horses and more owners than ever before and although many of those within the business realized bloodstock values were sure to level off eventually, few were prepared to believe in any predictions of an impending crash. The bloodstock business appeared likely to continue to prosper as long as the benign stance of the taxation laws was maintained, and as long as there was an international demand for bloodstock. At the same time the entertainment side of the industry appeared to be a in state of steady decline, a decline which was manifested both in racetrack attendances and the betting turnover. The Breeders Cup was conceived as a response to this state of affairs.

Astute American breeders realized the boom would not last for ever, and that their business relied upon racing remaining a popular entertainment. There was much soul searching and nostalgia, and even some new ideas. In New York there was an experiment with off-course betting, and new multiple bets were devised which offered the possibility of fantastic winning odds, and which encouraged the participation of gangsters and sundry race fixers. Racetracks with less innovative flair gave away T-shirts and other souvenirs to anyone who

*The report was commissioned by the American Jockey Club and carried out by R. H. Bruskin Associates, a market research firm.

turned up ready to gamble. John Gaines, the owner of Lexington's Gainesway Farm, came up with an altogether more imaginative idea. Indeed when it was first proposed in 1982 most of those in the business dismissed the Breeders Cup as being purely fanciful. The idea was for the bloodstock business to invest some of the abnormal profits which its members were making at the time, in marketing racing to ensure they would still be able to make profits in the future. The aim of the Breeders Cup was to stimulate an interest in racing among as broad a range of people as was possible, to attract people to the sport, rather than to help in the short run those who were already established within it. John Gaines' suggestion left behind the appellation of fantasy and was first put on display at Hollywood Park in November 1984, at the end of what turned out to have been the peak year of the bloodstock boom. There could not have been a better time to ask the industry's members to stop pontificating and to start helping themselves.

Breeders and stallion owners across America were invited to contribute to the cost of putting on one day's racing every year. On this day, which was billed as "The Day of Champions", there would be a race for two-year-old colts, for two-year-old fillies, for sprinters, for milers, and for older fillies and mares. Then by way of a climax there would be a race run like the European Derbys over a mile and a half on turf, and the final contest would be, like the Kentucky Derby, over a mile and a quarter on dirt. The prize money on offer was to be of a sufficient munificence to attract all the best horses in North America and many of the better horses in Europe as well. Most importantly of all, the whole event was to be televised live across the nation.

The intention was, of course, to create stars. If the television companies and national newspapers, who were giving racing extensive coverage for the first time, were to interest the audience they would have to differentiate between the contestants and explain to the non-racing fan why these particular seven races were so exciting. As a result there were stories about each individual horse, owner, trainer and jockey and when it was time to report on the winners there was more to say than simply the number six horse had beaten the number four horse. Besides this coverage immediately before and after the big day, the event was designed to be the climax of the entire year's racing. Horses would have to qualify by winning races throughout the year in order to be selected to run on Breeders Cup day. Races which were once major events themselves were to become merely preparations and rehearsals for the big day itself, when the nation's media were focussing on racing.

To finance all this and an extensive advertising campaign, breeders were asked to pay $500 to nominate each of their foals for the Breeders Cup and stallion owners were asked to contribute a sum equal to the advertised nomination fee of their horse. To persuade the industry's members to pay up, the entrance fee for a selected runner who had been put down for the Breeders Cup at birth was set at 2 per cent of the purse for the particular contest, whilst the owners of a selected horse who had not been nominated would have to pay between 12 and 20 per cent of the purse. As an additional incentive these supplementary fees are not added to the purse but are held over and added to the following year's fund.

The Breeders Cup has been a brilliant success. Breeders Cup Limited collect around $20 million in nomination fees each year, of which $10 million is spent on "The Day of Champions". The Breeders Cup Classic is the world's richest horserace with a total purse of $3 million, of which the winner receives $1,350,000. The Breeders Cup has lived up to its championship billing and there can be little doubt that at the 1986 renewal all seven of the races were contested by horses of the highest international class. In the Breeders Cup's first three years there were three European trained winners and numerous European based challengers, including such famous horses as Dancing Brave, which has given the event an international standing as well. The National Broadcasting Company is reported to be well pleased with the viewing figures for its four hour Breeders Cup telecast, and the day's proceedings are duly reported in many American newspapers. The remainder of the $20 million is spent on an advertising campaign which is sustained throughout the year, and on giving premiums to Breeders Cup nominated horses in four hundred races run throughout the country. Those who contribute most to the Breeders Cup Limited's funds express themselves as being well satisfied with the return on their annual investment.

In Britain and Ireland there was no immediate need for an initiative on the scale of the Breeders Cup, but in both countries the bloodstock boom has been accompanied by a boom in corporate sponsorship.* The five English Classic races are now sponsored by the General Accident Insurance Company, Ever Ready and Gold Seal Batteries which are owned by the Hanson Trust, and the brewers Holsten Pils. The profile of racing's sponsors has changed and what was once the domain of the bookmaking companies, breweries and other companies whose products were consumed on the racecourse, now attracts companies whose own business has flourished with the bloodstock boom

*In 1980 sponsors contributed £1,600,000 to the added prizemoney for flat racing, which was 17 per cent of the total. In 1987 the figure was £4,100,000, 28 per cent of the total.

and others with no connection with horses or racing whatsoever. Those within the business—stud farms, stallion syndicates, bloodstock agencies, bloodstock auctioneers and trainers—all sponsor races in the hope of gaining publicity and fostering goodwill within the racing world itself. Robert Sangster, Prince Khalid Abdullah, the Maktoum family, Robert Clay, Johnny Jones Jr, Paul Mellon, William Farish III, the Matchmaker Group and Tattersalls all sponsor Group races in England. For these companies television coverage is probably incidental to the decision to sponsor, as most of their clients will spend much of their time on the racecourse or thumbing through the Racing Calendar and the form book.

For the companies without a racing connection, television coverage is a more important factor, but in many cases this is only inasmuch as it helps a director with a particular interest in racing sell the idea of race sponsorship to the remainder of his board of directors. Although it is foolish to make generalizations about sponsorship, for each company decides to enter the field for its own peculiar reasons, in many cases the decision is taken for internal rather than external reasons. Sponsorship of horseracing has, like sponsorship of theatre, opera or classical concerts, become a means of entertaining employees and clients, rather than a form of advertising. This is why most corporate involvement in European racing is in the form of sponsorship, rather than ownership. A sponsor will be given a marquee or a private box in which to entertain hundreds of guests, while an owner is given two, or at the most four, free entry tickets. In Ireland the surge of sponsorship has been even more marked and the country's major races are now supported by some of the leading companies in the bloodstock business, like the Coolmore, Airlie, Gilltown and Moyglare Studs, the auctioneers Goffs, American businesses like Budweiser and Heinz and the Irish-American firm Jefferson Smurfitt.

However, the most important change in the pattern of British, and indeed of European, racing in recent years has been the formation of a new body from within the industry which has become by far its largest sponsor. The European Breeders' Fund was originated and set up by the British Thoroughbred Breeders' Association with the cooperation and collaboration of its French and Irish equivalents. The idea of the European Breeders' Fund was to raise a sum of money each year which could be distributed as prize money by persuading stallion owners to contribute to a central fund. Each stallion syndicate was asked to make an annual contribution equal to the average price paid for a nomination to their stallion. There had to be some way of persuading such a disparate crowd to pay up, other than by appealing to their charitable feelings, so it was decided to restrict 50 per cent of all maiden two-year-old races to the progeny of those stallions whose owners had contributed.

The next problem which confronted the Fund's organisers was to find some way to allow American bred horses to compete in European Breeders Fund races, for otherwise the restriction would have become untenable. As a result a deal was struck with the Breeders Cup Limited whereby European Breeders' Fund nominated horses were eligible for the Breeders Cup races and premiums, and Breeders Cup nominated horses were able to run in European Breeders Fund races. In addition the two organisations agreed to give each other $7\frac{1}{2}$ per cent of the money they raised in contributions from stallion syndicates each year. This means in effect that the European Breeders' Fund receives $800,000 from American stallion owners every year. In its own terms the European Breeders' Fund has been a resounding success. Some 800 stallions are nominated to the E.B.F. each year, with the result that in 1986, 89 per cent of the two-year-olds who ran in Great Britain were eligible for E.B.F. races. The money is collected centrally and then divided between the member countries. In 1986, from its 45 per cent share of the total, the British European Breeders' Fund was able to give £580,000 towards prize money for two-year-old races, support 64 weight for age races for older horses, a few Group races, some jumping races and as well as all this to donate some money for veterinary research. The fund is also set to grow, for in 1988 Italy and Germany will become full members.

The success of the E.B.F. is a reflection upon the perseverance and persuasiveness of its trustees and the T.B.A. To have persuaded so many stallion syndicates to support, or at least comply with, the scheme in the space of a year, with only one notably vociferous exception, is an extraordinary feat. One can only presume that stallion owners are a relatively prosperous race if they are so ready to give up what must be at the very least one fiftieth of their income and in many cases must constitute a larger proportion. Unlike the Breeders Cup, the E.B.F. was not a response to a crisis, there was no felt need to attract a new audience, the only intention was to raise money and give it away to owners. This apparent generosity is more easily understood when the deal with the Breeders Cup Limited is considered in detail. Many of those Americans who are aware of the terms of the agreement feel the Europeans were let into the Breeders Cup on the cheap, and presumably those South American and Australian Stallion owners who nominate their horses to the E.B.F. would agree with them.

America is the most important market for bloodstock in the world. The influence of the Breeders Cup through the "Day of Champions" and the four hundred other races to which they give premiums is so pervasive that a horse who is not nominated will lose some of its value on the American market. Without some cross registration agreement few American breeders would have been interested in using European stallions or in buying European bred horses, which does of course explain why so many stallion owners have been happy to support the E.B.F. The Breeders Cup could easily have become a protectionist measure, diminishing the American demand for bloodstock imports. It seems likely that those of an internationalist stance who helped found the Breeders Cup were keen to avoid this eventuality and so were happy to allow foreign bred horses to become eligible for the Breeders Cup without demanding the $500 from every foal, a sum which most European breeders would not have been prepared to pay. In order to persuade those who were not so interested in Europe the E.B.F. produced a letter signed by Europe's leading bloodstock agents and trainers saying that unless there was a cross registration agreement they would have to reconsider their policy of buying American bred yearlings and horses. This was surely a brazen bluff, but it worked. Incidentally it is clear that, as the country which produces the best thoroughbreds, the United States would lose the most from any suspension of the international bloodstock trade.

The E.B.F. is then an example of international cooperation and the rewards of clever diplomacy. In Britain the fund has the added significance of being a major source of prize money which is not directed by the Jockey Club. The first chairman of the E.B.F.'s trustees was also a member of the Jockey Club, but the trustees have acted as though they have their own distinct ideas about race planning. At the time the E.B.F. was founded the Jockey Club decided independently to reduce the amount of prize money distributed to two-year-old races, so the E.B.F.'s formation negated any effects that such a reduction might have had on the bloodstock market. The E.B.F. may yet use its power in a more startling manner, for it is a uniquely unselfish sponsor with no desire for publicity or entertaining opportunities; the trustees are motivated by nothing more than a desire to test their own ideas and priorities.

The Breeders Cup, the European Breeders' Fund, marketing sophistication and the surge in corporate sponsorship of racing, these are all products of the bloodstock boom and they have all, and will continue to, attracted money and people to the business. In 1987 stallion owners also contributed £405,000 towards the $1 million of prize money for the Festival of British Racing at Ascot in September. A brochure was produced for the event, containing stallion advertisements each of which cost about £10,000, providing the prize money for the six races. In many ways the full potential of horseracing as an entertainment business is only beginning to be realized both in the United States and Europe. In the short run the bloodstock boom created tensions which debilitated the horse and tarnished the thoroughbred business's public image. However in the long run it seems that the horse, the bloodstock world and the public are all set to gain as this potential is exploited.

═══ Ten ═══
Things to Come

To conclude this discussion of the thoroughbred business it will be interesting to consider briefly the two possible events which those within the business consider to be potential disasters: the introduction of artificial insemination and the withdrawal of the Arab investors. The prohibition on those racehorses which were bred with the aid of artificial insemination is comparatively recent, for in 1934 Federico Tesio produced by such methods two horses which subsequently raced in Italy. He had sent two mares to Ireland to be covered by Manna, the English Derby winner, but neither conceived so, "... he ... reluctantly consented to the artificial experiment, being convinced that in the absence of the natural act, a part of the nervous influx would be lost."* Tesio no doubt considered the fact that neither Iacopo Robusti or Leandro del Sellaio, as the horses were named, were particularly successful racehorses as circumstantial evidence to support his theory. However his worries were but superstitions, for there is no means by which the manner of conception can affect the product of a union.

Moreover there are many things to be said in favour of the introduction of artificial insemination for thoroughbreds. International epidemics of equine venereal diseases would disappear, for there is no reason why a broodmare should ever leave the farm at which she is boarded. The sperm would be brought to her so there would be no need for her to travel to the stallion. A.I. would therefore reduce the cost of breeding, particularly in Europe, for a mare would no longer need to be boarded at a stallion farm for the period of foaling and

*Franco, Varola, *The Tesio Myth*. op. cit.

202

conception. The mare owner would also gain from having the opportunity of using stallions which are based on different continents or the other side of the world, without having to pay for the transport and board of his mare. As for the stallion owner, it is hard to see that it would affect the fashionable stallion at all. Either the fashionable stallion's owner would decide to ignore the savings of A.I. and continue to use hand-held breeding, or he would decide carefully to ration and limit the supply of the stallion's sperm. The products of the less fashionable stallions might well become cheaper and more abundant, for their sperm would be demanded by those who bred for pleasure rather than for speculative ends.

When the introduction of A.I is considered it is usually assumed that the same number of thoroughbreds would be produced as before, but with the assistance or compliance of a much smaller number of stallions. This seems to be an unlikely outcome. The introduction of artificial insemination would be preceded by, or swiftly followed by, a final dispelling of the myth of the stallion. When the name of the stallion will no longer be a decisive influence upon a yearling's commercial value, then breeders will be happy to experiment with unfashionable or foreign stallions. The introduction of A.I. might also increase the demand for thoroughbreds, and by reducing the cost of producing them encourage new investors to take up private breeding.

Those who object to the introduction of A.I. usually open the case for opposition by saying it would demean the noble thoroughbred. This is a specious argument, for one reason for introducing A.I. would be to prevent a repetition of the abuse of the thoroughbred which was induced by a combination of hand-held breeding and an obsession with short-term commercial ends. A.I. would obviously bring about a dislocation of the breeding business and its resources would have to be redistributed in a new pattern, but such disturbances are not on their own an argument for rejecting it, for the introduction could only be gradual and would take place over a number of years.

The problems which would be raised by A.I. are those of fraud and of the belittling of the *image* of the thoroughbred, rather than the horse itself. Sam Shepard, the secretary of the British Thoroughbred Breeders' Association, has said that he can envisage A.I. being used in order to control disease, but of course only with the strictest of supervision.

In such circumstances the primary prohibitions would be no splitting of ejaculates nor freezing of sperm. At present freezing equine sperm is problematic, but if there was a commercial demand for an accommodating technique it would surely be only a matter of time before it was perfected. Sam Shepard also believes there are thoroughbred breeders using A.I. both in the United States and Europe. Preventing the splitting of ejaculates would be an attempt to diminish the possibilities of fraud. Sperm is not easily identifiable, without exact information and laboratorial analysis, so it is easy to conceive of sperm being fraudulently classified, or of a single ejaculate being purchased and then split up and resold clandestinely. If such behaviour were to become widespread it is possible that the concept of a stud book and carefully recorded pedigrees would have to be abandoned, an inestimable loss which would impoverish the whole thoroughbred business.

The possibility of freezing sperm poses an even greater threat. Without the inconclusive nature of its precepts, its mystery, its emphemerality and the play of information and misinformation, the thoroughbred business would be little more than a self-aggrandizing lottery. It must be possible to anthropomorphize the horse and ascribe moral qualities to it, otherwise one might as well race something which is cheaper and less time consuming to raise and look after. The progression of the horse from birth, to education, to a brief period of physical exertion, to a longer period of procreation and finally retirement, is one which is parallel to man's own. If it was possible to freeze sperm this progression would disintegrate and the pattern of the horse's life would be transformed. Once a colt had proved itself on the racecourse a large sample of its sperm could be collected before it was gelded and sent back to race against its children and grandchildren. Once a colt was unable to race it would have no further use, as its sperm could be collected and stored. A.I. raises the same spectre as embryo transfer, for until man uses cybernetics himself its introduction to thoroughbreds would destroy the thoroughbred's symbolic value and horseracing's popular appeal.

The effect the withdrawal of the Arab investors would have upon the bloodstock business is less clear, but then it is a less likely event, as no one has a financial incentive to attempt to bring it about. Indeed it is hard to imagine what would precipitate such a withdrawal, for it seems unlikely that, for example, either Sheikh Mohammed or Prince Khalid Abdullah are suddenly going to become disenchanted with the game. If some of the Arab investors were forced to become emigrés it is far from certain that they would withdraw from the business, and in any event the strategic importance of the countries from which they come is such that their political stability has a wide significance and many governments other than their own have an interest in maintaining the status quo. Nonetheless it is interesting to speculate and it must be possible that the period when the Arab investors had a critical influence has already passed.

There is a sense in which the Arab investors only speeded up a transformation or cycle which would have taken place without their assistance. The bloodstock market will continue to grow increasingly integrated and international, whether or not there are Arab investors in Europe. Americans are becoming more interested in and knowledgeable about European racing, while there must be a chance that New Zealand and Australia will soon become part of the international bloodstock market, while many of the new generation of international millionaires will be used to going racing in Tokyo, Hong Kong or Singapore. Nevertheless many participants in the business in Europe rely upon the Arab investors directly, while many more in the United States do so indirectly and any sudden disappearance would increase the costs and difficulties of this transition from the short to the long-run perspective. There can be little doubt that Great Britain is the country which stands to lose the most, but then the British thorough-bred business has been both boosted and deadened by the substantial Arab investment in it.

The irony of the prosperity of the British thoroughbred business in the mid 1980s is that it was largely the result of an impermeability which has enabled it to resist any flow of change. Fads come and go, but it seems the traditional pattern of the British bloodstock business has a lasting appeal. The participants in the British business missed out on the profits which they could have made during the peak years of the boom, but they will also avoid the bankruptcies and forced withdrawals on the scale which is inevitable in the United States. However such an inadvertent success encourages complacency and serves to deaden any impulse to innovate. The list of participants who are entirely beholden to the Maktoum family is long and steadily growing, and already includes many of the trade's newspapers and magazines, the leading bloodstock agencies, horse transporters and equine advertising agencies, and of course all of England's leading trainers rely upon one Arab investor or another. The complacency and the wish to contract such obligations are of course understandable, but it would be foolish to ignore the need to attract and appeal to newcomers and outsiders.

During the years of the bloodstock boom the appeal of the game upon which the thoroughbred business is founded was threatened by those who believed they were gambling, not for pleasure, but for the sake of short-term financial rewards. For a time the spectacle of racing itself was diminished as those who owned racehorses obeyed the commercial imperatives and planned their horse's racing careers for the purpose of acquiring prestige and "black type" and of maintaining their potential, rather than realizing it. The horse itself was abused when it was young and after it had retired to stud to procreate, for the only period of its life when its own needs were in conjunction with man's demands was while it was being trained to perform on the racecourse. The sales yearling and the fashionable stallion were seen as gambling chips and mistreated for the sake of short term financial gains. Bloodstock auctions were manipulated in order that they might resemble the poker games some considered them to be, rather than a means of distributing and valuing thoroughbreds.

However, the actions and practices of the gamblers and speculators proved to be self defeating for in each field their behaviour went beyond the sensible, the acceptable, and the commercially efficient, to be revealed as folly or rather as practices which were designed to fool and disinform. None of the individuals named in this book was connected with any of the practices which have been criticized.

Psychoanalytical studies of the gambler usually conclude that he will eventually reveal his wish to lose or, despite his initial caution, finally risk sums he cannot afford to lose. Most racing people would probably reject psychoanalytical explanations of gambling as preposterous and absurd, but before dismissing this particular trait in such a manner it is interesting to look again at those who bought and sold fashionable yearlings, demanded millions of dollars for a single share in a stallion, or paid a million dollars for a single season. They were not all fools or idiots; many of them had years of experience of working with and breeding thoroughbreds. Yet they were prepared to take such gambles when they must have realized these valuations were based upon a combination of myth and ignorance which could not possibly last indefinitely. They indulged because they are gamblers, and some went too far and others were caught out when the rules changed, because that is the nature of gamblers. A gambler knows a winning streak will end but he is prepared to bet that it will not end with the next play or game.

The horse has been seen as a symbol of both power and lust, a combination which is entirely appropriate for the thoroughbred, for both are emotions which are said to motivate the gambler. The racing game is so intertwined with gambling that any predictions about its future developments are likely to be invalidated swiftly. However, the central appeal of racing and the thoroughbred business will always be its role as a form of oracle. All participants in the thoroughbred business whether they are racegoers, trainers, breeders or bloodstock agents ask questions of the thoroughbred which can only be answered with equivocation. No event is conclusive, and after each race or auction, whatever its outcome, they will return to the oracle and ask again. To fulfil this oracular role the thoroughbred must retain its mystery and its aura of sanctity. The thoroughbred fulfils man's desire for the oracular and the gamble, both of which are of course closely connected. However, this strange nature makes it difficult to rationalize about the thoroughbred business or to conclude this discussion with any definite statements, other than that horseracing is both an odd business and an odd sport.

⟹ Bibliography ⟸

Steven Crist, *The Horse Traders*. New York: W. W. Norton & Co Inc., 1986.

Jon Halliday & Peter Fuller, eds, *The Psychology of Gambling*. London: Allen Lane, 1974.

William E. Jones, *Genetics and Horsebreeding*. Philadelphia: Lea & Febiger, 1982.

Sir Charles Leicester, revised by Howard Wright, *Bloodstock Breeding*. London: J. A. Allen, 1983.

Sir Rhys Llewellyn, *Breeding to Race*. London: J. A. Allen, 1964.

Jack Lohman & Arnold Kirkpatrick, *Successful Thoroughbred Investment in a Changing Market*. Lexington: Thoroughbred Publishers, Inc., 1984.

Ernst W. Mayr, *The Growth of Biological Thought: Diversity, Evolution, and Inheritance*. Cambridge, Massachusetts: Harvard University Press, 1982.

Jocelyn de Moubray, *Horseracing and Racing Society*. London: Sidgwick & Jackson, 1985.

Peter D. Rossdale M.A., F.R.C.V.S., *The Horse From Conception to Maturity*. London: J. A. Allen, 1985.

Marvin B. Scott, *The Racing Game*. Chicago: Aldine, 1968.

Wray Vamplew, *The Turf: A Social and Economic History of Horseracing*. London: Allen Lane, 1976.

Franco Varola, *Typology of the Racehorse*. London: J. A. Allen, 1977.

Franco Varola, *The Tesio Myth*. London J. A. Allen, 1984.

Moyra Williams, *Horse Psychology*. London: J. A. Allen, 1976.

Index

Horses' names are *italicized*

Acton, Robert 189
Adjal 139
Adstock Manor Stud 114
Affirmed 177
Aga Khan III 11, 17, 45, 60, 83
Aga Khan IV 83, 100, 114, 121,
   179, 188, 191
   breeding operation 96–7
Agence Française de Vente du
   Pur Sang 124
   Invitation and Select Sales 127
Ahmed Salman, Prince 103
Ahonoora 171, 186
   success as stallion 158–9
Airlie Stud, nr Dublin 82, 113,
   115, 130, 171, 175, 198
Alexander, Hamish 117
Alexander, Perry 40, 182
Alleged 38, 89, 111, 112, 117,
   172, 184
Alphabatim 150, 190
Althea 110, 151
Aly Khan 45
Alydar 55, 84, 90, 110, 177,
   184
   economic rent 87
American Institute of Archi-
   tecture 38
American Jockey Club 194
   report on racing industry 194–
   5
American Quarter Horse
   Association 31
Aqueduct racetrack, US 60
Arch Sculptor 174

Aristotle 29
   theories on breeding 11, 163
Arlington racetrack, US 62
Artificial insemination 19, 22, 36
   advantages 202–3
   destruction of thoroughbred's
      image 203, 204
   early use 202
   eradication of disease by 202,
      203
   freezing sperm 203, 204
   objections 203
   problem of fraud 203, 204
Ashford Stud, Kentucky 44,
   172, 174
Assert 186
Aston Park Stud, Oxfordshire
   41, 97n, 165–6
Astor, Sir John 116
At Talaq 175
Authaal 117, 148

Ballymany Stud, Ireland 45
Ballymoss Stakes 182
Baroda Stud, Ireland 115
Bathurst, David 140
Be My Guest 172, 173, 174
Beaverbrook, Lady 115
Belmont Park racetrack, US 62,
   194
Benson, Martin 75
Bering 178, 181
Blackwell, George 148
Blenheim 83

209

Christie's, New York 140
Claiborne Farm, Kentucky 25,
    38, 45, 83, 176, 177, 178
  stallion barn 38
Clay, Robert 26, 39, 111, 112,
    122, 161, 177, 181, 182, 187
career as commercial breeder
    178–80
Cleveland Oaks 101
Clore, Alan 142
Codex 151
Collins, Joss 147, 150
Combs family 176
Combs, Leslie 179
Commanche Run 174
Conquistador Cielo 90, 178
Contagious Equine Metritis 80
Coolmore Stud 19n, 82, 171–5,
    198
  international promotion 173–
    4
  stallions 174
  stud fees 173
  syndications 173
Cooper, Dr Wendell 33
Cooper, Tom 147, 150
Craddock, Richard 173
Critique 182
Crofter 174
Cromwell Bloodstock Agency
    147
Crystal Springs Farm, Kentucky
    110
Curragh Bloodstock Agency
    (C.B.A.) 79, 136, 147, 167
Cuthbert, Bernice 165, 166, 167,
    180

Dahar 82
Dalham Hall Stud, Newmarket
    122, 189
Damascus 178

Dancing Brave 8, 21, 90, 111,
    122, 150, 178–81 *passim,*
    188, 189, 197
  value of shares in 164
Danzig 55, 90, 108, 110, 159, 178
Darby Dan Farm, Kentucky 40,
    114, 177, 188
Darley Stud Management 146
De Burgh, Hubert 146
De Chambure, Comte Roland
    111, 181
De Moussac, Paul 113
Deep Diver 174
Deep Run 19n, 174
Delahooke, James 8, 114, 148,
    150, 190
Deputy Minister 178
Derby, the 67, 76, 100
Devil's Bag 161
Dickinson, Michael 175
Diesis 38
Dingwall, Charles 103
Dominion 41, 165, 166–7
Doncaster
  St Leger Sales 71
  two-year-old in training sales
    117
Downes, 'Tote' Cherry 149, 151,
    152

Eaton-Williams Farm, US 111
Economist 17n
El Gran Señor 174, 178
Ela-Mana-Mou 150
Elders Pastoral 126
Electric 38, 167
Elegant Air 41, 165, 166
Elizabeth II, Queen 112, 180
Englehard, Charles 175
Epsom racecourse 67
Equine Fertility Unit, Cam-
    bridge 31

Index

Index

factors in demand for season 157, 158, 161
factors in demand for share 157, 158, 161
failure of majority 159, 162, 174
fixing share price 158
gamble behind investment in 156
growth in number, mid-1980s 160–1
importance of inelastic demand for services 155
improvement in lot of 37
indications of commercial standing 159–60
insuring 34–5
Irish farms 171–5
maintaining image of 159, 160, 162
myth of prepotent stallion 18, 19–20, 21, 163–4
policy of covering as many mares as possible 162
reducing risks to 35, 37–8
risks and rewards of investment 161–2
role 34, 37
shareholders' profit from right to seasons 157
shares in 156–7
Sire Production Index 77–8
temptations of short-term policy re 162, 163
theory re age of 12
unpredictability of performance 158–9
US farms and management 88, 175–87
Stone Farm, US 177
Stoute, Michael 149, 179
Stroud, Anthony 40, 108, 146, 189

racing manager to Sheikh Mohammed 147–9
Stud farms
administration 95–6
advertising methods 106–7
Arab owners 97, 121
cost of land 95
cost of raising horse 97–9
definition for tax purposes 109–10
drugs to boost growth 104
economies of scale 96–7
equine services 95
equine treadmills 105
exercise by hotwalker 105
long-term investment 96, 97, 98, 100
losses made 109
pastoral image 43–4
pinhookers 117, 118
preparing yearlings for sale 104, 105
presentation of horses on sale days 107–8
scientific services required 95
selling foals 117
substitution of barns for stables 26
successful racehorse v fashionable yearling 99–100
surgery on yearlings 104
traditional 38, 45
training horses 103
well known British farms 114–16, 122
well known European farms 113–14
well known US farms 11–13, 122
Stud management
calculated risks 27–8
commercial considerations v horses' welfare 36–7, 40

Index

Stud management—*contd*
countering parasitic infection
24–5
dealing with equine V.D. 80–
1
embryo transfer 31
horse pastures 24, 25–6, 27
horses' diet 24, 33
increase in mares' fertility
since 1920s 31–2
outside rearing 27
paradox of infertility and
overproduction 81–2
perpetual pregnancy for
mares 32
precautions during copu-
lation 36, 42–3
problem of infertility 30–1
response to commercial incentives 23
shortage of skilled staff 39–40
teasing 35–6, 42
use of artificial light to
encourage sexual activity 33
value of broodmare 29–30
vet's importance 30
walking in mares to stallion
farm 41, 109n
weaning 27
yearly foaling for mares 29
Sun Prince 174
Sure Blade 189
Sushila 116
Swale 34
Sweeney, Brian 182

Tank's Prospect 151
Tap On Wood 171
Tattersalls 124, 125, 126, 130,
131, 139, 143, 198
commission 125
conditions of sale 128, 138

December Sales 81, 122
Highflyer Sales 7, 71, 125, 127,
130, 136, 144, 152
Houghton Sales 77, 116
Irish division 125
October Sales 125, 127
prohibition on 'by bidding'
137
sales pavilion 135
turnover 125
Tavistock, Lady 20, 25, 107
Taylor, Charles 112, 127, 178,
183
Taylor, Duncan 111
Taylor, E. P. 75, 113
Taylor, Joe 111
Taylor Made Farm, Kentucky
25, 111, 122
yearling barns 26
Taylor Made Sales Agency 147
Taylor, Mickey 178, 179
Terlingua 151
Tesio, Federico 4
belief in soft inheritance 12
on the cavalry horse 29
use of A.I. 202
Thatch 174
Theatrical 180
Thorn, Sir John 116
Thornton Stud, Yorks 122
Thoroughbred Management
Services 167, 168
Thoroughbred Record, The 77,
173
Three Chimneys Farm, Ken-
tucky 111, 112, 113, 122,
177, 179, 180, 187
exercise for stallions 39
shares in *Dancing Brave* 164
stallions' accommodation 39
To-Agori-Mou 150
Top Ville 189
Troy 34

220

Index